ExtraImperial

Danielle K Girl

Chapter 1

Ryder

The pale blue muck pressed to Ryder's lips not only smells foul — like burnt popcorn and blue cheese — but it's the consistency of over-cooked rice. There is no way it's going down her throat. Even if there wasn't a lump the size of Texas there already. But the Zentai guard is insistent. He has propped a hard pillow behind her shoulders, raising her into a semi-seated position on the wide hard platform she's lying on. Thanks to the senlier that rests like a cruel crown around her head, Ryder's body is held in a vice. She's as helpless as a baby.

The black-eyed guard has said just one word. Over and over. *Cessner.* Not English, of course, but it doesn't take a rocket scientist to work out what the alien is telling her to do.

Eat.

There is as much chance of that happening as there is of Ryder being able to throw herself off this bench and run screaming from her cell. Which is exactly what she wants to do right now. Run. Not eat blue goop. Or drink the syrupy, pink liquid the guard has also been trying to get her to take. She just wants to run. Far, far away from this place.

This world without Sophie.

Tears sting her eyes again. Her hair is wet at her temples. She's been crying for forever. Or a few hours? Ryder's not certain. The room hums with a vibration that borders on hypnotic. She slept at some point, utterly exhausted. In mind, and body. Yet how long the restless snooze lasted she has no idea, but it's left her more exhausted than before. Traumatic dreams of those moments at the bridge played over and over. Ryder's fight to keep Jack's helicopter from crashing. The nightmare that followed.

Sophie's gone.

And it's Ryder's fault.

But not just hers. It's the Presider's fault.

Ryder shifts and winces at the weight of the senlier, far too tight around her skull. The pressure only seems to be increasing. She stares up at the face leaning over her. Black pools regard her. The Zentai has no discernible iris and pupil, just one solid colour. Ryder is a long, long way from home.

"Cessner."

It is gently spoken, but Ryder frowns as hard as her barely-controlled muscles will allow. She shifts her head and her neck muscles spasm. Her cry doesn't make it past the lump in her throat. The Zentai lifts his hands, an elegant, flowing movement, and Ryder's not certain for a moment if it is a he, at all. A solid jawline and broad forehead say yes, but the brow is soft, shoulders and arms slender. And something about the lack of ear lobes thing just blurs the gender lines. All Ryder knows for certain, is that everything has changed. Her world is unrecognisable. Full of holes, and things she doesn't understand.

The Zentai rises, speaking as he does. A deep, decidedly male voice, by Earth standards anyway. Ryder decides her guard is a *he*. She needs to be certain of something. While she can't understand anything he's saying, it's presumably some kind of goodbye because he gathers the stinking blue stew, and leaves. Propped up as she is, Ryder sits eye level with the only window on the far side of the room. It is a low, narrow pane, not unlike the rectangular panel on the door she found Lucas behind at Tarraleah, where he was held bedridden and captive, just as Ryder is now.

Pinpricks stab at the back of her eyes. For all she knows, he's exactly like that again. Only this time with the Zentai. Through her agony, Ryder clearly heard the Commandant issue the order as they left Earth: *continue hunting for him.*

The memory of the Zentai leader's piercing jade-green eyes sends a shiver through her body. Even if Lucas is being helped back in Tasmania by Benjamin Cooper, how much protection can the boss of C-21 offer? He couldn't prevent monsters getting into Tarraleah.

Ryder stares through the narrow panel barely noticing the dull view. Her thoughts are back in the underground levels of C-21 headquarters. Back where she somehow managed to destroy the Epseen, the disgusting spider-like thing that came at them from the shadows.

She holds her breath. The memory is seared bright and clear. The weapons moving at her command, pulled from the guards' hands and barreling towards the Epseen. The remains of the creature peppering the walls like paintball stains.

What did you do? Blane's assistant, Marlee, had demanded, struggling to catch her breath, too weak to stand without leaning against the wall. *What did you do?*

Ryder had hurt them. Taken something from them. The guards kneeling on the floor, one clutching at his head as though he'd been struck. Shrinking away from her when she asked if he was okay. And Sophie trembling hard, a fragile smile clinging to her lips.

Ryder's light-headed from the memory. She needs to take a breath, but can't move. The Epseen wasn't the only monster in that corridor. And worse was to come.

Her chest is tight, desperate for that gulp of air.

"I'm so sorry, Sophie," Ryder whispers.

Her gaze drops to her hands. The Zentai have removed the elthar bracelets. Taken away her weapons. So they think. She closes her eyes and rolls her head as far from side to side as her restraint will allow. It can't be possible. How could the Beckoning be a part of her too?

The door to the room slides open, a sound like wind rustling through reeds, but Ryder keeps her eyes closed. Someone paces across the glass-like floor, the soft pad of their shoes marking a quick tempo.

"Ryder."

Now her eyes open, wide at first, but quickly narrowing into an angry glare.

"Get away from me," Ryder says.

Blane Cooper glances back at the door. Two guards stand in the corridor outside, hands braced around what appear to be weapons. Odd-looking weapons, shaped like French Horns, black as tar and with a series of pulsing red lights where brass valve caps should be. The door slides shut.

"Ryder, are you all right?"

"I said get away from me."

Blane hesitates, a step away from the edge of the platform she is lying on. Sweat gleams on his forehead, and several strands of his hair are plastered down the left side of his face.

"Are you in pain?" His amber eyes fix on the senlier around her head. His hands lift, then fall again. As though he's uncertain whether he should touch her or not. The answer is a very definite not.

"What have you done with her?" Ryder fights against her own stubborn muscles, trying to lift herself higher and draw eye level with Blane. "Where is she?"

He frowns. "Ryder... Sophie's gone... I'm so—"

"Where is she?" Ryder shouts through the pain that comes with resisting the senlier. She manages to rise. Sits up for a whole second, maybe two, before her stomach muscles twist into a knot that seems certain to tear her in half.

"Stop, stop, Ryder. Don't fight it." Blane presses his hands to her shoulders.

The reeds rustle again and the door opens. The two awaiting guards shout something incoherent. Blane shouts right back, waving them away.

"I can handle it. It's what you wanted me here for, right? A doctor for the human?" He throws curt words like bullets. "Get out. Just get the hell out of here. You want to see how human hearts react under duress? You'll give her a heart attack if you don't get the hell back."

One of the guards tosses his head, sending his thick dreadlocks jerking over one muscled shoulder. He shouts again, a sharp snap of sound that says he's not impressed with Blane's tirade, but the door closes. Ryder's chest heaves, her breath rasping up a dry throat.

"Take it easy, Ryder. Just take it easy." Blane pushes her hair from her face, tucking it behind her ears. "I'm so sorry about Sophie. I'm so, so sorry that I couldn't help her. But I am going to help you, okay?"

"Why are you here?" Ryder's voice wavers, and the tears that had barely stopped falling, threaten again. "Why are you helping them?"

Blane takes her hand and places his fingertips against her wrist. His brow furrows. "Try to calm down, Ryder. You need to get your heart rate down."

"Sure. No problem," Ryder snaps. "Why are you here, Blane."

And why didn't you save Sophie? Just the thought is unbearable, there's no way the words are going to make it out.

"I had to do something, they were going to tear Tarraleah apart. I had a lot of people down there, and I wasn't going to watch them die." His grip on her wrist tightens. "I told them… I told them about Sebastien, and that I could lead them to him. It was all I could think to do. I had no clue where Ben had taken Lucas." He hesitates, lifting his gaze to the ceiling, before continuing. "But I did know where Sebastien was. And I hoped he would be enough to make them back off. Daenara and your grandad had just left before the main attack began so I told the Commandant I could track them. I figured Jack had gone to find you. And from what I'd seen, wherever you were, then… Sebastien would be."

Blane's words do nothing to lower her heart rate. Her chest aches from the thumping. "You could have got Jack killed," she hisses.

Ryder tries to pull her wrist from Blane's grip, managing to jerk her hand a fraction but nothing more.

"And I'm truly sorry he and Daenara got caught up in that. But they are okay, thanks to you." Blane sets her hand down, laying her arm gently at her side. "Whatever you did, saved them. But it also drew a lot of attention." He tilts his head towards the door. "And got you in a whole new world of trouble. I'm sorry for that, I knew you were different, but I had no idea just how much. I don't think these people… aliens… did either. They didn't want you dead. I knew that much. So I did what I could. Told the Commandant she needed me to keep you healthy. Human anatomy and all that. I couldn't believe it, but it worked. They seemed keen to make sure you stay alive. Even more so now." Blane pauses. "Something's happened, something that has got them really spooked."

Ryder's tired body tenses. "What? What's happened?"

"Someone has died. Someone they called the Laudess?"

There is no thundering heart beat now. Ryder's heart and body frozen. Numb. "Olessia?"

Blane shrugs. "Do you know who that is? It seems like it's a really bad thing that they are dead. Who was she?"

It's all Ryder can do to push out two simple words.

"My friend."

A sudden jerk tilts the craft. Hard enough to topple Ryder from the platform.

Blane dives. "I've got you," he says.

He catches her, but lands hard on his right shoulder, Ryder's weight on top of him.

The room erupts. Alarms holler with a loud and steady beat. The craft jolts back in the opposite direction. Blane, with Ryder cradled in his arms, slides helplessly across the glass-like flooring. The tilt steepens, rushing them faster. Slamming them against the far wall. Their faces pressed up against the pane of glass. Ryder stares outside.

Swirling currents surround them. Churning streams of mustard-yellow, and weaker threads of sun-kissed orange. Ryder is hit with a terrible sense of *déjà vu*. She is back inside a river.

"What's happening?" Blane cries.

"We're about to crash."

Chapter 2

Ryder

The Zentai ship tilts heavily right. The lighting flickers. Once again Blane and Ryder are slipping across the floor like two eggs in an oil-drenched pan. Headed straight towards the platform she had been lying on. Blane grunts and manages to swing around on his butt, protecting her from the impact. Leaving his own back to take the brunt of it. The shock of the sudden stop jerks Ryder's head, hitting him squarely on the chin.

Blane lets fly with a handful of curses, and Ryder's thoughts turn to Sebastien.

"Sebastien." Her tongue barely does as it's told, slurring his name. "We have to find him."

There's little chance Blane has heard a word she's said above the din of the alarms, echoing off the walls around them. The lighting struggles to illuminate the room, wavering like candles caught in a breeze. Blane grabs the edge of the bench with one hand, Ryder flopping like a ragdoll in his other arm.

Ryder's jaw is clenched; she is utterly useless. A few hours ago she was fighting off an invisible monster and bringing down Jack's helicopter safely. Now she's struggling to co-ordinate her legs enough to find her feet as Blane rises to his. A cruel, quiet voice reminds her she did a lot more than that a few hours ago.

Terrible things.

Things she can't take back.

And now, Olessia is gone too.

A crazy thought strikes Ryder. Perhaps Sebastien learned what happened to Olessia and this is the result. He's found a way to bring the whole ship down.

She wouldn't blame him. If Ryder didn't have the senlier clamping down on her head, chances are, she would do the same. For Sophie. For Olessia.

"We need to try and get to the door," Blane shouts. He leans them against the platform and lifts a hand to the senlier. "How do we get this thing off?"

His fingers dig against her forehead, trying to work their way in behind the thin band of metal. All the attempt achieves, though, is a tightening of the band.

"Stop. That hurts." Ryder winces. "It won't come off like that."

He mutters something, but it's lost beneath the alarms. Blane gathers her tighter to him and pushes off from the platform. The doorway sits at the high end of the tilted room. Trying to reach it is like climbing the side of an icy hill. Blane manages a few strides before they are once again on their knees, sliding backwards. Ryder manages to curl one hand into a fist. Without her help, Blane's got no chance of getting them across the open space.

Not until the craft makes another jarring change of direction. The nose suddenly lifts, a lurching movement that reverses the tilt. Caught off-guard, Blane's hold on Ryder slips, and she is the first to go hurtling across the floor. Straight towards the door. Head first.

"Oh my god,no," Ryder cries.

Just as she is about to face plant, the solid metal door it glides open, and she arrows straight through. She squeezes her eyes shut, certain the wall across the corridor is about to bring her to a dramatic and painful halt.

But it doesn't happen. A strong hand grips her shoulder, dragging her out of the way of Blane's own headlong slide. No-one is there to stop him, and the doctor cries out, hitting the wall feet first. Hard enough to buckle his knees.

The hand that found her now drags Ryder to her feet. Rough enough to make her shoulder joint crack. The Zentai with the heavy dreadlocks glares down at her. He shouts something, but it's as indecipherable as anything the gentler Zentai with the terrible-smelling stew said.

"Let go of me." Ryder imagines herself lashing out, punching at the wide-shouldered alien who stands over her. Her right arm lifts, just a fraction. As big a threat to the guard as a feather to an elephant's hide.

The Zentai is untroubled by the dramatic lean of the craft, and definitely not troubled by the protesting human he's carrying. Lifting Ryder off her feet and bundling her beneath one arm, he strides down the lilting corridor. The craft sways left, levelling them out enough that the wall is no longer as good an option to walk along as the floor.

"Put me down," Ryder screams.

If the Beckoning is a part of her, if she somehow has extra-terrestrial mojo in her blood, then let it ignite now. Right here. Fire up along with her rage. That's what happens with Olessia. Whenever she gets angry, she is powerful. Olessia would be bringing everyone here to their knees. Making them wish they'd never set eyes on her. And Ryder would be at her side, doing whatever it was that just being there seemed to do. Balancing it all out. A team. Weird as it was. They were a team.

Ryder's own anger falters, and the fight slips away. They *had* been a team.

Olessia *used* to be powerful.

The Zentai strides along the corridor. Ryder stares down at his boots. They are crazy thick, more like moon boots. The click and clunk as they hit the floor and then release is audible over the still-wailing alarms. It's also why he is completely unbothered by the lurch and tilt of the craft. The boots suck at the surface, holding him firm until the pull of his foot releases it. Ryder watches every rise and fall, every step. Focusing in on the dark metallic material. Giving up her pathetic attempts to struggle against him.

She's such an idiot. How could she have possibly imagined she could fight against any of this?

Fight against the ruler of an alien world? It was a pipe-dream to begin with and now, without Olessia, it is complete insanity.

Lucas. I can't do it.

She can't hold on, not here. There is nothing to hold onto.

The Zentai stops briefly, before his purposeful stride continues, carrying them into a wider space. The bulky alien shouts out a garble of words she can't make head or tail of, but his pace quickens. Ryder lifts her head. The weight across her brow presses down over her eyes, and for a second, she doesn't trust what those same eyes are showing her. The Commandant and Sebastien stand in front of two huge triangular panels of glass, three times the size of the observation windows in the Aventar cabin. The world outside is a turbulent mish-mash of dull colour. Sebastien's at a control panel of some kind, two dinner-plate sized discs sit to either side of him, hip height. As the Commandant looks on, the two Zentai guards either side of him try to force his hands against the discs, but Sebastien resists. Loosened hair shifting with the effort, mouth working, laying out a serious helping of his favourite curses. The craft shudders, and leans. First to the right, then left. Not as violent as before but enough to be still be frightening.

The jade-eyed Commandant gestures to the Zentai carrying Ryder, then to Sebastien. He turns, knees bent as he fights to pull away from the guards man-handling him.

"Sebastien." Ryder's cry escapes as little more than a whimper.

The Zentai guard releases her and Ryder lands in a heap. She ignores the shock of her knees against the hard floor, refusing to take her eyes off Sebastien. Just in case he vanishes. A figment of her overtired, cracking little mind.

The guards release him. Sebastien stands frozen, a scowl on his face. Watching her. The Commandant yells words spoken in the twisting, guttural Zentai language. Sebastien turns on her. Fury the only thing Ryder can decipher in his reply. But he shrugs off the guards and places his hands against the discs. The guards step away.

Sebastien's shoulders lift as he takes a deep breath. Two flattened columns, half a metre wide and etched with a series of dashes and dots, rise from the floor either side of him, stopping just above hip height. A faint haze appears around his legs. The guards that had been bothering Sebastien move from the front of the cabin, revealing a second control panel not far from where the Guardian is standing. Manned by a Zentai, a slender figure with a single braid hanging down almost to their backside. Their long neck smattered with dark brown freckles. The craft drops, and so does Ryder's stomach. She braces her hands against the floor.

The Commandant appears from nowhere, right at Ryder's side. Towering over her. Reaching for her and tugging her to her feet. The Zentai speaks in short, snappy sentences, pulling Ryder to the right side of the cabin. Dots of blinking, fuschia-coloured light spreads out in a frantic pattern across the walls of the cabin. The light reflects off the Commandant's skin, highlighting patches where the pigment is much paler than the majority of her deep olive skin. Especially on the top of her bald head. It's a feature Ryder hadn't noticed before, but harder to miss now when she is practically cheek to cheek with the Zentai.

"Preston-ka mehet." The Commandant gestures to a space on the floor. A space where an oval outline brightens in the smooth panelling. The section opens and what looks like a baseball rises from the gap. A pure white baseball that bloats to the size of a basketball before it begins to peel open. A blooming flower whose petals elongate, writhing and curving to merge into a new shape. A bucket seat. Like something you'd find in a race car, with a raised, curving arch that protects the back of the head and short panels at shoulder height to keep anyone sitting there from shifting about.

"Preston-ka mehet." The Commandant repeats, more forceful this time. She doesn't give Ryder any time to protest or do as she is told. The Zentai plants a firm hand on Ryder's shoulder, shoving her into the seat that floats above the surface of the floor with no visible ties to either it or the high-domed ceiling of the cabin. Restraints slide into place over Ryder's shoulders, much like those in the Aventar, and she is locked into place. Good timing. The craft loses altitude in another gut-wrenching jolt. The Commandant takes her seat, another blooming basketball moving in a whip-fast motion to redesign itself.

In fact, everyone but Sebastien and the slender Zentai are seated. Their gazes fixed on the windows. Bodies leaning this way and that, hands pressed against the discs.

"What is he doing?" Ryder whispers.

"Teren, teren, teren," the Commandant calls out.

And the penny drops. Loud and clear. Ryder doesn't need a Zentai dictionary to work it out. And she's been on enough flights to understand.

Brace, brace, brace.

Sebastien is piloting the ship.

Outside, the curtain of swirling colour rips open and they shoot out into a fully formed world. One that is rushing up way too fast. Ryder's scream thunders up her tight throat and rushes past her clumsy tongue. The ground races towards them, the entire craft vibrating so hard her teeth rattle. Panic burns its way through her body. Her blood on fire. Pressing against the back of her eyes so hard she's certain they are about to pop from her head.

But it's not her eyes that shift. The senlier loosens, and sharp pain replaces the pressure as the barbs pull from her skin.

The Zentai craft hits the ground.

Ryder's world goes black.

Chapter 3

Olessia

A pair of attendants flank Olessia. One of them directs her to raise her arms, and she does not protest. Both attendants are clothed in swathes of a pale-blue material that conceals all trace of skin. Darker coverings rest over their heads and faces. A meshing that cloaks their eyes from view. They are considerably taller than Olessia, standing a head higher. The concealed faces, the formidable height all by design, Olessia is certain. Her Father finding every way possible to belittle her. Intimidate.

Olessia drew back her shoulders the moment she was ushered from the aircraft that bore her here, and has not wavered in her poise since. Not even as the attendants removed the Yentern clothing Sen-bay provided and began to redress her. Admittedly, they have done so with care. Though in utter silence. The material they wrap around her, and slip over her head to settle on her shoulders is unfamiliar. A far cry from the usual hard lines and starched material of her uniform whose harsh military design is in stark contrast to the layers of heavy fabric, a blood red that holds the faintest of sheens. Twisted and wrapped around her, tight about her stomach and chest, with looser folds encasing her shoulders and covering her arms. A skirt in the same material cascades from her waist, and sits in folds against the floor, a trail spreading out behind her. Ridiculously elaborate, and hence, a frustrating hindrance. The Presider adding another layer of difficulty to any escape plans Olessia may be courting.

She is uncertain where the costume originates — from what plundered world it has been taken — but does not doubt this, too, is intentional. She cannot dress like the Laudess of Bax Un Tey because the Laudess of Bax Un Tey is dead.

Best they make her ghost less familiar.

Olessia touches at her wrists. Bare. Only her Father could have removed the elthar but she does not recall when this occurred. The journey is hazy, pock-marked with periods of blackness. Whatever device he used upon her on the journey from Zentai to Kinna-Bray, it was unrelenting. And overwhelming. Giving Olessia the barest margin in which to take a breath. And remain conscious. No chances were being taken when it came to ensuring she could not rail against her fate.

And show the people of Siros that word of her death was vastly over-exaggerated.

"Is that too tight, my Higher?"

Olessia shakes her head, keeping her eyes locked on the far side of the room where shadows darken a corner of the lightly-furnished space. My Higher. Her attendants address her as they would a member of the Claven. Do they truly not know who stands between them? Or have they been frightened into ignorance?

The attendants fuss over her, tucking material here, adjusting a length there, until Olessia must clench her hands to fists to prevent herself from screaming at them to leave her alone. She lowers her arms as instructed, and a frown settles on her face. The Beckoning is quiet within her, just a distant hum at her core. As it was when she was taken from the Turning. What has her Father done to her? And how did he do it? She suffers no bruising, no punctures to her skin. No senlier or inhibitor necklace to constrict her. It seems the Presider has spent as much time developing technology to enable him to control his own daughter, as he has to defeat his enemies. Unease ripples through her, a discomfort beneath her skin. A sensation far stronger than the muted presence of the Beckoning.

"We are done, my Higher." The attendant to her right nods once, but no more. There is no bow, and no obligatory balled fist to the centre of the chest. Familiar signs of deference to the Presiderline Olessia has known all her life.

She chews at her bottom lip. Her born role as Laudess of Bax Un Tey is a burden she has sought to discard. But not like this. Forced to relinquish it when she knows her friends suffer to protect her. Olessia's shoulders drop. Christian and Sen-Bay were dragged aboard the vessel too. She closes her eyes.

When she first learned she was a creature to be feared, the loneliness suffocated her, but that pales in comparison to the isolation that grips her now.

"This way, my Higher."

Olessia's eyes flutter open. One of the attendants sweeps a hand towards a narrow doorway, barely discernible in the gloom of the room. The moniker of room hardly befits the place. The walls appear to be of natural materials – white rock, streaked with veins of a golden hue that has been carved and hollowed to accommodate living, breathing occupants. Intentionally or by natural process, the roughness of the design makes it hard to discern. Adjusting her posture, shoulders once again set back, Olessia gathers the folds of the skirt and follows the attendant into the orange glow brightening the exit.

A brief study of her prison has Olessia deciding this place is both man-made and naturally occurring. The attendant leads them through several corridors, all the same white rock with golden veins, and none containing viewing panes which might have granted her a glimpse of the outside world. The twin-confels do not cast any light here, neither is their stored energy used in artificial lighting. Everything in these corridors is bathed in light cast purely by vintinum. A mineral that emits as strong a light as anything manufactured in Siros, so long as the vapours in the air are thinner than those without. It explains a certain breathlessness she has retained since she was brought here. One she had attributed, until now, to the substance used to restrain her.

They reach a set of stairs, a flight that sinks deeper into the ground. Where they lead is cloaked in blackness, and Olessia falters. One attendant moves down a few steps. The other remains behind, and places a firm hand to the small of Olessia's back.

"Don't touch me."

The steep flight has a handrail on one side, and the air at the open side is as dark as that which awaits below. The knowledge she is likely underground, and being taken down even further, causes the pulses in Olessia's body to quicken.

"Apologies, my Higher. But you must continue."

In another circumstance, the attendant's voice might be soothing. A musical note to its rise and fall. But this is not that circumstance. Olessia leans back against the firm hand, refusing to take another step.

"You must come with us, my Higher." The attendant who has begun the flight down, turns to wave her forward. "If it is of some comfort, you should know that your companions await you. Down there."

"What? What did you say?" Olessia takes the first step. "Christian? Sen-Bay, they are down there?"

But the attendant has already moved on and offers no reply. Olessia hurries after her. Her skirt catches at the railing, causing her to stumble. She curses beneath her breath, pausing to gather as much of the cumbersome material as she can, exposing her lower legs entirely. She continues the march downward. The attendant sets a quick pace. Evidently this is not the first time the woman has taken this journey, and Olessia struggles to keep up.

The steps are narrow, and she must take shortened strides for each one. The muscles in her legs are soon screaming for respite, and her chest aches with each shallow breath. Her physical fitness leaves much to be desired. Using elthar to travel has done her few favours. The oddest thought flits through her mind. Perhaps when this is over, Lucas can show her how to ride those vehicles — a bicycle — he appears so fond of.

Olessia adjusts her hold on the bulky mound of material in her arms and refocuses. She evidently did not get enough restoration time back in the cluster; her fatigue still inciting delusional thinking.

The steps soon curve right and widen. Olessia's hand aches from clenching the smooth, metal handrail but at least the darkness that lay heavy at the base of the steps has peeled away. The end is actually in sight. And it is armed.

Alkell Guards, clad in their customary cloaks – a material the shade of the twin confels. And the Presider's eyes. His personal force. The Alkell wait either side of a triangular doorway, a light grey metal door stark against the white rock framing it. The entrance sits a generous distance above the ground. With no visible steps to reach it.

"Where am I?" Olessia whispers.

It is the first question she has asked of anyone since her arrival. Refusing to allow her voice to betray her fear. But now, down here, where the air is barely breathable and filled with the dust coming from the sheer white walls, Olessia can no longer keep up the charade.

There is no answer. Just a gesture. The attendant who whispered of her companions, the one who has refused to say another word, points towards the doorway. The Alkell take a step out from the door, turn in unison towards one another, shifting the jern shields they carry and placing the weapons across their chests.

The triangular door lowers from its apex, the narrow point moving towards the ground. The door is thick, rivalling the breadth of the shell of an Aventar, and looks to be made of the same near-impenetrable material. Pliotine. As the tip continues to lower, the room beyond comes into view. One that is as badly illuminated as the room where she was dressed.

Olessia squints, trying to make out the shadows moving within.

"Hey, I know you. Don't I?"

One of the shadows rushes towards her, stepping into a brighter section of the room, and Olessia's concerns about what awaits her dissolve beneath an overwhelming wave of relief.

Christian stands at the centre of room.

Now, instead of coaxing her forward the attendant must step hurriedly aside as Olessia rushes past.

Chapter 4

Olessia

Olessia's dash is short-lived. She is barely inside the chamber when she draws to a sudden halt. The Presider is seated on a low, backless chair just off to the side. Hands folded in his lap, he sits as still as the rock around him. Clothed in the angular lines he so favours, the woven metal of his vest forms sharp points at his shoulders, smaller jagged points encircle his wrists. Dashel stands close by, his Zentai clothing replaced with the far more familiar uniform of the Claven, a shade that is reminiscent of an Earthen forest. Olessia's stomach performs an unpleasant dance. Dashel is not the traitor she believed. He and the Presider are far worse. Destroyers of hope. Working to ensure no peace can exist between Zentai and Siros.

"Welcome, Olessia. I trust your journey wasn't too unpleasant." The Presider's expression doesn't alter from flat indifference, and the flinty gaze from which so many recoil, is fixed hard on her.

Olessia's gaze darts between her father and Christian. The human boy's appearance is dishevelled to say the least. His clothing is torn, scorch marks mar one pant leg and his feet are bare. The markings beneath his eyes are almost as dark as those of Sebastien. But it is not artificial colour beneath Christian's lower lids. It is exhaustion. And fear that sucks at his cheeks. There is no sign of the Yentern, an absence that only adds to Olessia's unease.

If terrible things have befallen Sen-Bay, the fault rests with her alone.

Christian clutches at his hair, the same mannerism he practised on Earth when under duress. "Can you help me?"

He frowns as he speaks, as though his words confuse him. Olessia sucks in the thin air. His words do confuse him. She worked a barrier around so many of his memories, took Ryder from them, with no time to complete the task with any finesse. His mind may be a labyrinth of memories, all disjointed and confusing.

"Christian, just keep calm," Olessia berates herself for the weak advice. "I will help you."

"Oh, truly? How do you intend to do that, Olessia?" The Presider sounds as though he is smiling but his lips do no such thing. She cannot recall when they ever have.

"Father, release him. I will submit to—" Olessia's body lifts into the air and races towards the domed roof. She cries out but once again finds herself helpless, unable to control her own body. A body that hits the metal plated ceiling with breathtaking ferocity. Before she can draw a full breath, she falls. Barely finding time to brace before her feet impact the floor.

"Submit?" Her father has not left his seat, his hands remain clasped in his lap. "The Laudess of Bax Un Tey will simply just submit for the sake of this?" The Presider sweeps his hand towards Christian. The terrified cry that leaves the human's lips stirs something cold and hard in the pit of Olessia's stomach. But it is not the Beckoning. That force does not shift, even as Christian screams and drops to his knees, clawing at his head. Olessia's fury warms her, but the Beckoning does not rise to the lure of it. Remaining deep, in a place she does not know.

"Stop, Father." Olessia rises onto unsteady legs.

"Or what? What will you do, Olessia?" The Presider tilts his chin. His eyes glint beneath the flicker of the golden veins criss-crossing the walls around them, turning his irises into pools of flame. Christian groans, rocking forward over his knees.

Olessia falters at her father's question. What will she do? What can she do? Olessia has no elthar, and the Beckoning is a dull weight within. The force that bent to her will at the Turning now barely a whisper inside her.

Olessia has no way to help Christian. Not down here in this void of a place.

"You wanted to use me, and you have done so," Olessia says. "This human, and the other, the Yentern that you tortured..." She directs a look towards Dashel that she hopes is laden with as much hatred as she intends but his smug, contented smile doesn't leave his lips. "I was your target. They have no place in this."

Dashel rests his hands behind his back and walks in slow, deliberate steps around Christian. His limp is evident; Olessia hopes the old injury is causing him discomfort. "Truly? They have no place? Come now, Laudess. If that were the case, then you would not be so clearly distressed by this boy's unfortunate plight." He stops in front of Christian and every fibre of Olessia's body tightens with alarm. The boy raises his head, tears dampen his cheeks and his breathing is violent, his chest heaving in sharp movements.

"I don't understand where I am," Christian says. "What is happening?"

Dashel crouches beside him. "Well that's exactly what we would like to know, you see. The Laudess cannot help you, in fact, you can blame her for the uncomfortable position you are in now."

"Laudess? I don't... I don't understand." Christian stumbles over his confusion. Two clear lines of fluid run from his nose. Tears still flow.

"I found a curiosity in the mindreach with the Yentern. Something that interests us more. Now that we have found what we truly sought." Dashel lifts one brow, nodding at Olessia. "And I'm hoping you can satisfy my curiosity. You told the Yentern about some friends of yours, in the Iondar realm. Who are Ryder and Sophie?"

The thin air vanishes altogether, and Olessia's legs threaten to buckle.

Christian screws up his nose, his eyes darting in a maddened pattern over Dashel's face. "Ryder? Friends? I don't... I've never..." He presses fingers to one temple. "Sophie... she's... a friend… a friend, I think." His chest rises and falls in quick succession, his distress growing. "But Ryder… I don't know… oh god." He covers his nose with one hand but Olessia spots the blood. Running in a narrow rivulet.

"Inel, stop," Olessia pleads. "The humans are weak creatures—"

The Presider hasn't moved from the position he retained when she raced in. "I am well aware, Olessia, of just how pathetic the species is. Is that why you left him with them?" Now the Presider tilts his head, a bare fraction to the right, considering her.

Her gut is awash with unsteady churning. "Left him? Who? Do you mean Christian, with the Yentern?" It is a fight to retain an outer calm, but Olessia is determined not to allow her trepidation to betray her.

"No. I do not. There is an absence here that is notable. Your Guardian. Sebastien, was that his name?" The Presider knows full well her Guardian's name. Olessia waits for him to continue. "Your little human boy here, spoke quite openly with the Yentern. Assuming you cannot be understood will cloud your judgement of what is wise to disclose. The Yentern might not have understood, but Dashel did. Quite clearly. And found something very interesting. Your human said that friends of his on Earth were being looked after by Sebastien. From the way he spoke of this, Sebastien, about how arrogant and quick-tempered the boy could be, and the tendency this Sebastien person had to morph his elthar into blades… Well, you can see where I might make the connection."

The shock of what the Presider is telling her freezes every joint.

"Come now," he says. "Enough of this, Olessia. You will tell me why your Guardian remains on Earth, watching over two human children instead of being at his sworn place. By your side. Or has Sebastien abandoned you? He will suffer the consequences for such a betrayal—"

"No," Olessia shouts. "He has betrayed no one."

"Then what has he done, Olessia?" The Presider's voice rises. No one else might notice the increase in volume, as subtle as it is, but Olessia has spent her life listening for the indicator that marks a corresponding rise in his temper. "What exactly did you and Aresh do in the Iondar realm?"

"I can assure you we did nothing as monumental as what you have done here. Creating a war where none should exist."

"The only thing I am creating is the environment to take what should be mine. Bax Un Tey needs one ruler. A strong ruler. It belongs to the Presiderline. And I will have it. You will have it."

It would be wise to stay silent. Christian's life is more endangered here than on the Zentai border, but still she ploughs on. Her father is threatening every single soul of importance to her. Even those he does not yet fully understand. He has Ryder's name. It is far closer than Olessia ever intended he get to her. She stumbles at one agonising thought. Aresh. Has he used her as well? Destroyed her in order to destroy the peace she fought to build?

"I'll take nothing from you." Olessia glares at her father, all too aware of how meaningless that title is. Olessia was not raised like the common people of Siros, or the Yentern in their Turning. Certainly not like the humans, with their family units. Nurturing, guiding, accepting the failings of one another. Olessia understands why Aresh could not set Earth from her mind. Could not resist embedding herself in its customs. Neither she nor Olessia were born of a union between two living beings. In a sense, they were manufactured. The Presiderline is a production line. A blending of cells and merging of genetic material designed to produce enhanced, powerful rulers. A fact that had been untroubling to her previously. Before Olessia found herself a part of the contrasting lives of others.

"I would rather see the Presiderline fall than take what you offer," Olessia growls. "I will give you *nothing*."

Dashel heaves a deep breath and looks to the Presider. "Shall I begin?"

The Presider's nod is barely perceptible. "You do not need to give me anything, Olessia. Aresh refused me also. But I have reason to believe all I need is right here. Inside this human's mind. Do you think me a fool? That I don't see you have created a Blackwall in this child's mind? You have hidden something behind that wall, and we will break him open to find it."

Dashel plants his hands either side of Christian's head, forcing her friend's chin up. Christian pulls his hand from his bleeding nose, and pounds at Dashel.

"No," Olessia cries. "No. Stop."

But her words disappear beneath Christian's fresh screams as Dashel launches his mindreach. Christian's body jerks, and his back arches. The blood flow from his nose surges, crimson fluid gushing over his lips and chin. His cries tear at his throat; a coarse, harsh sound.

The Blackwall Olessia imprinted on his mind is strong. And Dashel is brutal. The combination will likely kill Christian before they find any trace of Ryder's true identity. Olessia sucks in her breath; Christian may not even know that truth. So desperate to protect him at the Turning, Olessia didn't pause to think clearly. How much does he actually know of Ryder's abilities and her past? But Dashel will dig until there is nothing left to dig through.

Desperate, Olessia searches wills the Beckoning to rise to her command. It flickers, and for a delirious moment she believes it might listen. Only for the beast to sink deep and return to its slumber. Christian's cries grow weaker, gurgling up from his chest.

"Lucas!" She screams, offering up a sacrifice. "Sebastien is protecting Lucas. Not those girls. Lucas is not human. He is the surviving son of the Reigner."

Dashel pulls his hands from Christian's head and the boy slumps to the floor. Olessia stops herself from rushing to him.

"The Reigner? You speak nonsense, Laudess," Dashel sniffs. "For the Reigner to have a child of that Zentai's age, he would have had to have borne him when he was a child himself."

Fixing her gaze on the Presider, Olessia gives up Aresh's precious secret. "I'm not talking about the current Reigner… Lucas is the son of Reigner Bladen."

"Bladen?" Dashel's surprise brightens his dark face. He glances at the Presider.

"There, you see?" the Presider says. "You did give me something after all, Olessia. You have given me the proof I have sought. Now there can be no doubt. Laudine Aresh has long worked against me. She is a traitor."

Chapter 5

Ryder

Someone is groaning. Really close by. Ryder tilts her head away from the sound, and the simple movement sets off a painful eruption in her head. A headache that's a marching band against the back of her eyes. Her eyelids are lead-heavy, and the thought of trying to open them makes her head ache even more.

Something bad has happened. The memory is slippery and Ryder frowns as she tries to latch onto it.

"Sebastien?" The word bubbles between her lips. He was here, wasn't he? They were together. Ryder touches her bottom lip and her fingers come away damp. The fluid is on her chin too. Suddenly she wishes she didn't have to open her eyes. Ever. There are bad things beyond the darkness. Horrible things. Clawing at her. Niggling at her head where the ache grows stronger.

The groaning beside her stops, but there is no silence. Other sounds reach her. A hissing. A metallic clang of metal against metal. Footsteps.

Get up, Ryder. Go.

Ryder's eyes fly open, her unease thrown aside.

"Padellah?" Whatever is on her lips, sprays with the cry. Flecks of something dark.

But it wasn't Padellah's voice in her head. She knew that even before she uttered the name. This voice is fainter, a higher pitch, and singular. Not a bunch of voices whispering at once. Ryder runs her tongue over her lip, tasting blood. A wide cut, right in the middle of her bottom lip stings with the contact.

Eyes now open, there is no hiding from where she is – still strapped to her seat in the cabin of the Zentai ship. The Commandant hangs limp in her seat, eyes closed. Several cuts marking her bald scalp but no drastic bleeding. The cabin is chaotic, filled with debris that shouldn't be here. Branches and pebbles. So many pebbles. The lighting is out in most of the cabin, a few of the surviving veins providing the only illumination. The wall to her left has a massive dent at its centre, and one of the wide panes of glass is gone altogether while the other has more cracks than substance.

Ryder takes a breath, readying to call out.

For Sophie.

The recall hits like whiplash, taking Ryder's body and trying to snap it in half. Sophie won't answer. Ryder bites into the cut on her lip, pressing back the anguish.

"Ryder, are you all right?" Sebastien staggers to her side. He cradles one arm against his belly, and wide flows of blood run down either side of his face. His blood is so much darker than hers. Dark enough to appear black in the dimness. Seeing him, it all comes back in a rush. What Blane told her.

That Olessia is gone. Just like Sophie. Sebastien doesn't know. Ryder's certain of it. He might have been frustrated, angry, when they were forcing him to pilot the craft but he wasn't inconsolable. Furious beyond all calming. And that, she is sure, is how he'll be if he hears about Olessia.

Ryder shakes her head; decision made. "I'm okay, but what about you?"

She can't do it. Tell him about Olessia. Not yet. Besides the pain it would inflict, Ryder just can't bring *herself* to believe it. Something about the news unsettles her. Doesn't sit right.

Sebastien waves off her question. "Can you move? We must go. Quickly."

She hears his sharp intake of breath as he leans forward, a quickly stifled cry as he searches for the release on her harness. "Sebastien, you don't look okay."

"I should have actioned my elthar earlier, but I was pre-occupied with trying to avoid the impact altogether. It all happened so rapidly."

He runs his hand over the top of the chair's headrest and her harness whips away. Ryder pushes herself to her feet, expecting something to hurt. Wanting it to hurt. Anything to distract her from where her thoughts refuse to be distracted. But she really is okay. Aside from the headache, and a cut lip, Ryder doesn't have a scratch.

"What happened? Did you... did you do this on purpose?" she says.

Ryder's actually relieved to see Sebastien's familiar scowl return. The way he is moving so gingerly gives her a prickling sense of alarm.

"No. I would not risk your life that way," he says, his voice strained. "That was river turbulence like I've never seen before. The craft's systems couldn't accommodate such powerful unrest. The secondary pilot was incapacitated, I wasn't informed how, but they seemed to believe that I was better equipped to handle the turbulence than any other Zentai on board." He shakes his head, but only the once. Wincing. "I did what I could but we were hopelessly out of control by the time we exited the River." Sebastien moves to the Commandant, who is still unconscious. He removes several pieces from her utility belt. "Still, it has afforded us a chance we must take. I've taken care of those in this room who were not knocked out in the crash, but this is a large ship, we won't be alone for long. Move, Ryder."

Ryder isn't about to scan the room too closely to find out just what he means by 'taking care' of the others. She follows direction, heading to where he points – the shattered front window. A sense of déjà vu coming over her. This is not her first escape through the front windows of an alien aircraft, with an injured Guardian. And she would give anything, *anything*, to be back in the Paldrian River. She'd go into that river a million times over if it could alter the events that came after.

Losing Sophie.

Losing Olessia.

Ryder has run several paces before she realises Sebastien is lagging behind. A very obvious limp keeping his pace far slower than normal.

"Sebastien, you're hurt."

"Of course I'm hurt," he snaps. "While you were secured in your seat, I was being flung around the cabin as though I were made of enyos."

"You sound like you wish I had been hurt."

"Don't be utterly ridiculous. Just go, get out of here." He spits the words, far more riled up than the situation warrants. Which makes Ryder certain of what she only suspected before. He's hurt worse than he's letting on. "Don't wait for me."

"Yeah, right. Now it's your turn to be so utterly ridiculous." Ryder makes a mess of mimicking his voice; that arrogant, haughty voice. But he must have hit his head harder than she did if he thinks she'll leave him hobbling alone. Ryder back-tracks and grabs one of Sebastien's arms, slipping it over her shoulders. He tries to cover up his cry but does as bad a job of that as she did with imitating him.

"Sorry." Ryder adjusts her hold. "That better?"

"Yes." He relaxes against her, tension suddenly evaporating. "Let's go."

They crunch through debris littering the apex of the cabin. The tip of one of the triangular levels that makes up the craft, has arrowed into the ground, collecting dirt and other things, objects Ryder doesn't recognise: something that might have come from a willow tree, if not for the curious dots that mark the length of the branches, and a moss-like substance whose tendrils are far curlier than anything on Earth.

Ryder holds Sebastien a little tighter. This time, when she steps through the shattered windows of a spacecraft she is not stepping into a river. And she is not stepping back into her world. The thought makes her heart race.

The moment they clear the framework, Ryder gets her first glimpse of exactly what world she is stepping into. And she's never seen anything quite so beautiful. Soaring mountains rise either side of the downed craft, but they are unlike any she's seen before. These are sunset pink, glowing with a soft light in a world that is otherwise pitch dark.

"The Dovers," Sebastien says. "At the Greater Reach, if I'm not wrong. We are close to the Arlion Xhentex."

"Is that a good thing?"

"It is better than being on the doorstep of Falllyn, but I don't know yet if it is a good thing."

"Falllyn?"

"The Zentai Complex-Main. You would call it their capital."

Ryder shivers, but aside from having just crash-landed on an alien world, there is no reason to feel a chill. The atmosphere is uncomfortably warm, her armpits growing damp by the time she and Sebastien move just a few metres from the craft. Her black long-sleeved shirt clings to her, her jeans too heavy a material for the heat.

You need to move faster. Ryder jumps and Sebastien curses low and vehemently.

"What is wrong?" he says.

"You didn't hear that?" Ryder asks. Though the answer is fairly obvious.

"I hear concerning sounds emitting from the Baershard."

Ryder keeps peering into the dark, looking for her whisperer. "You are really going to have to work on the translation thing."

"The ship. The Zentai call those larger vessels Baershard. Move faster."

It's not Ryder who needs to move faster, but she stays silent and, practically lifting Sebastien off his feet, quickens their pace. The ease with which she can raise him catches her off-guard, and she glances at his wrists to see if Sebastien's using his elthar. He's not. And with her own bracelets removed by the Zentai, there's no chance it's her. Maybe gravity is different here. And she's a pro-lifter all of a sudden.

"Why did they let you keep your elthar?" Ryder says.

"Let me keep it?" Sebastien grunts with the effort of matching her pace. "They have little choice. Unless they decide to amputate my arms, which they may have viewed as an option, I suppose. My elthar cannot be removed as easily as your bracelets. Wait… Ryder… the senlier. You are not wearing it.”

“It fell off, just before we crashed,” Ryder replies, her attention on their surroundings. The speaker whispered so quick and breathless, so low, it was like hearing a murmur from the other side of a wall. “I guess with everything going crazy, they lost control over it too.”

Sebastien stays silent, and she can feel his eyes on her. The senlier thing is weird. She knows it without him saying a thing. If someone like Olessia can’t remove the terror-tiara, then Ryder sure as heck can’t.

A loud over-revving sound comes from the Baershard. Engines straining higher and higher. Like someone’s foot is coming down hard on the gas pedal. The vessel is huge, easily five times the size of the Aventar. Well, was huge. The impact has broken it in two. And the front half seems to have continued its journey a little longer than the rear section which is some way back, caught in what might be a rock formation. It’s kind of hard to make out, mostly because the whole thing is on fire. Incredible flames of powder blue rise and writhe more like smoke than actual flame. Ryder’s blood seems to chill.

“Blane. We’ve just left him there.” She fights to keep her aching thoughts from the other person they have left behind.

“He was no ally,” Sebastien says, bitter. “I will take no risks for him. Keep going. Head over there, see that large fissure in the outcrop?” Sebastien points but doesn’t hold his arm up long enough for Ryder to make out what he’s referring to.

“Where? I can’t see—”

The rear part of the Zentai ship explodes in a catastrophic fireworks display of brilliant blues and subtler orange light.

“Go, go!” Sebastien shouts. “There will be a chain reaction.” He shoves Ryder ahead of him.

She bolts for the nearest rock cluster shaped like a collection of anthills. In the near-blinding brightness its evident the rocks are crystal of some kind. Whatever they are, Ryder hopes they are strong. She slides into a gap between the two greater piles of crystal, her knees shredded by the rough ground. But it’s a lucky find, the 'ant-hills' form a low curved wall around the open space she crouches in. A natural mini-fortress.

Sebastien wasn't wrong about the chain reaction. Ryder watches the blue flame chew up the distance between the two sections of the craft.

"Sebastien, move faster. Use your elthar."

He's broken into a run but he's still too far away. Ryder jumps to her feet, ready to rush to him.

The flames engulf the front portion of the Baershard with a roar, and terrible sounds pour from the stricken vessel: the shattering of a felled tree, the scream of tortured metal. Magnified until they are deafening.

Sebastien isn't going to make it. He's screaming at her to get back. At least, that's what she assumes he's yelling, but the catastrophic sounds coming from the craft obliterate everything else.

The flames around the vessel suck in on themselves. *Backdraft.* Readying for the big bang.

Without warning Sebastien flies at Ryder and she leaps aside to avoid the impact. Sebastien's eyes are wide, his mouth gaping. No elthar glows at his wrists.

He hits the ground, and rolls. Shifting to his knees just shy of the v-shaped entrance to the shelter.

"Quick, get in here," Ryder shouts.

He is barely inside when the Baershard explodes.

Everything is blue. Smurf blue. No other colour exists. The ground shakes with a growing fervour. Sebastien leans over her, his shoulders and chest forming a makeshift roof. The shock wave buffets the crystal mounds. Ryder's hair whips against her eyes, making them water. Elthar peeks from the collar of Sebastien's army-green t-shirt, and layers his bare arms. Something digs into Ryder's ribs but she's not about to move. Debris slams to the ground around them. Pieces of metal falling dangerously close for comfort. One clips the peak of the closest 'anthill', and crystal shards coat them like candy-floss coloured rain.

"Oh my god." Ryder digs her fingers into crevices in the rock.

The entire world seems intent on shaking itself apart. The rumbling drags out for what feels like a terrifying eternity but must only be a few seconds. Finally, the light wavers, like when a cloud passes quickly across the sun. The Smurf-blue glow vanishes. Once again there is heavy darkness. Even the weak sunset shimmer coming from the mountains seems to have paled. Sebastien sits back on his heels, the elthar's glow already vanished.

"Are you hurt?" he says.

Ryder shakes her head. The air is thick with dust and it sticks to the inside of her nostrils.

"You?" She coughs.

"Fine. We need to keep moving. That blast will be noticed, even if by some great chance the crash was not."

"No kidding." Ryder uses the crystal as a prop to haul herself to her feet. "Hey, what happened back there? You kind of flew through the air but your elthar wasn't—"

"Activated, no." His brow furrows. "It must have been the build up from the explosion. I felt the pressure at my back."

Even he doesn't seem convinced by his explanation, but he's not prepared to discuss it, apparently. Sebastien turns on his heel and heads away. But Ryder lingers a moment. She brushes her hair back from her face, her fingers tangling in a bunch of knots. The copper tang of blood is fresh in her mouth again, the cut in her lip reopened. The odd blue flames, or smoke – she can't decide – are thick around what is left of the ship. Whatever fuel the craft used has done a thorough job of destroying it. There's a portion of framework still visible, curved sections of metal that lie like a dinosaur's rib cage, but aside from that the Zentai craft — and its contents — have been obliterated. The dust works its way into Ryder's eyes, and tears blur her vision.

"Ryder, I'm sorry. But we have to go."

Sebastien says it gently, carefully. No hint of his usual impatience. And his softness only makes the tears fall faster. Ryder swipes at her face, using the edge of her dirty sleeve to clear the tears. She turns away, leaving the ruined ship and its cargo behind.

Chapter 6

Ryder

Sebastien and Ryder walk along the valley floor, searching for some kind of cover. Well, Ryder walks. Sebastien hobbles, insisting every time she asks that he is fine. A lie, of course, they both know it, but she's not about to push the point. It's way too hot to argue anyway. It's too hot to think straight. Which is kind of a blessing, considering where her thoughts continually venture.

For half an hour there has been nothing but a squishy moss-like ground cover and random mounds of crystal. None of them tall enough to hide behind. The ground-cover sinks beneath Ryder's feet. Trudging through it is as difficult as walking through deep sand, and her calf muscles are screaming at her to take a break. The humidity is energy-sucking, her clothes stick to her body in damp patches, and the sweat running down her face always find the cut on her lip.

On the plus side, it is very dark, and they are very much alone. Not even the chitter of insects disrupts the silence. Nothing in the sky, no sign of searchlights trailing from behind. If that's how they search here. Do insects actually exist in this place?

It even smells different here. The air holds an odour almost like cut grass. Almost. So much about the place is 'almost' like home. But back home the mountains don't shimmer at night, and the moss doesn't go pale beneath the pressure of your feet.

Ryder hugs herself, keeping her eyes fixed on the ground, trying to make out the terrain in the darkness. Twice she's stepped in a hole and almost turned her ankle.

This is not the sort of place you want to injure yourself. Ryder's spent a good part of the last thirty minutes trying to stop her brain from working. Keep it quiet. Hoping to keep it from throwing images of Sophie at her. And Blane.

"Here, we will go right." Sebastien set off at quite the pace earlier, maybe adrenaline pushing him on, but it's definitely worn off now. And despite the darkness, Ryder can tell from the sway of his body that the limp has gotten worse.

"Maybe we should take a break—"

"No."

End of conversation. The trudge continues. Up ahead, a dark mass seems to coalesce. As they near, Ryder sees that Sebastien is headed for a forest. Or at least a cluster of trees. Tall and dense. Rising into the night sky, their tops lost in the darkness. Some have incredible twisted trunks, reminding her of a lollipop twirl minus all the hyperactivity-inducing food colouring. With so little light, she can't make out what colour the trunks actually are. Everything is some shade of grey or black. Sebastien doesn't stop when he gets to the edge of the forest, just ploughs straight in, pushing through the mess of vines and reedy undergrowth that hug the base of the trees. Ryder follows, glancing one last time over her shoulder. Blackness eats everything. Even the glimmer of powder-blue light they had been able to see for a while has completely disappeared. Perhaps someone has made it to the wreckage. Put out those weird blue smoke-flames. Whatever the case, it's as though the crash site never existed in the first place.

If only.

Ryder turns and smacks straight into a hanging mass of reed-thin branches.

"Ah!" She hits out at them. But it's just a plant. Nothing is attacking her. Not yet. She slaps out again. Teeth clenched so hard it hurts her jaw. Ryder grabs a handful of the helpless branches, wrenches them free. "Get away from me. Just. Get. Away. from. Me."

She stomps on the fallen foliage, grinding her sneaker into the slender fronds.

"What's wrong?" Sebastien hurries back to her, his footfall cracking the undergrowth.

"Nothing, nothing." Ryder's breath comes quickly, and the sweat gathering at her temples finds its way down her cheeks. "I'm fine. Just fine."

Sebastien pushes through the damaged hanging plant and grips her shoulders. "Ryder, look at me."

But she doesn't want to. She needs to make sure every bit of this stupid plant is ground into nothing. Heat builds in her chest, and weaves its way up her neck, finding its way into her aching head. The added heat makes the air thick as a blanket against her body. Stifling her. Drowning her.

"Ryder." Sebastien raises his voice and his fingers are digging through the material of her shirt. "Ryder, stop. Look at me."

He shakes her. Hard. And she snaps her head up to glare at him. Before she realises what she's doing she's raised her hand. Aiming to strike. Lashing out at him like she did the hapless vines. But their eyes meet before she takes a swing. The air cools. Those twin pools of grey find her, even in the darkness, and Ryder sinks into them. She lowers her hand, bringing it to rest against her mouth, trembling so hard it's difficult to keep it steady against her lips.

"I'm sorry," she mumbles.

Sebastien's hands fall from her shoulders. There is the tiniest moment of hesitation and then he wraps his arms around her, bringing her in closer. Pressing his lips to her forehead. Ryder closes her eyes, and takes deep, shuddering breaths as she tries to keep a grip on the floodgates that are desperate to open. She keeps one hand against her mouth but presses the other against Sebastien's chest. A faint and unfamiliar rhythm vibrates against her palm.

"I am the one who is sorry," Sebastien whispers, his lips still against her skin. "Sorry that you must endure the loss of a friend."

Ryder bites her tongue to stop the sob escaping her. Now. Now is the time to tell him about Olessia. But the words won't come. They can't find a way past the sob. And she can't bring herself to dump this pain on him. Because no matter what Sebastien may say, or how he acts, he will hurt as keenly as she does now.

Long seconds pass, and finally Sebastien steps back. Ryder's eyes flutter open. As her eyes adjust, something shifts in the shrubbery off to Sebastien's right, a sideways movement of shadow. Ryder blinks, goosebumps rising on her arms. A light breeze toys with the foliage, setting off a tinkling musical sound as branches sway. She can just make out the twisted trunk of one of those strange trees. Two branches stick out at an angle, about halfway up the trunk. They look a heck of a lot like arms, waving to her with the help of the breeze. Ryder sighs and rubs at her temples. The marks of the senlier are tender spots on her skin. She'd almost forgotten how it slid from her head right before impact.

"We'll rest here a moment," Sebastien says. "I'm going to find a hydration source. Do not leave this location."

He's gone before she says a word, as though he can't get away quick enough. Leaving her in the dark, in this alien world. But Ryder is too exhausted, too drained to much care. She sinks to the ground, leaning against one of the lollipop trees. She expected the trunk to be like wood, but it's another stark reminder she's a long way from home when she finds a far softer texture. She could be propped up against a body pillow. Ryder rests her head on it, tilting her chin so she can gaze up at the canopy. Not that there is anything distinguishable to see there. The darkness is like spilled ink above her. The mountains are hidden, and their soft light has no chance of getting through the barrier.

All around her the low melodic sounds of the wind moving through this strange forest fill the air. And still not a hint of any insects or animals moving in the undergrowth. Ryder sits up. Now there's no sound at all. No singing branches. No crunch and crack of Sebastien moving through the undergrowth, but instinct holds her back from calling out and drawing attention to herself while she's sitting her alone in a place that is as foreign as a dream. A place that seems to be holding its breath.

She squints, peering hard at a particularly black section of darkness. Down off to her left. There's a solidness to that patch that isn't noticeable elsewhere, but unlike when she mistook the tree for a person, there is nothing about this shape that makes the hairs on the back of her neck stand up. Not yet anyway.

Ryder settles back against her botanical body-pillow, but her eyes don't leave the dark mass. As her spine finds the softness of the tree, a light appears within the dark patch. Subtle, super subtle. Ryder blinks quickly, trying to work out if it's real or if her eyes are just playing tricks on her.

No tricks.

The air is brightening in that solitary patch of dense black. Right at the core. Subtle tendrils of light easing outwards, as though a tiny sun were pushing through cloud.

"Padellah?" The word croaks out of her, probably incoherent to anyone listening in. If it is the Cyne entity, then this is not her usual way of appearing. This is… weak… far too understated. And everything around Ryder is far too still. Padellah seems to enjoy a bit more of a grand entrance, throwing around whatever is nearby, or stirring up the breeze.

Ryder.

Ryder pushes forward onto her knees. The voice echoes, bouncing so rapidly she can't make out where it's coming from. Inside her head? Or out?

"Ryder."

She jerks her chin. The sound is definitely coming from behind her. Definitely outside her own head.

Sebastien stands just clear of another low-hanging mass of vines, and he's not alone. A hooded figure stands with him, a panel of mesh hiding any sign of a face. Where eyes might be there is a single panel of glowing green. And they are very clearly holding something against Sebastien's neck. Short as a pen knife but with two blades instead of one. Sebastien's captor issues a deep cawing sound followed by gun-fire like clicks.

"Ryder, stay still." Sebastien's hands are raised but his voice is low. Steady. "No sudden movement."

She freezes, halfway to standing. An uncomfortable crouch that's going to be super hard to hold if this goes on for long. But moving even just the tiniest inch seems like a terrible idea.

A humming noise comes from the figure holding Sebastien, followed by more clicks. They swing their head side to side in three jerky movements. The drape of material that covers the weapon falls away. Ryder keeps her expression neutral, at least that's her intention, but it's hard not to react to the sight of the appendage that grips the weapon. No fingers, just a claw. An over-sized scorpion's tail. The needle-point just inches from Sebastien's neck.

The cloaked figure is half a head taller than him, and they lean forward, peering over Sebastien's shoulder. The glowing rectangular shape at the centre of its face panel casts light against the guardian's face. His expression is totally unreadable. No fury, no concern. Nothing the captor could misinterpret and over-react to. But it means there is nothing for Ryder to read either. No hint of what Sebastien wants her to do.

"Ryder, move slowly, raise your hands," he says. "Show we mean no harm."

She searches his face for some sign of what's to come. Smooth indifference stares back at her. "I don't—"

The captor makes the same twitching head movement to one side, and all at once it dawns on Ryder. They are indicating a direction. The direction they want Ryder to follow, but she's frozen to the spot. She needs something from Sebastien, anything, to tell her what to do. Her hands stay at her sides. Knees still bent.

"Ryder," Sebastien says. "I believe our visitor here would like us to come with them."

"Sebastien, what do we—"

The *visitor* twitches their head yet again. But this time it's a sudden jerk forward. They tilt their head down further over Sebastien's shoulder. The odd movement suggesting a much longer neck hides beneath the layers of clothing.

"Seeebasstien." They drag out his name, pulling it like toffee, distorting it until it's barely recognisable. "Guaaardiaaan. Yeeeessss."

Ryder's heart seems to stop mid-beat. A frown shadows Sebastien's brow. But he seems as uncertain as Ryder and doesn't reply.

All at once, the visitor releases him. Raising long, sinewy arms. The breeze returns, and sets the cloak billowing, pressing back against an almost skeletal frame. The material at both arms slips free, revealing talons and skin the colour of mould on bread. The visitor bleets. There's no other word for it, a staccato hammer of beats that mark the air. They raise the weapon, and though Ryder braces, Sebastien seems to relax. A hair's-breadth release of his shoulders. The visitor turns the weapon upside down, and bleets again. The blades vanish beneath the folds of the cloak.

Ryder's still crouched, her thighs burning and trembling.

The visitor lets loose a caw, and this time there is no mistaking what it wants from them. No jerky head movement this time. Instead, a lengthening of one arm, with a crescent-moon talon waving them forward. The cloaked figure does a half-turn, gestures again, crow-calls.

Sebastien's arms are still raised, and his frown deepens.

Ryder licks her torn lip before speaking. "Sebastien, I think it wants us to follow."

"I have established that, Ryder."

"Okay, well have you *established* what we do?"

The visitor uses both arms now to urge them forward, adding a new gesture. Both talons jab at the sky. The cawing gains a higher pitch. It wants them to move from here. And move right now.

Sebastien places himself between Ryder and the hooded figure. "We will follow. But be prepared to run."

Chapter 7

Olessia

Olessia sits at the heart of her domed cell, cross-legged, the lengthy folds of crimson spreading around her like a pool of blood. She lowers her head. The Presider and Dashel removed themselves within a few moments of her blurted declaration.

Olessia betrayed Lucas. Gave him up. And that knowledge sits as heavy as the immense layers of Pliotine that imprison her. A burning sensation deep in her gut has grown stronger with each moment she sits here. But it is not the familiar lurch and pull of the Beckoning. This is somehow even less pleasant, pushing a hard lump to the base of her neck. Its width grows with each swallow. In time, it may restrict her from breathing altogether.

Much the way this confined space does. They have accommodated her with one paltry length of bedding, a panel of foreen that is unyielding against her body. The floor would be a kinder option for a restorative slumber. There are no obvious hydration sources. Nor any amenities that would offer the opportunity to relieve herself if the need arose. This space has not been created to hold anyone for great lengths of time and survive.

Olessia's back straightens, taunt with a sudden, violent thought. Is it possible? Would the Presider stoop to this level? Restrict her from all life-sustaining privileges until there was no life left to sustain? The fire in her belly spreads its claws at the thought.

Olessia should be able to throw off the question with a caustic, reassured no. *No.* Her own father would not end her for the sake of his own thirst for absolute power.

Confine her. Yes. Spread false word of her death, yes. But end her?

"I don't know." Olessia presses her palms against the natural unevenness of the floor. It is solid beneath her touch, but she is unsteady. A tremor starts at her core, her aching burning core, and flows through her veins. Finding its way to the tips of her fingers.

The Presiderline heirs are created. Her Father, Inel, could create another in her place to further the line. The birthing would take time, the growth longer still, but it is not an impossibility. The Presider is many things, including robust and unplagued by any ill-health. There are many more visn in his future. He has time.

Olessia folds forward, covering her face with her hands.

The vision she held of wielding her power to end her father's reign now appears utterly childish and fraught with impossibility. She knew the Presider had a role for her, that he hunted her for a purpose, but for too long she assumed it was her Beckoning he sought. Failing to notice his use for her may be far simpler still. He needed a reason to declare war.

Instead of ending his reign, she provided him with ammunition. And now Lucas is compromised. Perhaps Ryder too.

Olessia remains on her knees. Face covered, eyes and body smouldering. Rocking in gentle movements. Isolated. Alone. The sear of heat in her belly grows stronger; the obstacle that rests in her throat growing larger.

The door to her cell emits a rush of air before it begins to lower. But the new arrival does not halt her slow swaying. The clatter of footsteps suggests more than one person has entered her space, but the patter of multiple feet quietens, until only one set is audible. One set that approaches. A platter is placed on the ground before her. Olessia peeks through her fingers to see it is covered with an elaborate lid of plestex crystal, etched with a design she recognises readily enough. This has come from Kinna-Brey itself. She has eaten more than one meal from such a platter. But still, Olessia does not raise her head.

"We will return on the half-liss to clear away the refreshments, Laudess."

Her rocking halts, but her head remains lowered. That voice.

"Ensure you have fully sustained yourself, Laudess. It would serve you well to retain your strength." The speaker halts for several pulses, then continues. "It would please the Presider."

Olessia's fingers press at her cheeks. Perhaps Inel does not wish her non-existence after all. She admonishes herself for the brief flutter of relief. Even if that were so, her survival would not be fuelled by an affection on her father's part.

The speaker steps away. They pause once again. She feels their eyes upon her but Olessia has neither the desire or inclination to raise her head. In time, the visitors retreat. And it is only at the very last moment, when she hears the door begin to rise once again, that Olessia glances up.

Her ears had not deceived her. The voice is as familiar as the face that stares back at her. Gone a moment later as the thick slab of Pliotine closes into place.

Sentinel Teler. The Sentinel appointed by Aresh, years ago, to train Olessia in tactical defence and survival. She crawls towards the platter, her pulses suddenly alight with hope. She raises the lid and breathes in deep. A blend of sweet vir and tart msonal. She grasps the edge of the platter until it pains her. This is her favoured meal. A preference known by the very few who bothered to discover what she enjoyed eating.

The Presider cannot be counted among those few. Certainly not Dashel.

The message is loud and clear. Olessia is not as alone as she feared.

Chapter 8

Christian

C hristian hauls against the hand gripping his arm. Twisting and contorting his body until a muscle in his back spasms, and he gives up the fight. For now. Just while he catches his breath, which he can't seem to do no matter how deep a lungful he takes. But wherever these freaks in their body-hugging grey uniforms and stupid golden cloaks think they're dragging him, they've got another thing coming.

"Let me go. Put me down."

Fear is making his voice pitch and tilt like crazy, and he's fairly certain the guy on the left — the one that could be a Legolas stunt double from *Lord of the Rings*, with his long white hair and chiselled jawline — actually smirked at one point. Amused.

Not worried in the slightest. Not like him. Christian is shaking so hard even his thoughts are jumping around inside his skull. They've probably been telling him to shut up, they've occasionally muttered something at him, but Christian can't make it out. Russian, he thought to begin with, but this doesn't feel at all like Russia. Not unless they like to build diamond-shaped corridors and tile them with a million tiny black tiles so the whole place feels like walking through a black hole. There's no obvious light source, no fixtures on the walls, but the whole length of the corridor is bright with light. Almost as though the air itself is glowing. Maybe that's why he can't breathe properly in this place, why it feels like he's been punched in the chest. But so far these guys haven't done anything more than drag him along. Maybe he's sucking down particles of light, not oxygen.

Definitely not Russia then. Nausea does a trapeze act in his stomach.

Christian has no clue *where* this place is, or why he's in it. And that doesn't sit well. He's spent his time shouting and kicking and lashing out, trying to shove his thoughts off the rail road track they're hurtling along. Screaming straight towards terrified-mess station. He's never been so frightened. It's official. And he's been fighting the urge to throw up since he woke up on that… what? An airplane?

One hell of an airplane. Not like anything he's seen before. Nor was the young guy with him. What was his name? Sun? Sentai? The guy had no ears! Nothing on the side of his head. Bizarre, and again, definitely not Russian. But if Christian was deciphering hand-gestures and facial expression clearly enough, then the guy didn't intend to hurt him. At least, not at that point in time. The earless stranger was gentle when he touched Christian's cheek, caressed it, and there was sadness in those strange dark eyes — irises and pupils merged into a singular ball of black. Christian felt the oddest tug of familiarity. And the even odder urge to grab him in a hug and hold on tight. Like this odd-looking stranger was someone he should never let go. Or out of his sight. But neither of them had any say in the matter. The guy with the missing ears was gagged and rough-handled off the… plane… as soon as they touched down.

The guards pause at a crossroad in the corridors. Narrow walkways run off in about half a dozen different directions. They hold Christian between them like an old coat while they seem to try and decide which way to proceed.

"You need to let me go." Christian needs to be doing something, anything, or he's not sure he won't start bawling like a baby and never be able to stop.

They continue on as though he's not said a thing. He's shaking so hard they have to be able to feel it. No wonder they aren't reacting. They know he's as big a threat as a sack of jelly.

Christian's been shouting to be let go since they dragged him out of that metal cave. Where that girl with the incredible violet eyes was screaming at those two older guys to let Christian go.

Just thinking about those men now makes his guts flip. One of them, a bald guy with a touch of white hair around his jawline, just stood there. Staring down at Christian like he was a slug he wanted to grind under his heel. He wasn't a tall man, in fact Christian was certain he was taller but he'd been kept on his knees from the moment the guy entered the room and there was no chance for real comparison.

The second man wasn't built like a tank either, in fact at first glance he was as intimidating as Christian's old geography teacher, Mr Bronwin. Which was to say, not at all. But first glances can be deceiving. Not with Mr Bronwin, he wouldn't hurt a fly, but this guy was a different story. From the moment he settled himself on the solitary chair that occupied the barren room, the air changed. The temperature notched up, dank and uncomfortable, just like it had been outside this place. The sudden warmth dragged down the air, making it thinner than it already had been. The moment this man entered the room Christian's fear grew wilder, goosebumps marched across his skin.

Christian swallows down the memory. The guy had eyes like flames. The outer tip of his almond-shaped eyes seemed to stretch all the way back to his temple. Kind of reminded Christian of the ancient Egyptians, but where they had used dark eyeliner to achieve the result, this guy's seemed to be all natural. The girl that joined them had it too, the elongated sweep, only not quite as exaggerated. And her eye colour was an insanely bright shade of purple. Like amethyst stones had caught on fire. He could have sworn that for a second, her eyes turned into mini-windmills. The colour of the irises rotating.

When he first came too, on board some kind of high-tech aircraft, Christian thought for a moment he'd been taken to Asia somewhere. Japan maybe. But it was a fleeting thought. A closer look at everyone on board — with their luminously pale skin and angular features — told him that wherever he was, it was a long, long way from Tokyo.

And Russia.

Christian swallows hard. Earth.

He's a long way from *Earth*.

The guards pick a direction, finally. And they are on the move again, their orange cloaks flowing behind them. They lift Christian between them so his feet don't even reach the floor now. Impressive considering he's taller than both of them. It must take some significant strength to hold him up, but neither of them appear bothered. They nod at a passing guard, dressed in the same wet-suit tight grey uniform and flame-coloured cloak, who gives Christian an unreadable look before passing by.

No. This is definitely not Russia or Tokyo.

Or Earth.

Christian moans. One of the guards, his white hair braided in a tight, winding pattern over his head, throws him a look that might be inquisitive. Or might be a warning. Shut up or we'll cut out your tongue kind of thing.

Maybe Christian hit his head. Hard. Really, really hard. It still aches. And everything about this place has the strangeness of dreaming. A messed-up nightmare, that's what this is. He's still unconscious. In a heap somewhere after... after what? Doing what? Christian grimaces and squeezes his eyes closed. Bits of his brain seem to have come loose. Rattling around in his head, sending shooting bolts of pain through to his temples.

No. Nightmares didn't have pain that was so real. When that bald-headed guy clamped his hands on either side of Christian's head the agony had been unbelievable. Christian's head was a walnut and that guy's hands were nutcrackers. The pain was staggering. Even the broken arm when Christian was a kid, doesn't compare. Not one little bit. But she stopped it. Somehow. The girl with the violet eyes.

Screamed at them to stop. He didn't need translation to work out what those cries meant. And if Christian wasn't mistaken, she was terrified they wouldn't listen. Her name shoots out of the muddle in Christian's head.

Olessia.

His rattling brain throws a few daggers at the back of his eyes. Why did that girl care?

The guards come to an abrupt halt, releasing Christian. He sways on his feet, knees weak with expectation of what might come next. Apparently, they have reached their destination. It's a dead end up ahead. A wall of sparkling black tiles blocking the way.

A voice filters down the corridor but Christian doesn't turn to see who is approaching. He can't. Any attempt to move will topple him. He's a shaking, solid mass. Certain the bald man has returned to finish off what he started.

Words are exchanged between the guards and the approaching stranger. The higher rise of a female voice reaches them. But Christian's fear-struck body doesn't find any release. He's being held against his will, in a secluded, dead-end corridor on the orders of that fire-eyed man. And that can't mean anything good.

Nothing about that guy seems good. He's a thousand headmasters, a hundred bullies and a dozen angry parents rolled into one.

The guards step away, disappearing behind Christian. But he remains with eyes locked forward, swaying. His back to whoever approaches. His breath comes in ragged gasps. The woman speaks again. And Christian dares to imagine that maybe it's the violet-eyed girl. The stranger brushes past him and positions herself in front of the wall. He can only see the back of her head, but Christian already has his answer. It is not the violet-eyed girl. This is a grown woman, reed-thin. She is about the same height as the girl, with the same pale skin and jet-black hair, but her tresses cascade to the base of her spine, and is woven with glistening threads of varying colours: jade greens and coppery reds, baby pink and a sky blue that glints brightest of all.

The woman glances over her shoulder but looks past Christian. Doesn't seem to notice him at all. Her eyes are the same sky blue as the jewels in her hair, and her eyebrows have been plucked into a criss-cross pattern. Whatever she is looking for she seems to find, turning her attention back to the wall, raising her hands, palms facing the tiles. Christian is light-headed and unsteady on his feet.

In all his life, he's never stopped to wonder how he might die. But if he had, he would never have imagined this scenario.

"A dream… let it be a dream." It is more escaping breath than fully-formed words.

The woman presses her hands to the wall. The silence cracks. And thumps. Christian lets out a choked cry. A tear falls.

Veins of light form in the wall like a jigsaw puzzle revealing its pieces. The wall retracts, pulling pieces of the puzzle outwards, creating a space big enough to walk through.

"Val tarn." She waves him forward. "Val tarn."

It is a *follow me*, he's certain. But even if he wanted to, his legs won't allow it.

She steps closer, her hand surprisingly gentle at his wrist. Her blue eyes are speckled with dots of white, reminding him of a summer sky.

"Come. With me."

Surprise takes Christian's attention and he forgets his inability to breathe long enough to gasp. She just spoke English. Heavy with an accent he doesn't recognise, but English. It's enough to bring more tears. He sobs as she leads him through the opening and into a brand new, and equally strange world. Overhead the sky holds a pair of streaking comets, the same colour as the intimidating man's eyes. But it's not that odd sight that sends a fresh wave of goosebumps across Christian's sweat-coated skin.

It is the soaring framework of steel overhead. Long lines of metal that stretch from the ground and curve until they touch the ground somewhere beyond an array of low-set buildings forming a semi-circle in the distance. Between each column of thick metal there is a shimmering mesh of fine light. A hum sits low on the air. Several people pass by. Wearing matching clothing. Stiff jackets and pants all in a jet-black material that is threaded with lines of silver. And at their hips, what can only be holsters. Loaded weapons' holsters. The woman has led him into a prison.

Awake or not, this is a fully-fledged nightmare.

Chapter 9

Ryder

The hooded, talon-handed stranger powers through the forest at a formidable pace. An hour at least so far, taking all that is left of Ryder's energy. Her damp shirt plasters her, the material tugging uncomfortably as she moves. She's ripped one of the designer tears in her grey jeans open wider, trying to get some air beneath the fabric. Ryder reaches into one of the jean pockets and pulls out the strange crystal Sebastien gave her. A vrean, he called it. Like that explained it all. The fragment resembles a translucent miniature acorn, one that's been crushed underfoot. But it's actually a miniature miracle. Ryder bites down on an edge. A piece breaks away and hits her tongue. Dissolving, and producing way more liquid than seems possible for such a small portion. The fluid is as fizzy as mineral water. Tepid but still soothing. And a far better thirst quencher than any energy drink she's ever tried.

Focused on her liquid heaven, Ryder stumbles over a root, or rock, she can't make it out in the darkness. She's stumbled more times than she can count. So has Sebastien, his limp growing more pronounced as they continue. But his eyes haven't left the stranger.

As for that stranger, as they weave through the thick shrubbery it's clear they have done this before: the way the slender body shifts between narrow gaps in high-reaching trees, and then alters course well before they pass a deep hollow in the ground, one that Ryder can't make out at all until they are on top of it.

She edges closer to Sebastien and whispers, "Is this really a good idea? Do you have any idea where we are going?"

Her answer is a slap in the face. A branch Sebastien had pushed aside to get past, releasing it before she's done the same.

"Nice."

"It was hardly intentional," he replies, smooth as silk. "And no. I do not know where we are going. But our options are limited. And this being has shown no sign of aggression—"

"They held a knife to your throat—"

"But they could have used it elsewhere and killed me immediately." He pauses. "I was caught off-guard by their approach. Their stealth capabilities are impressive."

Ryder kicks at the undergrowth, trying not to focus on the fact Sebastien just admitted he got pretty close to biting the bullet. Her insides are already a mess, and the idea of losing him wants to melt pieces of her away. She watches the guide up ahead. Sebastien's right about the stealth. Even now, as they push through shrubbery that reaches as high as any of their shoulders, the cloaked figure's footfalls and sweeping arms barely make a sound. It's like a shadow moving through the forest.

"Not only did they retract their aggression, they have left themselves vulnerable." Sebastien waves a hand at the dark figure up ahead. "They have their back to me and have not checked to see if I am armed. Whoever this is, they are not of military background."

"Couldn't you just, you know, use the elthar—"

"Of course I could. But an attack seems unwise, and the use of elthar brings with it the risk of discoverability. We are without shelter or direction out here. To go about bringing down any being we come into contact with, especially those who appear to know who I am and have not made a move to kill me, does not seem prudent."

"Fine, whatever." Ryder wipes at her eyes where sweat stings the corners. "Well, do you have any idea who they might be?"

"I don't know *what* they are. Let alone who."

"You don't have people with claws for hands in Siros?" A whisper of wind, warm and not at all refreshing, stirs around them.

"No. We do not. Neither does Zentai."

He hasn't taken his eyes off their guide for more than a few moments the whole time they have been on this crazy safari through the alien Amazon.

"Then where the he-"

"I don't know, Ryder."

Sebastien pauses and rests his hand against a low mound of something soft and feathery. He is breathing almost as heavily as she is. And he rubs at the side of his left leg, shifting his head so his hair falls across his face. Covering up the grimace of pain she's certain is there.

"You doing okay?" Ryder says.

"Fine." The guy is officially a terrible liar.

Ryder rubs at the rush of goosebumps that dot her arms. Up ahead the figure has stopped. Watching them through the mask, the panel of light the only brightness in the gloom. Waving them forward, it bleets, though this time it is a low, hushed sound.

Sebastien raises his own hand and nods. "We are coming."

Cloaked-stranger seems to approve and continues on.

"Is it possible?" Sebastien says. Under his breath. So low it's pretty clear it wasn't meant to reach her ears. But it did. And Ryder isn't about to let it go.

"Is what possible?" she says. "Sebastien, please. I'm going to lose it if I... please... just tell me. Something..."

Ryder lets her plea fade. She is burning up, exhausted, hungry and so damn petrified it's a wonder she's not curled up in a ball beneath one of those twisty trunks, refusing to go any further. Her world hasn't just turned upside down, it's disappeared altogether.

Sebastien clears his throat. "There have always been stories of this place, tales of creatures that move within these clusters. Fearful creatures they call the Distant who would set upon any who trespassed. I always assumed the tales were designed to frighten the young and ensure those who use the clusters to run contraband across The Dovers were not disturbed."

"Tell me you still assume those things," Ryder says.

"I do not believe we can assume anything anymore. No one is quite as they seem," Sebastien says. His fleeting glance stings as much as the sweat against the cut in her lip. Mostly because she can't read into it. He knows what happened to Sophie. Does he look at Ryder and see a fearful creature? Is he wondering when she'll hurt him too?

Ryder falls back, putting space between them.

Maybe she should slip away. Disappear into this haunted forest. Where she can't hurt anyone else. The heated wind presses at her back, the wall of warmth pushing her forward, and lifting the dirty, tangled strands of her hair. The foliage shifts beneath the change in pressure and whispers mix in with the musical brush of branches. Ryder pauses then turns to stare into the deep inkiness of the forest behind them. Nothing moves. No sway of branches, no sway of the shorter shrubs that have made walking so difficult. Ryder tugs a strand of hair that has lodged against her dry lips: the only evidence the gust of wind existed at all. Maybe she needs another one of the vrean things. Dehydration isn't great for the brain. Plays tricks on the mind.

"Ryder. What are you doing?" Sebastien's voice comes from a distance but it still makes her jump.

She turns on her heels and pounds her way through the undergrowth. How did they get so far ahead of her? She could have sworn she only stopped for a second. The silence blankets the forest yet again. The musical notes gone.

"Coming, coming." Running in this heat is a terrible idea. By the time she reaches Sebastien, her heart is pounding and her lungs feel fit to burst.

Their guide is staring off into the distance. Their head lifted upward as though sniffing the air, or maybe staring into space. It's impossible to tell with the covering over their face. After a few quiet moments in the deathly still, they grunt and lift an arm, pointing a claw towards the shrubbery ahead; a slope of that butter-coloured feathery moss that was abundant where the ship went down. The slope is steep and rises to at least double Ryder's height.

"Wert, wert." The guide jabs a claw towards it.

"Enter?" Sebastien says.

The cloaked head nods vigorously. "Wert."

The guide rushes towards the wall, and at the moment it seems the creature will run straight into the solid mass. It raises their talons and presses them together, like they are about to launch into prayer. The guide swipes down through the moss, creating a narrow opening, and disappears inside. Sebastien doesn't hesitate, following immediately.

Ryder should follow his lead. If Sebastien thinks it's safe, then who is she to doubt it? But she can't bring herself to move. The forest shifts behind her, that dank, heated wind rising up once more. So, she hadn't imagined it. And once again it's pressing her forward, a force at her back that's out of sync with the gentler sway of the trees.

Ryder shrugs against it and sweeps her hands through the mossy curtain. Stepping inside. It's darker in here, and there is the hint of moisture on the air. Best of all, the temperature is noticeably cooler.

"Sebastien?" Her voice has a subtle echo.

"This way." His voice floats towards her, and she follows the sound. She passes through a soft, dark curtain and steps into a brighter, more open space. Ryder shades her eyes. After the pitch black, her eyes water. When everything draws into focus, she gasps.

She's stepped into a crystal cave of rose-coloured rock. Glowing like a sunrise, just as the mountains did. It is breathtakingly beautiful. And it takes a second to register there are more than three bodies in the room. Two figures, both clothed like the guide. Dark cloaks with hoods, and meshed veils across the face. The panels of light — where eyes might be — differ on each, one figure has glowing red orbs while the other has multiple amber-coloured diamond shapes spread across a white veil. It's not the only difference between them. One is petite, while the other is a formidable hulking shape, reminding Ryder of a wrestler.

"Sebastien," she says slowly.

"It's all right," he returns, standing stock still in the centre of the room. But the soft blue glow of elthar at his wrists tells her he's not so convinced.

The petite figure turns their head toward their larger companion, and whispers something. The hulk shakes their head side to side, lifting a hand, a gloved hand with fingers. Ryder counts at least four fingers before the hand is lowered into the folds of the cloak once again. Whatever the smaller figure wanted to do, the answer is clearly no. And they don't seem too impressed. The smaller companion shifts their weight, presumably from one foot to another but the long layers hide every part of their body.

"We have nothing of value, if that is what you seek," Sebastien says, in that low, utterly calm voice he uses on rare occasion.

Their guide bleets and caws, but the vocalisation is directed at the wrestler. The hooded head nods, the red eyes glinting, and they utter a series of caws in return. Ryder frowns. Red-eyes definitely didn't have claws. Doesn't seem to be the same species at all.

Sebastien's patience is fading, he's shifting from foot to foot in much the same way the smaller companion continues to do. The elthar flows, heavy around his knuckles.

Ryder can't help but wonder if the petite one is getting ready to attack. She and Sebastien are sitting ducks here. In a confined space, outnumbered. The heat seeps down into Ryder's bones, finding its way deep into her core. She's too far away from Sebastien. Ryder steps forward.

"No, Ryder," he says. Still in that monotone voice. "Stay where you are."

The elthar forms short blades over each of his knuckles.

The wrestler takes a step towards Sebastien, arms raised. "No harm is intended. You can disengage the elthar."

It's subtle, but Ryder catches the brace of Sebastien's shoulders. Then it strikes her. The hulk just spoke English.

"Who are you?" Sebastien demands it this time, the calm evaporating.

The wrestler makes a small sound, and to Ryder's ears at least, it could be a chuckle.

"I am not the enemy you have always supposed." The hulk lifts one hand, raising it towards the veil.

"Choose your next action carefully," Sebastien growls. "Do not test me."

"Well, then don't brandish those blades my way. The knuckle blades always were your favourite." There is a pause, and a softening of voice. "You will come to no harm here."

The room may as well be full of statues. No one moves. Not even the short figure who was so fond of fidgeting a moment ago. Ryder doesn't dare breathe. But it's not just because of the standoff. Her gut burns like she's swallowed a plateful of jalepenos, and her skin tingles with the unpleasant sting of warm water on sunburn. Ryder recalls all too well when she last felt this way.

At the bridge, with Sophie.

She grinds her teeth. It may be cooler in this sheltered space, but the tension sits as heavily as the heat ever did.

"Who, are, you?" Sebastien repeats. It's clear he's not about to do so a third time.

"It would be best if I show you." The hulk remains with a single hand raised, waiting on Sebastien's reply.

He doesn't say anything, just nods. Hands braced like a boxer waiting on the starting bell. Fear stokes the fire that's consuming Ryder. It's tinder dry in here, and any second something is going to spark. It had better spark soon. Her head spins as she continues to hold her breath. She's not going to exhale. That might be all it takes to throw things out of her control. Again.

The hulky figure grips the edge of their hood, and with the barest of pauses, sweeps it back. The veil drags up their face, revealing inch by inch who lies beneath. But it's no monster. At least, not an obvious one. Not one with scales and scars and a thousand eyes. This monster has a sharp square jawline, full lips, and eyes the colour of Arctic ice. Ryder stares. Their body shapes aren't alike but focusing on the face alone, this guy could be some long-lost relative of Sebastien's.

"Sebastien." The newly revealed monster says. "It has been a long time."

But for Sebastien it seems even longer than that. Like, never. If it's a relative, it's one he's never met. Sebastien shakes his head. Ryder can't see his face from where she stands behind him, but he hasn't lowered his elthar-covered hands. The blades are still being brandished. If he does actually recognise this guy, he doesn't like who he sees.

Ryder's vision speckles with tiny black dots, and there is a ringing in her ears which is getting louder. But still she holds on.

"I don't…" Sebastien begins, pausing to shake his head again. "I don't know you."

Ryder shifts her weight but Sebastien must think she's about to make a bolt for it because he sends a daggered glance her way. "Ryder, stay where you are."

"Ryder?" The small figure blurts out. Female. And speaking English. Suddenly Ryder is front and centre, a gloved finger pointed her way. "Your name is Ryder?"

"Quiet," the man with the ice-eyes hisses.

"How is this possible?" The small one has no intention of being quiet. "How is it possible that you are here? It has to be you, right? I mean you're human. And my mum said it was an unusual name in our world. It kind of sticks in your head, you know." Her words rise in an odd pitch, and it's only when the sound continues that Ryder realises what she's hearing. The cloaked figure is crying. They reach up and tear away the white veil. A dark-skinned girl, perhaps a few years younger than Ryder stands with tears glistening on her cheeks. She has everything you'd expect of a human, and all of it in the right place: ears, a wide flared nose, and thick lips, a head of spiral curls that jut out from her head. Inside her airless cocoon Ryder struggles to take in what she's seeing.

A human.

Here on Bax Un Tey.

Chapter 10

Olessia

Olessia stands at the dead centre of her metal cell and calls out to those she knows to be watching. The portals through which they monitor her are well concealed, but she does not doubt their existence.

"That meal was hardly adequate. If my father wishes to bring about my end through slow starvation, then he is on course for his desired result."

She is keen to allow reason for Sentinel Teler to return, but in truth, the thought of eating sickens her. War has been declared in her name, a fact hardly conducive to appetite. Downing the first meal brought to her had taken every ounce of will she could muster. Favoured meal or not, the scents failed to raise her hunger. She has had no desire for nourishment in some time. Not since her last meal in the Iondar Realm, an overly-seasoned mixture Sophie called 'Chinese'. Even in the Turning, in the relaxed company of the Yentern and Christian, she had to force her mouthfuls down.

Olessia lowers her head, seeking to hide the swirl of violet that plagues her each time she wonders at the fate of those two - the human and the Yentern. The innocents who are at the mercy of one such as the Presider, simply through the sheer misfortune of having met her. She hears it, even now. Christian's cries echoing around her. Dragging at her. Olessia's temper rises, a warm fury that seeps through her. But it is eagerly swamped by a hollowness that fills her belly, pressing at the food she consumed earlier and giving rise to a wave of nausea.

Olessia runs her hand over her stomach, her brow knitting. Not once in her lifetime has she regurgitated nourishment, but it appears that fact is about to be altered. She clamps her mouth shut, a hand covering her lips, searching the room for a vessel that might accommodate what is about to be ejected.

But just as the sickness overcame her anger, now it, too, is submerged.

The Beckoning, finally, begins to stir. Smooth ribbons of warmth rise from the abyss in which the beast has hidden for too long. Olessia places both hands against her belly, and the barest of smiles brushes her lips. Likely it is the first time the beast has brought on such an expression. But it is short-lived. She lowers her hands. Her father's hold on the Beckoning may have been released, but how? And for how long? She is still unaware of how it was controlled to begin with. As Dashel faked her death, both Olessia and the Beckoning were immobilised. Her lungs barely allowed enough freedom to ensure adequate intake of air. Dashel had placed no instrument upon her. No senlier. No lelle-car to control her.

Olessia paces her circular confines, the red folds of her dress billowing around her, rustling against the ground. What has brought on the sudden withdrawal of the restraint? Her eyes dart to the place on the floor where the plestex crystal tray had been set down. Was it possible it contained far more than pleasing sauces and delicate layers of axen?

Olessia recalls Sentinel Teler's words when he laid the tray before her. Encouraging her to sustain herself. That it would serve her 'well to ensure your strength is retained'. He insinuated it would please her father if she were to do so, but he was being watched. Teler would hardly advise her outright that an antidote laced her nourishment. That she should eat quickly so the Beckoning might be freed.

Olessia halts her steady march around the cell. Considers for a moment, then sends out a mindreach, searching for Sebastien, using the well-worn synaptic path they have long shared. Olessia winces, touching fingertips to her forehead. The mindreach swallowed by a formidable artificial Blackwall. Hardly a surprise that such technology should exist in a prison. It is no difficulty to line the walls with a substance that prevents telepathic transfer. Even the natural environment of Bax Un Tey is intent on preventing mindreaches. The Dovers are notorious for scrambling transmissions and reducing messages to garbled nonsense.

No matter.

Let them come. The next time that entranceway emits its tones and begins to lower, Olessia will find her own way to freedom.

Despite her demands for further nourishment, nothing arrives. And over the lengthening of time, her dread reawakens. This is her tomb. Not her prison.

One last meal served before she is left to starve in solitude. The Beckoning ignites, punching at her insides with a ferocity that doubles her over.

Although the blow pains her, it also fortifies her. She is not entirely alone. Though it may not be a company of her choosing, the beast has not abandoned her. For so long she has viewed the Beckoning as her enemy, Olessia could not have imagined a moment like this. One in which she would welcome its discomfort.

Deceptively dulcet tones echo through her prison. The door is lowering. The process is infuriatingly slow, and in that dragged-out pause her plans to dash to pieces whoever awaits her on the other side, falter. Olessia has no clue where she is or how much effort it would take to return to somewhere she does recognise. Is she even being contained at Kinna-brey? Or, is this labyrinth somewhere far more distant? Though Sentinel Teler's presence suggests this is not the case, Olessia recalls the advice given by the Sentinel himself an age past. Know your environment. Study it. Find the weaknesses and advantages it offers.

Taking down those who are about to enter her prison will provide nothing but chaos. And severe repercussions if Olessia does not gain the freedom she seeks.

By the time the door's apex touches the ground, Olessia's back is pressed against the cool metal of her confines, as far from the opening as she can manage, her eyes wide, fearful.

Let them believe she quivers at their arrival.

The Alkell who stood guard outside, step into the chamber. They are joined by a third figure, and Olessia's eyes widen further.

A Claven member; his clothing tells her that much. Clad in the familiar high-necked jacket that sweeps low over matching pants, both items sewn from the enduring thick brown skins of the leaping pell. One shoulder is draped with a wislayer — a material woven entirely from the silky nests of the rare hantegran of the Greater Luxesand. It is dyed to denote the Crest from where the Claven member hails. The wislayer is secured to the hip by a glistening square of elthar, engraved with the Moniker of the Claven member's Crest: in this case, a white cube whose tips are a crimson not dissimilar to Olessia's gown. If she didn't already recognise the Crest, the man's appearance would allude to it.

The resemblance to Verran is startling. This man shares the same wide girth and imposing height, along with Verran's features – hair the dark shade of dayfall and eyes to match. A needling intensity is evident in the few strides he takes towards her, another trait he shares with his relative, but this Sirosian is far younger than Verran.

"Olessia." The man's gaze meets hers.

And Olessia understands how dire her circumstance has become. Eye contact is forbidden when addressing the Presiderline, and only allowed once Olessia or Inel have acknowledged the presence of the speaker. This man acts as though he does not address the Laudess of Bax Un Tey at all.

He halts in front of her, again abandoning protocol when he stands far closer than is permittable and leaving Olessia with a sense of being pinned to the wall.

"We have not met before. I am Kileen. I believe you may have known my father, Verran." His pale skin highlights a cluster of markings to the side of his right eye that resemble freckles but such a skin discolouration is unheard of on Siros. Zentai skin tones have a much greater degree of variation. This man's markings are likely scarring from an injury. Olessia can barely drag her eyes from them. Her thoughts moving to Lucas, and a terrible realisation dawning. Her desperation has made her utterly foolish. She sought to protect Christian and Ryder, but in doing so has failed to protect their world. Lucas is on Earth.

Olessia presses harder against the metal, a sense of lightness coming over her. After all Aresh did to draw the Presider's attentions away from Earth, Olessia's revelation about Lucas's true identity has given Inel fresh reason to menace that world. And to label Aresh a traitor at the same time.

"Are you listening, Olessia?" Kileen draws out her name as though to highlight the fact he has failed to use her title. "My father died trying to protect you. But don't worry, I hold only one person responsible for his death. And though your actions were foolish, the blame can only lie with Aresh."

Olessia pushes away from the wall and is pleased to note that Kileen edges back.

"Watch your tongue, Kileen—"

"Or what, Olessia? You will call on your inept Guardian for assistance? I see him nowhere near you… abandoned you as his brother did, no doubt. Another piece of puppetry on Aresh's part. Do you not see that? Do you not see the Presider only seeks to protect you? Protect us all from the treachery that surrounds us?"

"Protect us?" Olessia releases an indignant laugh. "Do you not see me? Alive. Here in front of you, while out there I am mourned, and the worlds go to war?"

"A war that was inevitable. Simply a matter of waiting to see who landed the first blow. The Zentai have always eyed Siros with great intentions, but who imagined they would receive help from within the Presiderline itself? Whatever your reasons may have been for traversing to the Iondar Realm, do you deny the Zentai took you by force from Earth? Or has Aresh succeeded in converting you to her cause? There is talk Sebastien's brother was no traitor at all. That he was removed at Aresh's behest so she could place another Guardian at your side. One who would work with her, one who would make you vulnerable. Turn a blind eye, perhaps, when the Laudess crossed borders she should never have crossed." Kileen's thumb traces a repetitive path over the white cube Moniker at his hip. "Enabling an opportunity for the Laudine and the Crown to gain hold of a powerful hostage. At the cost of

Verran's life. But if I am wrong, if the Zentai did not take you by force from Earth, Olessia, and you travelled with them freely, then perhaps it is more troubling than we imagined. Perhaps, I stand before another usurper."

Olessia stares at him, aghast at the words falling from his lips. Even the Beckoning — swirling deep and low within her — appears subdued by the magnitude of the Presider's capacity for manipulation.

Aresh sought to protect Olessia, concealing her disappearance so as to avoid the Presider's wrath. Doing her all to return Olessia undetected. And the Presider knows this. He must know this. Dashel — his carefully placed spy — saw first-hand how Aresh struggled to return Olessia to Kinna-brey. But her efforts have been manipulated into treachery.

The Presider has always been a master at keeping people under his sway, but truly he exceeds himself now. To have them convinced the Laudine is a traitor, that perhaps Olessia herself is too, is breathtaking.

Kileen dives on her silence. "You are uncommonly quiet, Olessia. I see I present some uncomfortable truths."

She draws herself to full height, and her eyes must churn like raging storms for the pain they give her. "I have this to say to you, Kileen. I am sorry for the loss of your father. Even more so because he knew the truth of all this. And he would have made you see it too. There is treachery here, that is most certain, but it does not come from the source you believe. The Laudine and I are, and always have been, at my father's mercy. As are you all. Where is she? Where is Aresh?"

The Beckoning rises, reaching into coals of fury burning deep within her. No longer subdued.

"Calm yourself, Olessia." Kileen smirks. "You should consider carefully before you attempt to drain me of life. I am Claven, and even the strength of a Beckoning such as yours will take some time to affect me. The power runs in my veins too, after all." He jerks his head towards the Alkell. "They are elthar clad, which will give them more than enough time to incapacitate you before they, too, are drained. Reserve your strength for a more meaningful task. The

Presider has a need of you yet. I should have you understand that your co-operation will mean the difference between great suffering or less uncomfortable circumstances for the traitor you seem so very concerned for."

His smile is devoid of any warmth, a mechanical lift of his lips that bares too many teeth. "Personally, I would prefer you didn't co-operate. Aresh's actions took my father from me. I have no concern for her comfort."

Olessia does not try to halt the storms of violet she knows to be swirling in her eyes. The Beckoning dances beneath her skin. And her visions shifts. Adjusting to the greater sight that allows her to see the life-energies around her: Kileen's blue-green aura with its sparks of onyx bursting like tiny fireworks within the paler shades, denoting the faint trace of Beckoning in his bloodline, and the plainer white auras of the Alkell. The Beckoning gathers intensity. Olessia braces for the effort it will take to subdue the beast and is surprised when it stills quickly.

"You would do well to hold your insults. And remember that you speak to the Laudess of Bax Un Tey." She laces her words with acid, but Olessia is filled more with fear than rage. "To question my loyalty to the Presiderline is a dangerous path to take. What does my father wish from me?"

What *more* does he want?

"I will show you how you may prove your loyalty. You are to contribute to the war effort." Kileen gestures to the Alkell and they move to flank her. One of them reaches to touch her, and Olessia sets him back with a glare.

"I do not need to be dragged," she says. "Lead, and I will follow."

"A promising start, Olessia." Kileen nods. His blue-green aura reminding her of the storm clouds over Hobart. "We will begin."

Chapter 11

Ryder

R yder and Sebastien step no further into the confined space they probably shouldn't have entered to begin with.

"What's going on?" Ryder says.

The young girl, the *human* girl, fixes pleading eyes on the older man. "It must be her, don't you think?"

"Carlsson, that's enough," the man growls.

Ryder exhales, and the world spins. "Carlsson?"

"Yes." The girl nods so hard her hood slips from her head. "Yes, that's the name I was given. In memory of a woman my mother admired, they were in the Collective together. They escaped together too. Her name was Evelyn Carlsson. You're her daughter, aren't you? You have to be."

The fire inside Ryder retreats, disappearing into the cracks from where it crawled. Now there's only a chill. Ryder doesn't realise she's staggered until Sebastien's hand find her arm. Steadying her.

"Evelyn Carlsson..." Ryder baulks at saying it aloud. "She was... here?"

The older guy, the one with pretend eyes of ruby fire, frowns. One corner of his lip raises. A near perfect imitation of Sebastien's preferred facial expression.

"There was a human woman of that name, yes. She was held by the Presider in the Collective, but—"

"Enough!" Sebastien moves, faster than she's ever seen before, and the elthar blades are fully formed in what seems like the blink of an eye.

"Sebastien-"

"Quiet, Ryder."

She bristles at the sharp command, but decides, for now, it's best to listen. Sebastien's tension fills the space, sparking off the air, a sense that he might explode as bright as the sapphire light dancing off his blades.

"State your name." Sebastien's order crawls across the space separating the two.

"Come now, you must understand already who I am, brother."

"Do not address me as your brother," Sebastien hisses.

Ryder drags herself from the haze of her own thoughts. Brother?

Maher scratches at the back of his neck. "How then should I address you? Guardian? To address you by your title is not only rather formal but seems unwise in our circumstance." The man attempts a small smile, but it wilts beneath Sebastien's glare: grey eyes tumultuous storms. "Very well. I am Maher of Nevin Rea."

Sebastien hadn't exactly shared his life-story with Ryder but she knew this guy existed. And also knew Sebastien wanted to pretend Maher didn't.

"You're his brother," Ryder says. A statement. Anyone with eyes could see the similarities.

Maher nods, but his eyes don't leave Sebastien. "Despite how Sebastien may despise the fact, it remains. I am his brother. I don't suppose he spoke to you of me. I am not given high regard in my family."

"You are given none," Sebastien spits.

Ryder frowns at the tightness in Sebastien's voice. He's hardly the most patient guy in the world, but this encounter has another level of tension to it. She's half expecting him to start slashing and pounding their way out of here. And that's not what she wants. Nor what he needs. His pant leg is a bloodied mess.

"Sebastien, there will be a time for us to discuss old wounds, but right now we should attend to those much fresher injuries." Maher gestures towards the injured leg, keeping the movement slow. Like he doesn't want to frighten a skittish horse. "You are both in need of refreshment and you, brother, are wounded."

"I will take no aid from you."

Maher releases a deep breath. "Brother—"

"Stop calling me that." Sebastien's protest rings petulent. Almost childlike.

"That's what I am, Sebastien. You can't remove that fact by sheer will. Now listen to me, I am not your enemy. But you have them, that I know. More so now than ever. These are very dangerous times. Btet advised us of the Baershard crash, told us she was tracking you. You make quite the pair. A human and a Sirosian racing away from a downed Zentai craft. And not just any Sirosian. The Laudess of Bax Un Tey's Guardian. Brother, why were you not at the Olessia's side? Perhaps things would have—"

"Stop." Ryder's command seems to surprise everyone, her included.

"Are you okay? You look kind of pale… paler than before." It is Carlsson addressing her, but her voice comes from miles away. The ringing in Ryder's ears buries the sound.

"I want to speak to Maher. Alone."

"There is no way—" Sebastien begins.

Ryder steps between him and Maher. "Stop, Sebastien. Just stop. Whatever issues you have with your brother, they need to wait. I want to talk to him. And I'm going to talk to him. Alone."

And not just because he seems to know about Olessia, but because of what he knows about her mother.

"Why?"

"Just… I need you to just trust me. Okay?"

Sebastien hisses, digging one hand into his hair. If Carlsson thought Ryder was pale, she must be thinking Sebastien is downright ghostly. There's no doubt his wound is bad. He's weak and angry, and right now would be a terrible time to tell him about Olessia. It would break him, and Ryder has no intention of letting that happen. Not until she knows for certain Olessia is truly gone.

Ryder places a hand on his raised arm. "Please, Sebastien. You need to get those injuries looked at. Let them help you. If they wanted to hurt us, wouldn't they have done it by now? He's your brother."

A brother Sebastien clearly despises, but Maher isn't giving off the same acidic vibes. There's a tinge of sadness to his expression that cinches Ryder's decision. They are staying.

Sebastien shifts his head, glaring at Maher from beneath limp, dank hair. He doesn't just need first aid, he needs a shower. A really long, hot shower. Ryder's about to repeat herself when he nods. Just a jerk of his head, but it's enough.

He turns to Maher. "Harm her, and I will—"

Maher raises his hands. "Your intentions are clear, Sebastien. But know this brother, I will do likewise to you if any harm comes to those in my care." His eyes flit to the human girl, and the still-cloaked Btet. "Ryder, will you come with me? There is a place where we can speak."

Ryder lets her hand fall from Sebastien's arm. He goes to reach for her. Stopping himself and folding his arms instead. "Do not linger, and call for me at the first sign of—"

"I'm good. I know you're right here. I'll call if I need you."

Chapter 12

Ryder

Maher of Nevin Rea leads Ryder to the back of the chamber. He seems set to collide with the wall before making an odd jerk left and disappearing altogether. Ryder draws closer, and the optical illusion is revealed. A section of the crystal sits forward of the rest of the wall, concealing the open space behind. Sebastien's eyes bore into her all the way across the chamber. Carlsson asks him three times if he will take a seat and allow her to tend to the wound on his leg. Her questions get more and more pointed as he continues to ignore her.

Ryder edges around the section of rock, and hurries after Maher, who strides down a candy-pink tunnel.

"My brother is greatly protective of you, Ryder." Maher glances back at her.

His features are as sharp as Sebastien's, the resemblance undeniable, but now it's clear just how drained Sebastien is. Ryder curls her fingers into fists. Maher's cheeks are hollowed where his brother's are full, and there is no darkness of fatigue beneath his eyes.

"We've been through a few things," she says.

As hostile as Sebastien might be towards him, Ryder doesn't share the animosity. Maybe it's the controlled, steady manner Maher has, or his concern for Carlsson and Btet, but something about the guy is reassuring.

"It would appear so," he replies.

The question about her mother sits on Ryder's lips, sharp as knives. Her mother. Here. Ryder shakes her head, trying to clear her thoughts. Truth be told, she's too afraid to voice the question. If she asks Maher why he said her mother was held by the Presider, then he might take her away from Ryder again. Was held. Not anymore. So she starts with something else.

"What's a Collective?"

"One of the Presider's pet projects. He enjoys collecting specimens from realms his teams Traverse to. They usually abduct creatures who exhibit abilities considered abnormal in the worlds in which they are born. Telepathic or telekinetic abilities, for example," Maher says. "Souvenirs. Examples the Presider likes to use to assure himself no one in the known realms is yet as powerful as he, or as the Presiderline is."

Silence settles as Ryder considers his words. Abnormal abilities. Did that include her mother? She clears her throat. "And some of them... I mean... Carlsson said that... her mum escaped."

Maher eyes her over one shoulder, slowing his pace. "With aid from the Laudine, that is correct. Evelyn Carlsson. She was your mother?"

Ryder's toe catches at the ground and she stumbles. "That was her name, yes, but I don't know if this person was actually..."

Her thoughts dry up her words. It's just too crazy. That it could possibly be her mother they are talking about. Here. But is it any more crazy than Ryder somehow finding her way from Hobart to this place? A world in a universe no one knows exists?

"If she is your mother, I'm sorry, Ryder." Maher focuses on the tunnel once again. "I cannot tell you for certain that she still lives and that we could not prevent her recapture."

Ryder fixes her gaze on the ground. She can't think about that. Not now. She's already as fragile as a glass full of cracks. Forgetting the injury to her lip she bites down, and winces, but says nothing as they continue on. Ryder shoves all thoughts of Evelyn Carlsson down into a deep pocket in her mind and seals it. Later. Worry about that later.

When she's certain they are far enough away from the others, Ryder quicksteps to draw closer to Maher. "Sebastien doesn't know about Olessia."

Maher stops dead and turns to her. "Why did you stop me informing him? He should know."

"So he'll go on a rampage and get himself killed?" Ryder glances back up the corridor and lowers her voice. "I'm guessing you guys haven't seen each other in a while, I mean, I haven't known him long but he won't take this—"

"Well? No. He will not." Maher's smile is gentle, and desperately sad. "I have not seen my brother in a while, this is true, but I have kept track of him. He has been burdened with a role that should have been mine. I hope one day he can forgive me for what I did. Abandoning him and my duty. But what I feared from a young age, the tyranny of the Presider and his Claven, is to be feared even more so now. With the Laudess's death, his desire for war can be realised."

Ryder shakes her head. "No. I don't... I don't believe it. That she's gone." She lifts her shoulders; her uncertainty is a physical weight she just can't shift.

Maher leads her around a curve where the tunnel begins to slope upwards.

"It seems, Ryder, that Olessia's death pains you as greatly as it would my brother."

Ryder bites at the inside of her cheek to distract herself from the curl of something unpleasant in her belly. Olessia's not gone. She can't be. They have things to do. Together. Ryder can't lose Sophie and Olessia.

And her mother.

All at once.

How could Ryder ever breathe again? Ever stop feeling as though she's teetering on the edge of an abyss.

Absorbed in her thoughts, Ryder bumps against a now stationary Maher. He's stopped inside a room about half the size of the main chamber. The effort of moving uphill has taken more from Ryder than she realised, and she takes a shaky breath to try and steady her pulse.

The room is a haphazard shape, reminding her of an upside down bird's nest. There's no glowing crystal here, just a thick mass of plants, vines and hanging branches that form a dome overhead. Ryder weaves to avoid dangling curls of green, following Maher. He kneels by one of two large holes in the living walls. There is a thin film of translucent material across the opening. Outside, a valley. Not unlike the one she and Sebastien traipsed through after the crash. She ducks down, trying to see what lies even farther. The sunset-pink mountain range is visible, and she tracks its great rock face. Ryder can just make out another valley carving its way through the range. Perpendicular to the one where Maher's hideout is located. The edges of the valley, all the way to the peak of the mountains, are tinged with emerald green, reminding her of the Southern Lights sometimes visible in Tasmania. A delicate veil of light stretches the width of the valley, hiding what's behind.

"What is that, down there?" Ryder says. "The light."

"The Arlion Xhentex," Maher says. "The very outer edge of it at least. The Xhentex is a Meshed area that came about after the Arlion between the realms of Siros and Zentai collapsed, creating a singular realm – Bax Un Tey." He makes a dismissive sound. "My apologies. That must make no sense to you—"

Ryder kneels beside him. "No. It's fine. I've had a bit of experience with a Meshed area." The viewing window is large enough that a metre of empty space still sits between them. "But you said it collapsed, so there's a river or slipstream between the worlds now?"

Maher raises a fine eyebrow. "Well, normally yes, there would be. But the Arlion Xhentex is an anomaly. The collapse was catastrophic, a level of destruction never witnessed before. It is a Mesh like no other. Of course no one living was present at the actual event, but we make what we can of the information that has survived. The Laudine has always held a special interest in the Xhentex's creation."

He literally bites his lip. Staring intently out the window.

"You know Aresh?"

Maher jerks his head to stare at her. Both eyebrows high. "You know her?"

Ryder sits back, frowning at a tear in her dirty jeans. "Oh yeah. We go way back… apparently. Is she… I mean, do you think she's okay?"

Ryder's hardly had a second to wonder where Aresh is in all of this.

Now it's Maher's turn to do an uncomfortable shuffle. He sucks at his teeth. "I do not believe so. No. The beings in my care, Btet and Carlsson and others, all gained their freedom because of the Laudine, but I fear it is she whose freedom is lost now. I've not heard from her, and I cannot reach her."

They sit in a long silence. The sounds beyond the veiled window drawing in; ticks and clicks, like the forest is dotted with a hundred tiny clocks. It's not quite as dark as when she and Sebastien stumbled around earlier.

Ryder snaps the loose cotton around the tear in her jeans. "Did my mo… did the woman Carlsson is named after… did Aresh give her freedom too?"

Maher squints at the view beyond the window. "That human woman is the reason anyone found their freedom from the Presider's Collective. Aresh had never approved of the Collective, but nor had she gone to any lengths to try and cease its existence until a Traverse to Earth came back with several humans. She never voiced the details to me, but I sensed an anger in her that was not present before. I was in exile, but she had helped me find a location to live. Aresh got me out of Siros before the Presider could list me as a traitor." A small shake of his head. "When she asked me to conceal some of the inhabitants of the Collective, I was not about to refuse her. But the whole mission was far more fraught than she intended, and it was decided the casualties were simply too high to risk any further attempts. That's what she told me." He pauses. "I could not help but feel the truth was different. Evelyn Carlsson was among those freed. I believe that ultimately, her freedom was the only one the Laudine desired. But that poor woman, the human, had endured a loss that drove her near to madness – the loss of a child for whom she would not stop searching. I don't know the details, I wasn't there, but they fought, the Laudine and the human, and the next we knew, the human woman fled from the safety Aresh offered. Word came soon after that she had been recaptured."

Ryder sits in the soft light, gazing out on a world she doesn't recognise, listening to a story where every word chips away at her.

"Ryder," Maher's voice startles her from her thoughts. "I think perhaps we should be very honest with one another. You have come to our world at a dangerous time, and yet I cannot help but feel that is no coincidence. Clearly, you were in Olessia's company. When the Laudess ran to your world she did it of her own free will, I know this. Aresh told me so. But the Presider is claiming she was held there by the Zentai, and that she was killed attempting to escape when they tried to return her to the Crown. Now Aresh, who knows the truth, has disappeared. And here you are, in the company of my brother, both of you prisoners aboard one of the Commandant's Baershard vessels. Forgive my bluntness, but what reason do the Zentai have for transporting a human? Did they seek to use you as proof the Presider lied about Olessia's situation on Earth?"

Two humans, Ryder wants to shout at him. Two humans were transported, stolen from their world. Three if she includes Blane. Ryder presses her fingertip to the bridge of her nose and stays silent, not trusting herself to speak without bursting into tears.

Maher rises to his feet and moves to the second viewing hole, taking him further away from her. "Your kind seem to be right at the heart of this upheaval. If Olessia had not been so foolish as to use the Beckoning to save that boy and the Yentern, then perhaps —"

"Boy, a human boy? Was he someone from the Collective too?"

Maher cranes his head to peer out the window. "No. When I found Olessia she had been in the company of a Yentern youth, and a human boy. She was greatly concerned about them, and entrusted them both into my care—"

"Christian," Ryder breathes.

Maher breaks from his surveillance to stare at her. "Yes. I believe that is the name she gave one of the two."

"Oh my god, oh god. No." Ryder pushes to her feet, leaning against the wall for support. "Where is he now?"

In her head, Christian has been far from all of this. Safe. Hidden. On Earth.

"Ryder, I'm sorry but—"

She sinks back to her knees, all the strength torn from her. "Oh god," she groans.

"No, no. Taken," Maher says, quickly. "He and the Yentern were taken by the Zentai. The Protectorate had been interrogating them both, and I could not stop Olessia from going to their aid. But they were alive when I saw them taken on board the ship. It seemed strange at the time, considering what the Zentai had just done to the Laudess. To take prisoners, instead of… well, instead of resorting to more dire solutions."

They would only keep them alive if Olessia was still alive too. Insurance.

The voice is loud, and right up close to her ear. Ryder lets out a scream, jerking backwards. Her shoulder hits a low shelf behind her and an array of ornaments tumble to the floor. She only glances at them for a second but when she turns back, someone stands right in front of her.

Ryder blinks. The image is blurred and it takes her a moment to realise it's not her eyes that are to blame. Everything around the silhouette is crystal clear, including Maher who hesitates halfway across the space that divides them. Frowning at her.

"Ryder? Is everything all right?"

In the distance footsteps pound down the tunnel, and she recognises Sebastien's unmistakable sharpness. He shouts at someone to let him be, and Btet's caws and bleets follow.

No. Is the answer to Maher's question. Everything is not all right. Ryder's mind is breaking apart. She tries to reply but it just comes out in little gasps, like she's choking. She tries to tell him who is standing there, right in front of her, as though they hide behind a thin wall of water. But it would take ten Niagara Falls worth of tumbling water to prevent Ryder from recognising this figure.

Superhero red hair glints from behind the veil, a bright yellow cardigan with a bluebird over the left breast, and pink paisley-print pants. An outfit guaranteed to make the eyes water on any occasion, but this time the tears that spring from Ryder's eyes are for a different reason entirely.

"Sophie," she sobs. "Soph."

That's it. Ryder has lost her mind. But if it was going to happen, then this is the best way to go. At least she gets to see her best friend again. The image dances. Actually dances, jumping from foot to foot, arms waving.

About time! You can see me? Can you see me? Tell me you can see me.

Ryder winces, pressing her hands to her ears. But it won't help anything. Sophie's in her head. And she's mega-phone loud.

"Yes. Yes, keep it down, Soph." Ryder laughs.

Sorry, sorry. This is hard work. Oh, man it is so good to see you again.

Ryder's laughter hurts her chest, making her whole body shudder. "You too." Even if it means that she is falling apart.

Sebastien enters the room, throwing a scowl at his brother, and pacing across to where Ryder sits on her backside grinning up at a watery Sophie. He walks straight through the image, making it ripple like a puddle of water.

"Sebastien, don't you…" Ryder lets her question fade. The answer is pretty obvious. He doesn't see her.

"Ryder, what's wrong? Ryder look at me." He crouches before her, blocking her view of Sophie.

He doesn't see me.

"No," Ryder whispers.

Sophie's voice is so clear in her head. As clear as Padellah's. No, clearer. Just a single voice. There's a slight echo but nothing compared to the multiple whispers of the Cyne entity.

"No what, Ryder?" Sebastien asks, his tone gentle. His grip easing. "Are you okay? Did he do something?"

Ryder shakes her head, leaning to peer around him. Her stomach sinks. Sophie is gone.

Leaning into Sebastien, she presses her forehead against his shoulder. "You didn't see her."

"See who, Ryder?" He runs his hand down the back of her head, the caress feather-light against the messy knotted nest her hair has become. When she doesn't reply Sebastien turns his questioning to his brother. "What happened, Maher?"

"I'm not certain. I told her of a human boy I had seen…" He falters. "At a Turning not far from here. He and a Yentern were taken captive by the Protectorate—"

"Christian?" Sebastien says. He edges Ryder back, and his grey eyes search hers. "Christian is here? How is that possible?"

Maher scratches again at his neck, obviously deciding on how he will answer. Ryder watches and listens, tucked in a cold cocoon of shock. She barely feels Sebastien's hands on her. Can't sense the floor beneath her. And has a vague sense that she doesn't want Maher to speak.

But he does.

"Brother, he was in the company of the Laudess Olessia."

From her distant place, Ryder feels Sebastien's grip on her shoulders tighten. "Olessia? What are you talking about? Why would she be in a Turning?"

"She sought to hide him there." Maher hesitates. "But when the Zentai attacked the Turning she would not be talked out of returning—"

Sebastien releases Ryder and shoots to his feet. "You have seen the Laudess? Why would you not tell me this immediately?"

"Sebastien, please—" Maher begins.

"What have you done, Maher?" Sebastien's fury resonates through the room. "Where is she?"

He turns on the figure hovering by the doorway. And Ryder's eyes widen. Btet has removed the hood and cloak, revealing a green rough-skinned creature with three onyx eyes and a gash of white where a mouth and nose might be. But even the sight of something so alien isn't enough to rattle Ryder out of her shocked state.

"I've been an utter fool," he growls. "We are not guests, we are prisoners. You have betrayed Siros, again. Is that not right, Maher? You allowed the Zentai to take her."

He doesn't give Maher a chance to answer, launching himself at the older man. Sebastien's elthar gleams, racing to form a long, jagged knife.

"Brother, no." Maher raises his arms, a paltry defence against the coming attack.

Sebastien lunges, driving the blade at his brother, who backs away, arms raised to show he has no way of defending himself. Ryder finally shakes free of her shock-cocoon.

"Sebastien, stop!"

Something rushes from behind her, whistling past her ear so fast her hair shifts. A short-legged stool. Right on course to slam Sebastien in the back, but at the very last moment it whips around him and pummels into his outstretched bladed arm. The stool splinters into a dozen pieces. The sudden, unexpected attack isn't enough to harm him, but certainly throws Sebastien off centre. He lashes out wildly with the other arm, whirling around and seeking out his attacker.

Honestly, he's got to calm down.

The voice is still too loud, and this time Sophie's watery image doesn't join it, but Ryder fights to keep from bursting into a maniacal fit of laughter, again.

She's not crazy. Everyone saw that piece of furniture move on its own. Sebastien definitely felt it.

Whirling pools of grey find her. Shock parts his lips.

"Ryder, did you just throw that at me?"

I'm kind of glad he can't see me, really.

"Yes." She clears her throat. "Sebastien, Maher isn't the bad guy here." She turns to Maher. "You said you wondered why they didn't kill them, Christian and…"

"The Yentern boy? Yes, go on." Maher keeps one wary eye on Sebastien. At least the knife is gone, though the elthar still sheds its blue light around the room.

When's the penny going to drop with this guy? They wouldn't keep hostages, not ones like that, if Olessia were dead.

"Oh man, I hope you're right," Ryder mutters. She coughs, focusing back on Maher. "You said it yourself that keeping them alive was weird. After…" She flutters her fingers, "after they took Olessia. And you saw yourself how worried she was about Christian, that she was trying to hide him. Keep him safe. What if the Zentai know he's important to her, and took him and that other guy as leverage? You said the whole reason she got… caught… was because she tried to rescue them. What better way to keep someone like her under control than by threatening to hurt someone she cares about."

A frown creases Maher's normally unlined face. His eyebrows raise a fraction. He nods in a slow deliberate rhythm. The penny has just dropped. The more she considers it, the more Ryder is convinced Sophie's right. Christian is here, somehow, in this world. Alive. And so is Olessia. Ryder has no idea how her friend ended up so far from Hobart, but she has no doubt Olessia would do anything to keep him safe. The Zentai must know that. And so long as they need Olessia, they need Christian.

"The Zentai have Olessia?" Sebastien touches at his arm. He would have barely felt the impact from the stool, that's not what's unsettled him. Ryder recognises the lopsided frown, the one that wrinkles up the left-side of his face. He's uncertain.

"They have Olessia, and they have Christian," Ryder says, casting fleeting glances around the room. But there's no sign of her puddly friend. "We need to find out where they've taken them, and we need to go there."

Soph? Ryder tries telepathy. *Can you hear me?*

If she can, she doesn't answer.

"The Presider has declared war. Regiments are already making their way towards the border," Maher says, glancing at Ryder. "With the Laudess as their… captive, the Zentai are bound to take her to Icewynn. I see nowhere else capable of containing her."

"We are at war?" Sebastien frowns.

"Soon to be," Maher says, grim-faced. "All the more reason for you to have your injuries seen to. Please, Btet is an able medic on her homeworld of Treznor, it was her role. Your Laudess needs you, brother."

For whatever reason, exhaustion, confusion, or perhaps, just knowing Maher is right, Sebastien doesn't protest. He is hardly friendly in the way he stares at Btet, but he follows the creature back into the tunnel and disappears from view.

Another figure takes the creature's place in the doorway almost immediately.

Carlsson. Ryder swallows hard. She's shoved the whole 'my mum might be here somewhere in this alien world' thing down somewhere deep till she has time to process and ask the hard question. Is her mum still alive?

"So, anyone hungry?" Carlsson glances down at the ruined furniture but doesn't comment. "I've got some epexs boiling. War or not, you're going to need to fill-up before you head out to find the Laudess, right?"

Before Ryder can answer, her stomach growls. Embarrassingly loud. Carlsson offers her a friendly smile, and Ryder returns it, blushing as her stomach continues to gurgle.

"Lead the way."

Chapter 13

Christian

Thinking makes Christian's head hurt, but he's finally decided on one thing. He is a long, long way from where he should be. In his world – the place he should be – there's only one sun in the sky. Not two. He stares up at the two blazing patches of fire-red and molten-orange. More like comets than suns, really.

And they are bone-sappingly hot. His hair is plastered to his head with sweat, and the stink coming from his armpits is getting more nose-wrinkling by the second. It is testament to just how exhausted he was, that he was able to sleep after the woman led him to a tee-pee like structure and directed him towards a pile of rugs - incredibly soft and smelling of lavender.

He slept like the unliving, according to Sen-Bay. And for quite some time. Twelve hours maybe. No one seems to have any watches or clocks that would tell him for sure. But Christian's back aches as much as his head, he's been lying down for way too long.

"Christian." Sen-bay offers him a slice of something that has the glistening blackness of licorice, but a few bites reveal a taste more like key-lime pie. Delicious. "At least your appetite hasn't changed."

The guy grins, and his eyes sparkle. Christian gives him a lop-sided smile in return. "So we know that much then, I'm always hungry."

"Correct. But you may wish to control your intake of drin. It is delectable, but quite rich, and may not agree with all stomachs, or…"

He gestures to his butt, grin widening. Christian stops mid-chew, spitting out what's left. Sen-bay bursts into a fit of laughter.

Finding Sen-bay is the best thing that's happened in far too long. Though the reasons are fuzzy, just out of reach, Christian felt immediately at ease when he spotted the long silver braids and the multitude of bracelets and beaded chains around the stranger's dark arms. Christian's spine-melting panic subsided beneath a blanket of familiarity.

This guy isn't a stranger. Christian is filled with doubt about so many things, all the pieces in his head that don't quite fit, but he is certain about this fact. He can trust Sen-bay. And he wants to be near him.

They sit at the edge of a small pond formed from rust-coloured rock that bubbles like a volcanic hot-spring. But the scent stirs memories of a pine forest, and Christian's pretty sure volcanic hot springs back home are a lot less pleasant.

Back home.

He can see it, in his mind's eye. The sky is blue, not tinged with hints of pink and yellow like here. And there aren't creatures like the ones in this place. Almost-human beings that walk on both two and four legs, or have eyes of total white, or gills where ears should be. Or no ears at all, like Sen-bay. But if that fact ever bothered Christian before about his companion, it doesn't now. In fact, he finds himself having to stop sneaking a glance at Sen-bay. Heat filling his cheeks every time he does.

Sen-bay burps then pulls another twist of the drin from a bowl that rests in his lap. "I don't understand how it has happened, but I'm grateful we comprehend one another other now, Chris-tan. You were not particularly good at hand signals."

Christian groans, nudging his shoulder against Sen-bay's own. "There's so much I don't understand, I've kind of given up trying to make sense of some things."

His hand falls to the chain around his neck. It is super-fine, and a tiny cross dangles from it. But hard as he tries, he can't recall who gave it to him. Or when. Did he get it recently? Or did he arrive with it? He's pretty certain he's never been to church. Well, definitely not when he was super young. Christian frowns. Yet again, thinking too hard is not a good thing. The clamp fixes on the crown of his head, crunching down on his thoughts.

"Are you well?" Sen-bay touches his hand to Christian's chin. "Chris-tan?"

"Yeah. I'm okay. I guess." Christian gazes around them, taking in the cluster of buildings that sit right under the apex of the domed metal that cages them here. There's more tee-pees, made from a white Perspex-like material, along with other structures that remind him of the temporary buildings used on construction sites, or schools. Single-level, squatting on stumps that keep them a couple of metres off the ground.

School. Christian went to school. Goes to school? Memories rise without trying to slice his brain in two, but don't seem to fit right. He's young. Much younger than he is now. Couldn't be more than eight or nine. But if he pushes any further, looks for something from more recently, then things really start to ache.

"Are you recalling something?" Sen-bay takes his hand.

Christian shakes his head, conscious of how cool Sen-bay's skin is against his. "Nothing important, I don't think. Stuff about another place."

"Nothing about Olessia?"

The hair on the back of Christian's neck stands to attention. The violet-eyed girl. The one who stopped those men hurting him. The girl who seemed to be their true target.

The Laudess, Sen-bay calls her. Someone important. A princess, from what Christian can gather. But why does a princess care what happens to him? And weirdest of all, Sen-bay has been trying to convince Christian that he arrived in this world with Olessia. That Sen-Bay watched her pull Christian from the wreckage of an aircraft after they crashed landed, fleeing a Zentai attack. The Zentai are Sen-bay's kind, but he tried to help Christian and Olessia. Only, they were discovered, betrayed by someone Sen-bay had once called a friend in his village. And now, both he and

Christian are here. In a place called Siros. The Laudess's own home.

But it doesn't make sense. If Siros is Olessia's home, then why does the Laudess seem as much a prisoner as both he and Sen-bay?

Christian can still feel the agony of that encounter with those two men, the ones who seemed to want to peel open his skull and take a look inside. Olessia called one of them Father. But what sort of father tosses their kid around like they were a rag-doll? And says some pretty nasty things to her?

"I still don't understand." Christian shrugs off the uncomfortable recall. "Why are they keeping us here? I mean, this is her home, right? Wouldn't she just tell them we're not enemies? Why are we in here?"

Sen-bay still clutches Christian's hand. Now, he tightens his grip. "We are not the enemies, no. I think the enemies are much closer to her. I had no idea who she was when I first found you. She was in hiding, that much is clear. And I thought it was from the Zentai, from the Crown and Reigner who would hunt her down if they realised she had crossed the border. But I'm not sure that was the whole truth. I can't help but feel she hid also from the Presider himself."

"The Presider? That's her father, right?"

"Yes." Sen-bay pulls away, letting his fingertips brush the length of Christian's own.

"Man, that guy… he's something else. Both of them were. That other one… Dashel… he just…" Christian stops, his guts roiling. The encounter is way too fresh. Sickening.

"The one who laid hands on you?"

Christian nods. The one who brought on a wave of agony like nothing he'd ever known. Whatever Dashel did to him, it went deep. Carving through Christian's insides like a hacksaw, in search of something. Both he and the Presider had thrown names at him. Demanded to know about people Christian's never heard of.

Ryder. Sophie.

A stab of pain shoots at the back of Christian's eyes. He cries out and hunches forward, covering his face.

"Chris-tan?" Sen-bay sounds alarmed.

"I'm okay." Christian speaks into his hands, muffling his words.

"No, you are not. I must get you help."

"No!" Christian drops his hands, grabbing at Sen-bay. "No, I'll be okay." He squints, eyes watering against the light. The needle jabbing harder at the back of his eyes.

"You are not well—" Sen-bay moves to stand.

"I don't want anyone to touch me," Christian shouts,then sighs. "Please," he whispers. "What if they take me away… I can't… I don't want to go."

Sen-bay drops down beside him, grasping him in a tight hug, pressing his hand against the back of Christian's head. "It is all right. They will not take you. They will not hurt you again, Christan."

Christian's head is pressed to Sen-bay's chest, his nose tilted at an uncomfortable angle but he doesn't move. His heart races with panic, his mouth suddenly bone dry. The magnitude of what's happening to him, sinking in.

"I'm so scared," he whispers.

"I know. As am I." Sen-bay's voice rumbles against Christian's ear. Strong, close, clear. "But we live. And we are by each other's side. There is strength in that. You have survived much, and will continue to do so."

"Everything all right, Sen-bay?"

The feminine voice comes from right overhead. Christian jerks upright, and Sen-bay's arms loosen to allow him to move. A woman. A human woman, stands very close by. The bubble and pop of the restless water cloaking her approach. Christian's breath comes in rapid, unsteady gulps. But Sen-bay actually exhales what sounds like a sigh of relief.

"It is you. Can you help him? He is one of your kind, is he not?"

"Human. Yes. He is," she says, her warm brown eyes taking in every feature.

Christian stares at the woman as she settles on a flattened section of rock beside them.

"Christian, isn't it?" She smiles at him. "I'm so very glad to meet you. Sen-bay has been worried about you, thought he wasn't going to see you again. He's been a pretty happy guy since you arrived yesterday." Her laughter is light and soft.

She speaks in English, with an Australian accent just like Christian's, though hers holds the hint of some other twang, something vaguely familiar. Sen-bay rests his arm around Christian's shoulders.

"She has been looking forward to meeting you, Chris-tan, but I wanted to give you time to adjust here first."

Christian doesn't acknowledge he's heard Sen-bay speak. He's too busy staring. A niggle at the back of his head threatening to turn into something far more painful, but he can't stop his thoughts racing.

"You're human, too?"

The woman nods, sending long waves of brown hair dancing. "I am. How are you feeling, Christian?" She tilts her head and looks up at him from beneath a furrowed brow.

"I'm…" Christian's dry throat swallows up the rest of the sentence. There is something so familiar about the look she's giving him. The rich brown of her eyes. He touches a finger to the back of his head. The niggle has shifted into a squeeze. "I'm… you seem…"

He strains to catch the memory dancing just out of reach. Dangling in the shadows, taunting him. The back of his skull cracks. Or so it seems. Christian screams. Sen-bay's hand comes down tight across his mouth, pushing the sound back.

"Christian," the woman says. "What is it?"

"Go, just go," Sen-bay hisses. "It is too much for him. Go."

"I'll find some medication to help him."

"Yes, yes. But please, Evelyn, go now. We will discuss the rest later."

Sen-bay's arm is tight around Christian, pressing him in against the Yentern's body. Great spots of black fill Christian's vision, and the headache that just exploded at the back of his head creeps across his crown.

"Chris-tan," Sen-bay whispers at his ear. "You are safe. Calm yourself. They watch us. Please, Chris-tan."

He continues to mutter, soft and gentle against Christian's ear. Telling him it's okay. They are okay. No one will take him away. Christian focuses in on the sound of Sen-bay's voice. Monotone, unwavering, soothing. Gradually, the pain eases. Sen-bay removes his hand from Christian's mouth, and cups his chin. Christian blinks, and the dots in his vision scatter. The world is bright and clear again.

Several of the other inhabitants have paused to watch the spectacle; a couple of creatures that could be mistaken for Bigfoot, and a four-legged being with a shelled back and elongated neck topped with multiple small heads. At a greater distance two of the guards survey them. Sen-bay raises his hand, gesturing to the guards. "He did not take well to the drin."

One of the guards speaks in return, telling Sen-Bay in a not particularly friendly way, that any mess Christian makes will be his problem.

Sen-Bay sighs and mutters under his breath. "Truly, the Sirosian's are vulgar creatures."

But Christian doesn't respond. The accent that clings to the guard's words is the same one that mingled in with the Australian accent of the human woman. She must have been here a long time, to pick it up. Christian sucks in his breath, searching for the dark curls and soft, wide eyes but the pressure in his skull begins to rise, and he exhales against it. Letting all thought of the woman go.

The latest brain-melt was by far the strongest. Does that mean this woman has something to do with why his brain is so scrambled?

"Who was she?" he says, letting Sen-bay help him to sit. In truth, the drin isn't resting all that well in his belly. "That lady?"

"I was informed she was one of the longest surviving beings in this place. When I realised you and I had been separated, and I had no clue where you were, I sought her out hoping she may know more than most appear to do here. Little did I know she was one of your kind. Until a day ago I was unaware your kind existed at all. Now I am in the company of two of you."

"Why is she here?"

"Olessia's father enjoys collecting things. Alive or otherwise. Willing or not. This is, apparently, the Collective."

Christian's stomach does a disconcerting roll. "He collects people?"

Sen-bay runs a finger against Christian's cheekbone, pushing back the hair that has matted in the sweat. "Do not concern yourself with that now. How do you feel?"

"I'm fine." Christian presses a hand to his stomach. "Fine. But I need to speak with her again."

"With Evelyn?" Sen-bay's heavy brow rises.

Christian's answer is stifled by the approach of the two guards, who seemed to have changed their minds about not wanting to see Christian hurl. They stride towards the pond with a purpose that has them at the bubbling water in a few short moments.

Sen-bay waves them off. "He will be attended to, rest assured. You need not worry yourselves."

But the guards don't seem to like his response and shout back at him in a stream of words that are lost on Christian.

"On your feet, Chris-tan," Sen-bay says hurriedly. "They want us to follow them."

"Why?" Christian's insides start to shake again. "What's wrong?"

"I'm not certain. Perhaps nothing. But for now, we will do as we are told."

Chapter 14

Olessia

Olessia follows Kileen across the chamber towards a panel of onyx lights that brighten a section of the wall directly opposite to the now-closed entranceway. Under different circumstances, Kileen would prove no real threat to Olessia. The Claven, though they will never admit to it, are technically biological failures. Generations ago, the Beckoning flowed along multiple genetic pathways. Few survived in any great strength, most died out altogether, wilting under the strain of carrying the Beckoning.

The Claven are remnants of bloodlines that did not succumb entirely, holding a whisper of the power that flows through the Presiderline – the singular bloodline that thrived. Olessia's father, his mother before him, and her father before her; each of their carefully-sequenced offspring not only capable of carrying the Beckoning but wielding its power in ever-increasing levels of strength.

That power stirs within her now, far more awakened than it has been since her arrival. If Sentinel Teler truly aided her, his assistance has been successful.

But for now, Olessia presses the Beckoning down. And with a speed and ease that surprises her,heeds her command.

Kileen disconnects the Moniker from the elthar clip at his hip and holds it up to the lit panel. The onyx lights pulse.

"You would be wise to come closer to the wall."

Barely is the warning uttered before a large circle of pliotine dislodges from the roof. Plummeting towards them. Olessia presses up against the wall, a movement mimicked by the accompanying Alkell. The panel's rapid pace slows almost immediately and lowers in a controlled movement, coming to a stop a fraction of a teslos from the ground. Above, a tunnel lit with specks of vintinum has been exposed, boring up into the exposed white rock, blackness at its far reaches.

"Come." Kileen steps up onto the wide panel of pliotine, and waves Olessia forward.

The Alkell, composure recovered, move to herd her in Kileen's direction. Olessia delivers a glare that stops them in their tracks. She gathers the folds of her skirt, and steps onto the panel. It rises as quickly as it had first descended, and Olessia staggers, shoved against the expressionless Alkell at her right. For a shocked moment she believes him about to tumble from the moving platform, but his body is jerked back by an unseen barrier, and he rights himself. His bland expression does not shift, and he doesn't utter a sound.

The platform's rapid rise continues; does not stop as they reach the roof of the chamber. They continue upwards, right into the white rock itself, the veins of gold turned a greenish hue by the pockets of blue vintinum illuminating the interior of the tunnel.

Olessia takes shallow breaths, due as much to the rapid pace as to the lightness of the air. The platform hums, offering the only sound in the confined space. The journey unsettles her but she refuses to allow Kileen to note any sign of her distress. She keeps her chin raised, eyes fixed on the darkness high above, where the vintinum does not yet reach.

But the silent, lengthy ride erodes her resolve. This could well be her final journey. Olessia's thoughts are as dark as the reaches of the tunnel itself, when all at once the blackness is swamped by bright light, a parting of rock that sends them rising into an open space. The section of pliotine they have travelled on becomes a panel of the floor in a room constructed of the gold-flecked white rock. Shimmering panels on one side of the dome allow a view of the surroundings.

Olessia's vantage point rests halfway up a slope of yet more of the gold-veined white rock, though much of it is covered in a layer of weering. The dome overlooks a settlement similar to Sen-Bay's Turning.

"Olessia, we are most pleased to see that you did not show resistance to Kileen's instructions."

Olessia starts, turning to find Dashel watching her. She meets his gaze steadily, allowing the Beckoning to whisper up its resting place.

"Where are we?" she demands.

"Oh, so the Laudine never saw fit to bring you here?" Dashel runs his fingertips across the short crop of white hair at his chin. "I'm surprised. As she did seem so fond of coming here for quite a time." Dashel sweeps his hand towards the view. "This is the Collective. All the finest specimens that have been retrieved on Traverse are kept here."

Olessia steps closer to the shimmering viewing panels, barriers of the same type that enclose her compound at Kinna-Bray. The panels afford an almost unimpeded view, but those without see only a distorted wall, like a cascade of fluid pouring from an invisible source. Olessia leans in close, trying to make sense of what she sees.

The settlement is clearly occupied, but by whom she is uncertain. The creatures that wander between the low-level buildings and triangular unmay — portable shelters usually reserved for use by the border patrols — are certainly not from Siros. Or Zentai.

"Why are they here?" Unease cradles Olessia, and she finds herself reaching for the Beckoning. Seeking assurance from its presence.

"A variety of reasons, only one of which you need concern yourself with." Dashel jerks his chin towards Kileen. "You have informed the Laudess of our concerns?"

"Yes, I have. And that her co-operation would be appreciated."

"Good, good."

"Stop with the ridiculous games, Dashel." Olessia's temper flares. "What do you want from me?"

Dashel eyes her. "Simple. Your power is great. Even those… restraints… I placed upon you appear to have weakened. You have recovered rapidly, faster than we had estimated. That power is needed. Today. To aid the war effort—"

"You are just repeating Kileen's words, which mean nothing to me." Olessia's eyes burn. Auras spring into existence around her, Dashel's as bright as the twin confels that blast the sky overhead, speckled with the flecks of jet black that mark the Claven. "Where is Aresh? What have you and my father done to her, Dashel?"

He adjusts the lavender-hued wislayer draped across his shoulder. "What we have done is contain a threat. A threat that will be dealt with when we are not pre-occupied by the war the Laudine herself has stirred into being."

Olessia lunges at him, hands shaped into claws. Not content with using the Beckoning, she wishes to feel her nails rake his cheeks. Before she can reach him, Dashel lifts something from his pocket and flicks it into the air. An image appears between them and Olessia stops dead.

Aresh. Floating on her back with no visible support beneath her. Her eyes are closed and her skin is so pale the scarring on her face is accentuated. Her hair hangs vertically beneath her.

"Listen to me very carefully, Olessia." Dashel peers at her through the slowly rotating image. "You cannot reach her, but you can ensure she does not disappear altogether. A war of this scale requires an extensive arsenal, and as you well know, the Beckoning provides us with that. The energy it drains is the very power that fuels Siros technology. But the Presider's time and energy are required for the war, so you will share his burden. You know what is expected of you. The Presider attempted to teach you at Vale Leven. To harvest, rather than destroy."

Olessia recoils, tugging at the folds of material wrapped around her midriff. Too tight against her body. "Harvest?"

"We have developed ways to utilise the energy that brings life. And the Beckoning enables us to harvest that energy." Dashel paces to the viewing panels, arms folded. "Removed in controlled assaults, the subjects are weakened but not eliminated. There would be little point in decimating our energy source. We don't wish another Vale Leven, if you can avoid it. But I believe you have far greater control of the Beckoning now, don't you, Olessia? And those in the Collective are strong, believe me. They are well used to this procedure."

Olessia tears her gaze from the image of Aresh. "You want to use the Beckoning to steal—"

"Not steal. I consider it payment for their upkeep. Think of them as a dairy herd from your beloved Earth. They are milked each day with no adverse effects, while benefitting the greater good. The situation is the same here."

"Have you and my father lost your sense entirely?" Olessia cries.

Dashel ignores her, and nods at Kileen. He waves his hand over the floor. A small section folds open, and a pyramid-shaped structure rises from the ground. Half Olessia's height, it is constructed of a matte-black material that reflects no light against its dull surface. The structure's peak sits at Kileen's hip level, and floats with his light touch as he guides it to the centre of the room.

"You will draw the auras to you, and the energy will be contained in the Qarnam. Ready for processing."

Olessia shakes her head. "This is… it is…"

"It is what the Presider demands," Dashel says, nonchalant. "And it is what you will do. Do not entertain any idea of using the Beckoning as your means of escape, that would not bode well for the Laudine, or for them." He flicks a finger towards the settlement, turning away before Olessia can follow the direction. But it is clear who he is indicating. A pair of Sentinels push two figures up the slope of the hill towards Olessia's new prison. Her expression is held smooth but within, her pulses are erratic. Relief and terror quicken them, as she stares down at the Christian's spray of stark white hair, and Sen-Bay's long swaying grey braid against his rich, dark skin.

The pair are alive, something she feared may no longer be the case. But now they are directly in harm's way. Her way.

Christian and Sen-bay do their utmost to impede their forced journey up the slope, actually dragging their feet. Christian may be considerably taller than the guard, but he is not stronger, and the Sirosian's pace is unaltered by Christian's struggle.

Dashel appears at her side, and Olessia's near empty stomachs twist with his proximity. "Do not imagine you can outmatch Inel, child. You have seen how we can reduce you to nothing. It will take far less to do so to these two. Now, begin. Tread carefully, Laudess. The Presider would not be pleased if you were to harm his Collective residents. They are so precious after all." He smiles, without a trace of anything resembling mirth, and Olessia must use some resolve to restrain the Beckoning as it feeds on her anger. To lose control now would only result in greater harm to those she wishes to protect. Vale Leven cannot occur a second time. She will not allow it.

"Direct the energy here." Kileen touches the point of the pyramid. "The Qarnam will contain it as soon as the energy comes into contact with its surface. Simple really. All you have to do is retain control of the Beckoning." His eyes move to the slope where Christian and Sen-Bay rest on their knees. Christian's head darts frantically back and forth, as though he searches for escape. Sen-bay appears to be speaking to him, steady where he kneels with the Sentinel at his side. But escape is not yet an option. Olessia understands this, even though it pains her. She must understand her environment. She must collaborate.

The inhabitants of the Presider's Collective are being gathered at the base of the slope. She counts fifteen figures, perhaps more, being shoved and cajoled into a rough semi-circle by a group of weapon-laden guards. One drives a vet-kray arch into the back of a hunched creature with a bulbous head, forcing the being's jaw to widen in a jagged tooth-baring cry.

"Begin, Olessia. There is no further time for delay." Dashel crosses his arms behind his back, bracing his feet apart. His pose was not so dissimilar the day he stood behind the Presider at Vale Leven.

Olessia turns away, tilting her head so he might not notice the close of her eyes, forcing back the memory of that day. Her eyes reopen, and she places her hands on the pyramid. The surface is the same temperature as the viewing room, far cooler than beyond the panes. Some of the captives fan themselves against the weighted heat, and Christian tugs at the high collar of the Zentai vest he still wears. The clothing Sen-Bay provided in the Turning. How Olessia longs for that brief time of respite and safety.

She centres herself.

Forgive me. She sends out the thought, knowing it will not reach them but needing to set it free all the same. Olessia breathes in deep, just as Sebastien taught her. Finding her focus, just as Sentinel Teler drilled into her. The time of Vale Leven is long past. Olessia has controlled the Beckoning on more than one occasion since, in situations of extreme duress. Certainly, she is capable of it now.

The Beckoning senses its impending release. Rising fast, heat flooding her body. But Olessia does not stop it. Nor even attempt too. She waits. In a pool of total stillness. Not the flurry of panic and resistance she has so often exercised before. Before she met Ryder, and the calmness her presence brought with it. Olessia's eyes sting with the churn of colour there but she ignores the discomfort. Ryder may not be here now, thankfully, but she has already shown Olessia what she is capable of.

Olessia focuses her concentration on a place of clarity. A space in her consciousness where she builds a barrier, and braces for the impact of the beast. That moment is not long. The Beckoning shudders against her inner resistance, her body alive with the heat that comes with the release of the entity within. Auras flare, radiating from Christian, Sen-bay and all the living beings that huddle at the base of the hill. Combining all colours imaginable. Pulsing, radiant shades that twist and dart and intertwine.

Olessia's breathing quickens but retains its rhythm. Her calm seems to unsettle the beast. Confusion rattles through her, and her nerve endings flare in a brief moment of recoil before the Beckoning steadies itself.

One breath in, another out. Both slow. Sustained. Controlled.

The Beckoning flickers, as though it does not recognise its new surrounds, its heat dimming for a moment. The auras dim accordingly, only to flare immediately again. With her next breath, Olessia releases the beast, allowing it to draw on the world around her. Christian and Sen-bay are the first to be touched. They kneel, on their own, on the slope. The Sentinels who watched over them, and the guards who herded the Collective residents into place have moved to a safe distance. Relying on the wex barrier — an electric fence of sorts — that surrounds the group to ensure none of them attempt to escape their fate.

But no one looks even remotely like they will. Shoulders droop, and heads are bowed. Some even sit upon the ground.

They are well used to this procedure, Dashel told her. And, Olessia realises, they are resigned to it.

A subtle colour, the shade of a clear Earth sky, flows from around Christian. He presses a hand to his chest, the fear in his expression causing Olessia to falter. The Beckoning claws at her, angered by the sudden halt.

"Now, now, Olessia. You were doing so well," Dashel says. "Don't disappoint us now."

But doubt plays with her. Tears a hole in her calm. Christian is frightened. And now, so is she. The auras from the larger group flow like a great river up the slope, moving right through Christian and Sen-bay, swallowing their life-forces. The sheer mass of energy catches her off-guard. Usually her management of the Beckoning is so barely in control there has been no time to consider how much energy she can manipulate. Olessia balls her hands into fists. The beast's hunger roars through her, chipping at her control.

Sen-bay takes Christian's hand in his, speaking to him in words that do not reach Olessia, but she doesn't need the sound to make out the words formed on Sen-Bay's lips.

You will be okay.

His gaze does not leave Christian, and he repeats the words. Christian nods, his face clearing.

Olessia has no idea whether the Yentern understands what is happening, or that she is even here. But his certainty is contagious. And it is all she needs to re-centre herself. Flames lick at her insides, and sweat coats her body, but Olessia rebuilds her place of clarity, reins in the Beckoning and leads it to where she directs.

The auras' volume increases, a river flowing in reverse. Finding its way across the distance between host and thief. The pyramid's surface shines as the first of the auras make contact. Dashel and Kileen move around her, their excitement palpable, their voices muted beneath the hum of the Beckoning as it works with her.

Olessia widens her eyes. The beast is working with her. Heeding her direction, moving at her behest as she gathers the lifeforces to her, capturing them within the Qarnm. It is a momentous realisation but she can afford it no time. Her attention must be on the auras and the people she takes them from. These are beings from a variety of worlds with varying levels of fortitude against such a force as the Beckoning. Olessia must heed the smallest sign that limits have been reached.

And she finds it in the shape of a woman. A human woman. With chocolate brown hair that sits in waves around a face that causes Olessia to gasp.

Her alliance with the beast falters. Just as the woman does. She collapses against the scale-covered being that stands beside her. A being shorter than her, and with their weakened energy, both are unable to stay on their feet. The human woman and her companion hit the ground.

"Enough." Olessia snaps off the Beckoning's connection. Faintly registering that it does so with the barest hint of resistance. She rushes to the viewing pane, her skirt billowing behind her. She cranes her neck, hoping to catch another glimpse of the woman's face but the group has gathered around them, many showing obvious signs of fatigue. A creature with a pair of elongated limbs jutting from its side, ones that first appeared to be very long arms, suddenly drops and uses all six limbs to edge away. Another, with a hair-covered body and hunched back, sways back and forth on its broad feet. Dazed perhaps.

Sen-bay helps Christian to his feet, staring up at the dome. Olessia presses her hand against the viewing pane, ignoring the sharp tingle it sends through her skin, willing him to see her despite the barrier between them. The Sentinels and guards return.

Sen-bay swipes at the guard who tries to take Christian's arm, shouting something at the armed escort that sees them back off, and he guides a stumbling Christian back down the slope.

Olessia's chest burns with the lingering touch of the Beckoning, but the ache that runs to her core has less to do with the beast, and everything to do with the distance growing between her and those below. Eyes stinging, she searches for a sign of the woman.

"Impressive. Perhaps your escapade to the Iondar realm was even more useful than we first thought." Kileen stands over the pyramid, touching at a panel that has appeared on one side. "I'll advise the Presider that we are done here. He'll be most pleased with the results, I believe."

"Come, Olessia," Dashel says.

But she does not move from where she stands. Will not until she finds trace of that woman again.

"Olessia?" Dashel's voice is laden with warning. "I will not ask again."

And he does not need to. Olessia catches a glimpse of wavy dark hair. The woman is being assisted by one of the guards, her arm slung around their neck. But her face is concealed from Olessia's view, and she cannot be certain of what she saw earlier. A face with such familiar features, it took Olessia's breath away. For a moment she believed the worst had happened. That Ryder was one of those held in the Collective. But the woman is clearly older. Slender to the point of under-nourished.

A new possibility births itself, and it is a singular point of light in the darkness of Olessia's world.

Ryder's mother did not abandon her on Earth. She was taken. Added to the Presider's collection.

Ryder's mother is alive.

Olessia gathers the folds of her crimson skirt, turning her back on those she has stolen from.

Ready, but not willing, to be led back down into the depths.

Chapter 15

Ryder

The meal isn't terrible, so far as eating ingredients that don't even exist in your world goes. But Ryder prefers to eat without an audience that watches her like a hawk.

"So, what did you think?" Carlsson is a bouncing ball of energy on the low ottoman-like nearby. She's been watching every mouthful Ryder's taken, which hasn't exactly been a relaxing way to have a meal. "Just like home? My mum hunted for the right ingredients for a long time, trying to get it right. What do you think? Just like lasagne you would eat in those… oh what are they called, the places where you pay people to bring you things."

"Restaurants?"

"Yes." Carlsson claps her hands, like Ryder was a baby speaking her first word.

Ryder raises another mouthful of the gloop that smells a little too much like socks. "Sure. Yeah, it's just like lasagne. She did well."

Actually, not even remotely well. The pasta sheets are definitely not pasta. More like grains of sand clinging together. The bechamel sauce is an off-putting grey, and there are strands of weird hexagon shaped leaves that have a furry covering and make her want to gag. Ryder stalls for time, picking at her teeth where something that might be a very distant relative of the tomato has lodged between molars. On the plus side, there are no signs of anything meat-like.

Apparently, this gang of jungle-dwellers isn't big on hunting. In the scheme of things, the vegetarianism probably isn't so noteworthy, but Ryder finds it oddly comforting.

"When you're finished," Carlsson declares. "You can tell me all the latest news about Earth."

Ryder gives her a dismissive grunt. "All of it, huh? That will be a long conversation."

The plastered smile on Carlsson's face wavers. "Yeh, I suppose you're right."

Ryder shifts the topic, hoping it will shift Carlsson's melancholy. "So, you were born here?"

"I was. My mother was pregnant with me when she was taken." Carlsson jabs her finger into the green liquid in the pewter cup in front of her. The drink is almost the same emerald shade as the glow of Ryder's elthar.

Ryder rubs at her wrists, missing the coolness of the metal there. The moment sits ripe and ready for her next question. About her mother. She opens her mouth, but the moment is snatched away from her by the slam of a heavy cup against the table. Though the rectangular table could pass as wood it rings with a metallic sound.

"I am not Aresh's Guardian, I am Olessia's." Sebastien shoves his plate of half-eaten 'lasagne' away, using enough force to nearly send it off the other side of the broad table. "I will go to Falllyn if that is where you believe she has been taken. Or is that a deception too, brother? How can I trust that you are, as you say, an ally to the Laudine?"

Maher takes his time with an answer, letting the tension simmer and cool. He gathers up his plate, reaching across to collect Sebastien's. "With Aresh gone, I have no way to prove it to you, so you will have to have some faith in my intentions, Sebastien. I desire what you do. To have the Laudess returned to Siros so we may have hope of preventing the breakout of war. Believe me, I do not doubt your ability, brother. You may have not seen me in many tar, but that does not mean I have not watched you. The Laudine has kept me informed of your development and how you have risen to the challenge that was presented to you—"

"That *you* forced on me—" Sebastien's eyes darken, his jaw tight.

Maher sighs. "True. I passed on the burden of this role to you. But now, seeing you as I do, your strength and loyalty, I believe I did not do the Presiderline the disservice I intended." His smile is tinged with a pride that reflects in his eyes. "Aresh has told me she believes I could have done nothing better than betray them. That my anger towards the Presider would have presented in the way I treated Olessia. But your anger, it was directed elsewhere. Not towards our masters, but towards me. I was your enemy. Not the Laudess. And as a result she has been receptive to what you teach her."

Sebastien sniffs. "If I were the Guardian you claim me to be, then she would not be a captive. I am going to Falllyn, I am going to find a way into Icewyn, and there is no point—"

"Wait. I'm confused," Carlsson says. "You're talking as though the Laudess is still alive. But you saw it, Maher—"

"Carlsson, no—"

"But you saw it. They killed her when she was trying to save that human boy. And you heard the Protectorate declare that she was dead—"

The lasagne flips in Ryder's stomach.

"Stop! Carlsson, please. Stop," Maher says.

But it's way too late.

Sebastien hunches, pressing his fingertips to the table-top as though the air just got knocked out of him. Which, of course, it did.

Ryder's been dancing around this moment since Blane told her what he'd heard. Refusing to believe it, convincing herself some strange sixth sense told her it hadn't happened. Maher went along with the delusion. Forgetting to mention he'd actually *seen* it happen.

"You didn't tell me…" Ryder's words vaporise the moment they are free.

She may as well have not spoken at all. No one looks her way. Maher stares at Sebastien, his jaw working as though he's attempting to speak but no words come.

"Why…" Sebastien's voice cracks, and he pauses. "Why would you not tell me?" He's speaking low and slow and it's more terrifying than any of the times he's shouted. He doesn't wait for Maher to answer, turning on Ryder.

She wants nothing more than to lower her head and not have to look at those eyes. The grey irises so pale his entire eye appears white. But it's not the strangeness of them that has her wanting to avoid his gaze. It's the pain there. The hollowness of Sebastien's cheeks as the shock drains them of all colour.

"You knew," he says, in that dangerous whisper.

Ryder winces. "But I didn't believe it—"

Does she now?

"How long, Ryder. How long have you known that Olessia…" His eyebrows knit together, as though he's burned his tongue on the words.

Ryder holds his gaze. "Blane. He told me just before we crashed… but Sebastien I don't believe it." She takes a step towards him. And it is a step too far.

"No. Leave me. Both of you." Sebastien raises his hands, balled into elthar-covered fists, and slams them into the table, breaking it in two. Carlsson screams, and dashes in behind Ryder.

"Sebastien, stop. Enough." Maher begins, only to find himself at the business end of the same blade Sebastien directed at him earlier.

"You had no right," Sebastien shouts. "To keep this from me. No right. I am her Guardian. The Laudess's safety is my responsibility." He clutches at his head with his free hand, A short moan escapes him before he storms towards the far wall, where the concealed entrance lies. "Let me out. Now."

"I don't think—"

"Let me out," Sebastien roars, his words coarse with rage. "Now."

He lashes out with the blade, and crystal flies in chunks from the wall. As he moves to swing again, the concealed entrance glitters and the archway that leads into the outside world appears. Sebastien is gone before Ryder can catch her breath. Her heart bangs out a beat against her ribs. Carlsson is clutching at her arm, trembling.

"I'm sorry… I didn't know." Tears stream down her face.

"His temper is not your fault, Carlsson," Maher says. "The blame is mine. I should not have withheld the information from him. Whether we believe it is true or not, we should have told him."

Btet stands in the archway just beyond him, her long limbs wrapped around her torso. She sounds off with a couple of sharp, high-pitched bleets, and Maher nods.

"You did the right thing, Btet. Letting him go. There was no reasoning with him. I will follow after him—"

"No," Ryder says. She's not sure if it's just Carlsson shaking, or her. "I don't think that's a good idea. I'll go."

Maher stoops to pick up the plates that lie scattered around the broken table. "Btet said he's used his elthar, he's headed towards The Dovers. I have a garreson… a vehicle, that will enable me to track him through this terrain."

"Please, Maher." Ryder is already striding to the entranceway. "Just let me handle this. I'll get him back. I promise."

He won't go far. She's certain of it. He won't leave her here.

Ryder is going whether Maher likes it or not, but still, it's a relief when she looks over her shoulder and finds him giving her a grim nod. "Fine. But take these with you."

Maher heads for the copper-coloured crate sitting beside the entranceway to the kitchen area, but Carlsson is one step ahead of him. She pulls out a pair of goggles that would look right at home at a steampunk convention; elaborate etchings on the surface, and a braided strap whose clasp glints with a stone that could pass for a ruby.

"These are called an anvel—" Carlsson says.

"They will enable you to see your way out there. We will sync it with Sebastien's tracker. Then you just need to follow the display," Maher says, frowning. "Are you certain—"

"When did you put a tracker on Sebastien?"

"Btet did, when she first came across you. A precaution."

Ryder nods. A precaution that has come in quite handy. "Do I have one too?"

Btet emits a low gurgling sound, one claw touching to the side of her elongated neck.

"You did, but the device must have been faulty. She says the signal wasn't clear, and it managed to come loose before you got to the shelter." Btet's gurgle rises to more of a throat clearing, and Maher screws up his face. "Btet is somewhat insulted I believe. Her tech is usually outstanding."

All three of them, Maher, Btet and Carlsson stare at her. Like Ryder sabotaged the green-skinned, claw-lady's tracker on purpose.

"What?" she says. "I didn't break it, I didn't even know I was being tracked. Look, this is a great chat and all, but I have to go."

And without waiting to see if that's okay with them, Ryder heads out.

Chapter 16

Ryder

R yder stops just outside the camouflaged hideout. The coolness of the shelter gives way to sticky heat. The forest is a dark blob before her, night still hugging the air. Ryder tugs on the goggles. Not made of metal as they first appeared, but a spongy material that is soft around her eyes. The strap is too tight but she's not going to waste time adjusting it. The minute she places them over her eyes, the world around her draws into focus. Infrared but better. Like someone has switched on a low light to lead her through the forest. Everything in true, but dull, colour. She lifts her head. A thin winding light snakes its way through the foliage overhead. She pulls the goggles away from her eyes, and the light disappears. It's on the lenses themselves. And, she's guessing, is the path that will lead her right to Sebastien.

"Too easy." Ryder settles the goggles back into place and sets off at a run. Jumping over fallen trunks, odd piles of moss that look too much like cow pats, and haphazard clumps of that pale pink crystal of the mountains – the Dovers. All the while glancing up to make sure she's still following the trail. Sebastien's airborne path is giving her a crick in her neck. Every now and then Ryder calls his name, but the silence sits heavy around her.

Anything but a slow walk is incredibly unpleasant in the heat, but Ryder keeps up the fast pace until her head spins. She stops, and leans her hands on her knees, struggling to suck in enough air to fill her lungs.

"Oh man, you are not making this easy," she coughs.

That's exactly what I said when you ran off into the paddock that time.

Ryder's stifles her squeal behind a cupped hand. Her already racing heart kicking up a notch. "Sophie?"

She whirls around and comes face to face with her friend. In perfect clarity through the anvel lenses.

"Oh my god, Sophie." Ryder reaches for her. "You're really here. How is this possible?"

Ryder. Finally. You heard me this time. Sophie's grin is wide, her eyes dancing with delight and she lifts her arms.

Ryder's hand sweeps straight through her. "Oh." Ryder snatches her hand back against her chest. "What's happening?"

Sophie's smile drops away. *I don't know how this works, Ry. But I think I'm terrible at it.*

"No, no, you're doing fine," Ryder falters. She has no idea what 'it' is, or how she can help her friend. All she knows is that it's agony. To be so close and not be able to give Sophie a hug. "Are you… are you okay?"

Aside from the obvious. The missing body, for one. Ryder drowns out the inner voice telling her this is all wrong. None of that matters. She hadn't imagined it when she heard her friend's voice in the shelter. Sophie really is here.

Yeah. Yeah, I think so. I mean I feel fine. Kind of.

Sophie's image — hologram, spectre, astral projection whatever it is — isn't quite as clear as Ryder first imagined. The trees behind her are shadowed through her form. *Padellah found me, I'm not alone, Ry.*

"Padellah? Where is she now?"

I wish I knew. She could give me some more tips on being ghostly. Sometimes you can see me, and hear me, other times I'm just shouting into a void. A really big void. Sophie shudders. *It's crazy, Ry. There's like this black hole here, and I should be scared of it, but… I dunno… I'm not. I kind of want to just, sink into it like it's a big cosy bath of tar… weird right? Did you see anything like that? When you were, doing your astral projection thing?*

Ryder takes a second to answer. The Rising had a black hole. Just like Sophie describes. One that Ryder could have quite happily let herself drift into. Lose herself in entirely, if Padellah hadn't hauled her back from the edge. Warned her away from the abyss.

"Don't go near it, Sophie. Are you listening to me? Just stay right away from that darkness. It's not somewhere you want to go. Stay here, with me."

Sophie nods, her hair wafting around her face in slo-mo, like she's stuck in a weird shampoo commercial. *Well, it's almost impossible not to. Stay with you, I mean. You're like a sun in here. You should see yourself, Ry. You are haloing the heck out of this place. A golden sun with pretty rose-pink edges. But I keep losing the connection with you, sometimes you can't hear me calling, and when that happens they kind of fade, the pink edges. But when I reach you, they are like the most amazing sunset you've ever seen. So beautiful.*

Rose-pink. The colour of Sophie's aura. A chill settles on Ryder, despite the warmth of the air.

"Sophie, where is Padellah now?"

I don't know. I remember us being dragged up towards that ship, then everything went black. Next I know, Padellah is there, telling me I'm safe. And then she left.

Sophie's seen Padellah more recently than Ryder in that case. Padellah got Ryder's help shifting that creation out of the Paldrian River and that's the last she's seen of her. Ryder was angry about it earlier, but now, if there's the chance that the Cyne has somehow… saved Sophie, then all is forgiven. Is that what this is? A crazy miracle? Maybe Blane found a way to revive Sophie, or the cryo-stasis the Commandant wanted her kept in, actually kept her alive?

And Ryder just ran. Leaving Sophie back there at the crash site without a backward glance.

Ryder stifles her stampeding thoughts, and starts walking. Quickening her pace, as though she can out step the thoughts altogether.

"Well, you're here now. And that's all that matters."

Sophie's smile beams. *My thoughts exactly. Plenty of time to work out the details.*

"Plenty of time." Ryder sucks at her lip, fighting the tears. They can cry this out later. "Soph, I have to find Sebastien before he does something stupid. He thinks Olessia is dead."

But didn't you tell him about our theory?

"I tried, so did Maher, his brother."

He's really quite lovely, don't you think? Sophie giggles. *Maher I mean, Sebastien's pretty, sure, but even if he was my cup of tea, he's totally taken.*

"Seriously? Right now?" Ryder shakes her head, cheeks burning.

What better time? There is a lot of tension at the moment. Which reminds me, how long are you going to wait until you ask about your mum?

Ryder stops dead, turning to face her friend. There is nothing behind her but an unfamiliar forest.

Over here, Ry. One thing I am getting better at is focusing on where I want to go, and how fast.

Her laughter is light against Ryder's mind. Ryder turns. Her friend is just ahead, giving her a salute. All at once, Sophie doubles over, her red hair covering her face.

"Sophie." Ryder rushes to her side, flailing her arms in a useless attempt to take hold of Sophie's hand. "What is it? Are you okay?"

I don't know. Ouch. This is not fun. She jerks upright. *Oh, whoa. Can you hear that?*

Ryder holds still, straining to catch any sound. "Nothing, just you. Why?"

Sophie purses her lips, nodding intently.

"Sophie?"

Sophie holds up her hand, and the signal is clear. Be quiet. Ryder does as she's told, tapping her toe impatiently against the roots underfoot. In the distance, a low rumble catches her attention. She tries to follow the sound, staring out through the night goggles. A shiver runs across her shoulders. The ribbon of light indicating Sebastien's path has disappeared. Ryder curses under her breath.

Ryder, we've got a message incoming. This may sting a little.

"What?"

The pain arrows through Ryder's skull, moving from the back of her head and slamming between her eyes. She cries out, clutching at her head. Staggering in the uneven undergrowth, Ryder's heel catches on something and she topples onto her back.

Ryder. Aresh's smooth voice moves with the pain.

Aresh? Where are—

The Crown must know of my brother's deceit. Aresh's voice rises and falls in volume, making it difficult to catch all the words. *Go to the Crown.*

The crown? Isn't that the Zentai leader?

But Aresh's words keep coming. As though she didn't hear Ryder's question.

Go only to the Crown. Megnastin. Must... The volume dips super low, barely above a whisper. *Take... to Megnastin.*

An odd click sounds inside Ryder's head, like someone tapped her skull, and then, just as abruptly, the pain vanishes. Ryder groans, blinking her eyes open. "Aresh? Sophie?"

The lenses on the goggles are cracked, and she is surrounded by darkness. Inky black. Ryder tugs at the anvel, letting them dangle around her neck. She is alone. In the forest and in her mind. She rolls onto her side, picking out flecks of stone and dirt from her shirt, squinting into the darkness.

"I don't understand. What was that? Guys, you need to help me out here."

There is no reply. And she can't shake the sense that the message was more like voicemail. One-sided. Aresh didn't respond to Ryder but spoke over the top of her.

The forest is silent as a grave. But whatever that just was, it means Aresh is alive. The thought helps chase away the quiver of unease that comes at being stranded in the pitch black with no idea where home is. Aresh is alive. Whatever the Presider might have done to her, she's survived it. Somewhere. In Megnastin? Or is Megnastin a person? Someone who can help? Ryder staggers to her feet. She needs to find Sebastien. Now.

"Sebastien," she yells. "You need to come back."

The ground shudders beneath her. Ryder braces herself. Wondering if the ground is about to open up beneath her. Off to the right, somewhere in the distance, a cracking filters through the forest, followed by a heavy thud. The rhythm is repeated. *Crack, thump, crack.* Something enormous is headed her way. And it's tearing the forest down to do it.

"Sebastien, where are you?" Ryder yells, twirling around in a messy pirouette. She has no clue which way to go. "Sebastien!"

She picks a direction, the only one that doesn't seem to reverberate with sound, and runs. As fast as possible, which is snail's pace thanks to the undergrowth, and the low hanging sweep of branches that tug at her hair, and try to poke her eyes out. If she stares down hard at the ground, she can make out the terrain, and be almost quick enough to avoid holes and tangles of roots. Almost. Her ankle, the one she busted when she landed badly carrying Sebastien, turns in a divet of squelchy mud and she hisses at the dull pain. What Ryder wouldn't do to have her elthar right now.

"Sophie, are you with me?"

But no one is with her. Except for whatever it is that's thundering through the forest behind her. There's an echo to the sound, as though it's bouncing off the mountain range that's around here somewhere and back down into the valley. But then the truth, and a thorny branch intent on taking her hair out at the scalp, hits her and digs in. Ryder yanks the branch from her hair, wincing as a few strands get left behind. It's not one thing thundering behind her. There's a whole bunch of massive, stomping *things.*

Ryder forces her feet to move faster but her lungs are on fire, and she can't keep the sweat from pouring into her eyes. As though the darkness wasn't bad enough, she's practically blind. Pretty soon it's going to be more than a twisted ankle that sends her flying. But the monsters behind her are fast. And gaining. The forest is alive with their destruction. Her unsteady course sends her headlong into a huddle of those weird twisted-trunk trees. She cries out, narrowly avoiding a full-on collision, but unable to avoid slamming her shoulder against the outer most trees. There is a cracking sound that might be the tree she just hit or the breaking of her collarbone, but Ryder pushes forward. *Worry about that later.*

Jelly seeps into her legs, and her heart feels like its sitting at the base of her throat. There's been plenty to be scared about recently but right now, Ryder can barely stop herself from screaming with the terror. Her bones want to jump out of her skin, and her skin wants to tear itself free of flesh.

Run. Run. She chants to herself between desperate breaths. Breaths that are way too shallow for this much effort.

But it won't be fast enough.

The devastating thought pulls a cry from her – a wailing, desperate sound that lifts from her core, rising over the cacophony and filling every inch of her exhausted body.

The alien forest comes alive with colour, as though someone just threw the main switch. The shades spill from the odd shaped trunks, and crazy angled leaves.

Auras. Shimmering, dazzling and lighting the way ahead of her in a rainbow of colour.

Ryder stumbles, reaching for the nearest support. A clump of candy-floss pink crystal. The moment her hand touches the jagged pieces the crystal brightens, beaming out a pink that's near to fluoro. A coolness flows through her, rushing in at her fingertips, finding its way through her in the blink of an eye. It chases away the jelly legs, allows her lungs to expand fully, and take in the deeper breath she desperately craves.

Ryder tugs her hand off the crystal, and the shimmer dulls. *Maybe…* Ryder takes the few paces needed to reach a shrub that has leaves as hard and pointed as a Holly bush. She snatches a handful, ignoring the subtle sting of the barbs against her skin. The bush's subtle yellow glow lifts, brightening to rival a morning sun. Her heartbeat slows, the thudding in her ears fades.

The cool chill beneath her skin spreads further. Finding its way down her spine. Ryder's body buzzes with energy. And the sensation is not unfamiliar. It was there at Willow Court, when she lifted the bed and threw it at the spider-creature. It was there at Tarraleah, when Ryder drew the cart with Sebastien's antidote to her. It was there when she safely brought down the helicopter carrying Jack and Daenara. And killed Sophie.

The cluster of crystal explodes in a violent burst, sending shards of shimmering rock flying in all directions. Ryder dives for the nearest cover, though it's barely good enough to be called that: a clearly dead tree, a slender trunk surrounded by long, flowing fronds of brittle leaves. Another explosion hits just off to her right, giving Ryder no chance to see what, or who, is firing at her. Ryder covers her face, waiting for the spray of debris to settle before she risks a glance. She should have kept her head down.

Pushing its way through the rainbow-coloured landscape is a giant metal crab. At least, that's Ryder's first thought on seeing the disc perched low between four spindly legs. A multitude of joints run down each leg, where cogs turn and spin. The rim of the disc contains sapphire squares of light that dance from one side to the other, increasing in speed until a single line of blue sits across the entire rim. Uh oh...

The craft fires.

A massive bolt of blue shoots from the disc.

"No!" Ice shifts deep inside her, and Ryder raises her arms, creating a pathetic shield. But she notices the storm cloud of light hugging her skin, touched with every colour imaginable.

Her own aura.

The cloud thickens, and a barrier grows around her, its chill chasing away every trace of heat. At her core, a familiar niggling. Not the harsh clawing that came when she brought down the helicopter, this is more subtle. More under control.

In the middle of the chaos she is calm. Focused.

She must survive. And she wills it to happen.

Ryder shifts her hands towards the wave that pummels towards her. Grits her teeth, readying for impact.

The sapphire blast rushes at her. Closer. Closer...

The light shatters, exploding into a thousand tiny dying fireworks that fall harmlessly to the forest floor.

"Holy..." Ryder whispers. "I did it."

The crab still stands. It's not done with her yet. The lights form again along the rim of the disc.

A *metal* disc.

Ryder sucks at her lip. The cut stings, but she's focused on the craft. She seems to have a thing with metal; the bed-frame, the cart. The helicopter. She glances at her surroundings. The only thing that will get hurt here are the trees. And her, if she doesn't do something fast. Ryder presses a hand to her stomach, there is a fluttering there. But it's not nerves.

"Help me out here, okay?"

She rises to her feet, and the swathe of heavy auras lifts with her like the skirt of a technicolour ballgown. Ryder exhales, and focuses on the craft. There's no sign of any inhabitants, which fills her with relief.

In, out. In, out. The odd meditation begins. Ryder pictures the craft lifting. Pictures it moving back through the forest. Back to where it came from.

Ice spreads through her body, as though butterflies have taken flight. Moving into her limbs. But she doesn't shiver. No goosebumps rise. She's never felt more comfortable in her life.

She continues to picture the craft lifting from the ground. The rumble of the engines waver.

A dull ache presses at the back of her skull but Ryder breathes through it. The butterflies tremble their way through her, and for a moment it feels like it's her, not the craft that is about to float away.

The crab teeters to one side. The front right leg rises. Ryder draws deeper, and that sense of being no longer flesh and bone returns. No longer anything solid. She is fire and ice and things she does not understand, carried by a million powerful butterflies. Propelled towards the craft that is trying to destroy her. Whatever she is.

"Go."

The word flies from her. And the mass of steel and bolts and firepower is enveloped in a storm of colour, catapulted back into the forest. Tearing down the same pathway it created to reach her. She was right to assume there was not just one monster hunting her. The other stands right in the path of the disabled craft.

The explosion shakes the entire world it seems. The shockwave hits before Ryder can even think about shielding herself. Heat blasts through her, melting all the ice. Ryder drops behind the fallen tree, and it rocks against her with the force of the blast. She needs to move. No matter how leaden her body suddenly seems.

She staggers to her feet. The forest is alight with a strange silver fire. Flames lick at the scar in the forest, the open corridor that leads right to where she is. The place must be tinder dry, with the pace the silver tongues are devouring the forest. She needs to move. But now, back to good old flesh and bone, Ryder can barely blink, let alone run.

Something dark and heavy falls from the sky between the fire and where she stands. An aircraft, a helicopter that's been stripped of its blades, with a snub nose and stubby tail. Silver perhaps, or it is just the flames colouring it.

Before Ryder can even think about putting one heavy foot in front of another, a door on the side of the craft slides open.

"Ryder, get in. Quickly." The speaker waves frantically, the aircraft hovering unsteadily just above the ground. "Ryder, come on."

Her eyes narrow. "Blane?"

But she can answer her own question. There's no doubt it's him. Somehow, he survived the crash. She can't see the pilot of the craft, the cockpit panel is dark, reflecting the silver flames making their way towards them at a cyclonic pace. There's a chance she could use her... power... to douse the flames. But the auras around her are just thin shadows of what they had once been, and that niggle inside, the flutter of something that isn't quite her, has vanished.

Ryder vaults over the fallen alien tree, dashing towards the craft.

Chapter 17

Olessia

Returning to the depths of her chamber, gathered on the panel of Pliotine, Olessia does not make eye contact with either Dashel or Kileen. But she does acknowledge the praise being directed her way.

"The Presider is pleased to learn of your compliance in this matter, Olessia." Dashel's words crawl over her, but she allows none of her discomfort to show, just tilts her chin in recognition of his words.

"It was not as unsettling as I had first believed." She readies herself for the effort it takes to continue. "My father's highest goal is to protect Siros, I understand this, even though I may not agree with his methods. The peace and safety of Siros is what I desire most of all as well. Though my critics may choose to believe differently." Now she does allow her gaze to shift and take in Dashel.

"Oh course, Laudess," he says. His smile lingers a parn too long. "So you understand that protecting Siros, in turn means protecting the Presiderline at all costs. You and your father are the very heart of our power. Our strength, my lady. Our methods may not meet with your approval, but to be pre-emptive is to be the wisest of all. The Zentai may not have claimed your life this day, but there is little doubt that it is what they seek in time." He fixes cold eyes on her. "We are merely speeding up what would have occurred, only on this occasion it is on our terms. And you are unharmed. The Zentai *did* pursue you in the Iondar Realm, even you cannot deny this." Eyebrows arched, Dashel pauses, but when Olessia remains silent he shrugs and continues. "I infiltrated their ranks, only as a means to see first-hand how far the Crown would go to bring down the Presiderline. It was with no small degree of horror that I learned the Crown did not work alone. That the Laudine had led them to you. Aresh's supposed desire for peace between the Realms is little more than an illusion. What you told us of the Zentai boy Lucas, only serves to confirm this. She has been working with the Zentai for some considerable time. In order to achieve what she desires – the removal of Inel from his rule."

To reply would betray Olessia's simmering anger. Dashel's words are beyond outrageous. Remaining tight-lipped and simply nodding, Olessia steps from the panel. Setting foot once again in her Pliotine prison. The chamber is not as sparsely furnished as before. She's been afforded some privacy with a screen surrounding a wide resting platform.

"Your impetuous nature almost brought the fall of our realm, Olessia," Kileen declares with an overly dramatic toss of his head. "By running away to Iondar, you made not only yourself vulnerable, but the Presiderline. An opportunity for the Crown and the Laudine to reach their common goal. To rid Siros of its true leader, and its heir. And install Aresh in their stead."

Olessia smooths her frown. She adjusts the folds of her gown, allowing herself opportunity to calm. What Dashel proposes sets her screaming inwardly. The insanity of the idea that Aresh would wish true harm upon her, too much to bear. But it is not so difficult to believe the Presider would do such a thing. He has declared her dead. Declared Aresh a traitor so he might remove her, and her defiance, entirely.

Olessia's hand freezes against the smoothness of the material. This is what he attempted to do at the Treating Signing on Zentai. Many visn past. The attack on the Laudine had never come from the Crown. Just as the Crown said. Repeatedly. Denying any knowledge of the assassination attempt to this very day. Olessia shifts her hand, conscious she is standing far too still. Remaining outwardly calm. Understanding more clearly how she must fight this battle now. She must assume all the Claven are as brainwashed as Kileen. Unable to heed any protest she may utter. If she were even afforded the opportunity to speak with them to begin with.

Olessia allows a worried scowl to mar her features, eyes widening. "I had not given the Presider's intentions the considering it deserved. My father has protected me. He has removed me entirely, thereby eliminating any chance the Crown had of being able to blackmail him through negotiations for my release. I cannot be used as a pawn." Olessia nods. Allow them to think she understands the method in this madness. "And now, he can deal them a mortal blow in this war. Our military and our technology clearly outweigh anything on offer by the Crown and Reigner. Even I will not argue that." Olessia lifts one corner of her lip, casting a furtive glance from beneath lowered lashes.

Kileen's smile is quick to form. "And the Claven believed you too immature to be convinced of the reasonableness of this cause."

Olessia's laugh is bitter, and brief. "The Claven do not know as much as they think they do. Kileen, I would never intentionally cause harm to our people. It is my father I have issue with. Not his passion for protecting us all. He expressly forbade me from Traversing, so I defied him. As I have done many times before." She shrugs. No one, especially not the Claven would deny she has always fought against her father's directives. Even Dashel smirks at her words. "But, I will admit, I struggle to truly believe the Laudine seeks to overthrow my father. She Traversed to the Iondar Realm to retrieve me, not harm me."

Olessia chooses her words carefully. To make too great a change of heart will not sit well with Dashel, he will notice the deception. She must protest a little.

"Aresh has concealed her true nature from you, Laudess. You did not bear witness to her fervour when she returned to Siros, having abandoned you to the Zentai." Kileen is nothing if not passionate about what he believes. Olessia fully expects spittle to fly from his mouth. "Telling us all that she had fought to return you safe and well but that you had been snatched from her. Feigning great distress at your loss. It was truly a great performance."

Olessia bites her tongue. Stopping the shower of curses and shouted explanation that seeks to burst from her. What point with the truth here? Dashel's gaze is sharp upon her. Olessia retains just one goal here. Find out where Aresh is being held.

She tilts her head, as though considering a new possibility. "There is truth that we were separated. She forced me to move through a slipstream while being restrained by both a lelle-car and a senlier. Something that struck me as strange at the time. I was next to helpless in that condition." Even now, it is difficult not to clench her fists in remembered anger. "We lost contact and I believed it was due to the instability of the slipstream. But Aresh's power is great, great enough to overcome such an obstacle."

It is Olessia's turn to lie. Aresh's power is great, but something even greater tore them apart in the slipstream. The Cyne have not reappeared since that incident, but Olessia clings to the hope that Sentinel Teler is not her only remaining ally. She paces the length of the room, the skirt whispering against the ground. Olessia still knows nothing of Aresh's whereabouts.

"Tell me, the former Reigner's son, Lucas," she says. "What do you believe are Aresh's reasons for concealing him on Earth?"

"Not all in the Crown's council share their leader's desire for total rule." Kileen jumps in eagerly. "The current Reigner has long been an advocate for peace. Perhaps Aresh sought to install Lucas as a Reigner more sympathetic to their cause. One who had been raised with some loyalty to the Laudine."

Olessia narrows her eyes, seemingly repulsed by the idea. But inwardly her mind races. They have an explanation for everything. But she knows full well Lucas had been groomed for nothing save blending into the human population so well, no one knew he existed.

"Aresh appears to have succeeded in that regard," Olessia wrings her hands. "Lucas was particularly close to her."

Because Aresh had saved his life, protected him, and given him his freedom. Trying to repay a debt she felt she owed. Olessia sees it all too clearly now. Aresh understood the truth. Lucas's family lost their life because of the Presider's deceit.

Olessia plays at being shocked at Kileen's suggestion. But it's the shock of the truth that catches her breath. Aresh's attempts to protect them all — Ryder, Lucas, and Olessia — has cost her everything. Every move she's made in the past, now colours her in a dark shade of guilt. But to declare Aresh guilty of treason is one thing. Would the Presider take the next step and eliminate her entirely?

The Beckoning slumbers, a dull and distant weight within her. And it strikes Olessia that her effort to remain in control has succeeded on a level she would not have thought possible a short time ago. But right now it is grossly inconvenient. She wishes to appear angered beyond belief. The Beckoning would assist greatly in the charade.

"This is truly infuriating." She folds her arms tight across her belly. "It would seem the Laudine's ambitions have burned for a long, long time."

The Beckoning serpentines from its dark place, moving in a slow roll through her, and Olessia almost cries out in delight.

"Far too long," Kileen says. "I doubt your true Guardian, Maher of Nevin Rea, ever refused to take his place at your side. Aresh insisted Sebastien be offered the role, but everyone could see he was far too young. Too unpredictable. Far too pliable to a traitor."

"Kileen, this is of little importance—"

"I beg to differ, Dashel," Kileen declares. "I see clarity coming to the Laudess, a true understanding of the deception that surrounds her. She should know of all of it."

Dashel's eyes narrow. He sees something coming to the Laudess, that is clear, but Olessia does not trust that he believes it is clarity. It is time for her to let the control slip. Even just an inch. She pictures Christian in her mind. The agony that scorched his face as Dashel tried to pry open his weighted mind. The Beckoning lunges for the bait she dangles, roaring through her. And the sudden churn within her irises is sharp.

"I do not enjoy being deceived. This much I share with my father," Olessia growls. "I can only hope the Presider's punishment is fitting."

The Beckoning billows from her, and there is no doubt the men sense its presence. Kileen takes a step back. The satisfied smirk upon Dashel's face suggests she has succeeded in convincing him her anger is directed at the Laudine alone.

"Of that, you can be assured, Laudess," Dashel says.

It's one of the rare times he's addressed her by her title since this began. Olessia risks one more question.

"Does she live?" The Beckoning reaches into every section of her body, and Olessia fights to hold it in check.

"For now," Dashel says.

"But she is held far from here," Kileen says. "Laudess, you are safe from her connivings—"

Dashel glares. "Kileen, that is enough. We will leave now."

The entrance to the chamber peels open, as though reacting to his words. A young girl carrying a plestex crystal container, and a small tray set with a single bowl, enters. Halting just inside the door upon noticing those in the room. She stumbles over her apology and moves to back from the room.

"No, come forward. Bring the sustenance." Dashel waves her in. "She will be needing it."

She. No title this time. Olessia grinds her teeth. Dashel and Kileen stride past the girl who has to dodge to avoid them, her long woven hair swinging like a pendulum at her back. The cup on the tray tips over, spilling its contents. But the Claven members reach the door and disappear without so much as a glance at the sound.

The girl is little more than a child, and the tray rattles with the tremor running through her. Her eyes are wide, and the colour of the plestex crystal she carries.

"Wh-where should I place this…"

Olessia waves absent-mindedly towards the only possible place to lay such an object. A low-set block near the resting platform. But the girl does not go where she is directed. Instead, she moves close, too close, tripping on the long folds of Olessia's gown. Sending the spilt broth flying over the material, and landing hard against her.

"I'm so sorry, I'm so sorry, Laudess. Don't hurt me." The child bursts into tears. Clutching at Olessia's waist. Pressing her face against her belly.

"Enough, enough. There is no harm." Save for the stains on a dress she did not care for.

"Sorry, sorry." The child backs away and scampers from the chamber. Leaving Olessia alone with the mess she created.

Her hands are dripping with whatever liquid spilt from the bowl, and she wipes them against her waist.

Her fingers brush at something hard and raised, where the skirt's material gathers in a bunch at her hip. Olessia catches herself before she peers too intently at the item. The tingle through her fingertips tells her all she needs to know.

Elthar. And not just any. *Her* elthar. Pinned to her dress, in the guise of a small brooch.

Chapter 18

Ryder

B lane hauls Ryder into a dimly lit capsule. A space barely big enough to accommodate the two of them, with a narrow bench seat that is hard against her backside.

"Where is Sebastien?" Ryder says. "Is he with you?"

"Sebastien? No."

A hiss and muttering comes from the front of the cabin, the pilot.

"Here, pull this down over your shoulders," Blane struggles not to push against her as the pilot jerks them into the air. He lifts her hand, placing it on a thick harness that sits above her, like something you'd find on a roller coaster ride. "Are you okay? Are you injured?"

He slumps into the seat beside her. One of only two, so close together Blane nearly elbows her in the face as he pulls down his harness.

"I'm fine."

Probably. There hasn't been a chance to think about it. Ryder grunts, struggles to latch the heavy harness into position. Blane moved it as though it were light as a feather but it's like a curve of lead for Ryder, and she strains to shove it into place. Blane reaches over and with just one hand pushes it down. There is a satisfying click as it snaps into place. Maybe she's not as fine as she thought.

The ice butterflies are gone though, and her eyes are kind of itchy, but aside from that she's in one piece.

The pilot is hidden behind a high-backed seat, only one of their hands visible where it lies against a silver orb the size of a soccer ball. They tilt their hand against it, and the aircraft shifts. Following directions.

"Who's flying this thing," Ryder asks.

The hand has fingers. No claws. For a crazy second, she checks for sign of elthar. Like maybe Blane lied and Sebastien is doing the flying. But the fingers are too fine. She bites the inside of her cheek, trying not to think too hard about where he is right now.

"Someone who knows what they are doing," Blane says, at the exact moment a violent change of direction shoves his head against the solid curve of the harness. The thump and his curse fill the cabin.

Outside, there is only silver. Flames engulf the craft. A chaos she created.

"Blane—"

"Just hang on, Ryder. We're going to have to trust her on this one."

Her? The aircraft shudders and their altitude drops with stomach churning speed. Ryder squeezes her eyes shut, hands tight against the harness. Adrenaline pumping making her dizzy.

"Are we crashing?" she shouts.

"Hopefully not."

"Bledis ben," comes the hoarse cry from the pilot's seat.

"We're under attack," Blane says, but he's clinging just as hard to his harness, the whites of his eyes showing.

The sound of high-pitched pulses fills the cabin. Ryder tilts as far as her harness will allow, and catches sight of racing darts of red, jettisoning from the nose of their craft. The light vanishes into the wall of flame, and a moment later an explosion rocks them.

"Benesdin bin don art."

Ryder looks to Blane. "The Presider's troops are closing in on us. I think she's trying to hide us in the flames, but not sure it's working."

There's a nasty burn on the side of his face that she didn't notice earlier.

"You understood her? How is that possible?"

Blane lifts his curl of hair above his left ear. There is an imprint on his skin, a white pattern reminding her of the veins of a leaf. "Translator of some kind, the Commandant had it put on me when I first went on board."

Ryder's eyes dart to the pilot seat. "That's the Commandant?"

"Verd." The pilot snaps.

Ryder doesn't need a translator to understand what was just said. Yes. Ryder is right back where she started. A prisoner of the Zentai. She leans her whole body weight against the harness, trying to force it loose. This can't be happening.

"Blane, why?" She wriggles against the harness but it's clearly going nowhere.

"Ryder, calm down. It's not what you think—"

"Not what I think, Blane? Want to tell me what the hell it is then?"

He doesn't get a chance to answer. The pilot releases another battering of firepower, and the aircraft rolls. A full three-sixty rotation that makes Ryder's eyes bug out of her head. Her chest feels fit to burst, and the contents of her stomach are ready to make an appearance by the time they level out. The flames are gone, and ahead stretches a wide open plain. A desert with no dunes. No sign of anything at all so far as Ryder can see.

The pilot - the Commandant - lets loose with a long stream of sounds, some of which, Ryder's pretty sure, are not friendly.

"What's going on?" Ryder hisses.

Why could she understand what was being said to her on board the ship but now can't understand a word? It's not only weird, it's extremely annoying.

"I think we've outrun the last of them." Blane rubs at his neck where a dark bruise spreads down beneath his collar. "She didn't think they would follow us too far into Zentai territory, looks like she's right."

"So where are we going now?" Ryder tries to add an edge to her voice she's not really feeling. Sebastien is somewhere back in that blazing forest. So are Maher, and Carlsson, but at least they had the protection of the bunker. Sebastien had nothing. Would Maher go looking for him, now all hell has broken out?

"Eeesen brant fra." The Commandant twists in her seat. Jade-green eyes fix on Ryder. She stretches out her hand, something clutched in her fist.

"Take it, Ryder," Blane cries.

But Ryder presses back against her seat. Certain the sour Zentai soldier is about to shoot her, or taze her. Something unpleasant.

"Eeesen brant fra," the bald-headed alien says, this time with a smouldering anger that is unmistakable.

Ryder freezes. No superpowered butterflies now. She's just plain frightened. And helpless.

I got this, Ry.

Sophie megaphones her way into Ryder's head. "Ouch, damn it." Ryder hunches her shoulders.

The Commandant's patience is wearing thin. She shakes her hand, shouting almost as loud as Sophie did. "Eeesen, Eeesen." Her hand jerks and she makes a startled sound. The device drops from her grasp, hitting the floor with an odd dull clink. Two thin bands of elthar.

Done. Oh. It's your bracelets, Ry. Elthar.

But Ryder can already see that. Maybe Blane is right. This isn't what it seems. The Commandant just handed Ryder a weapon.

The Zentai barks out several more unpleasant sounding words, the only one of which Ryder can make out is Blane's name.

"Ryder?" Blane says. "What did you do?"

"I didn't do anything. She must have dropped them."

The Commandant's voice lowers to a growl, her words muttered under her breath. She settles back into her seat.

Why is she giving you elthar, Ryder?

"I don't know," Ryder cries. "Why is any of this happening? Where did you go, Soph—"

Ryder snaps her mouth closed, all too aware that she's just had a very vocal, nonsensical conversation with someone other than the two seated with her.

Blane's expression holds way more pity than Ryder is comfortable with. He releases his harness and leans down to grab the bracelets. They are too far out of reach so he has to leave his seat to retrieve them. Blane shifts onto his knees in front of her.

Seems an odd time to propose. Sophie giggles.

"Stop it," Ryder hides the words in a cough, wondering not for the first time why she can't seem to contact Sophie via a mindreach.

I'm freaking out, okay. About so many things right now. Stupid jokes calm me. That much hasn't changed.

"Ryder, I know you are frightened. I am too." Blane's hand shakes as he holds the bracelets out to her. It strikes Ryder that she hasn't once assumed he might be terrified too. His smooth demeanour has barely wavered in all this. "But I'm guessing it's nothing compared to how you must be feeling… with all that's happening… to you… the things you can do."

Ryder takes the offered bracelets. The narrow bands are dull, reflecting none of the light of the cabin.

"You have no idea." She slides the elthar on, the bands snug but comfortable around each wrist. It gives her that same kind of sensation after you find the phone or wallet you thought you'd lost. Total relief, every tensed muscle releasing.

"No. I don't," Blane settles into his seat. The craft glides along so steady it feels like they aren't moving at all. The chaos lost behind them. Ryder's moment of relief fades. Sebastien is back there. And with every moment she's on board the distance between them grows.

I'm here, Ry. For as long as it's possible. I'm sorry, Aresh's message kind of blasted me away.

Ryder rubs at her eyes. *God, I'd forgotten about that.*

Believe me, I have not. It was like getting caught in a tornado. Ryder! You didn't say that out loud. I heard you! Do you think it's the elthar? Can you see me, now?

Sophie's questions pepper her like mental gunfire. But Ryder is only interested in the last one. She scans the cabin. It's hard to get her tongue around the words. *No. I can't see you.*

Blane's hand touches her arm. Drawing her back to reality. But she keeps on searching, just in case.

"Ryder, just hang in there, okay?"

She smooths her expression. "Blane, what is going on? Where are we going?"

He opens his mouth to reply, but the Commandant beats him to it.

"That is a question whose answer will have to wait," she declares. "Do not harbour any ideas of escaping, now that the elthar has been returned to you. You would stand little chance of survival in the world out there, no matter what you might be capable of. Do you have any idea where the Guardian might be? Does he live?"

Every word is clear. Recognisable. Ryder glances down at the elthar, rubbing her thumb across its matte surface. "Why would I tell you anything? Last time we met, you tried to kill me."

"I did no such thing, don't speak with such ridiculous elaboration. I merely contained you, and the Guardian, in order to return you to Falllyn. Following orders. Which in turn has apparently made my life forfeit."

Ryder glances at Blane, confused. He hesitates, waiting to see if the Commandant says anything more before he speaks.

"She thinks the ship was sabotaged."

"I don't *think*, I know. That vessel has been under my command for many visn. The secondary pilot was my most experienced, and more than capable of guiding us through the extreme turbulence we encountered. That is why they were removed from the equation. I believe they were killed."

Ryder blinks. "Killed?"

"Ketn was no traitor. Loyalty undoubted. Which means that by abandoning their post, I can only surmise Ketn was killed." The Commandant is matter-of-fact. "The systems were also seriously compromised. Catastrophic failures that were just too far ranging for it to have been anything but purposeful. We were meant to lose our way, permanently, in that river. The Guardian's skills prevented that from happening but were not enough to save the vessel. As you well know."

God, I'm glad I got that stupid tiara off your head before that thing crashed, Ry.

That was you?

Yup. It stung like a thousand bee bites but I had to get rid of it. Tiara's really aren't your thing.

Ryder stares at a spot on the curved wall, hoping against hope that maybe Sophie stands there. *Thank you.*

Well, you're welcome. But compared to Padellah, I didn't do that much.

Padellah?

This green-eyed lady isn't kidding, you were going down in that river. And I'm pretty sure it wasn't just Sebastien's skills that got you out. Things got kinda crazy, I don't know how this floaty, ethereal thing works but I'm fairly certain Padellah shoved me out of the way, just before you catapulted out of the river. The blast sent me who knows where. It's why I took so long to get back to you.

"Ryder." The Commandant snaps. "Are you ill? Blane, is she broken? You're the human doctor."

"I'm not ill," Ryder says.

"Then answer my question."

"Which was?"

Jade-green eyes narrow. "Is the guardian alive?"

"I really hope so," she whispers. "But why do you care if he's alive? And why did you ask him to help land the ship?"

"Because my known enemy could be far better trusted than the one I do not know. The one who sought to bring down the Baershard." The Commandant pauses and only the hum of the external engines provides any sound. "Sebastien's level of concern for you ensured he was not about to do anything but bring us through the River safely, if it was within his power."

But Ryder's stuck on something the Commandant just said. "Who do you think brought down the Baershard?"

The Commandant swivels her seat, facing towards them now, those jade eyes needling into Ryder. "I sent a distress signal when our predicament worsened, but no one heeded the call. Just a short time later, the Siros Bexsron arrived. Unchallenged, despite being well inside the Zentai border." Her face grows hard, her long neck twitching with tense muscles. "The Bexsron were exterminating those who had managed to survive the impact. I was outnumbered, intervening would have been foolish, but it took me some time to realise that. I got close. Close enough to overhear something said by the Bexsron leader. Make sure they are both dead."

"Both?" Ryder shakes her head. "Who were they talking about?"

"Me, of course." The Commandant shrugs. "That is to be expected with a person of my rank. But I could not understand, who the other was they searched for. I thought perhaps it was you, but that struck me as odd considering I had told no one of your presence on board. Then, the fools actually said his name."

"They were looking for Sebastien too, Ryder," Blane interrupts. "Looking for a body. I heard them as well, they weren't exactly being discrete. They had orders to make sure—"

The Commandant's cold stare lands on him and Blane settles back. "Sorry, I just..." He falls silent.

"They wished to kill your precious Guardian. Olessia's guardian. His own people had been ordered to prove him dead." She tilts her head, a crow-like move that makes Ryder's skin crawl. "Now isn't that curious. Almost as curious as to why Presiderline troops found our location before the Zentai did. The Reigner ignored my emergency signal because he did not expect the Baershard to ever make it that far. But when we did, he advised the Presider exactly where we had come down. That imbecile is everything I believed him to be, and more."

Reeling from what she's just heard, Ryder whispers her question. "What did you believe him to be?"

"A man with his own agenda. One that has never been aligned with the good of the Zentai people."

Oh geez. Sophie squeaks. *Is she saying what I think she's saying? The Reigner guy and Olessia's dad are working together?*

That's exactly what she's saying.

And the Commandant isn't happy about it. Not one little bit, judging by her fierce expression.

"So... you're not taking us to the Reigner, are you?" Ryder's pretty certain of the answer but a niggle of doubt won't let go.

The Commandant tosses her head. "Of course not."

Then who? Sophie's voice ripples with her frustration.

"Then who?" Ryder says.

"The only one I trust in all of this insanity. We are going to Icewynn, and I am taking you directly to the Crown."

Chapter 19

Christian

Christian is shaken awake by a gentle hand. His eyes flutter open to dim surroundings. And a peculiar roof. Thatched strands woven in intricate patterns that he might compare to straw, if it weren't for the fact they are semi-translucent. Christian gazes up at twin blazing comets moving across a bruised sky. Body as jittery as it was before he drifted off, like he's gone too long without food.

"How do you feel, Chris-Tan?" Sen-bay lies beside him, propped up on one elbow.

Christian gives him a faint smile. "Kind of wiped still, but okay. What about you?"

"I have greater fortitude, it would seem. And did not require the amount of rest that has been necessary for you."

Christian's gotten used to the easy way the truth just rolls off Sen-Bay's tongue. "How long have I been out this time?"

"Out? You have not left this area." Sen-Bay's puzzled frown makes Christian laugh.

"Asleep. How long have I been asleep this time?"

Over the space of about twenty-four hours, so far as Christian can tell, they have been herded to the base of the hillside three times. He's struggled to keep his eyes open in the hours between.

"Ah, I understand," Sen-Bay declares. "Well, you have been out for just a short while."

Christian sits up, leaning into Sen-Bay as he helps him wriggle out from beneath the layers of bedclothes. The under-blankets are like the foil sheets emergency services use back on Earth, but the topmost layer isn't like anything he's seen before. If Christian were to take a wild guess, he'd say it was a flattened covering of tree bark, like something off a white gum. He grips a handful of the rough material. White gum. That tension at the back of his skull hasn't shifted with sleep, and now the knot tightens with his thoughts. White gum. The pain is distant, like a tooth ache that hasn't set in properly, and he lets the thought go not wanting the pain to notch up again.

Sen-Bay doesn't notice Christian's hesitation. He shifts off the side of the low-set bedding. "The advice is that you do not remain asleep for too long. It is best to revive the body sooner rather than later once it succumbs to the fatigue brought on by a Beckoning."

"A Beckoning? Is that what happened to us?" Whatever *that* was. Christian hunches his shoulders; now that experience he does remember well. And wishes very much that he didn't.

"Yes. An occurrence experienced many times by the beings held here."

"Why? What did it do? Apart from make me feel… drained…"

They had been forced into a pack. A pack of creatures of all shapes and sizes, all with one shared emotion – fear. It had been palpable, but there was also resignation. The barriers set up around the huddle had been almost pointless. There was surrender in the air. The sense that fighting was useless. And it had scared Christian every bit as much as not knowing what was about to happen.

"That is exactly what the Beckoning does. Drains you." Sen-Bay hands him a shirt, a white long-sleeved tunic that is a size too big and threatens to slip from Christian's shoulder. But it's clean. Which is more than can be said for the vest it replaced. "The Beckoning is the Presiderline's greatest weapon. An ability to extract the very energy that gives us life, and utilise it for other purposes."

Christian rubs at his arms. The shirt is soft as satin but looks like white denim. "Extract our life-force?" Yet again, the niggle at the back of his head starts up. But it's more of a pulse this time. Like his heart in miniature, stuck inside his brain. "Are you kidding me? They have a machine that can do that?"

Sen-Bay considers his reply, staring down at the floor, a surface covered in a layer just like the blanket. "Not a machine, Chris-Tan. The Presider himself wields that power, so too does his heir. The Laudess." He searches Christian's face. "Olessia."

Christian lowers his head, studying the same patch of floor Sen-Bay had done. "That's a pretty full on talent to have."

"Indeed, it is."

A woman — he assumes from her voice — pushes aside a drape of patterned material that conceals the entranceway, and steps into the shelter. Christian blinks with the light that moves into the space with her. She allows the drapes to fall back into place. The entrance isn't the only thing covered. She has a mesh veil over her face, distorting her features.

"Evelyn, do you wish to frighten him into recognition?" Sen-Bay asks.

Her easy laughter flutters around them. "The exact opposite, I hope. Sorry, Christian but I didn't want to upset you again. Not so soon after a Beckoning, it could be dangerous if your strength levels are low. But having said that, you're looking okay. How do you feel?"

With all the questions about how he's feeling, it's kind of like being in a hospital. But he doesn't voice his thought. Instead Christian gets to his feet.

"I'm good– Whoa!"

The room tilts, the ground giving way beneath him. At least, that's how it feels. The woman, Evelyn, reaches for him but Sen-Bay is already there. Holding Christian steady, making the world solid again.

"Okay, sit down. I've got something that will help." The woman gestures to the bed, and Sen-Bay helps Christian to sit. "Your body will build up a bit of a resistance to the Beckoning, which isn't as great as it sounds. It simply means they can take more from you, and for longer the next time. And the next time." She pulls a black packet from beneath the fold of her draping white and grey speckled top. "You were lucky, the Presider is going easy on us, for now." She pauses, her fingers dipped into the small black packet. "That first Gathering, I didn't really believe my little charade of feigning collapse would work to stop it. I'll admit I was pretty pleased with myself when it did, but I have my doubts my theatrics had little to do with it." She tugs what could be tobacco strands from the packet. "These Gatherings since you've arrived, are the gentlest we've had in a quite a long time. I don't think that's a coincidence. Here, hold out your hand."

Christian darts a glance at Sen-Bay and getting a nod, lifts his hand. Evelyn places three squiggly strands of the black substance in his palm. It certainly could pass for tobacco, but the odour is sweeter. "What is this?"

"It'll get rid of the strange jittery feeling. The teek speeds up your recovery. Recharges you, if you will."

"But have I lost years or something?" He'd been exhausted to ask many questions earlier.

Evelyn isn't as quick to shake her head as he hoped she might be. "I don't think that's how it works, but I have to be honest. I'm not sure. I can't say for certain if it's the Beckoning, or the living conditions here that are taking their toll. Mortality rates are depressingly high. I tend to think of the Presider as a vampire. And if he drains too much blood, we die."

"Vampires?" Christian mulls the word over, and the memory doesn't take much coaxing to drift free. Fictional monsters. Written about for hundreds of years, and still getting air time in TV shows. TV. Yes. He definitely likes TV. "Netflix. I really like Netflix."

He makes a self-satisfied sound. And pops the teek onto his tongue. The fibrous strands sting far more than the memory did. He winces.

"You all right? Got some head pain?" Evelyn chews at her bottom lip. "I don't know who Netflix is—"

"It's not a... No. I'm good. And I mean it this time." Christian fights to keep a straight face, even though the strands are hot as jalapenos. "Tell me more about the Beckoning. Why are they doing it?"

Draining people's lives. It's something out of a horror movie. And he's trapped on set. The fire in his mouth fades as quickly as it began.

"Power." Evelyn shoves the packet back into the folds of her shirt. "Actual, power. Fuel. They've found a way to integrate the energy into some weapons. Giving them a unique firepower capability. And now, with the war, I suppose he will be coming to us even more often than before."

"War?" The bedding had managed to cool Christian's skin but now the heat rushes back. Olessia and the man with fire eyes talked about a war.

"The Presider has declared war on my people," Sen-Bay says.

"And in Olessia's name," Evelyn sighs. "All of Bax Un Tey believes the Laudess is dead, and the Presider is going to tear the realm apart to avenge her. Forward lines have already been deployed. It's begun."

Christian picks at the strand, now dull and flavourless, embedded between his teeth. "Olessia?" Maybe he misheard. Or is totally confused, which is highly likely. "But the Presider knows she's not dead, I was there when he was talking to her."

Yelling at. Throwing her around. Not exactly dad of the year.

The drapes at the doorway swing open, and a tall, broad man steps into the room. His bulk crowds in on them, his face dark against the light behind him.

"Keep your voice down. The truth is no friend at this time." The man steps super close to Evelyn, but she doesn't seem to mind. In fact, Christian's pretty sure she just took a step closer. "Why have you kept that?"

He lifts fine fingers, almost too slender compared to the solidness of his body.

"This?" Evelyn touches at the mesh that covers her face. "I suppose I always hoped I'd need it again one day, because it would mean I was free again. And that time will come very soon, will it not?"

"I need you focused, Evelyn. These are dangerous times, concentrate on the task at hand," he says, stern as a headmaster. His jet-black eyebrows are carefully sculpted to rise at the outer edges, matching the line of his eyes. And contrast his cropped hair, which is snow white.

His harsh tone doesn't seem to bother Evelyn. She places a hand on the man's arm. Her petite fingers made to look even tinier against the thickness of his forearm. "Trust me, Teler. I have never been more focused. I haven't had a chance to fill the boys in yet but they are both well. With enough strength for us to begin. What about our other young friend?"

He towers over her, intimidating if it weren't for his expression. Christian and Sen-Bay both glance at each other. Sen-Bay sees it too. The only intimidation going on here would be directed at anyone who tried to harm Evelyn. The way he touches her, traces a finger along the length of the veil is enough to make Christian squirm.

"All is as it should be. She is ready." He shifts, readying to leave, but Evelyn doesn't let go of his arm. "I must continue with my round, I cannot be seen to favour your residence."

"A touch too late for that. I think they'll be suspicious if you leave quickly," Evelyn says.

Christian's cheeks grow uncomfortably warm, but Sen-Bay smiles.

The man ducks his chin, eyes the colour of the Sahara lowering to the floor. "Evelyn."

Evelyn throws back her head laughing, loose curls cascading down her back. The laugher is caught between a giggle and a breathless gasp. The sound brings a smile to Christian's face. He knows someone who laughs just like that. Does he? Maybe?

"Oh god." Christian doubles over, clutching at his head.

"Chris-Tan!" Sen-Bay, who hadn't left his side, plants his hands over Christian's. "Look at me, Chris-Tan."

Not an easy thing when your own head keeps wanting to explode, but he grits his teeth, and lifts his eyes to find Sen-Bay.

"I thought you said they were ready?" Teler says.

"This is nothing to do with the Beckoning," Evelyn whispers, crouching beside Christian. "Did the Presider do anything to his mind, you said he interrogated this boy? This has happened before, it's why I hide my face. What was it, Christian? Do you know what is causing this?"

The pain is fading and Christian doesn't want to tempt fate and bring it on again, so he shakes his head. "Not sure."

The large man leans over Christian, blocking what little light there is. Before Christian, or Sen-Bay, can protest he presses his palm to the crown of Christian's head. And all at once it's as though big chunks of wax have shifted in Christian's ears, the world all muffled and dull. He tries to edge out from beneath Teler's firm grip.

"Stop, stop now." Sen-Bay pounds his fists against Teler's arm, and the guy uses his free hand to shove him away. Sending him tumbling backwards into an unceremonious pile on the ground.

"Take it easy, Teler," Evelyn cries. "He's just protecting his friend."

But Teler ignores her. He has his eyes closed, and his grip on Christian's head is tightening, though not unbearable. The memory flashbacks have been way worse. Teler eases off, taking a step back from Christian, a frown lining his already gullied face.

"A Blackwall," he says, as though that explains everything.

"Blackwall," Christian mutters. He rubs at his hair, which has more knots than he realised. Pretty soon he'll be sporting dreadlocks just like Sen-Bay. "I've heard someone say that before." He hesitates. What if trying to remember who it was brings on another mega-brain attack? But the name slides into his head without an ounce of pain. The Presider. He said it, right before he ordered the other guy to lay hands on Christian.

"Who?" Teler demands.

But Christian hesitates. He has no idea who this giant is.

"Christian, it is all right. Teler can be trusted. So can I. I wish we had some way to prove that to you, but for now, you have only my word." Evelyn's gentle voice is persuasive. And Christian is too tired to think straight.

And once the decision is made to confide, the words rush from him.

"The Presider said it to Olessia, said she had created a Blackwall... in my mind..." The horror of that moment had buried the memory from him, and now when it rushes free, he shivers. Christian knows for certain nothing has ever scared him as much as those two guys. "He wanted to know what she was hiding… and the guy with the Presider, I don't remember his name, but man he had the creepiest eyes I've ever seen, like tar pits—"

"Sounds like the Protectorate," Sen-Bay says. "He laid hands on me at the Turning, and my thoughts were not my own. He pulled them from me—"

"A mindreach?" Teler tugs at his collar, his gaze drifting to a dark corner of the shelter. "The Protectorate has no such ability, and his eyes are the shade of a Placer's tongue." Whatever that shade is, Teler is clearly not impressed. His gaze lifts from the shadows and falls back on Sen-Bay. "The Zentai hold no such telepathic capabilities. That was not the Protectorate."

Sen-Bay scratches at the crux of his arm. "Then it was not the Protectorate who killed Olessia."

"She's not dead—" Christian begins.

"We know that, boy," Teler snaps. "It was a ruse for war. What I had not gathered is who had the power to enable such a thing. Now I know. Dashel, the Presider's most trusted Claven. You two grow more important with each passing moment. Not only are you the Presider's guarantee to ensure Olessia's compliance, you are witness to the full truth of what began this war." He turns to Evelyn who has her fingertips touched to her lips, she nods before he says another word.

"Was that what Olessia had hidden?" she whispers. "In your mind, Christian? Was she trying to keep what you saw from him, so he could not remove the truth from you?"

Christian swallows. If he stops to think things through too long, he'll either pop an eyeball, or just curl up in a screaming ball.

"Lucas," he says quickly. "Olessia told them that was what she'd blocked in my head. I guess I knew him, maybe? The name is familiar." But he's not going to risk thinking too hard about it. "Anyway, she gave them that name. And they stopped hurting me."

Sen-Bay's lips are pressed tight, muscles in his neck working.

"Lucas?" Teler scowls. "Who is Lucas?"

Christian glances at Evelyn, and she squeezes his hand gently. "Go on. Perhaps, it is someone I know? Is that why my face brought on your pain?"

But trying to put a face to the name sets off an uncomfortable tightness behind Christian's eyes, and he baulks.

"Do not push yourself, Chris-tan," Sen-bay's hand rests on his thigh, and Christian takes hold of it to stop himself shaking.

"There is no time for careful measure." Teler's patience is drying up, if it was there to begin with. "Not now. Who is Lucas?"

Christian breathes against the rising ache. "I don't know any more than what Olessia said. That Lucas was the Reigner's son?"

Teler scoffs. "That would hardly satisfy the Presider, he knows as do we all that the Reigner has no—"

"That's what they said," Christian butts in, shrinking back, half expecting a swipe. But it doesn't come. "Both the Presider and Dashel said that this Reigner person doesn't have a son. But Olessia said it wasn't the current Reigner she was talking about. Badden? Burden? I don't remember the—"

"Bladen. Reigner Bladen," Teler says. The mood has shifted, there is a simmering tension around the big guy now. "The one accused of being behind the assassination attempt on the Laudine Aresh."

Evelyn's head jerks up at the mention of Aresh. But for Christian, there is no penny drop moment, just more aching.

"It can't be possible, surely?" Evelyn shakes her head. "All this talk of the Laudine being a traitor, of plotting against her brother —"

Teler's bulk seems to grow larger. "Never doubt the Laudine again."

For the first time Evelyn does not appear quite so carefree in Teler's presence. "Doubt her? You know I would be the very last to ever—"

Teler takes a step towards her and Christian holds his breath. But there's no need for alarm. Teler presses his lips to her forehead in a brief kiss before he pulls away. "Forgive me. I know your friendship with Aresh is deep. I should not have said such a thing."

"We are both worried, desperately so. Does she live?" she asks in a low voice.

"She must," Teler growls, cracking his knuckles. He hisses something that Christian doesn't catch. "The Presider has set a bounty on the Laudine, he has officially declared her a traitor, but I will not believe he would end her life. I cannot believe it, and there is only one who is capable of locating her. We will free Olessia, or I will die trying. I have done what I can to ensure the Presider's poisons do not weaken her further. She is ready, more so than I dared to believe. Olessia's control over the Beckoning has increased to an astonishing level, you have seen how she restrains herself at the Gatherings."

"One moment," Sen-Bay says. "The Laudess is responsible for the latest Gatherings?"

Teler nods. "They force it from her. Using you two. Forcing her to aid her father's war effort." He turns to Evelyn. "The time is upon us. Await the signal, Evelyn." His voice drops on her name, as though speaking too loudly might cause her to drift away. "And be safe. All of you."

He's out the door before anyone can draw breath. Evelyn's veil flutters with her exhale.

"Signal?" Sen-Bay ventures.

"You're freeing Olessia?" Christian says. "How?"

"Well, I'm not. Not directly. We are going to be a distraction," Evelyn replies. "A very large one if all goes to plan."

"What kind of distraction?" Sen-Bay asks.

She lifts the drape, and light pours in. "Oh, you'll know it when it comes. And I want you two to stay with me, no matter what happens. We are leaving this place together."

Chapter 20

Olessia

Olessia is certain her pacing will wear away the metal floor eventually. Her body is humming, brimming with the residual energy that cloaks her from the last Gathering. She has discarded her footwear, desiring the coolness of the ground against her heated skin. A platter of nourishment has been left for her after her last trip to the surface, but Olessia has not touched a morsel. Could not do so, even if she were requiring sustenance. The Gathering upsets all her systems, most of all the digestive. Eating would not be a good idea right now.

She paces the length of the chamber and touches her fingertips to the wall. One digit at a time until all are pressed to the metal. This must be at least the tenth time she has done so. Walk, tap, press and turn. Olessia has lost count. But the routine is oddly soothing. Christian, too, has such a repetitive routine. Twisting the ring of silver that hangs at his eyebrow. He told her once that it was called a habit. And it helped to ease his tension. Olessia turns and paces back, hands raised, fingers at the ready to repeat the process at the far wall. For those brief seconds, as she counts the press of each finger, her mind quietens. Nothing but the numbers in her head. It is a momentary respite, but very welcome.

Her steps falter. It was not wise to allow Christian to enter her thoughts. His presence there always causes her pulses to quicken, her fear for him making her breathless. Three times Kileen has taken her to the surface and watched with a crex-like intensity as she manipulates the Beckoning and draws from the living souls beneath her. On each occasion his praise grows more pronounced, and she senses a certain awe in his tone. Remarking on how much more able she is at handling the Beckoning. Though he does not say the words, Olessia hears them in the lilt of his voice. Vale Leven is on his mind.

It is certainly on hers. As she gazed down on them, the creatures herded before her, imprisoned and at her mercy, Olessia fights to stave off the memory of that day. To see Christian and Sen-Bay among that group paralysed her altogether. Until she realised that such a paralysis would do no one any good. Least of all Christian.

They have used him to force her hand. To protect him, she must act. Put on a show that will mesmerise all those who watch her. And keep their attention firmly away from a human girl who must never, ever reach her father's attentions.

Three, four, five. Olessia pushes away from the wall and begins the return trek.

Dashel did not appear the second and third times she was taken to the dome. A fact that has brought Olessia both comfort and concern. She has sifted through her own memories of her time on Earth, searching for evidence Dashel may know something of Ryder from his time there. Olessia touches at the folds of her gown, where the brooch sits hidden in the voluptuous folds of material. She has checked it remains hidden far more times than she has paced the room; her elthar delivered by a stranger.

Is this a test of some kind? To see if Olessia is coming around to her father's master plan in the way she professes? Should she ignite the elthar and attempt escape, she would reveal categorically her true stance. And even if she did, how far would it truly take her? Olessia knows so little of the layout. To escape from the metal cave is one thing but where to next? Straight into the arms of a dozen Sentinels, most likely. And to attempt an escape on the surface may lead to the death of those she has worked so hard to keep alive. Not just Christian and Sen-Bay, but all those souls whose life she drains away. On the surface, the Presider has dozens of hostages to blackmail her with immediately.

Olessia starts a new count. One, two… she punches her fist against the metal. The wall is unforgiving, and her knuckles ache, but she punches at the surface again. Indecisiveness and uncertainty is driving her to distraction. She is far too used to impetuous decision-making. Far to used to simply running away from her troubles.

A process that has resulted in calamity, and eroded her confidence in her own choices.

Olessia readies herself for another blow. The doorway to her prison makes the delicate rustling sound that indicates it is about to open. She does not turn, keeping her back to whomever enters, but tilting her head in order to establish if perhaps Sentinel Teler has returned. There has been no sign of him since the delivery of her first meal.

Olessia does not need a full view of the entering figure to know it is not the hulking silhouette of Sentinel Teler. A woman enters. A Claven. Her delicate features and slender figure are faintly recognisable though Olessia would have no clue what her name might be. She has never given the Claven much thought or time. Always assuming they only spoke to her to either curry favour or spit venom. But Aresh would know this woman's name.

Olessia's hands fall to her sides, a hollowness filling her. All attempts to source Aresh's location have come to nothing. At least she still lives. For now. Dashel took great delight in telling Olessia that much. The dark inference in his words most clear.

"Laudess, my name is Dara." The woman's hair, as dark as Olessia's own, hangs all the way down her back, resting at the base of her spine, and the strands are intertwined with cords embedded with flek stones. She presses a fist to the centre of her chest in the gesture of acknowledgment to the Presiderline. "Arrangements have been made for you to cleanse. Would you come with me?"

She speaks so faintly Olessia finds herself leaning forward to catch the words falling from pale pink lips. "Cleanse?" It is not what Olessia expected, and she abandons an attempt to appear nonchalant.

"Indeed. Or would you prefer to remain here?" The woman's pointed side glance at the metal cave suggests she personally could think of nothing worse.

"No. No I would not prefer that." But cleansing seems a luxury Olessia assumed she would not be afforded. In fact, even when they made her change into this ludicrous dress, there was no option to cleanse. Her thoughts go to when she last had such an opportunity. In Sen-Bay's home, under that strange device that seemed to want to blow her skin off her body. The memory only increases the hollowed-out sensation sitting at her core.

"Then please, come with me." The woman moves with a fluid grace that is mesmerising to watch. She is barely taller than Olessia but there is little doubt she is more advanced in age. Serenity such as hers is rarely found in the young.

The two Alkell flank them but keep a discrete distance. A distance made all the more necessary by the long flow of Olessia's gown. She darts glances at the woman beside her but Dara's eyes, the blue of a clear Earth sky, remain fixed on the hallway ahead. They do not move towards the towering flight of steps that led Olessia into her prison. Instead they travel in the opposite direction, where a spiral staircase greets them at the end of the corridor. Vintinum is imprinted into each of the steps, lighting their way.

"This way please." Dara gestures, pale fingers pointed to the steps. She allows Olessia to take the lead.

The moment pressure is placed on the steps, the vintinum brightens. Olessia sucks at the thin air, the warmth in the corridor far greater than that in her metal cave. Far less pleasant. She grips the handrail with each step, only partly to keep her balance. Her senses are piqued, her nerves on edge. This strange procession unsettles her; the lack of others in the area, the cool detachment of the woman, the lack of any restraints on Olessia. A senlier at the very least would seem prudent. Perhaps Olessia's apparent willingness to accept her father's plans has proved convincing enough.

Or, more likely, he tests her. Watching from a distance. Dara communicating with him in a mindreach. Both of them enjoying her unrest.

"Come this way."

Olessia starts, too buried in her own thoughts to realise she has reached the top of the stairs. Dara stands to the right where there appears to be a dead end. A solid panel of pliotine, just like those that line her cell.

"Where exactly are you taking me?" Olessia shifts her shoulders, trying to increase her height to at least that of the woman. "I've done everything my father asks of me, do not think that you—"

Dara places her palm against the wall. An entranceway brightens beneath her touch. The edges are undulating and even Olessia will need to bend to accommodate the low height.

"Your father is pleased with you, Laudess. There is no need for alarm." Dara indicates the entranceway. She wants Olessia to go first but Olessia holds her ground. And the look on her face must indicate her hesitancy because Dara offers a soft smile. "Laudess, I had a hand in the construction of the Collective, I can assure you that nothing nefarious lies beyond this doorway. Simply a space in which to indulge yourself in a cleanse. Please." She gestures again. Olessia is about to take a step forward when the Alkell edge in closer behind her, the rough material of their cloaks giving them away. She whirls around.

"What are you doing?" she demands.

"Olessia, please. They are simply ensuring you follow my request." The sharp note in Dara's voice draws Olessia around. "Enter the cleansing chamber."

A flintiness has entered the woman's gaze. Olessia's caution lifts into concern. A low burn troubles her eyes, and the Beckoning raises its head in the abyss. Curious but not yet fully awoken. Whatever lies on the other side of that entranceway is not something Olessia wishes to see.

"Higher, do you require assistance?" One of the guards rumbles, lifting his jern shield, readying the weapon.

Dara gives Olessia a hard stare before focusing on the guards behind her. "No. I do not require your assistance at all."

And with that she raises her slender hand and fires two quick pulses. The guards drop to the ground without uttering a sound.

The Beckoning rises with Olessia's sudden panic. The elthar brooch is tangled in her skirt, and her hands snag in the folds as she struggles to reach it.

"Stay calm, Olessia," Dara says in a low whisper. "You will come to no harm. Do not use the elthar, not unless it is dire. Help me."

But Olessia doesn't do anything. She just stares as the slight woman grabs one leg of each guard and drags them towards the entranceway with a strength that belies her willowy body. The woman uses her palm once again to reveal an entranceway, one that whips upwards, revealing a room beyond.

"Assist me," Dara hisses. "We have one chance to break you from this place."

Now Olessia jumps to move. Her assistance isn't required though. Dara has the guards through the entranceway before Olessia can decide which body part to grab. Once they are all through, Dara pushes her hand against the inner wall. The entranceway seals off once again.

"Quickly, change into those clothes. You must be ready." Dara hurries over to a hinter, a storage compartment, and pulls an armful of clothing from its depths. Thrusting them at Olessia, who accepts them absently, absorbed in her surroundings. This is a cleansing chamber. Dara did not lie about that fact. An oval-shaped pool, barely big enough to contain one person, bubbles at the centre of the room. Though this is far more spacious that her quarters at Kinna-Bray, and with a view of the marbled expanse of the Gittren Mor that Aresh could never seem to admire enough.

"What is going on?" Olessia pushes her mind from thoughts of Aresh. "Tell me now, or I will not move another limb to aid you."

Dara's eyebrows — marked with the criss-cross pattern so many of the Claven women favour — rise high over her blue eyes. "Aid me? I'm not sure you have done any such thing to begin with. Get changed. And do not delay. Now, we await the signal. And when it comes, you must be ready."

Chapter 21

Christian

As instructed, Christian and Sen-Bay remain some distance behind Evelyn. Christian's mouth is desert dry, and the dank heat is only partly to blame. If he is honest with himself, and he's trying very hard not to be, he is terrified. Evelyn wouldn't elaborate on what is to happen next, aside from telling them to stay back but keep her in sight, and act normal.

Normal. Right. Christian tugs at the silky material encircling his neck. He can't seem to get the shirt to sit right against his body. The sweat keeps it clinging to him, bunching in uncomfortable folds. It's like being wrapped in beautiful cling wrap.

"Act normal," he mutters.

She's asking the impossible. Christian's an exhibit in an alien zoo. Where the animals are getting the life drained out of them.

"Here, have some refreshment," Sen-Bay offers a palm full of mauve pellets. They actually don't taste too bad, kind of like the candy bananas from home. But Christian pushes his hand away, scowling.

"I don't want any refreshments." Christian blushes. "Sorry. I just… I don't…"

Sen-Bay loops his arm across Christian's shoulders, and despite the heat and the humidity, it's comfortable. "I understand. Do not apologise."

"Thanks, I'm kind of freaking out."

"Does that mean you are experiencing severe levels of stress and anxiety?"

"Yep."

"Then I, too, am freaking out."

For a second the stress and anxiety disappears beneath Christian's smile.

Evelyn stops and, in unison, Christian and Sen-Bay do too. Christian's not sure they are about to win any awards for their ninja skills. Anyone paying them half an iota of attention would have found the sudden halt strange. Sen-Bay must sense it too because he suddenly bends down, studying an odd bunching of foliage, structured like a tiny, haphazard stack of yellow Lego blocks.

"Interesting," Sen-Bay muses.

"Yeah, interesting," Christian says with a nod. From beneath his fringe he scans the area. His chest is tight, a sensation he's slowly getting accustomed to, the air in this place has never quite managed to fill his lungs, but right now the knot in his diaphragm makes it doubly hard to breathe. "God, whatever it is, just let it happen and be done with it."

"I share your concern." Sen-Bay tugs a portion of the plant free and lifts it to his nose. "The anticipation is overwhelming." He makes a face and flicks the chunk of yellow away, muttering something that translates into gibberish in English. A curse most likely. "I do not believe that is plant matter at all." He wipes his hands furiously against the wrap of material that sits around his hips. A skirt, for all intents and purposes, with black pants beneath.

Christian doesn't ask what the Lego blocks actually were but judging by Sen-Bay's reaction they could have something to do with the pack of peacock-like creatures that wander around the Collective. Squat and round like a chicken, with similar short necks and jerky movements. Their long, flowing tails sit upright in a fan shape covered in colourful patterns. But unlike any peacock Christian's ever seen, the patterns shift and change, like something in a kaleidescope.

They are herded by lanky one-eyed beings that seem to walk as easily on four legs as they do on two. When upright, they must be at least eight feet tall, and they bay like hounds to communicate with each other. Christian can't make any sense of what they are saying, whatever enables him to understand Sen-Bay doesn't extend to these creatures. One of them gestures to Evelyn as it herds a barely-controlled flock of peacock-things right past her. It bays, a drawn out monotone that ends with a high shrill.

Evelyn ducks her veiled head, and then, to Christian's astonishment, bays right back at the droopy-shouldered being who is waving a stick at the stragglers in his herd. She holds the same note for a few seconds, then does the same quick shrill to end.

Whatever is going on, it's going down well with the shepherds. The shepherd who is trying to control the kaleidoscope peacocks, lifts its curious mushroom-shaped head, and hairy shoulders. Not so much baying now, as honking. Like a car horns is stuck in its narrow throat.

"I believe it is amused," Sen-Bay says, sounding equally as entertained.

"Great. At least someone is." Christian's mood is sinking, and he can't seem to stop it. The ache in his head is getting to him.

Evelyn continues across the open area, a kind of village square, surrounded by row upon row of shelters. She disappears around the tallest – a cube-shaped building built from smooth white rock. Christian breaks into a jog, but Sen-Bay slows him with a firm hand.

"She advised us to remain unobtrusive."

Christian's pulse pounds as though he'd actually broken into a run. Begrudgingly he slows, and lets Sen-Bay guide him, redirecting him ever so slightly on a different path, but still in sight of Evelyn, until they pass a lop-sided tee-pee that needs some repair on one of its sides. Clear of the structure, they catch sight of Evelyn again, who must have broken into the run Christian wasn't allowed, because she's a good twenty-metres away now. She turns and glances over her shoulder. And holds up her hand. Stop.

"Sen-Bay, do as I told you. Don't move," she shouts.

Sen-Bay grips Christian's arm and hauls him back a couple of paces.

"What does she—" Christian begins.

Evelyn is lost in the glow of a massive explosion.

"No!" Christian screams.

Sen-Bay shoves him to the rumbling ground, laying his body over Christian's. The shock wave roars past them, bringing with it a dust storm that makes keeping eyes open impossible. The sound of the blast fades, but another rises above it. A murmur of voices that grows louder and louder. Sen-Bay shifts and Christian scrambles to his knees.

"What was that?"

Shouts and cries come from all directions. Dust clouds the air but shadows move within the blurred light.

Sen-Bay grunts, his hand pressed to his upper arm. "Evelyn did not properly forewarn me of the ferocity of the blast."

"Evelyn told you this would happen? Why didn't she—"

"Your mind is compromised. The less you knew the safer all of us would be." He lifts his hand from his arm, revealing a nasty cut that's oozes with a rich brown fluid. "On your feet Chris-Tan. I will live."

He helps Christian to his feet. An acrid scent lies heavy on the air. There's no sign of Evelyn. The shelters in the area she had been standing have been hit hard by the blast. Not toppled completely but the three buildings lean at dangerous angles. All of them on fire. Well, what Christian presumes is fire for this place. The flames are barely visible, more like the waver of heat off a bitumen road in summer. With just the barest tinge of blue to highlight them. Exactly as it had been in the Turning. When Sen-Bay's home was destroyed.

"Now what? That was the distraction, right?"

Sen-Bay stands close but his attention is focused around them. Head turning, searching. "Yes. Come on, come on." His smooth skin is creased with a frown, and Christian's frantic heart can barely stand it. All at once, Sen-Bay braces, pressing Christian in behind him. Out of the dust a figure lopes towards them, low to the ground. But Sen-Bay doesn't push Christian to run. He steps towards the approaching figure, which stops just in front of him. Raising up onto two legs. It's the one-eyed shepherd. And it lets out a clicking sound, low and quiet, almost vanishing beneath the cries and screams coming from across the Collective. The shepherd raises a long arm and taps at its back, before dropping onto all fours. Sen-Bay seems to know exactly what it wants. He throws his leg over the creature's narrow back, and clambers onto the thing like it's a one-eyed pony.

"Are you serious?" Christian says. The inside of his nose burns, his throat red raw.

"Chris-Tan, hurry." Sen-Bay shifts back, patting at the empty space in front of him. "Overcome your fear."

Easier said than done. The fear monster is chewing on his insides. But Christian reaches for Sen-Bay's outstretched hand and uses the momentum to swing himself on board, settling in front of Sen-Bay on the shepherd's back. It's as uncomfortable as it looked. The creature's spine pressing between his legs, making Christian grit his teeth. He's given no time to readjust and they are moving.

"Oh man." Christian winces, the jolt of spine against butt leaving him breathless. He grips hold of what might be the shepherd's shoulder blades, two boy protrusions that rise out of long thin hair, like the fins on a surfboard.

"Hold on, Chris-Tan." Sen-Bay states the obvious, using his own body weight to press against Christian in an attempt to hold him steady.

Christian's thighs scream with pain as he grips hard against the shepherd's sides. They weave between the shelters at a pace that would be impressive if Christian wasn't so certain it was about to throw him clear. The shepherd races towards where the main body of the blast occurred, a place where all the shelters have been torn to shreds and are on fire. Up ahead, the ground is churned like a field ploughed by a drunk farmer. Creatures of all shapes and sizes spill across it. Headed for something Christian can't make out just yet.

Another explosion rumbles the ground beneath them. Further away this time. Too far to catch sight of the blast itself as the shepherd darts in behind a hill whose side has been scorched by the initial blast, speckling it with black. The sounds of horror and cries of alarm rise, seeming to come at them from every direction.

"There," Sen-Bay cries, right up against Christian's ear.

A section of the metal skeleton that holds them in the zoo, has been torn open. A hole a couple of meters off the ground punctured through the massive slab of metal. They are not the first to come across the sudden exit. Creatures spill through it, desperate for the freedom that awaits on the other side. The shepherd doesn't wait his turn in line, shoving his way through the throng, rushing forward until they reach the opening. Christian gasps, dropping down low against the creature's back, Sen-Bay doing the same behind him. The jagged edges of the hole find Christian's shirt, snagging momentarily before ripping free.

Then they are through.

Out of the cage.

Racing at break-neck speed across a wide expanse of open ground. Behind them, yet another explosion rips apart their prison.

Chapter 22

Olessia

The walls glow with a subdued vintium light, which catches on the sway of colour within Dara's eyes. She is unsettled, the churn of blue tells Olessia as much, but whether it is fear or anger that causes Dara's unrest, Olessia cannot be certain. The Claven clicks her tongue and places her hands on Olessia's hips.

"Unhand me." Olessia slaps her away.

"Fine. But you do not seem to understand the urgency here, Laudess. I beg you, change into this clothing." Dara turns her back on Olessia. "If you require privacy I can provide this much."

Privacy? Olessia has had no privacy since the day she was created. Even in her own cleansing room she would be attended by at least three certifiers. And this Claven woman would know that full well. Dara is either desperate or a fool. Olessia strongly suspects it is the former, considering the woman would also be fully aware of Olessia's power. Turning her back to the Laudess of Bax Un Tey in a situation like this is a dangerous move. Olessia makes a hurried analysis, deciding this woman is no enemy in disguise. She unclips the meshwork that holds the skirt in place. Far less cumbersome a clasp than the zippers of Earth, which are horrendous creations. The skirt falls from her waist, ballooning around her ankles. She rifles through the clothing, trying to decipher the outfit she has been given.

"These clothes, I don't recognise them," she frowns.

"Here, let me assist you." Dara reaches to take the item but hesitates and only moves again when Olessia nods. "They are not from Siros. Nor Zentai. We have sourced clothing from those in the Collective. So that you might blend in more readily."

"Blend in?" Olessia glances around the chamber to reassure herself that she is where she believed herself to be.

"Yes," Dara replies. And explains no further.

Dara gathers a circular length of green material in two hands, pulling at it so that Olessia might step into it. Her legs slide into a material far coarser than Olessia is used to. She grimaces as it scrapes her skin, where nerve endings sit on heightened alert, the Beckoning on a low burn beneath it. Dara must tug with some ferocity to raise the garment higher. It appears to be one whole piece of clothing, bottom and top united as one. The unpleasant material now covers virtually all of Olessia's body. Sleeves down to her wrists, and a V-neck that has a jagged edging. Like enormous teeth reaching up her chest and encircling her neck.

"Two more pieces to go." Dara drapes a finer material, white as Christian's hair, over Olessia's shoulders, and it hangs halfway down her back. She clasps it in place with a single clip, embellished with flek stones. "And the elthar?"

Olessia thought she had been discrete in removing the brooch from the dress, and concealing it in a fist. Dara waits with outstretched hands, and with some reluctance, Olessia places it in her palm, pulses thumping. Odd though, despite her trepidation, Olessia has no impulse to remove herself from Dara's presence. That subtle ring of alarm, an instinctual perception of danger, does not plague her here. At least, not so far as Dara is concerned. Olessia dares to allow herself to believe this is as it appears. An attempt to restore her freedom.

"What now?" She squares up to Dara, who's hard expression softens. Her smile is infinitesimal but it is there, nonetheless. Acknowledging Olessia's unspoken message: she will do what is asked of her. Dara lifts the last piece of clothing that remains. A headpiece, a drape of dark material that clings to the head, shaping itself around it. A finer, lighter material covering the face.

Olessia wrinkles her nose. "I am to wear that?"

"If there is to be a hope of our plan succeeding. It would be helpful. It is not uncommon to use some of the inhabitants of the Collective as certifiers, but many of them have an appearance that less than pleases those they serve."

"You wish me to serve? I am to be a certifier?" Indignation lifts Olessia's voice.

Dara reacts the way Aresh did when Olessia protested against being asked to do something she considered beneath her. Dara does not react at all.

"Today, Laudess, if anyone should ask, I will declare you are a certifier. So ensure you act as such and follow my instructions. Be sure to heed what I say, word for word. But if this goes as it should, then our partnership will be brief."

Before Olessia can question her, Dara slides the veil over her head, leaving Olessia in a blurred world, Dara barely a defined mass in front of her.

Dara adjusts the bindings at the side of the mask. "Very shortly, any attention we may draw will be directed away from us and settle on something far grander. But if we are stopped, if your identity is revealed Olessia, remember this. I am your enemy. A supporter of the Laudine, the traitor, as she has now been branded. I forced your compliance, manipulated you into following my direction. Perhaps appear non-sensical, whatever it is you feel you should do. If they come for us, let them take me. You must not give them cause to imprison you even deeper in the depths of this place. Too much depends on you."

She herds Olessia back from the edge of the steaming pool and dips her hand into the liquid, sinking her arm down deep, almost to her shoulder. Her hair slides forward covering her face, the tips of some strands touching at the bubbling water that now glows with a pale blue light, the shimmer of elthar. Olessia tugs up a corner of the veil.

The water level is depleting, the fluid draining away. In a few short moments the bottom of the pool is covered by only the barest layer. The base of the pool splits, two halves retracting, leaving a wide hole beneath. Olessia edges forward as Dara shakes her elthar coated arm, the sodden material of her gown sticking to the metal. A grim but self-satisfied expression on her face.

"Quickly, go," she says. "We should have advanced already."

Olessia catches sight of a stairwell that drops into darkness, and she is reminded of that long row of steps that took her down to the metal cave. But any thought of backing away is stolen from her. Dara grips her arm and drags her forward. Olessia must either move with the momentum and find her balance or topple helplessly down the stairs. Self-preservation sees her clambering over the edge and stepping onto the first step. The passageway does not actually descend into the depths, as she feared. But angles almost immediately into a corridor that runs just beneath the floor of the cleansing room. Olessia adjusts the headpiece which has dislodged to cover her right eye.

"Do not remove it," Dara whispers.

They hurry further down, the divided slabs of the cleansing pool rejoining, the trickle of liquid evident from up above. Dara hurries Olessia along the low corridor which only just accommodates the Claven's height. It is just as well Christian does not travel with them, he would be forced to bend at a most discomforting angle to make his way.

"I am not removing it," Olessia whispers back. "What of the guards? Do you not think they alone will give us away?"

"That was a hasty move on my part, I will grant you that." Dara's elthar, now a patterned cuff on her right wrist, lights their way forward. "But it will be some time before anyone dares to attempt to enter the cleansing rooms without invitation, especially with you in my presence, and even greater time still, if at all, before they will find the entrance to this passageway. And that, I hope, is all the time we will need."

"You keep insinuating something grand is to occur." The tension makes Olessia's words far shorter and sharper than she intends. "Are you going to avail me of this information? Or shall you simply keep me, quite literally, in the dark?"

She must lift the veil in order not to fall, the vintinum in the corridor far from adequate.

Up ahead the passageway breaks off into three different directions. Dara's pace slows and she lets go of Olessia's arm. She heaves a heavy sigh.

"This is where I berate my lack of commitment to the task I was given here," Dara says. "If I had not grown so disillusioned by Inel's rule, I might have completed these thoroughfares, and we would be able to depart in utter secrecy. But alas. That is not the case."

She heads down the central passageway. "Those other corridors lead nowhere. And this one… this one will take us out into the Nidrin, a thoroughfare that all who tend the Collective pass through at one time or another to get where they seek."

"We are to exit in such a place? That hardly seems wise."

The central passageway does not extend for long. Up ahead, a solid wall of pliotine awaits them.

"There is no choice. This will bring us closest to what we seek. Now remember, Olessia, once we exit this place you are nothing but a certifier. You pretended to be human once, a species you knew little about. I trust you can extend the deception to include that with which you are far more accustomed."

Dara's attention is on the wall and finding the space where she must activate the entranceway. A distraction Olessia is grateful for. She allows the veil to fall into place and does not advise the Claven that her attempt at playing human was nothing short of a total failure.

Chapter 23

Olessia

O lessia's breath is uncomfortably warm against her face, the slight weight of the veil enough to trap each exhale. Dara does not wait for her, nor turn to ensure she still follows. To do so would only draw suspicion. A Claven, Higher or otherwise, would not waste a moment of their time in ensuring a certifier is doing as they have been trained.

Follow.

Wait on the next command to be issued by one considered far above them. Olessia hurries to catch up, remembering to hunch her shoulders, remove the regal posture that might mark her as something other than an attendant.

Dara sweeps them through a series of wide corridors whose floors are inlaid with thousands of minute tiles, each illuminating a piece of a grander picture: the Crest of the Presiderline. It is as though many lifetimes have passed since Olessia last saw this Moniker – set on a background the hue of the twin confels – in all the corridors of Kinna-Brey. The Moniker represents elthar in its natural form; fluid, strands of dull grey that weave into one another, shaping themselves into what she learned on Earth would be called a star. Each strand is constructed from miniscule dots, so close together they appear as one solid piece, unless you are close enough to discern the subtlety. As Olessia is now.

She lifts her head, removing the Crest from her sight. Diamond-shaped windows rise from floor to ceiling at intervals along the passageways, allowing a glimpse of the external world. Olessia has moved through corridors just like this at Kinna Brey. Though on those occasions all who passed by would step aside for her, pressing themselves up against the walls, acknowledging the presence of the heir to the Presiderline. Not like now, where twice Olessia has been forced to step aside for a passer-by who does not seemed to have noticed she exists at all. And one of them was just an Uenar, the lowliest in the certifier hierarchy. Olessia's hands still clench with the indignation of it. She sidesteps as another collision threatens. An Alkell, whose presence causes the Beckoning to rise. The guard walks by, nodding to Dara, with no acknowledgment of Olessia's scrambling effort to get out of his way. Olessia presses her lips, an acidic remark on her tongue. The Alkell continues on down the corridor without a backward glance, and Olessia is struck by a wonderous realisation.

She does not exist here. Olessia is invisible.

Now her pulses thump with a fresh fervour. There is a chance this plan of Dara's will work. The Laudess of Bax Un Tey is a ghost. Just as her father wished. She smiles behind the veil. And when next they encounter a passer-by, Olessia does not alter her course, muttering an apology when she collides with a burly groundsman who heaps disparaging comments upon her. Berating her for her stupidity.

Then continuing on.

Another viewing pane draws level, and Olessia glances outside. This place, this fortress or prison, or both, looks down on the enclosed world the Presider has created. The Collective. The scale of the domain entrapped beneath the structured metal frame with its life-ending barrier, is far grander than she first imagined. The Presider does nothing in small measure, it would seem. Her body tenses as she catches sight of the dome used for the Gatherings and is grateful Dara is setting a pace that gives her no time to linger on it.

"Dara."

Dashel strides down the corridor towards them, clad in the Claven uniform, his sharp chin lifted. Dara's hurried steps come to an abrupt halt. Olessia stumbles, uncertain if she too should stop, or continue on as though her main task lies elsewhere. Her body is awash with panic as Dashel glances at her. But his interest is as short-lived as anyone else they've come across. He turns back to Dara. Olessia holds herself rigid, not just with the shock of the encounter, but in anticipation of the Beckoning reacting to her sudden shift in mood. To her surprise the beast's stirring is minimal. A flutter at most. As though it too wishes to conceal its presence from the man who blocks their way.

"Were you not attending to a more important task?" Dashel says.

Dara gives him a disinterested shrug. "I delivered the package to the cleansing room as instructed. I was not aware it was my duty to remain close at hand for what followed. The guards are in attendance, I will return momentarily to ensure a safe transfer back to the enclosure."

Olessia does not exist in their conversation, her name removed from it entirely. Talked about as though she were no more than a shipment of Pletherot. Dara raises her hand, flicking her fingers towards Olessia. "Why are you still here? I asked that you ready my chamber. Go."

The signal could not be clearer, but Olessia hesitates. Horrifyingly aware that she is not certain of the protocol expected of a certifier when they leave the presence of their Higher. There is one, Olessia knows for certain but she's never paid it full attention. Her body trembles. Dashel's gaze snakes over her.

"Dashel," Dara says at a volume that jerks the Claven's attention back to her. "There are certain… concerns I would discuss with you, should you have a moment. I have reason to suspect that Kileen's fondness for our… guest… sees him grow far too accommodating." Dara sweeps her arm towards a room that sits off the corridor. "Perhaps—"

"No. Not now. There is far too much—"

Whatever there is far too much of, none of them learn. A distant explosion sends a low vibration through the corridor. Squeals echo down the passageway, and those who had been moving come to a standstill, bracing themselves. Now Olessia has no choice but to remain still. Running while everyone else stands as statues strikes her as a terrible idea.

"Dashel?" Dara's voice rises with alarm. "What is that?"

"How would I know?" Dashel's, in contrast, brims with fury. "Get to the cleansing rooms. Take another contingent with you."

He strides with a rapid pace back the way he came, and Dara follows after him. Ignoring Olessia completely. Leaving her alone in the corridor, her pulses taking full flight.

As much as this place may resemble Kinna Bray, the unfortunate truth is that, whatever and wherever it is, it is not Olessia's fortress home. Now that she has been abandoned by her would-be rescuer, Olessia struggles to decide on a direction to take. The beast senses her discord and pushes against her control. Is this the distraction Dara spoke of? Why did she not inform Olessia more fully of the plans?

She tugs at the veil, pulling it from where it sticks to her lips. Perhaps she was right all along. This is another twisted trap, set by her father. The other occupants of the corridor find their feet, movement filling the broad passageway. Some run, others quick-step, all appear frightened. The corridor seems to have doubled in population. Olessia edges up against the wall. Common sense says she should continue in the direction Dara was taking her, but that is now the direction Dashel followed. Indecision wracks her, and the Beckoning warms her core, fighting to rise from the abyss. Olessia's eyes churn, set into motion by her consuming panic. The veil at least hides her signature violet irises, but to remain here like this, paralysed while everyone else flees, will draw undue attention. Olessia pushes from the wall and places one foot in front of the other. Continuing down the path Dara set. Olessia joins the throng of people rushing up the corridor. Stepping aside, as all others do, when a squad of Alkell race up behind her. Ordering everyone, in the name of the Presider, to clear a path.

Another tremor runs through the building. This one far less intense, perhaps further away, but significant enough to solicit cries from those gathered around Olessia. Is this a distraction, or an attack on the Collective? Olessia hisses with frustration. Touching at the elthar brooch. Dara warned her not to use the elthar, *until the need is dire*. Fine. But how does Olessia quantify the situation as dire? She struggles to calm her thoughts. Seeking some level of logic that might steady her.

Both Dashel and the Alkell have overlooked her so far.

There is her answer. The situation is not yet dire.

Olessia hurries herself into a quickened walk, one hand trailing along the wall. Mimicking what some of those who pass her by are also doing. Bracing themselves. She quickly gains on a small figure, a child perhaps, moving at a slow pace up ahead. Olessia shifts out from the wall to pass them by. But as she does so, a hand reaches for her, and clasps her wrist. Olessia starts, and jerks her hand free, glaring at the who touched her.

A child with eyes the colour of plestex crystal. The child who passed her the elthar brooch.

"This is the way." She tugs at Olessia's arm. "You are so close."

Olessia pulls back, reluctant. Close to what?

"I know you are frightened. As am I." The girl tries to take Olessia's hand. "Please." A note of desperation creeps into the single word. And she raises eyes filled with a fear that reflects Olessia's own behind the veil.

"Lead, and I will follow."

The girl nods. "This way."

She turns and runs, long braid swinging at her back. Olessia follows close behind. The girl makes an abrupt turn right, entering what is clearly a sustenance prep area. Section plates glow, nourishments lie in various stages of preparation upon a layout that occupies most of the centre of the room. But there are no techs present. The room is deserted. The girl heads straight for the door on the opposite side of the room, pushing it open.

"Come, come."

They step out into the glare of a confel-lit sky. Shading her eyes, Olessia surveys the new surrounds. The growing area for the nourishment supplies is abundant with drin, and little else. Affording a clear view of what lies beyond the growing lots. A wall, reaching skyward. Far too high to get over without the assistance of the elthar.

They have reached a dead end.

The girl digs into the folds of her skirt.

"What are you doing?" Olessia says. She takes a step back and allows the Beckoning more free reign. Surely, this child intends no harm?

Lifting cupped palms, the girl raises her hands. A whippernell sits in the bowl her hands have formed. Smaller and more delicate than the klix of Zentai, but similar in form, the petite creature spreads tiny gossamer wings and lifts into the air. Darting out of sight.

"What are you doing?" Olessia demands for a second time.

"He will come. We must wait."

Olessia takes a further step back, contemplating returning to confines of the building. The air lies hot and heavy, and silent. No further disquiet from distant explosions.

"He? Who are you talking about?"

The child smiles, and Olessia is stunned by the beauty of it. The lift of small lips causes her whole face to radiate.

"You will know him. And you will be safe." The girl curls up her tiny fist and places it to her chest. Lowering her eyes. In deference to the Laudess of Bax Un Tey. An odd tightness comes to Olessia's throat, and she busies herself with the folds of her cumbersome clothing.

"Look!" The child exclaims.

Olessia lifts her head.

A shape crests the height of the wall, soaring down towards them. A figure sits astride a garrison, dark cloak whipping at the air behind them. Before they have drawn close enough to distinguish their features Olessia is already certain of who approaches. It is a face difficult to forget after so many visn spent under their tutelage.

The garrison draws down, levelling out in front of them.

"Olessia, let us go." Sentinel Teler reaches for her, and Olessia does not hesitate. Taking the broad hand offered. Teler lifts her easily, and Olessia swings into place behind him on the garrison. It is a vehicle designed for just one passenger, but the way Olessia clings to Teler's solid frame there is little chance she will dislodge.

Teler manoeuvres the garrison back up into the air, leaning forward against the length of the machine. Olessia searches for the child, to offer her thanks, but the girl has already disappeared.

And a moment later, so too has Olessia. Teler guides them over the wall.

Freedom stretches out before her.

Chapter 24

Christian

Christian doesn't so much dismount, as fall off the back of the shepherd. His legs are numb from the ride, and the creature's sides heave, dribble running from the corners of its wide mouth. They have been travelling at a frantic pace for at least thirty minutes, and the shepherd's speed literally took Christian's breath away – the jarring motion of the bony back grinding at an unfortunate point between his legs. They travelled across a barren but stunning landscape. Waves of rock rising out of soft pockets of peach-coloured sand. No hint of green or blue. Anything that might be shelter or water.

There was a lot of water back home. A lot of water, and a lot of green. That much Christian remembers with clarity.

"Are you all right, Chris-Tan?" Sen-Bay's dismount is much more dignified, but even he winces as he stretches his legs.

"Yeah fine." Not entirely true, but Christian is tired of being the obviously terrified one.

The shepherd drops onto its belly, the hard pump of its breath shifting the fine sand. At least, it looks almost like sand, the grains are much coarser, larger, like they've been running across a huge expanse of rock salt that's tumbled out of an enormous salt shaker. The scenery, both in the Collective and in Zentai, has a vague sense of familiarity. *Almost* like something that might be on Earth, but not quite.

"Where are we?"

"I do not know." Sen-Bay stretches his arms over his head. "The shepherd chose our path, and I do not understand the language the being speaks."

"So, what do we do now then?"

The one-eyed creature that just got them safely away from the wreck and ruin of the Collective, looks utterly spent. If they are going to continue this journey it will be some time before that happens. Their stopping point is beneath a massive curve of rock that sweeps over them like a stationery wave, shading them from the blazing comets. The Collective was uncomfortable, but Christian realises now, it wasn't anywhere near as hot as it is out here. It's the only thing he misses about the place.

"I suppose we will rest." Sen-Bay doesn't seem convinced by his own words, and his gaze scans back and forth across their surroundings. As though he expects company. Not great company either, judging by his frown. Christian shades his eyes and tilts his head. The curve of rock sits just above a narrow gully. The wave-rock stretches about twenty metres in length, giving them ample hiding room, but the gully continues on much farther, curving away to the right another hundred or so metres up ahead.

"Do you think Evelyn is okay?" Christian says. Recalling how the blast enveloped her, sucking her into a blaze of light. He tugs at the hoop in his eyebrow. He's been trying not to think about her, doing so just intensifies the ache in his head.

"Yes. I believe she lives. She was expecting the explosion."

"Did she start it?"

"No. The other one did. Teler."

"Just to get us out of there?"

Sen-Bay settles down on a section of rock that offers a convenient backrest. "I believe their plans were grander."

Christian frowns. "Grander? What—"

The shepherd's head lifts, dust clings to the hairs covering its chest. A gurgling sound comes from deep in its throat. Sen-Bay sits bolt upright, gesturing for Christian to move closer. He does so, crouching beside the Yentern, the rock salt crunching beneath his shoes.

"Keep quiet," Sen-Bay whispers, laying a hand on Christian's thigh.

Christian's heartbeat sets off in a manic pace yet again. He holds his breath. Like that might make him invisible.

But whatever the shepherd heard doesn't reach Christian's ears. He strains to catch something, anything, that might tell him what's out there. And from what direction it's coming. But not only is this place devoid of trees, it seems to be lifeless. No bird calls, or insect shrills. Even the breeze has vanished.

The tension makes him want to scream. "Should we run?"

Sen-Bay's answer is to grip harder to Christian's thigh. Tight enough to make him bite his lip. The answer clearly no. Sen-Bay watches the shepherd, who in turn stares up with his single eye at a point on the rock roof. The creature hasn't shifted from his initial alert position, long body rigid.

Christian is certain his heartbeat alone is going to give them away. It thumps in his ears like bass drums.

The shepherd slumps to the ground, returning to the exhausted, heavy breathing pile of strange hair and skin. A fraction of a second later, a shadow dashes down from above, vaulting over the lip of the rock. Sen-Bay shoves Christian behind him, causing him to land awkwardly on his right wrist. A shadow lands like a gymnast on the rock in front of them.

"Eva-leen." Sen-Bay's voice pitches with recognition. And happiness.

Christian ignores the twinge in his wrist and scrambles to his feet.

"You're okay!" A smile jumps to his lips and won't let go. "We didn't know if you made it out of that explosion… well, I didn't. Sen-Bay was fairly certain. Everyone but me seems to know what's going on. But that's okay. I think it's better if I don't…" He stops himself, conscious that he's talking a mile a minute, all the tension rocketing his words from his mouth.

Evelyn smiles. He can't see her mouth, its covered by the folds of the dark material wrapped around her head, but her eyes are uncovered. And the sudden appearance of wrinkles around them tells Christian she's smiling.

Dark brown eyes, wide, and just a bit too big for her face. He gasps, grabbing at his head.

"Christian?" Evelyn says.

"Your eyes, Eva-leen," Sen-Bay replies.

"Oh god, sorry. I'm sorry, Christian."

He keeps his fingers pressed to his temples. Trying to breathe through the nail being driven into his head.

Get a grip, Chris. He's not going to die from a headache. Though it feels like his head is going to explode. Sophie's brother Kye used to get migraines, and once he tried to explain how it felt to Christian. Sounded horrendous. He even went blind with it sometimes. But it didn't kill him. Christian takes a breath and holds it. A picture of a girl's face fills the blackness behind his eyelids.

Red hair, goofy smile. Crazy bright clothes. Christian's skull balloons with the pressure. The weight at the back of his eyes is intense. But he keeps holding his breath.

Sophie. Tears sting his eyes.

"Sophie," he whispers.

His friend. Best buddy. An anchor when his world goes topsy-turvy. This is the girl the Presider wanted to know about. Sophie. But there was another one. Ryder?

A savage pain rips through his temples. He opens his eyes but the world remains black.

"Oh god, I can't see." Christian presses at his eyes, and someone tries to pull his hands free.

"Christian, settle down," Evelyn says. "You're okay. Just relax, it will pass."

"Chris-tan." Sen-Bay is firmer, both in voice and touch. "You are safe. Stop it."

The sharp command freezes Christian's hands in the air. And the breath he is still holding escapes him in a loud exhale. The light seeps back in. He blinks through tears and fading pain.

"I'm sorry," he mutters, cheeks warming.

"Nothing to be sorry about. I wish I knew how to help you." Evelyn has covered her eyes, with a thin gauze that distorts them.

She presses something into his hand, a small grey pellet. "A mild painkiller, it may help."

Evelyn kneels beside the shepherd, running a gentle hand down the creature's back.

Christian rolls the pellet in his palm. "I remembered some things… I remembered my friend, Sophie." His chest aches with missing her. "The Presider asked me about her. Said she was with someone called Sebastien? That seemed to really irritate him. Like he should have been somewhere else?"

Evelyn's hand hangs in mid-air above the shepherd's back.

"Indeed he should have," Evelyn says. "Sebastien is Olessia's guardian. To leave her side is tantamount to treason. If that is what he has done. Is the guardian alive?" Tension holds the words tight.

Christian shrugs. "I don't know… do you think I've met him?"

"It would seem so, if Sophie is a friend of yours. A human?"

Christian nods.

The shepherd coughs, a dry hacking sound that sends up a flurry of dust from among the pebbles. Evelyn murmurs to the creature, pulling something from a satchel that hangs at her hip. She wipes at the skin on the beast's shoulder and presses a rounded stone to the coarse skin near the shoulder blades. Christian edges in closer, staring down at the stone. The familiar niggling begins again at the back of his head, and he looks away. Not ready for another brain blast from his memories just yet.

"How long do we intend to remain here?" Sen-Bay stands over Evelyn as she tends to the shepherd. "The creature cannot take us further, should we continue on foot?"

"Not yet. We wait. Zagen has done a magnificent job getting you this far." She cups her hand to the shepherd's head. The beast makes a weak sound, the familiar bleating they heard in the Collective. "For that I hope to repay you one day, friend. But rest now."

The single eye closes, and the beast shifts its long limbs, curling them up high against its equally elongated body. Christian envies the creature. He's struggling to keep his eyes open, his body wiped of energy. Evelyn's declaration that they are going to wait isn't bad news so far as Christian is concerned, but Sen-Bay is definitely less pleased.

"We wait?" Sen-Bay says. "For what?"

"For Sentinel Teler." She rifles around in the satchel, removing a small onyx cube and placing it alongside the shepherd.

Sen-Bay shifts on his feet, folding his arms. "What is that?"

"This will shield us from external attentions… I hope. This rachmeed was smuggled out of the Sentinel weapons cache. We should be undetectable beneath the shield it will generate. Though this particular one was in for repairs, so, time will tell if the techs did their work properly." She laughs, a quick-dying sound.

Evelyn taps in a sequence on the cubes carved surface and a red light appears around all the edges of the device.

"Does that mean it's working?" Christian says. A yawn catches him off-guard.

"Yes. Rest, Christian. This has only just begun. It shouldn't be too long before Teler arrives. So rest, both of you. I'll keep watch."

Sen-Bay takes a bit of convincing but Christian settles down onto the smooth rock, wriggling and shifting, trying to find some place remotely comfortable. After a few unsuccessful minutes, he groans, rolling flat onto his back. Sen-Bay sits beside him.

"Do humans never sleep in external environments?"

"This one doesn't, no."

"Here." Sen-Bay stretches his legs alongside Christian. "You must rest."

After the briefest hesitation, Christian shuffles in, and lays his head on Sen-Bay's thighs. Not exactly pillow-soft, but it's better than the rock, and enough to see Christian drifting off to sleep just a few minutes later.

The dreams move in rapidly, storming into his unconscious and throwing wild images at him. Strange snippets of a world Christian doesn't recognise; shadowy figures dashing at him, a world that is almost entirely white, creatures that screech and bay and holler so loud they throw him out of his slumber and back into the steamy, humid world.

Christian's eyes fly open, and he sits up. The ear that had laid against Sen-Bay's thigh is dripping with sweat, which runs into his ear canal. Christian shakes his head, trying to clear it, but he is groggy with sleep. His eyes land on the shepherd. And the stone that Evelyn placed on his shoulder.

Ryder.

The memory shoots through his barely woken mind, tearing a path like a hot needle. Christian screams, trying to get to his feet, stumbling and finding himself sliding down the rock. The rough surface tears at his clothes, and his skin. But all he can focus on is the agony. Kye was wrong. A migraine can kill you.

Christian's head is finally going to split wide open.

He lands against something hard, and his freefall comes to an abrupt end. There are people around him, voices aimed at him, but none of them matter.

Ryder. Dark brown eyes. Evelyn's eyes. Curling waves of chocolate brown hair. Evelyn's hair.

Ryder's hair.

"Ryder," he cries.

The voices around him are close. Right on top of him. Huddled around him. Reaching for him.

"What did he just say?" Evelyn's voice.

"Move back. Move back," A new voice. And yet, not new.

But he can't process it. Can't think. Won't think. It hurts too much.

A face draws into focus in front of him. Violet eyes.

"Hold on, Christian. I will make this stop. Just stay with me."

The girl from the prison. The girl who protected him.

Chapter 25

Ryder

Ryder sits silently in her seat. So silent that Blane asks her a couple of times if she is okay.

"Yeah, great."

He says nothing in reply each time, leaving her alone with her thoughts. And they are a mess. Not least of all because of Sophie, who just can't seem to shut up.

Are you sure this is a good idea, Ry? Right into the lion's den? I'm not sure that's high up there on the list of brilliant ideas.

What is plan B then? You tell me. Ryder scratches at her cheek, her skin irritated by the constant humidity. *We're going to the Crown. That's what Aresh wanted right? In her mind text? Besides, not like I can just jump off this thing.*

Hmm, yeah. I'm pretty sure you can. You're like hella superhero chick now, Ry—

Sophie's comment draws a roll of the eyes from Ryder.

I saw that.

Ryder sits up in her chair, searching for her friend. The Commandant pilots the craft, as silent as Ryder has been. Blane beside her, dozing.

God, I wish I could see you. I don't understand why I could see Padellah but can't see you without those damn glasses... when they're working.

The glasses that are still around her neck. She lifts them and holds the lens that isn't cracked over her eye, just to make sure. But the glass is so darkly tinted that it's like trying to stare down a well. Ryder can't make out the back of the Commandant's head let alone Sophie in spectre form.

Well, I guess technically, I'm not Cyne… so maybe that's why you can't see me without some help. Come to think of it, I have no clue what I am right now.

She laughs, light and fluffy, and Ryder recognises that nervous sound instantly. Mostly from whenever Ryder has tried to make Sophie say hi to someone in a mascot costume. For whatever bizarre reason, about the only thing that freaks Sophie out is an over-sized head and a giant waving hand.

Well, you're not alone in the who-am-I club, Soph. I'm here with you. For better or for worse. We're together. And we just have to hang on to that for now, okay?

Ryder still clings to the idea that maybe Padellah can help them. Bring Sophie back… more permanently.

Your pep talks are really getting so much better, you know?

Thanks, Ryder laughs.

"Something amusing?" The Commandant's voice is low in the quiet cabin. Blane doesn't stir.

"No… not really." Everything is so far from amusing it's… well, it's laughable.

"You want to tell me where you managed to get hold of an anvel."

"A what?"

The Commandant gestures to her own long, slender neck but doesn't turn from where she sits, eyes on the darkness ahead. "The thing around your neck. I don't recall giving you one on board the Bauershard. Did the guardian steal from me?"

Ryder touches the spongy frame. Better that the Commandant think Sebastien's a thief than tell her about Maher. For now.

"I guess so. He gave it to me."

"Was he planning to drag you back to your world, through a slipstream?" The idea seems to amuse the Commandant. "The guardian has quite the reputation for being rash, now I see it is quite justified."

"What's that got to do with these goggles?"

"That model is usually found on board vessels designed for river and slipstream crossings. They enable the wearer to view greater depths there. Navigators use them. I think your guardian had grand plans of reversing our journey."

"He's not my guardian." Ryder's cheeks warm, despite the coolness of the cabin air.

"Oh I wouldn't be too certain of that."

Perceptive, I'll give her that much.

Shut up, Sophie.

Glaring at thin air, Ryder clutches the armrests. Sebastien is somewhere back there in that forest. Where Ryder left him.

You should tell her, about what Aresh said.

Sophie's voice jolts Ryder out of her guilty thoughts.

No way!

Why not?

Did you not hear what Aresh said? Tell the Crown. Not the Commandant. I'm sticking with the orders I was given.

If that's what you think is best.

"Thank you," Ryder says, sighing.

"For what?" The Commandant shifts in her chair, turning to glance at Ryder.

"For…" Ryder searches for something, anything. "For not making me give back the anvel."

And also Mrs Commandant, can you please fly this thing faster.

Sophie, stop it.

We need to get to the Crown like right now. Sophie's mindreach grows louder.

Stop. I'm serious.

So am I.

We need to get there, like yesterday. Don't tell her the details, just tell her we have a message from Aresh. One the Crown needs to hear.

No.

Argh, I hate being invisible.

I know. And I'm sorry, but we can't risk it till we know for sure that's where she's really taking us.

But—

"No." Ryder's frustration jettisons the word out of her head and into the cabin. Resulting in another quizzical head twist from the Commandant.

"No, what?"

Ryder scrambles for a reply. "Oh, I was just saying, oh no, the anvel… it's broken… do you think it can be fixed?'

"Depends what happened to them to begin with. Why are you so concerned?"

"It's just… they kind of…" Sophie is one secret that Ryder will never share. Not if there is the slightest chance that any of these aliens can take her away again. "They're a good luck charm, I think. Helped me, you know, do that stuff. Back there."

The Commandant shifts her shoulders. "You do understand that if you attempt anything untoward in Icewynn, your demise will be immediate."

"Untoward?"

"Attempt to use that *stuff*, as you call it, to launch an attack on the Crown. Nire is formidable enough, but there are many before her who will cut you down before she has need to."

Nire. It's the first time Ryder's heard the ruler's actual name. But she's more concerned with the 'cut you down' part of the conversation.

Whoa. That seems a little harsh.

And the Commandant isn't done yet. "They have been forewarned of our approach, and of your… display. Do you understand, Ryder, that I will not hesitate to—"

"I get it!"

Ryder's shout causes Blane to stir. He yawns, mouth wide, stretching his hands over his head. "Did I miss something?"

"Ryder and I have come to an understanding. Isn't that right?" The Commandant's tone leaves Ryder in no doubt the answer had better be a quick yes. But she surprises Ryder by offering a sweetener. "Take this if you like. Consider it a gift, in exchange for your co-operation."

She throws something in a backward underarm throw, not checking to see where it landed. But it's on target. Hitting Ryder's knee, and falling to the floor.

Another anvel. No cracks on this one, despite the sound it made as it landed. Ryder snatches it up, tugging the broken pair over her head. She pulls the new set down over her forehead, settling them over her eyes. Same soft material around tinted lenses, though these goggles are a deep green colour. Like her elthar when it goes supernova.

A beaming face appears in the space between her seat and the Commandant.

"Sophie," Ryder whispers, her smile a mile wide.

Oh, oh, oh I'm back? You can see me? She waves like her arms are possessed.

Ryder nods.

Blane, still bleary, blinks. "You all right, Ryder?"

"Yeah. I am now. I'm great."

"With the goggles?"

"Uhuh. With the goggles." And if Ryder has any say in it, she's never taking them off.

Blane nods, his expression serious. As if he totally gets it. Sophie leans over Blane, pulling faces about an inch away from his. It's juvenile, totally, and Ryder can barely hold in her laughter. She has to press her palms to the seat to stop herself from jumping up and hugging empty air. To see Sophie, translucent or not, looking exactly as she remembers — the tilt of her smile, the gestures and clothing whose bright colours are thankfully muted in the lens of the anvel — makes it hard not to start bawling like a baby.

"I understand," Blane smiles. "They make you feel safe, when everything else doesn't. A security blanket of sorts. I could do with one myself. They look really good on you, Ryder."

It wouldn't matter if they made her look like the monster she probably is, but Blane's words are kind of sweet, and she returns his smile.

"So, how are we doing? How much further to go," Blane asks.

A heavy impact shudders against the right side of the cabin, sending the craft into a spin.

"Brace, brace," the Commandant yells, as though anyone on board is doing anything different.

Ryder clings to the harness as the world spins around her. Alarms erupt on the control panel, alerting them to what everyone knows all too well. They are going down. Her stomach lurches to the back of her mouth, and the force of the spin presses her back against her seat.

Hold on, Ry.

But she shouldn't just be holding on, she should be doing something. Ryder tries to focus in on the elthar, but the speed of the spin makes it near impossible.

An explosion fills the air beyond the front windows of the cabin. The craft slides through it, and everyone is dabbled with white and gold light.

"Hold on." The Commandant's voice is impressively calm. "I'm taking us down."

There are approximately ten seconds before her declaration and the actual act. Set-down is violent, a thump against the ground that jars all the way up Ryder's spine. Her teeth clack, snipping the edge of her tongue. The warmth of blood in her mouth quick to follow.

The craft slides, still rotating but much slower now, and they skim along an uneven surface that pounds against the outside of the craft.

"Get ready to evacuate," the Commandant shouts.

The craft shudders to a halt. Ryder's head slams against the back of her chair, the shock of it leaving her gasping.

"Get out, get out." The Commandant has already followed her own orders, out of her seat and reaching for the panel to open the doorway. "They will be on us in moments. Go, go!"

Blane is the most dazed of them all, barely conscious. His hands trying and failing to find the release on his harness, swatting at the metal like it's covered in flies. The Commandant curses, the untranslatable words full of frustration, but she hurries to Blane's side, releasing his harness. Dragging him to his feet and hunching to accommodate her height in the low cabin. The entranceway retracts, and the heat thunders in.

"Go, Ryder," the Commandant shouts.

Ryder leaps clear, feet sinking beneath a layer of fine pebbles – speckled red and white, dulled by the anvel.

"Where do we go?"

They are in the middle of a vast, flat expanse of land. A desert devoid of anything to hide behind. The anvel allows her to see the horrible truth – there is nothing for miles and miles in every direction.

A high-pitched scream comes from a distance.

Need to move, now, Ry.

"To where?" Ryder cries.

"This is the Galian Span, there's nowhere to go. We must fight. Can you do something?" The Commandant handles Blane like he's no heavier than a rag doll. Dragging him along as she guides them all away from the craft. She brandishes a weapon in her right hand. Circular, with a grip for the hand. Like a killer frisbee. "This will only do minimal damage."

"Do something?"

"What you did back there, when you destroyed the Siros Bexsron. Can you do that again?"

"It's not that easy… I don't… I can't just…" Ryder's words back up against one another, mushing them together. There are no trees here to siphon energy from, no sign of life save for Blane and the Commandant. "It's too dangerous."

And there's no butterflies. There has to be butterflies. But her belly is a void.

"Ryder, that craft that brought us down, was a Caleax, a Zentai craft. We survived the Baershard, they will not allow us to survive this."

Ryder wraps her hand around her wrist, the elthar carries a dull green glow. Could she carry both the Commandant and Blane? But even if that is possible, where would they go?

The craft bears down on them. Crystal clear in the anvel lenses. The Caleax is a compact ship, triangular like the Baershard but far smaller. Soaring low to the ground.

Every muscle tenses, and finally movement stirs at Ryder's core. The elthar ignites, emerald green light reflecting against the red and white pebbled surface, flowing up over her lower arms. The heat of it filling her veins. She is as light as air.

You can do this, Ry. I'll do what I can.

Sophie! What are you doing?

"Act now, Ryder. Or it will be too late." The Commandant opens fire on the approaching vessel, but the pulses of silver fall far short, and the craft doesn't slow.

All at once, their own shattered vessel shifts, rocking as though something pushes against it.

Sophie?

I'm not strong enough, Ry. Her voice is heavy with frustration.

The Caleax is almost upon them, lights like narrowed cat's eyes moving in fast.

"Give me your hand," Ryder reaches for the Commandant. But she thrusts the semi-conscious Blane into Ryder's arms.

"Just one more shot." The Commandant takes her time aiming. The craft pierces the heated air, an enormous bullet aimed right at them. The Zentai craft fires. The Commandant does the same but it's such an uneven match it would be laughable, if they weren't all about to be fried.

Ryder!

The crashed vessel lifts onto its side, like a cumbersome over-baked potato. Taking the full force of the Zentai blast. Exploding into a thousand tangled pieces of metal. The blast throws Ryder onto her back, Blane landing hard at her side.

Soph, was that you? If it was, she's not taking credit for it. Ryder staggers to her knees, lifting Blane with all the ease the elthar gives her.

"Oh no," Ryder breathes.

The Zentai craft soars in a wide circle, angling back in on them from the other side of the silver-flame engulfed wreckage.

The Commandant races in front of Ryder and Blane. Feet braced, she fires round after round. None of them even hint at touching at the craft. She hollers, a guttural war cry that makes

Ryder's hair stand on end. Brandishing the circular device at the sky. She's out of ammunition.

The butterflies stir into madness. Ryder tugs the anvel from her face. Blane's aura drifts around the edges of his body. Wisps of it already moving towards her. What choice does she have?

"I'm so sorry," Ryder grips him tight. She exhales, and the butterflies dance their way up her spine, clawing up her ribs.

"Move!" The Commandant dives towards Ryder. "It's coming down on top of us."

The Zentai craft is down, its pointed nose piercing a scar through the pebbled ground. Moving is not an option. It will be on them before Ryder can gather Blane up.

"Get behind me," she shouts at the Commandant, who obeys her like she is the military general, and not a terrified kid from Tasmania. Ryder raises both hands. The elthar spills from her fingertips. Forming a shield. One wide enough to protect them all. Her fingers blaze, her joints ache like she's run two marathons. And the craft slides closer. But slower, and slower. Until there is no movement at all. The emerald shield vibrates, a transference of the trembling of Ryder's body. In the chaos the butterflies have sunk deep again. She's not sure how long she kneels there, arms raised, but when the Commandant touches her hand to Ryder's shoulder she jumps.

"What happened?" Ryder's dry tongue feels too big for her mouth.

"We survived. Thanks to you, and some very timely backup." The Commandant leans to one side and points an overly long index finger. Ryder blinks, not sure if she's still on some weird high from the stress of nearly being blown apart. Because if she's not losing her mind then it appears that a miniature submarine has just jettisoned up from beneath the pebbled ground.

The Commandant rises to her feet. "The Crown have come to us."

Chapter 26

Olessia

Olessia can barely bring herself to look at Christian. His appearance has been vastly compromised: hollowed cheeks, hair that has grown greasy with lack of cleansing, a haunted look in his eyes.

She takes her hands from his head. His trembling evident no matter how firmly she grasped him.

"Do you still harbour pain?" she asks, softly.

A tear runs from his eye, snaking its way down his cheek. "No. Thank you."

She presses her lips at his thanks. Olessia is to blame for the torment he endures now. He should not thank her. The Blackwall is cracking, splintering within his mind. She had not practiced on less robust minds, such as the humans. Such as Christian's. Her skills leave much to be desired. Olessia has repaired what she can, pushing his memories of Ryder back down behind the barrier.

"That is enough for now." Sen-Bay's voice is gentle but his hand firm upon Olessia's shoulder.

She nods, and the Yentern escorts Christian a short distance away. She suspects he would prefer to remove Christian from her presence entirely.

Christian is not the boy she remembers from that darkened house, Clarendon. When she stepped from that slipstream, using the memory she had stolen from Aresh, Olessia had no idea the consequences that would arise from her decision to flee Siros. Flee Kinna Brey.

Olessia thought of nothing beyond her own overwhelming desire to flee her life as heir to the Presiderline. Reinvent herself in a place that did not know her. Or fear her. She was a fool to pursue such an impossibility. Sebastien would not hesitate to agree with her summary of self. Olessia cradles her arms around her waist. Never would she have thought it possible to miss her guardian's dour companionship this much.

"Olessia? Is all well?" Sentinel Teler is an imposing presence. One that should offer security, and some comfort. In the past his aid and guidance has done just that. But Olessia finds little comfort now.

"Well? No. Very little is well." She lowers her voice. "I fear the damage I may have caused Christian. The Blackwall should not have splintered in this way."

"You were hardly in a position to proceed with caution at the time you implemented it," Teler says, his deep voice firm with certainty. "And though I understand you care for the human, we are faced with extreme circumstances. The challenges are great. And he is not—"

Olessia glares at him. "Consider your words, carefully Teler." Not important. That is what the Sentinel intends to say. "I am grateful beyond measure for your intervention. For all that you have done to enable my freedom, and I do not doubt your loyalty to the Laudine, but do not decide for me what is of importance."

Teler gives her a slow nod. "Of course, Laudess."

"What now?" Olessia says. "I am free but the Laudine is still missing, and my father's patrols march on the Zentai border as we huddle here beneath this lick of rock. Was there a plan beyond destroying the Collective?" Far too sharp, far too arrogant, but Olessia's uncertainty over Christian has her rattled. She peers over Teler's shoulder, searching for the other member of their small squad. The veiled figure who ran to Teler when he and Olessia arrived. Her words garbled by distress, but Olessia heard enough to know Sirosian was not her natural language. Olessia has not seen them since.

"Your companion, where have they gone?"

"Collecting nourishment."

No small task in this environment, which to Olessia's eye looks to harbour nothing more than rock and gree. "From where do they hail? They are not from Siros."

She is almost certain of their origin but wishes to hear it from the Sentinel.

Teler fiddles with the cuff of his heavy jacket. "She is human. Evelyn has been a part of the Collective for quite some time now. Aside from the occasion when she escaped."

"Escaped?" Olessia is impressed.

"Yes." He considers for a moment, then continues. "The Laudine had a particular attachment to this human. For reasons she never divulged to me. But I believe it was when Aresh learned Evelyn was a part of the Collective that she truly decided to put a stop to the Presider's practice. Aresh herself was unaware of the orders her Traverse crew were under to gather species. When she learned of it, she did what she could to grant freedom to some of those imprisoned. Evelyn was one of them. But there were problems, and she was recaptured. I have done what I can to make her comfortable. As the Laudine requested. Others though, remain free to this day."

"Did the Laudine never try again to free the prisoners?"

Teler frowns. "It would be a mammoth task to return them all to their realms, and the Laudine thought their living conditions adequate, aside from the Gatherings of course. So she focused on ensuring no new residents were added to the Collective. I believe she planned to try and give Evelyn her freedom again, several visn after she had been recaptured. But something happened..." he scratches absently at his arm, his nails rasping the rough material. "Her fervour to release the woman seemed to fade. She told me it was best Evelyn remained in the Collective, but she would not elaborate on why. I have reason to believe the Laudine imposed a Blackwall on the woman."

The crackling of stones underfoot reaches them. Someone walking in the gully below.

"She approaches," he whispers. "Say nothing of our conversation."

The veiled figure appears in the shallow gully beneath their sheltering wave of rock. Pulling herself up the short incline with admirable dexterity. Teler moves to the edge and reaches for her. Olessia's brow lifts. The Sentinel's stern expression softens as he leans down to take her much smaller hand in his. Pulling her up into the recess, one arm wrapped around her shoulders. An arm that does not fall away even when the woman is clearly stable on her own two feet. Olessia watches him smile down at her and cannot help but do the same. This is not the Sentinel Teler she recalls, the demanding trainer who shouted till Olessia's ears rang, the relentless teacher who instructed her into exhaustion.

"Evelyn, how did you fare?" The lightness in his tone confirms Olessia's suspicions. The hardened Sentinel is quite enamoured.

The woman lifts her veil, wiping her hand across a sweat-soaked face. The amused smile falls from Olessia's lips. This is the woman she saw at the Collective. The one who so reminded her of Ryder. The shade and wideness of the eyes, the curve of the jawbone. Olessia's pulse races. She is about to step closer, when another figure clambers up incline, pushing themselves easily up onto the wind-smoothed rock.

"Teler, look out!" Olessia rushes forward, the elthar that now sits in wide cuffs around her wrists, igniting. Flaring over her forearms.

"No, no, Laudess." The woman, veil lowered, steps in front of her. "They are allies."

Olessia draws herself up, indignant at being halted. A short-lived state. Over Evelyn's shoulder, the new arrival draws back the hood on their coat. And Olessia takes a step back.

"Maher?"

He wears none of the ludicrous costuming from their first encounter. Clad in all dark material, the multiple layers favoured by the Yenterns.

"Laudess. I am pleased to see you so clearly alive." He appears to mean what he says, his eyes solemn, some relief evident in the shift of his body weight.

"How are you here?" Olessia says.

Evelyn answers. "Because of this." She holds up a piece no larger than the elthar brooch Olessia was given. It catches the relentless light, shimmering as blue as Olessia's elthar. "Aresh gave it to me a very long time ago. Told me that if I was in danger, then I should use it and help would come. Someone I could trust, would come. I wasn't even sure it would still work, I've had it that long. And it was only to be used in the direst of circumstances. But Teler and I agreed I should at least try." She nods towards him. He's watching her with barely concealed adoration. "Because this all feels pretty dire."

"So, here we are." Maher spreads his arms. "At least, half of us. My brother refused to set foot here until he had monitored the perimeter. Ever the serious guardian."

They are allies. Evelyn's words when Maher appeared.

Olessia takes a step forward. "Sebastien? He's here?"

"With some protest, yes," Maher says.

Olessia rushes past the huddled group, her caution evaporating with a ferocity that takes her as much by surprise as it seems to do Maher and Teler.

"Olessia," Teler cries. "Where are you going? Stay within the Rachmeed barrier."

He moves to try and stop her, but Evelyn stays him with a murmur.

Sebastien. Where are you?

Olessia has sense enough not to go shouting inside the echoey funnels of curved rock, but a mindreach is probably equally unwise.

Sebastien?

When a figure swings from the overhead lip of rock up ahead Olessia doesn't break stride. Sebastien executes a steady landing upon the rock platform. And marches towards her. The same purposeful stride that has matched hers for more visn than she can recall. They both halt, a few short paces from one another.

"Olessia." His voice catches. Sebastien abandons his statue-like stance and rushes towards her. Enveloping her in his arms. Olessia sucks in a breath. In all their visn spent together, they have never shared such an intimacy. Olessia's arms raise, returning the embrace. They touch each other lightly. Cautiously. And in the foreignness of the moment, an absurd thought comes to Olessia. One that she voices.

"I think the humans would say we are doing it wrong."

Sebastien laughs. A wonderful, guttural sound that plays against the rock. She has never heard such laughter from him before. They release one another in unison.

"She was right. You are alive." Sebastien pushes his loose hair behind his ears. Wounds streak his skin, a gash at his cheek, several more along his neck. A darkening of his skin beneath his chin. Olessia's own thoughts darken.

"I am. But Sebastien, if you are here… where are they? Where are Ryder and Sophie?"

His gaze shifts away from her, fingers digging into the side of his leg.

Olessia's pulses race with manic abandon. The Beckoning unfurls itself from deep down, sniffing at her distress. "Sebastien?"

He raises his eyes to meet hers. Grey swirls move around a dark centre.

"The Zentai attacked us, in Hobart. Ryder did what she could, as did I. But it was not enough." A jawline muscle twinges. "Sophie is gone, Olessia. There was nothing I could do."

The forceful blow of his words resonates through her. Even the Beckoning shudders. "And Ryder?"

It is as though Siros holds its breath. No chitter of eegarn, no rise and fall of the wind.

"We were transported aboard a Baershard. It crashed landed when we cleared the river in Zentai. We survived, and that is when we located Maher. But…" Sebastien falters. "But Ryder and I became separated."

"How? How did this happen?" The words crawl out of her, flat with restraint.

Sebastien's expression has returned to one far more familiar. Unreadable.

"We were hidden with Maher. I was told of your… demise and required some time. To myself. But Ryder…" He clenches his jaw, pressing a balled-up fist against his thigh. "Ryder attempted to follow me. That girl never, ever does as she must." He gathers himself. "Bexsron attacked the cluster, I believe they still searched for survivors from the Baershard. I made my way back to Maher's quarters, unaware Ryder had followed me to begin with. If I had any notion that she remained out in the cluster…"

Olessia can offer no solace. She hangs in her airless world. Her body light. The only weight down at her core, where the Beckoning is ballooning with every word Sebastien speaks. "Does she live?"

Sebastien's expression is at once all too readable. Anguish, taking hold of every pore. "We searched and found no trace of her. Some of the survivors from the Baershard must have retained their weapons because both the Bexsron were utterly destroyed. The cluster was decimated."

The Beckoning flows, touching at nerve endings. Olessia braces, anticipating the harshness that would normally follow. Not desiring to stop it. But the beast is gentle. Almost soothing. Olessia touches a hand to her belly.

"My brother tortures himself. But that girl is still alive." Maher has managed to get right alongside Olessia without her noticing. "She wore an anvel when she went to search for Sebastien. I can't afford to lose track of such useful items, and some of my colleagues tend to be remiss in recalling where they have left things. We can activate a tracing signal on all our devices, so long as they are within a reasonable distance. I did so, not long after we detected the Bexsron. The explosions came and that signal still existed. Sebastien and I followed it, but it began to lead in an unexpected direction." He points skyward. "Then it disappeared. She had moved out of range. There was no trace of her anywhere near the Bexsron wreckage. I do not believe she was a casualty."

The Beckoning flutters, spreading out through Olessia's body like a swarm of iines. Soothing, yet again. Or is it something else? Olessia touches a hand to the base of her throat. Does the beast try to reassure her?

Olessia finds Sebastien. "Nor do I."

He gives her a grim-faced nod, and it's impossible to tell what he believes.

Maher clears his throat. "So you feel it too, Laudess? Like Ryder did for you? She was certain you were alive." He glances at Sebastien. "And she was right." Sebastien's lifelong anger at his brother is well known, but there are no signs here that it is reciprocated. Maher seeks to offer solace.

"Ryder believed I was alive?" Olessia says. The Beckoning still thrums. A patterned beat that is unfamiliar, but far from unpleasant. "What gave her such certainty?"

"I'm unsure. There is much about that girl I don't understand." Maher's grin lop-sides. Lucas's face fills Olessia's thoughts. She recoils from the image of his same uneven grin.

"Olessia?" Sebastien eyes her.

"I'm fine." She waves off the concern.

Olessia paces back towards the others. Sebastien matches her, stride for stride. Shadows hug the back of the rock curve, where Christian still lies sleeping. Sen-Bay awake and watchful at his side.

Teler and Evelyn have moved a short distance in the opposite direction, still beneath the barrier, but about as close to it as they can manage it. Both of them stand at an angle that does not forewarn them of Olessia's approach. Teler lifts the veil, touching at the back of Evelyn's head. The entire head covering comes free. And she tosses her head, uttering a sigh of relief.

Olessia and Sebastien stop mid-stride, almost in unison. Sebastien curses under his breath.

"Oh," Maher says.

Teler stoops to place the headpiece on the ground, and Evelyn catches sight of them. "Is everything all right?"

"You look like someone we know," Sebastien says quietly,

The woman tilts her head. "I do? Do you think it has something to do with why Christian can't seem to look at me? Who do I look like?"

Sentinel Teler takes her hand. "They're mistaken—"

"A human girl I met on Earth. Her name was Ryder," Olessia says, watching for the slightest sign of recognition but Sentinel Teler's reaction is far more obtuse than Evelyn's.

He glares at Olessia, giving a subtle shake of his head. "She doesn't know her. Evelyn has been away from Earth a very long time."

"Would you like to return there, Evelyn?" Maher speaks up.

Evelyn shakes her head in a very firm back and forth. "No. Not possible. I can't go back."

Olessia glances at Sebastien, his frown is as deep as hers. "Why not?" he demands.

"Enough with the interrogation, there are more pressing matters to discuss," Teler continues to glare, but Olessia is far more interested in Evelyn's reaction.

The woman presses her fingers to her jawbone, as though something pains her.

"I just… I cannot go back. That world is no longer mine. And it is…" She winces, pressing her free hand to her forehead. "It is not safe for me to do so. This is my home. Isn't it?" She looks up at Sentinel Teler, and he brushes a strand of hair off her face. There's a sadness in his expression that seems out of place.

"This is your home," he says quietly. "Now, would you begin food preparations, I will assist you momentarily. You should put this back on." He hands her the headpiece, and she accepts it readily.

"Of course. But don't expect anything too amazing to eat. I've got nothing to work with here." The shadows lift from Evelyn's face, and she heads back beneath the curl of rock with a lazy wave of her hand.

Sentinel Teler waits until she is lost in the shadow before he speaks. "Now is not the time to raise this. And it will do nothing but cause her unnecessary distress. Aresh is far more adept at Blackwall than you, Olessia. Evelyn's memories of her child are long buried. And no one but the Laudine can retrieve them."

"So it is no illusion then? This is Ryder's mother?"

"I did not know the child's name, but Aresh did this to keep that child safe. Erased the memory of her." Teler glances over his shoulder and edges closer to Olessia. "Isn't that exactly what you did with the boy?"

"But for so many years?" Olessia has never known a mother, certainly never experienced the bond that must exist between mother and child. But since the moment she learned Aresh was missing, an ache has not left her. A desperation that drives her. To imagine Ryder feeling this for so long causes Olessia a discomfort like she has never known.

"Evelyn agreed," Teler says. "She does not remember doing so, but she did not go into this Blackwall unwillingly. Aresh received her blessing before blocking those memories. It is true that Evelyn fought to return to her child. But the situation changed, I don't know what occurred, all I know is that this was deemed the right path to take, to keep that child safe."

"Well, she's not safe now," Sebastien says, hard and fast.

Olessia stares down at her hands. "We must find Aresh, for far too many reasons. And we must do it quickly. Do we have any idea of where she may be?"

"Megnastin," Maher says, dropping the single word as though it is the anchor they can cling too. "In Aresh's last mindreach with me she repeated that word several times. It was one of the few I could comprehend, the contact was fragile, distorted."

Olessia raises her head. "Megnastin? Is that a person, a place?"

Sentinel Teler steps up close to Maher. "The Laudine used that word?"

"Yes. Among others, but I could not make them out. She had not used a direct mindreach with me for many, many visn. Not since —" His gaze darts to Sebastien. "Not since I was first banished. Do you know what it is?"

Teler nods. "Megnastin is a place within the Arlion Xhentex," he says, face grave. "An anomaly within an anomaly. A point that has long been of interest to the Presider. He seeks to dominate the rivers and slipstreams and Sirosian capabilities within them. Megnastin is rumoured to be a testing ground. I believe, we have located the Laudine."

Chapter 27

Ryder

Ryder pulls the goggles free, letting them hang around her neck. She stares at the cylindrical vessel that rests on the desert surface.

"The Crown is in that thing?"

Twin prongs jut from the front of the vehicle, cogs still spinning. Presumably the digging tools it uses to burrow through the ground. The nose is equally as sharp and pointed, and constructed from a matte black material. Unlike the rest of the cylinder, which appears to be a giant mirror. Ryder stares at her reflection; she looks exactly as she feels. Like someone who's just fought for their life. The still-burning wreckage illuminates her bird-nest hair and smudged face. The craft is no bigger than the average sized car on Earth, but way quieter. In fact, there doesn't seem to be any sound at all coming from the vehicle.

It is quite the entrance. Ryder will give the Crown that much.

Soph? What do I do? You getting any vibes?

But there is no reply. Maybe the effort of throwing alien spaceships has thrown her. Ryder grips Blane's arm tighter, trying to decide what to do.

"Are you sure about this? I can get us out of here." Ryder figures there is enough adrenaline pumping right now to enable her to lift a school bus, let alone Blane and the Commandant.

"I am sure," the Commandant says. "The Crown heeded my distress signal."

Ryder takes in the smoldering vehicles. "And what about them? Did they heed it too?"

But the Commandant doesn't reply.

Ryder swallows against a dry throat, adjusting Blane's limp body against her side, still barely registering his weight with the elthar's still glowing.

A clunk and hiss precede the lifting of the front upper section of the vehicle. Part of the tip slides back, revealing an interior with just one visible passenger. Clad in what appears to be black leather of some sort, with lighter stitching along all the seams, the figure leans forward, like they are pressing against the body of a motorcycle within the confines of the craft. Their helmet is as tinted and reflective as the exterior, but much more fitted to the wearer's head than any helmet Ryder's seen, almost like a metallic balaclava.

The Commandant edges closer to the craft.

"Oh man, I hope that's a good idea," Ryder mutters.

Blane groans. "What's going on? Where are we?"

"Your guess is as good as mine," Ryder says. She eases him to the ground. "Take it slow, you had a bad knock to the head. And we've got company."

Rubbing at the back of his head, Blane lifts bleary eyes that soon land on the craft, then widen almost comically. "Who is that?"

"Hopefully the good guys."

The pilot sits up, and presses at the side of their helmet. The head covering folds away, pieces moving back against one another like origami, until only a slender section remains at the back of their head. The pilot is young. Perhaps not much older than Sebastien. Ryder winces. The guilt of being here without him drags heavy at shoulders. Knowing the Presider wants him dead, is an even weightier burden to bear. She clings to the one thing that provides a hint of comfort. Maher had a tracking device on Sebastien. He had a way to find his brother.

Ryder is distracted from her thoughts by the Commandant's sudden movement, a touch of one knee to the ground, and a hand to her forehead. She rises just as quickly, but if Ryder were to take a guess at what just happened, she'd say the soldier had just done a weird version of a curtsy. The young man lifts his hand, and traces a symbol in the air, but the movement is way too quick to work out the design. It seems to be the Commandant's cue to move again though, and she starts talking to him. Too faint for Ryder to catch. It's a brief conversation, with both the Commandant and the young man beckoning Ryder closer.

"Quickly, into the Taer-lon," the Commandant calls.

What's the alternative? Being left here in the broad, dark desert. Ryder takes a deep breath, gathers Blane against her, and heads towards the craft.

As she nears, it becomes clear that the pilot is younger than Sebastien – maybe mid-teens, just like her. But, unlike Ryder, he has the characteristic lack of ears. Strange how such a simple thing can be so unsettling. For the first time too though, Ryder finds a similarity between this Zentai and Lucas. This guy not only has a trace of auburn in his short-cropped sandy hair, there are a smattering of freckles visible on his pale skin. Just his cheeks though, his button nose is clear of any marks. There's a hint of the androgyny many of the Zentai have; full pouty lips topped with a very noticeable cupid's bow, and a fine chin that offsets his heavier cheekbones and brow. He's the first person she's seen so far that doesn't have striking eye colour; a good old reliable brown. Much like hers.

Ryder starts, realising he's scrutinising her every bit as much.

"Back there." The Commandant directs Ryder into the narrow cabin, where a couple more 'lay down' seats are positioned behind the pilot. "Quickly." She helps Blane throw a leg over one of the first padded seats, a single right behind the pilot, lifting his heels and settling his toes into indents either side of the burgundy-coloured cushioning. "Place your hands here."

She gestures to the front of the seat where two impressions of hand prints jut from each side. But Blane is apparently too slow to follow orders. The Commandant mutters under her breath, grabbing his hands and slamming them into the moulds. The moment his fingers make contact, a curve of metal slides around his midriff, locking him in place.

"Ryder, take your seat," the Commandant says.

The pilot has already taken his, without saying a word. Head once again hidden the intriguing helmet.

"Do we need to wear one of those?" Ryder jabs a finger towards the pilot's head.

"No. Quickly."

The external panelling slides down, sealing the cabin.

Ryder swings her leg over the very back seat. She adjusts the goggles so they sit at the back of her neck, and then lays forward. Her body sinks into the cushioning the same way it does at home on her memory-foam mattress, though this is, admittedly, way more comfortable than that expensive queen size. It's a little disconcerting to lift her feet off the floor and dig her toes into the grooves, like being on a strange surfboard in an ocean she doesn't trust. She places her hands against the moulds, just as the Commandant instructed Blane. It's cold as metal, but there's a problem. Her fingers are too long.

"Hey, my hands don't fit in this thing."

"Give it a moment," the Commandant says with a sigh.

A low buzz tingles through Ryder's fingers. The material beneath her hands softens, remoulds itself, shaping around her hand in a perfect copy.

"Oh." She tries to pull her hands away but it takes greater effort than it should, as though her skin is magnetised to the mould. "What is this?"

"A way to ensure your safety." The Commandant takes her position on the last empty seat, parallel to Ryder. "You will be held in place quite securely, which is vital for this type of journey."

Before she can ask what that means exactly, a low humming fills the cabin. Loudest of all from overhead. Ryder glances up, no easy task from her current angle. But the sight distracts her from the neck crick. The roof is shifting down. No. Not just the roof. The entire cabin seems to be retracting. The space where they edged past the pilot seat to reach their own, could barely accommodate a child now.

"Is this supposed to happen?" Blane's shoulders lift as he tries to tug his hands free.

"Hold still. Yes." The Commandant sounds mildly amused.

The retracting continues until the curved walls of the cabin sit right up against Ryder and the Commandant.

The pilot utters his first words. "This will feel quite strange I imagine. For first timers."

The ship tilts forward, and Ryder's grip tightens. But it's not necessary. Despite the angle, her body doesn't move an inch.

"You are fine." The Commandant watches her.

"I don't feel fine," Ryder says. She might not feel like she's about to fall out of her seat, but the blood-rush to her head is getting painful behind her eyes.

"We will level out momentarily." The pilot's voice is deeper, older, than he looks. "The Taer are not deep at this point."

"The what?"

The craft readjusts, settling back into a horizontal position. Ryder cranes her head, trying to see through the panelling but there is only her own reflection staring back at her.

"The Taer are the underground channels that criss-cross Zentai," the Commandant says. "J'salax is an accomplished pilot, we are in safe hands."

Ryder eases her tight grip on the handles. "And is… Jax, the Crown?"

"No. But the Regal J'salax's presence honours us."

"Nire And I are self-sames," the regal J'salax says. "All unions of the Crown produce dual lifeforms we call self-sames."

"Twins?" Blane says.

"Self-sames," J'salax returns, with the mildest hint of annoyance.

Blane casts Ryder a glance in the reflective walls. Ryder mouths, twins.

"Commandant, Nire awaits you with much impatience at Icewynn. The Presider moves already at the border."

"Yes. I am aware of that." The Commandant glances at Ryder. "We only just managed to out manoeuvre his forces ourselves. But I fear threats come from much closer to our core. Those were

Zentai Legions that attempted to destroy us back there, as you would know."

"Legions under the direction of the Reigner."

There is a lengthy silence, and the Commandant eyes do not lift from the cushioning before her. "It would seem so, yes."

Ryder bites at the corner of her lip, careful to avoid the cut. If the Commandant's assumptions about the Reigner having gone rogue are wrong, and that the Crown is in on the party too, then they may have just landed themselves in a whole lot of inescapable trouble.

"Nire's only regret is not heeding your warning sooner," J'salax says.

"I would not have expected her to rely on my word alone. The Crown is far more astute than that. But does she formulate a plan to contain this threat?"

"At this moment, we have decided on compliance. Act in agreement with the Reigner's calls for war while we set about determining who is upon whose side. This seems to be a conflict with many complicated layers. And humans appear to be an intrinsic part of it. That Legion that set upon you had actually just returned from the Iondar Realm. They were headed for Fallwyn and were redirected by the Reigner when he learned their location as so close to yours. You were attacked by a faction of your own contingent. The Legion you had directed to remain behind on Earth and search for the Zentai boy."

"Betrayed by my own Legion." The Commandant bites down on each word.

The craft tilts again, taking them deeper, but this time Ryder doesn't grip quite so hard or dig her knees in like she's on the back of a diving whale. And she's none the worse for it. Aside from the pressure behind the eyes, her body doesn't shift.

"Before you consider them harshly, Commandant, you should know the Legion were advised you had perished under a Siros barrage, and that an escape pod from your Baershard had been hijacked by the Laudess's Guardian with the intent of attacking Icewyn and killing the Crown. They were deceived. But then the Crown received your signal, and we realised—"

"Did they find him?" Ryder throws herself into the conversation. "Did they find Lucas? The Zentai boy."

The pilot lifts his head, using the roof's reflection to look her way but Ryder can't see his face behind the helmet's own reflective panelling. "That is what we believe. But the Reigner has succeeded in isolating the Crown." He resettles. Eyes forward. "Information is getting more difficult to come by, and those truly loyal to Nire are not as numerous as they once were. The Reigner has been very successful in using an age-old fear of the Sirosian's to further his own agenda. Many in the Vex have been persuaded to his chosen warpath. What should we know about this… Lucas?"

Ryder's heart is thundering. "Just that… he's a friend. My friend. And if anything happens to him—"

J'salax laughs. A light and high sound. "You will what, human? What could you possibly do? I'm very interested to understand why you are here, in the midst of this at all. You and your friend seem oddly out of place, yet the Commandant has gone to some lengths to keep you alive."

The Commandant opens her mouth, then just a quickly shuts it. When Ryder glances at her, she moves her head in a barely perceptible shake. So, it seems as 'honoured' as she may be to getting picked up by the queen's brother, the Commandant is hesitant to give too much away. Ryder gets it. She needs to shut up.

But now it's not only Sebastien, Christian and Olessia on Ryder's list of people to be worried about. It's Lucas as well now. Lucas who is supposed to be safe back on Earth. Hidden away with C-21. Instead, he's in the hands of the Reigner who is almost certainly working with the Presider. And neither of them are going to like the fact the real heir to the Reigner's, what… throne? High-chair? Whatever it is, is back. None of them are going to want to see a ghost. And that's exactly what Lucas is.

Ryder shifts, setting her shoulders back. "You have to stop the Reigner getting hold of Lucas. You have to get him out of there."

The craft shudders. Distracting J'salax for a moment. Their directions alters, taking them right. And the shuddering stops.

"Why would we wish to do that?" he says.

"I can't tell you."

"That's not a sufficient answer."

Ryder's skin heats with anger, and fear. "I have information you need, but I won't give it to you unless you promise—"

"Ryder," the Commandant hisses.

Ryder shrugs off her warning. "I have information the Crown is going to want. And I can't give it to anyone but her."

J'salax is slow to reply. Sweat beads against Ryder's top lip, and the cramped quarters seem to press in harder.

"There is undeniable proof now that the Reigner shares an alliance with the Presider. We both have much to share with the Crown and her true allies. But the human girl is under great duress, Regal," the Commandant says. "I assure you, she does not pose a threat to the Crown. In fact, I believe Ryder will be of great advantage to us."

"The girl is certainly forthright." J'salax seems unphased by her attempt at blackmail. The craft tilts yet again. This time though, they are headed up.

Ryder holds her breath, sending out one last mindreach, hoping Sophie might be there to talk her down from a really dumb idea.

Sophie? I think I need to tell them. Now. Otherwise it will be too late for Lucas.

But her friend is infuriatingly, and not a little bit concerningly, quiet.

She exhales. "Lucas is more proof. He was hidden on Earth for a reason." She screws up her face, giving herself a second to reconsider, then, "Lucas's father was Reigner when Aresh was almost killed at the Treaty Signing." The words roll from her like this story has been a part of her whole life. "She took him to Earth. To keep him safe. I think, even way back then, she knew it was dangerous…"

The Commandant's stare bores a hole in the side of Ryder's head. J'salax sits upright, bracing his hands against the cushioned seat so he can turn to face her. The helmet opens over his face. "The Zentai boy is Reigner Bladen's child? There have always been rumours of this. That the child was never located."

"Because Aresh protected him," Ryder says. "She didn't believe his father was behind the attack on her. And the way things are looking right now, she was right."

The gaze J'salax is directing at her is intense but she doesn't shift. The flare of anger is not meant for her. She gets that, but she sure wouldn't like to be on the receiving end of it.

"And with no surviving heir, Reigner Zetem was installed in the role," the Commandant says, slowly. "You are suggesting that as far back as then, the Zetem and the Presider worked in unison."

Ryder shrugs. "Honestly? I don't know. Until a few weeks ago, I didn't know any of you guys existed, let alone who was at war with whom. But if the Presider is capable of making it look like his own daughter died to get what he wants, isn't it possible he was somehow behind that attack too? Made a deal with the Zetem guy, get rid of Aresh, then Zetem gets to play Reigner. Blame it all on a dead guy. And now the Presider has a big IOU in Zentai."

Blane is the first to make a sound. "Please tell me we are never meeting this Presider guy."

The hum of the engines, soft and unobtrusive until now, seems to lift.

"If we do," she says. "I have a few things I'd like to say him." She touches at the goggle straps around her neck, her exuberance fading. One man has managed to make such a mess of her life, and she's never even set eyes on him.

The craft shakes, there is an audible screech from somewhere outside the craft, and once again they are horizontal. The sudden stop jolts her against the cushioned seat, hard enough to take her breath.

"What you have to say to the Crown is far more important," J'salax says. "I welcome you, humans, to Icewynn."

The walls pull away, the narrowed cabin returning to something more spacious. The ceiling panel slides open. Whatever force held her in position, releases. Ryder sits up, rubbing at her shoulders and gazing up at what is the most incredible treehouse she has ever seen.

Chapter 28

Olessia

Dayfall came as they made their laborious advancement across the Desner Coniva, plunging the landscape into inky blackness. The Desner Coniva is a remote area of Siros that Olessia has never viewed in person. A missed opportunity, she sees now. They weave the garreson through the wave-rock formations rising out of the undulating landscape. Many of the structures are as shallow as the one they had sheltered in earlier, but others cut paths so deep down into the pixelated feshn that even the drone of the garreson engines are sucked into the depths as they pass over them. Olessia had been quick to judge her world devoid of any true natural beauty, but she was mistaken. This landscape, with its hue reminding her of sunsets on Earth, and stark majesty commanding the eye, is by far one of the most incredible sights she has witnessed.

Dayfall, with its lack of light, brings some advantage. People's faces are blurred by the shadows the moment they stray beyond the low light of the elthar. A fact she hopes may spare Christian unnecessary pain. She worked on his Blackwall again, after Sebastien's arrival but Sen-Bay allowed her only the barest amount of time before he was pulling Christian away. Insisting that further interference was harmful.

Olessia did not protest.

Though dayfall may offer Evelyn the chance to raise her veil and find the slight coolness darkness brought with it, she has remained veiled.

With the arrival of Maher and Sebastien came the arrival of two further garreson. Including the vehicle Sentinel Teler used to rescue Olessia, they are now furnished with three means of transport. Four, if elthar is to be included. Which, Sebastian, Maher and Teler all agree, should only be used under the strictest of measures. The energy signature is far too unique and pronounced for such a clandestine mission. It would alert their enemies.

Alert the Presider.

Olessia is seated with Maher for now. Her fingers wrapped so hard around the hollow of metal positioned behind the small of Maher's back, she wonders if she will be able to pry them free when the time comes. Sebastien moves ahead of the group, utilising his elthar at the lowest ebb so as not to draw unwanted attention. He's on patrol. Out of sight.

Again.

Olessia is surprised at just how that fact irritates her. The moment Sebastien appeared at the hideout, Olessia realised a part of her has been paralysed. Lost. Since they separated on Earth, she's longed for the brutal honesty and ease of familiarity they share. She and Sebastien are in a deeply connected partnership, one she failed to see the beauty in, every bit as much as she failed to see it in the Siros landscape.

Teler assures them all that he knows how to reach Megnastin, but with the Presider's troops already active near the Zentai border, they must take a meandering route to ensure safety and concealment. He is unsure how long it will take. Megnastin engulfs the farthermost and highest reaches of The Dovers, a section of territory named by the Presider in true inflammatory style, as The Claiming. Zentai controlled for generations, until the Presider altered that fact, the region is notorious for an unpredictable quaking of the land; a restless anomaly that at once pushes at the earth, forming odd pillars and mounds before swallowing them in pits the following day. The Zentai did not fight hard to retain the land.

"What do you know of Megnastin, aside from its volatility?" Olessia shifts to gain a more comfortable perch atop the garreson, her view blocked by Maher's broad back. He is a far sturdier specimen than his younger brother, even though the age difference between them is not so great. "I cannot understand the link between Aresh and this place."

"Nor I. It is a dangerously unpredictable area. The few that have been recorded as venturing into it have never been recovered. You said Dashel told you Aresh was alive?"

"Yes. For now, those were his exact words," Olessia says. "Though whether they hold truth or were simply intended to unsettle me, I am unsure."

"We shall believe that it is both." Maher rolls his shoulders, taking his hands off the pronged controls to shake them. They have been traveling for several liss, and everyone grows weary. "I recall this Claven, Dashel. At least I recall the way he spoke to my father when Aresh placed me in exile. I was not more than a child when I refused the position, and yet, I feel Dashel would have preferred to see me pitterned until there was nothing left to banish." He laughs; a mirthless sound.

Olessia shudders, recalling what she has heard of pitterning. A punishment so vile many of her certifiers refused to believe it existed at all, simply a story told to incite fear. Just like the flesh-eating tales of the Distant. But having been at Dashel's mercy and seen how far her own father will go to take what he desires, Olessia's not so certain she can discount pitterning as myth.

Maher continues, "I am unsure what link Megnastin has to the Laudine, but I would venture to say it does not bode well. The Laudine's strength is formidable, a fact the Presider knows. She spoke to me of the divide between her and Inel, how it had only widened over the visn." He pauses. "Olessia, Aresh has long held suspicion that Inel was behind the assassination attempt on her at the Treaty Signing, not the Crown as claimed. Even I was not convinced of it, but I see now. The Presider is capable of anything."

"Except holding Wendera," Sen-Bay angles his garreson in beside Olessia and Maher. "The Presider failed at that at least."

Olessia grips the handle tighter, a swirl of violet in her eyes. "No. He could not." She watches Christian, alert to any discomfort, but he sits pressed up close to the Yentern, his arms about Sen-Bay's waist. The speed of the garreson pushes his hair clear of his face. And his expression is thoughtful, and for once, not fearful or pained.

"Wendera?" Maher says.

"Before I knew who Olessia truly was," Sen-Bay says. "I believed her to be Wendera. A petulant girl with some ability, who did not abandon us as she could have."

Olessia stares down at the ceaseless flow of rock and pebbled ground. She *did* abandon them.

"Your departure was calculated for us, not against," Sen-Bay says, as though sensing her thoughts. "And you returned for us when we needed your assistance. Even when you must have known it would imperil you. I wish you to know, Laudess, that you have my loyalty. For what it is worth, I will remain at your side for as long as you will have me by it." He pats Christian's hand where it lies on his stomach. "Even if all you require is a kreketet for this human."

"What's a kreketet?" Christian asks.

Sen-Bay laughs. A throaty chortle that is dangerously contagious.

"Essentially a babysitter, for particularly helpless young," Olessia suppresses her smile. "Thank you, Sen-Bay. But I did not manage this on my own, and I will need all the assistance I can gather if there is to be any hope of finding, and freeing Aresh."

Teler and Evelyn lead the line of garreson, and the shadow that Olessia knows to be Teler twists. She supposes to look at her, though she cannot make out his eyes in the dark. "Well, I do not imagine the Presider ever considered the existence of a group such as this. Two traitors, two humans, a Yentern and a Guardian, united." She is certain he is smiling, it is there in his voice. "You bring me great pride, Laudess."

It is tempting to bask in the praise, let it warm her where portions of her have gone cold with fear, but Olessia moves on. "We are yet to do much more than destroy his Collective. Teler, do you have any idea how he and Dashel kept me from utilising the Beckoning? I was powerless when they took me."

"The Presider, for all his glaring faults, is a brilliant man," Evelyn answers in Teler's place. "And he has multiple universes of resources at his disposal for his research. He definitely has a thing for biological warfare. Using viruses as weapons."

Olessia lowers her head, though it's doubtful anyone could note her expression in the gloom. "I have heard such things. Aresh told me of the Traverses he launched for such a purpose."

Maher glides ahead of them. "He favoured the Iondar Realms at one point, did he not? The place where Earth is located?"

Olessia stares hard at his back. "Perhaps."

"He's not content with just controlling other species," Teler continues. "The Presider puts effort into learning to control the Beckoning, too. As Evelyn said, the Presider is no fool. He is very aware the new generations of the Presiderline grow ever stronger. And we see now he has prepared well to ensure his place as leader. He utilised a strain of meir he located in the Preffren-bey Realm to sedate the Beckoning within you. Of course any pathogen requires an antigen. One I managed to deliver to you, but in truth, the Presider had already ordered it be administered. The long-term effects of the meir are unknown, and despite what he has led everyone to believe, he himself does not want you dead."

Not yet, anyway.

They approach a particularly narrow funnel of rock, one whose curve touches almost to the ground. Teler doesn't hesitate, moving into the inky blackness with Evelyn. Maher edges the garreson to one side, instructing Sen-Bay to follow Teler first.

Maher and Olessia find themselves in momentary isolation. "We have a moment to speak of the girl, Ryder. Is there something about her that we should know?"

"We should not allow too much distance to grow between us and the others," Olessia says.

"No, you are right. Distance is a dangerous thing," Maher says, but makes no move to set the machine forward. They hover close to the fractured ground, dark with shadows now. If she so wanted, Olessia could jump down without injury. "Do not let it grow between us, Olessia. If we are to achieve our goal here, we must trust each other. We must know that no vital information has been withheld."

Would it serve Ryder now to tell her story? Or at least some of it? Aresh trusted this man. Should Olessia?

Maher raps his fingers on the controls, an easy rhythm that is oddly musical. "Olessia, the destruction in the cluster was substantial. And yet, Btet detected no trace of any Zentai craft that would be capable of downing two Bexsron so utterly."

Olessia's pulses run riot. "What are you suggesting?"

He shakes his head. "I do not know, myself. But is it possible that… Ryder had something to do with that?"

"A human girl?"

"Is she though? The Commandant saw fit to bring her to Zentai, along with Sebastien. What possible reason could there be for her to do such a thing? They had Sebastien, why did they take her too? And what puzzles me even more, is that my brother was with her, not you. His loyalty to you is something that Aresh has long admired, and been thankful for. If he was not at your side, it was for good reason. Beyond what he feels for the girl. My little brother is quite enamoured with her."

"Yes," Olessia whispers. "He is. And no. Emotion was not the reason for his presence at her side."

The humidity presses down, the relentless heat not shifting despite dayfall.

"I understand you may feel you have no reason to trust me, Olessia."

But in that, Maher is wrong. Aresh trusted him. And, in an odd way, made him the Guardian he'd never wished to be, and entrusting him with the lives of those she saved from the Collective.

Olessia's tongue brushes her lips before she speaks. "My father's Traverses did produce results. As Teler said. And Ryder is one of those." Maher remains still and silent, gazing at the darkness that has swallowed the others. "And you are right. There is reason to believe she may have caused that damage in the

Cluster. I truly hope she did. It would mean she certainly lives. And that she is strong. Stronger even than when I left her."

The Beckoning weaves a gentle pattern at her core.

"Aresh knew of Ryder?"

"More than you could imagine." Olessia stops short of telling him that Aresh's blood runs in Ryder's veins. "Aresh has done everything in her power to keep Ryder hidden. And safe. By going to Earth, I undid all she had done there. And I enabled my father to commence a war he has long dreamed of. There is much damage I must repair. Aresh cannot be gone. I need her. I cannot do this alone."

The last two sentences spring from her like wayward klix released from their cages. Olessia touches her wrist, where a vibration teases at the nerves there. Not the Beckoning, though it dances around her insides at a quickening pace.

"You are not alone, Laudess." Maher drives them forward, manoeuvring through the narrowed entrance with a deft tilt of the handles. "We will find them. Aresh and your friend."

She does not acknowledge his words with any of her own. That is impossible. A thickening in her throat prevents all but the barest whisper of air to pass. The speed of the garreson pulls her hair back from her face, the rushing air seeming to whisper at her. The low hum of the engine echoes against the encroaching walls, bouncing the whispers with it. The beast sends out pulses of energy, not yet uncomfortable, but threatening the possibility.

Olessia tilts her head back. Hopeful the breeze may dry the condensation that is dense upon her face.

Hey! Olessia!

The mindreach is a thunderous screech in her head. Startled, Olessia's hands jerk from the handle, just as Maher negotiates a sudden turn in the tunnel. Olessia tumbles backwards off the garreson, and flips head over heels into the darkness that consumes the tunnel behind them.

Chapter 29

Ryder

I cewynn is a treehouse. A really elaborate, incredibly constructed, treehouse resting in among the thick branches of enormous trees. Like, *really* enormous trees. Ryder slides from her seat, peering up through the open roof of the Taer-lon in wonder at the twisting, curving pillars around her. The largest – three in total – have trunks the size of a road tunnel, while others are big as drains for a capital city. Their texture is rough like brushed concrete, though this concrete is all the colours of seaglass, not a drab grey; one aquamarine, one a frost white, the other a subtle green, like it's been gift-wrapped at Tiffany's. The three giant trunks intertwine, rising higher than Ryder can tilt her neck to see, disappearing into the heavy darkness of the night.

The less impressive specimens create a barrier around this central formation. The ground is covered in a mossy plant, the same frosty white as one of the trunks, but speckled with flecks of crimson, as though someone has bled all across it.

"Holy…" Blane lets the rest slide, shading his eyes to peer up. "This is incredible."

"I suppose it is." J'salax jumps from the Taer-lon. Easily clearing the distance between the craft and solid ground. The craft floats on a pool of clear, syrupy liquid that doesn't ripple as the craft shifts with the momentum of J'salax's leap. "I grew up in Icewynn, so I'm rather bored with the view. The place is more of a prison than a home, if I'm honest. Especially now. Though I don't say as much to Nire. She takes any slight to Icewynn very personally."

The Commandant exits the craft, standing on the pointed nose, and propelling herself forward as though of a diving board. Ryder follows their lead. She measures the distance and jumps. Landing on the soft, cushy bank. Blane isn't quite so graceful and doesn't use quite enough force. Teetering on the edge, his right foot slides back into the pool. The liquid is even thicker than Ryder imagined, sucking at his shoe. Blane swears, hands flailing and Ryder hauls him further up the bank. But Blane's shoe isn't so lucky, claimed by the goop.

"Forget it," the Commandant says. She at least has waited for them. J'salax is already out of sight. "They will supply you with another."

Blane stares down at liquid, rubbing his soaked sock against the mossy ground. "I've got it on me… is it safe?"

"Safe enough." The Commandant follows after J'salax, apparently knowing exactly where he's gone because she makes a beeline for the Tiffany box-coloured trunk.

As they walk over the softly undulating surface, Ryder gets a better look at the 'trunks and branches'. They've got none of the randomness of natural trees, no knots and gnarls in the wood, no peeling bark like she's used to on the eucalypts back home. She taps a knuckle against one the size of a pool noodle. The clang of metal rings back at her. Nothing natural about these 'trees' at all.

The Commandant and J'salax are waiting for them, at the Tiffany tree. An enormous structure whose circumference could easily hold three buses side by side. He doesn't touch anything, but a section of metal rises from the ground level until it has formed an archway wide enough and high enough for them all to walk through.

The Commandant steps past J'salax, entering the archway first.

"She's in a hurry I guess," Ryder mutters.

"Protocol," J'salax says. "I am not allowed to enter a location first. A tactic to avoid my demise, I believe." He raps his knuckles against the panelling at his chest, a layer of protective metal if the sound is a give-away. The material looks little different to the rest of the full-body outfit, if not a lighter shade of black.

Ryder blushes. "Oh, I was just… being… wait, this is your home isn't it?"

"Yes, but those in positions of power can never really be too cautious. Can they, Ryder?"

He follows after the Commandant, disappearing into the innards of the trunk. Did he just wink at her?

Ryder chews at what's left of a very bitten down fingernail.

"We going in?" Blane says, balancing on one foot, his goo encased sock raised. The guy must be as terrified as she is, but he's holding it together. The benefit of being in C-21, she supposes. They hunt for the stuff everyone else runs from.

Ryder pushes at her hair, and her broken nails snag in the tangle. She's about to meet a queen and she looks like hell. "Yeah, let's do this."

"Let me go first," Blane says. He puffs out a breath, like someone preparing to do an ice-bath, and steps into the trunk.

Blissfully cool air hits Ryder's skin, a welcome relief after the sticky heat of outside. The interior is bathed in a soft pink light emanating from a spiralling staircase set at the centre of the round space. J'salax and the Commandant are already halfway up to where a strange ceiling glints like a kaleidoscope a couple of storeys above.

"A greater speed would be appreciated," J'salax calls down. "Just step on."

The staircase is not stationary. It's a glowing spiral escalator. Blane steps on, and Ryder hurries to stay close. They twirl in a wide circle, moving upwards. There is no sound of machinery, not even a whisper of an engine. The entire thing is made from opaque pink crystal, whose glow bathes Ryder's hand when she places it on the handrail. Mined from the Dovers presumably.

"Look, Ryder. Have you ever seen such a thing?" Blane leans against the moving rail as they rise higher and higher up the trunk.

She shakes her head. "No."

The walls at this level are translucent. It's like looking out from a castle tower. And for a moment the stress and fear and desperation take a back seat to the view of this incredible but odd fabricated forest.

"I wish my brother could see this," Blane says. "He's searched for this his entire life."

"Jack would know the words to describe this place." But Ryder can't find them. The alien beauty is literally breath-taking. She sucks at her bottom lip, the sting of tears pushing close. A hand touches hers, and she lifts her head to find Blane giving her a sad smile.

"They're okay. I know it."

"But you don't…"

"I believe it, then." Blane's smile falters. "Whatever has happened."

Because something has. If Lucas is here.

Blane releases a choked cry, raising his hands above his head.

"What is it?" Ryder cries.

But she spots it before the question is done. The kaleidoscope ceiling she admired earlier is fast approaching, with no visible entrance for them to pass through. There's no sign of J'salax or the Commandant either. Ryder mimics Blane, cowering beneath her hands. All at once the pink glow is replaced with an emerald sheen. Her elthar's warmth sweeps through her, racing up her arms.

"Is this thing going to stop?" Blane cries.

"No idea." Ryder crouches beside him on the step. The escalator quickens its pace, still without a sound. The loudest sound is that of Ryder's heart thudding in her chest. Sweat beads on her upper lip, stress and the heat of the elthar. The flickering ceiling appears to be a type of crystal too. Solid. And right on them. The step hurtles towards it. Ryder lifts herself, enough so that she leans over Blane, her arms stretched to cover her own head. The elthar is all they have to protect them.

And it is totally unnecessary.

They pass through the floor. Not solid at all. At least, not the section they pass through. Just vapour that whirls around them, like the blast of a fog machine. The step they are crouched on stops and disappears. Leaving them kneeling on a now definitely solid floor.

They have emerged into a circular room where J'salax and the Commandant await.

A young woman stands alongside J'salax. Barefoot. Clad in a gold material with an opalescent sheen. The outfit is fitted around her legs and arms, long sleeves and calf-length pants, with a light and flowy tunic draped over the top, reaching to mid-thigh. Her hair is almost as wild and tangled as Ryder's, and it is a blazing shade of red. The type of colour Sophie would go nuts over. Ryder has no time to take in any other of her features. Her attention is drawn by a very unwelcome sight. About half a dozen soldiers surround them, clad in some serious exo-skeletons — jet black hinged metal over white suits beneath — with weapons pointed at Blane and Ryder. Orbs they hold in the palm of their hands. Darts of light pulsing out frantic rhythms on the smooth surfaces.

"Release your weapon," one of Exo-soldiers demands.

Ryder throws a furtive glance over her shoulder. But the space behind them is empty. Just another breathtaking view of the world outside.

"Ryder," Blane hisses. "He's talking to you."

"What weapon?" Ryder curses under her breath. Her elthar. The metal on her right hand has taken it upon itself to arm her. She's grasping an impressive sword. The swashbuckling kind. Like something she's seen in the old pirate movies Petra used to love so much. "Oh wow. This is new."

She lifts her hand, not entirely sure how to get rid of the sword.

The guards go into a frenzy of shouted commands. "Lower your weapon! Lower your weapon!"

"Ryder! Stop swinging it around," Blane cries.

"I don't know how to get rid of it." Frantic, she tries shaking it off. Flicking her hand. But she's freaking out so bad it only seems to make the elthar glow even brighter. "I'm not trying to hurt anyone."

"We will shoot if you do not remove the weapon," the lead guard shouts, the orb in his hand no longer has patterns on it. The entire globe is one solid colour. Ryder's guessing not a good sign.

"No. You will do no such thing." The wild-haired woman steps forward. And Ryder freezes, her hand lifted, the sword held across her body like a barrier.

"My lady," Chief Exo-soldier says, his voice gruff. "Remove yourself from the reach zone."

But the lady touches at her hair, a tilt of her head side to side. Kind of jerky, like a bird. One that watches Ryder like a hawk. "Come, come, Hrin-te. Clearly the child is frightened. And certainly no threat with a weapon. You see that as well as I. Now, your name is Ryder? Is that correct?"

Her speech is fluttery, rising up and down in strange places. But gentle, and the hawk doesn't look so much hungry as curious.

Ryder's breathless from panic and trying to manage the weight of the elthar, nods. "I don't want to hurt anyone—"

"Oh, my child. I fear you would will hurt yourself more than anyone." She doesn't smile but her eyes dance: jade green, like the Commandant's but with unusual smatterings of a red that rivals her hair. She has freckles along her jawbone, the rest of her skin marble white. "But this is decidedly interesting. You are human, the Commandant tells me, not Sirosian. And yet, here you stand with a glorious shade of elthar. One I admit, I have not seen before. And you appear unfamiliar with the elthar you bear?"

Despite the woman's reassurances, the guards still hold the orbs pointed in Ryder's direction. Blane stands in a no-man's-land off to one side, his eyes darting from the guards to the woman who address's Ryder. Ryder's answer is super slow to come. They shouldn't be discussing her terrible use of elthar right now. This woman needs to know about Aresh. But still, making sudden moves seems like a bad idea.

The Commandant speaks up while Ryder stands, mouth agape. "Forgive me, Lady." She inclines her head. "I desired to inform you of the human's unique abilities sooner than this, but while I returned from the Iondar Realm it became clear to me that Reigner Zetem's motivations were no longer in sync with that of the Crown. Until I understood the situation on Zentai, I felt it prudent to fail to relay certain information."

The Crown turns her sparkling eyes to the Commandant. "Your caution was wise. As it always has been. You have always held a distrust of Reigner Zetem. I should have heeded your advice earlier."

The Commandant bows low.

"Please, arise." The Crown flutters her hands. The thickness of her fingers contrasts the fineness of her wrist. "It is I who should be in deference to you. I know what you have endured, and your loyalty has not wavered. We suspected Zetem of rationing the information being received by the Crown. That he has long worked at eroding the commitment of the Vex to peace with Siros. But this, to cause the death of the Laudess, it is far beyond anything I believed him capable of. He has brought us unavoidable war."

Ryder shifts on her feet, knees dancing, like she needs to use the bathroom. But what she really needs, is to talk to the Crown. Now.

"Lady, there is much we must discuss." The Commandant rises.

No kidding. Ryder folds her arms… and doesn't stab herself. The elthar sword has disappeared. Only two cuffs of still-glowing elthar circle her wrists. She heaves a sigh, brandishing her wrists at the head Exo guy, but he's not even looking at her anymore. Everyone is focused on the adults. Talking about war. A war started by the death of a girl who isn't dead.

"We are in conflict not only with Siros, but within our own house," J'salax says. He now stands in front of several screens that have appeared out of thin air. Their surfaces filled with sharp-angled symbols "Commandant, you have returned to a coup. Reigner Zetem has isolated Nire at Icewynn, swayed the Vex to his side, and compromised our access to information."

"And I've been unable to reach the Laudine Aresh." The Crown frowns, chewing at the nail on her pinky finger. "A most concerning development. Her resolve to perpetuate peace between Siros and Zentai has never faltered. I only hope the death of the Laudess has not seen Aresh withdraw as my ally too."

"It hasn't." Ryder's voice booms around the room, and the orbs lift once again, lights dancing across their surface. "Sorry, it's just… it hasn't. Aresh needs your help. We all do. I really need to speak with…" She tucks one foot behind the other and bobs – her first ever curtsy. "With… your highness…, please."

The Commandant glares, not with any rage, just exasperation. Clearly, Ryder just breached some kind of royal etiquette. Too bad. J'salax and the Crown share a glance.

"That would be unwise, Lady," the ever-watchful Chief Exo declares.

Nire brushes off his warning, in fact she brushes him right out of the room. Ordering the small army of soldiers to leave them. She walks over to the long s-shaped couch that takes up the centre of the room, and flops onto it. The way Ryder used to do on her bed after school. Her bird's nest hair splayed against the white material, her feet lifted from the ground, the Queen of Zentai folds her hands across her stomach.

"Now, Ryder," she says. "Tell me what the Laudine needs."

Chapter 30

Olessia

Olessia's inelegant fall from the garreson is only ever briefly out of her control. Her elthar ignites mid-tumble, while her legs are above her and her head sweeps uncomfortably close to the hard ground. She rights herself with an indignant grunt, illuminating the confines of the tunnel with the glow of the metal.

"Olessia," Maher shouts from around the very same bend that used Olessia's distraction to dislodge her from the garreson.

"I am unharmed."

Sorry. My bad. But have you ever tried gymnastics?

Olessia spins, searching for the speaker. *Sophie?*

Sophie didn't make it. That's what Sebastien said. What Olessia has fought hard not to think of since he told her.

Yeah, it's me. I'm not so great at this. Ryder said I'm super loud. Am I super loud?

"Olessia." Unable to turn the garreson around in the confined space, Maher leaves it hovering and jumps clear. Racing towards her. "Are you all right?"

She waves him back. "Stop. Just stay there. I'm fine."

Sophie, how is this possible? How are you able to instigate a mindreach?

Hmmm, well... I'm not sure this is strictly... telepathy. Or mindreaching...

What do you mean?

Maher must wonder if Olessia has finally tipped into insanity, with the way she peers into the dark shadows. Feet braced, hands touching at the air. But he says nothing, watching her.

You know what, Olessia, we can deal with that later, okay?

There is an unnaturally high pitch to Sophie's thoughts, a ring of something troubling.

Sebastien's words return to her. Sophie didn't make it.

Sophie, how can I help you?

Don't worry about me. I have no idea how long we can hold this, so I need to make it quick.

We?

Padellah, I'm not sure if you know her, and the explanation might have to wait. But she needs you to hurry. You're getting closer, I think that's why I was able to reach you.

Olessia certainly knows Padellah. The Cyne entity enabled her to save Christian. But has not appeared again.

Sophie?

The long silence is frightening.

"Sophie?" she says aloud. Maher takes a step towards her, and again Olessia ushers him away. "I said I'm fine. Please. Just stand back." She searches for a sign of the red-haired girl she thought she'd lost.

She's running out of time. Aresh, I mean. You have to hurry. Padellah is doing what she can, somehow... but she's slipping.

Slipping? Who?

Aresh. She's trapped in there, in Megnastin. It's like some kind of black hole... wait, you probably don't call them that... but it's bad. He's got some kind of device locking her in there...

The girl's words come with gunfire rapidity. And something else. A harsh chorus of static that is growing louder. Readying to envelope Sophie's words altogether.

He? Sophie, you need to tell me—

I'm trying... your dad... have to hurry. They need you. I can't hold on much longer... I keep getting pulled back to Ryder...

The crackling, broken air eats at Sophie's mindreach. Olessia squeezes her eyes closed, fingertips to temples. Concentrating.

You've seen her? Ryder is alive?

She is. And with some guy called J'salax. Weird name... but that... The weakening connection crumbles, then revives. Sophie's thoughts blast Olessia's synapses. *He and the Commandant are taking her to the Crown. That's what Aresh wanted. Told Ryder to tell the Crown about Megnastin. She a friend? This Crown lady. Oh... I'm sorry Olessia, I don't know how to hold on here... please hurry.*

Sophie? Sophie? Though there is no reply, Olessia sends the mindreach anyway. *Tell Ryder I'm coming for her.*

Maher is still watching her, keeping his distance.

"Olessia? What do we need to do?" he says.

"Move faster."

Olessia does not reveal the true source of the message, mindful of the effect Sophie's name — and potential presence — may have on Christian. Her information about Aresh is absorbed by the party with few questions, though Sebastien's frown and knowing stare suggest he will interrogate Olessia further at a more suitable time. Right now, there is only time to heed one command: move faster.

Sentinel Teler does as instructed. Sebastien returns to scouting ahead. After a short while, the Desner Coniva reveals a surprise shift in terrain. Transforming from endless wave-rock and stony ground to another landscape altogether. One they hear long before they come upon it. A high whistle on the air. Monotone and constant. Growing louder and louder until the pebbled ground gives way to weeren-drenched slopes covered in one singular plantform. Kexen. Towering skeletons of stark white, faintly reminiscent of the trees of Earth, but the Kexen angles are too sharp to be mistaken for them. This forest holds a distorted interpretation of a tree: giant white structures faintly luminescent, with square trunks and branches sharp and narrow as swords. No leaves to rustle, or pliable limbs that bend with the weight of a breeze.

Not that a breeze is present.

"No wind ever touches this area," Teler says, as he winds them through the labyrinth. "It's as though the Kexen repel everything that attempts to enter their atmosphere. We are fast approaching the outer edges of the Arlion Xhentex. Strangeness is the only certainty from here on."

The lack of airflow not only makes for a denser heat — unbelievable considering how intense it already is — but it allows the unsettling whistle of the Kexen to dominate, ringing sharply against Olessia's senses. Even attempting to send a mindreach becomes near impossible, as though the whistling burrows deadens the mind. Olessia abandons her attempts to reach Sophie again. She has not yet conveyed the information about Ryder to Sebastien. As much as she desires to share the news that Ryder definitely lives, she's uncertain of how the guardian will take news she may be deep within Zentai territory. And now there is Evelyn to consider, with her own Blackwall.

Christian presses his hands against his ears.

"What is that noise?" he says.

Olessia brightens, diving on the question as an opportunity to converse with him. The first communication they've had since she repaired the Blackwall. But Sen-Bay steals her opportunity.

"No idea. But it is certainly not pleasant."

Olessia taps Maher's shoulder, gesturing for him to edge closer to Sen-Bay's garreson. "The Kexen are built by a… a parasite of sorts, and the creature produces that sound while it structures the interior of the plantform."

"They disturb my sense of wellness." Sen-Bay frowns. "If Siros is full of such things, little wonder the Presider seeks Zentai as his own. My apologies, Laudess, but the beauty of our landscapes transcend anything I have seen here."

"It is not the beauty of Zentai the Presider seeks," comes Teler's gruff reply. "It is the resources that dwell within that beauty."

Evelyn turns in her seat to take in the conversation, and her gaze falls on Olessia. "Well I believe Siros has beauty, there is always some to be found in nature." She gives Olessia a gentle smile. "I mean really, this is quite incredible. Like a forest of unpainted porcelain sculptures."

"Porcalin?" Sen-Bay says.

"Porcelain." Christian lifts one hand from his ear, frowning. "It's an Earth thing, a ceramic, super fragile normally. Evelyn's kind of right. This is like a forest of weird designer Christmas trees or something. My mum… she has a tree, plastic though, that is all angular like some of these… she was trying to be cool, I think. But none of us wanted it. Don't know what she did with that tree."

He falls silent, lost in the memory. Olessia tenses and is grateful when Maher brings the garreson right up alongside Sen-Bay and Christian. Although Christian's thoughtful frown remains, it doesn't deepen or morph into a grimace of discomfort.

Sebastien's elthar gives away his return, tinging the subtle white light of the trees to their right with sapphire.

"Halt, halt," he hisses, "Shut down, shut down."

Teler shuts off his garreson at Sebastien's first halt. Sen-Bay a pulse-beat after. Their vehicles sinking to the ground at the base of a Kexen, heavy with limbs that might cover them.

"What is it, brother?" Maher lowers the garreson but does not shut off the engine.

"Shut down, Maher," Sebastien glares at him. "Olessia, instigate your elthar shield. There is no time to set up the Rachmeed."

"But won't the elthar—"

Now Sebastien's hostile stare fixes on Olessia. "Do it now. Shield them, if you wish them to live. An armadel of Sretlan approaches. Our energy signature will be lost in the greater echo of the fleet."

He kneels beside Evelyn and Teler, who are huddled with Christian and Sen-Bay at the base of the Kexen. The plantform is certainly far heavier with limbs than any around it, and a good portion of those limbs drape in generous arches towards the ground. A feature that might afford some shade from the confels but will certainly not conceal the group entirely. Certainly not from an armadel of Sretlan, forward-advance aircraft renowned for their manoeuvrability and capacity to fly at astonishingly low altitudes.

Still, Olessia hesitates. "Are you certain they will not detect the elthar signal?"

"Of course I'm not certain," Sebastien shoots back. "But only one of those hundreds of pilots needs to notice an outstanding grouping of colour on the landscape below for our location to be detected. Their flightpath will take them directly over us. But the armadel is moving at a rapid pace, far too rapid for a sonic mapping. They are not searching. They will pass by here in a moment. Hold fast."

"Are they headed for Zentai?" Sen-Bay says.

Sebastien answers with a nod. Olessia allows the elthar to reach her shoulders and cover them. Providing more surface metal from which to emanate the shield.

A new sound joins the whining pitch of the Kexen, this one lower and far less obtrusive. The vibration that runs ahead of the armadel infiltrates the surrounding structures, rattling loose small fragments.

"Instigate the shielding," Sebastien murmurs.

Olessia has done so before he finishes speaking. The twin energies from each of their elthar form half a canopy that stretches over the group. Olessia's 'other' energy, the Beckoning, niggles but rises only with a mild curiosity.

Olessia glances at the others. Christian presses his forehead against Sen-Bay's back, eyes down. His back moves high and low with his deep intake of breath. In contrast, Evelyn looks skyward, a determined set to her jaw, as though daring what approaches to try and harm them. And yet again, Olessia is struck by the similarities that exist between mother and child.

"Hold steady, Olessia. Keep the elthar at its lowest ebb," Sebastien whispers from where he crouches the other side of the huddle. A mindreach is too dangerous, they do not know who rides with the armadel, but the shared creation of the elthar shield enables them to speak as though they were side by side.

"Perhaps we should split—" Olessia's words are drowned out by the drone of the Sretlan Armada. Single-pilot craft shaped like a human tear, and designed to travel at ludicrously fast speeds in short, sharp bursts. When travelling at a relaxed speed, as they do now, the machines growl with bone-shaking intensity. The Sretlan are used to breaking a path through enemy lines to clear the way for ground troops. This group fly desperately low to the ground, barely as high as the tallest Kexen, which to Olessia's mind is far from tall enough.

Olessia has never before viewed so many Sretlan in a single armadel. With the fuel-draining capabilities of the craft as renowned as their speed, there is little wonder the Presider required her assistance with Gatherings. The upkeep, and energy required to run this armadel alone would be astonishing.

The rumble of engines vibrates the air. Shattering several of the jutting branches of a neighbouring Kexen. Olessia's eyes churn. If one of the branches falls upon the shield it will draw undesired attention. The sparking of contact though dull, will still cause an unnatural brightness in this setting.

The overhead procession seems endless, and the vibrations caused by its passing put the Kexen forest under strain. The ground quakes with a low tremor beneath Olessia's knees. The natural world shaking beneath the weight of the parade of the Presider's might.

A might that will be Olessia's should she actually survive this war. A sobering thought.

"It is almost done, hold steady," Sebastien declares, peering up at the sky. Though how he might guess this, Olessia is at a loss to say. To her eyes the sky has been swallowed by the armadel. A destructive force, using her name to break its way into Zentai.

A Sretlan drops out of formation, sinking beneath the rest of the group.

"Sebastien," Olessia's hiss strains from her.

"Hold steady." His eyes do not leave the craft. The Sretlan is on track to pass straight over the Kexen they shelter under. If the pilot does not increase altitude, they will clip the highest reach of the structure.

Evelyn lets out a cry Olessia is close enough to catch. Sentinel Teler embraces her, directing a fierce frown towards the approaching craft.

Hold steady. Sebastien's order. And Olessia follows it to the best of her ability. Maintaining the ebb of the elthar. Her own vulnerability does not plague her, but that of the people she protects beneath a barrier of her making. Should it falter, should it draw attention, then the lives of those around her are in immediate peril. The Sretlan is almost upon them when the pilot adjusts course. Swinging wide to the left and lifting back up into the main body of the armadel. Olessia chokes on her rushed exhale.

"Almost done. Just a moment longer," Sebastien says through the connection.

And he is right. The air-shattering drone of powerful engines softens, and the sky peeks through the covering of Sretlan. No one moves even though the last of the Sretlan pass by and disappear, lights grown so faint in the darkened sky that Olessia's no longer certain they exist at all. The ground no longer shudders beneath them, but no one moves. The creatures within the Kexen are silent. Only Christian's breathing mars the unnatural hush.

"They are gone," Sebastien declares.

"We must keep moving," Teler says, following the directive Olessia herself gave him.

Sebastien deactivates the elthar, and Olessia follows suit. But as the others get to their feet, Olessia is slow to follow, uncertain her legs will bear her weight. She inhales deep and slow. The exhale even slower. Someone stands close to her. Olessia looks up to find Christian by her side.

"Are you okay?"

Not at all. The rumbling of the armadel still fills her. The closeness of peril. "Yes."

His gentle smile says he doesn't believe her. Christian holds out his hand, and Olessia wraps both of hers around it, taking hold of the support he offers. Using it to bring herself to her feet.

Chapter 31

Ryder

Nire sits up on her elbows, jerking her head to one side. And again Ryder is reminded of a watchful hawk. A really young hawk clad in gold.

"Aresh wishes us to go to the Arlion Xhentex?" She scratches at one of her tight sleeves. "More specifically, she wishes for me to take you there?"

Ryder nods, not blinking. The Crown's gaze darts momentarily at the Commandant, who shrugs as though to say, told you.

"It would appear you were most astute in protecting Ryder, Commandant."

The Commandant leans forward in a shallow bow. "Thank you, my Lady."

J'salax folds his arms across his armour-plated chest. "Why would the Laudine request we go there? Megnastin is among the most dangerous points of the Xhentex. Are you certain, self-same, that this is wise?"

"No, not at all. But at one point I was certain the Reigner would not betray us either. How wrong I was."

J'salax lets his arms fall to his sides, his hands balled. "But a human can't survive the Xhentex, much less serve us any purpose there."

The Commandant makes a small sound. "I dare say of those who stand before us, only one is truly human." She jerks her head towards Blane who scowls, scuffing his feet against ever-changing marks of the kaleidescope floor. Ryder stares into the morphing patterns. Splotches of powder blue curl in on themselves to form a string of Chinese-lantern shapes the colour of ripe lemons.

Blane is the only human here. Ryder doesn't even bother protesting the Commandant's statement. Why protest the truth? Ryder has slipped into a whole new category. And she has no idea what her label should be now. Ryder lifts her head; there's just numbness where some kind of emotion should be. The Crown's needling stare rests on her. Though intense it's not unfriendly; like how you might look at a unicorn the first time you see one.

"We will do as you request," the Crown says thoughtfully. "The Laudine entrusted you to me." There is a note of pleasure in her words. "And I will honour that trust. J'salax, you will see to it that my Qell-tri is readied for the journey?"

"Of course."

All the convincing and pleading Ryder expected she'd have to do, evaporates just like that. But she can't shake the anxious knot that comes with thinking about Lucas. They can't leave without him.

"And Lucas... did..." She hesitates, unsure how she should address J'salax. Ryder doesn't want to put a single toe out of line here. Not if it means getting them to help rescue Lucas.

"Nire has been advised of the Zentai boy's predicament and his identity." J'salax taps at the armour-like plate attached to the elbow of his bodysuit.

Green eyes, slashed with crimson, twinkle. "Yes, yes. And we are in the process of doing something about it." Nire pats the empty space on the couch beside her. "Come, Ryder. I wish to spend some time speaking with you. Alone. J'salax, would you ensure the Commandant and Mr Bane—"

"Blane," Blane corrects her, and his face grows dark with a blush. "Oh I'm sorry... I..."

"No need for apology," Nire slumps onto her back. The cotton-like fabric of the tunic shifts easily. "Blane. I shall endeavour not to pronounce it incorrectly again. Please, J'salax will you—"

"Right this way, my esteemed guests. How long has it been since anyone refreshed themselves?" He wrinkles his nose. "A long time I suspect. Refresh, sustain, and rest. Do it while you can, I suspect there will be little down time in our futures."

Blane hesitates. "Ryder?"

"It's okay," she smiles. "Let me know what's good on the menu."

Actually food would be a great idea. Her stomach is not so much growling as attempting to eat itself. Ryder has a horrible sense the last morsel of food that passed her lips was the blue goo the Zentai tried to force feed her on the Baershard. Decent sleep was an even longer time ago. Ryder's not certain lying down on a couch that is as wide as a king bed is such a great idea. Not if the queen wants conversation.

Blane gives her a nod and follows after the Commandant and J'salax, who again has not waited for anyone to follow. Moving towards a double archway that has opened onto a set of wide stairs beyond, he takes the stairs at least two a time and is quickly out of sight.

The archway evaporates, it's the only word to describe it. One moment it is there, the next the wall is solid again.

Ryder and the Crown are alone in a room large enough to accommodate at least twenty people. Jiggling her shoulders, Ryder settles into what is, admittedly, the most comfortable couch she's ever lounged on.

"So, Lucas," Ryder begins, tentatively. "You're really trying to rescue him?"

Nire frowns at the high ceiling. "Of course, it is my duty. Aresh has honoured me by protecting the true heir to the Reignership. The moment J'salax informed me of Lucas's existence, I utilised the few loyal associates I have within the Vex. We had hoped to intercept the Caeleax fleet bearing him back to Fallyn, but—" She lifts her hands dropping them heavily against the cushioned surface. "Pinpointing his exact location is problematic. I simply don't have the resources within Fallyn anymore. Fallyn is the Zentai Complex-Main."

Ryder nods, absently. "Yeah, the capital. Sebastien told me."

"The Guardian? You two are close, the Commandant informs me."

It's probably rude not to look at a queen when she speaks to you but Ryder stares up at the ceiling. She's already so tired, tears are just waiting at the ready for no reason at all. To start talking about Sebastien will tip her over the edge. Nire rolls onto her side, leaning up on one elbow.

"He is extremely resourceful, Sebastien I mean. Aresh always spoke highly of him, even if others did not," she says.

Ryder rolls her head to look at Nire. "He's not that bad."

She laughs, a tinkling, high sound full of amusement. And again Ryder wonders how old the Crown is. Hanging out with her feels more like hanging with a school friend than an adult. "And I see you shared Aresh's high regard of the Guardian. The Commandant told me as much but now I see it with my own eyes."

Sitting up, Ryder is ready with a dozen 'no way's'. But she swallows them back. What's the point? She shakes her head. "Yeah, I do. Care about him I mean." Saying it out loud is crazy simple. Why do the easy things take so much work? "And if anything has happened to him… I'm not sure." She slumps back onto the embracing softness of the couch. "I care about all of them, and I wish I knew that everyone was okay. Or at the very least, where they are. I can't stand it." Louder than she intends. "It's driving me nuts. Not knowing. I hate it, I hate this place. And I want to go home." She presses the heels of her hands to her eyes. Blocking out the light, the room. The alien world she's stuck in.

Christian. Olessia. Aresh. Lucas.

Jack. Her dad.

Her mother.

Sophie.

Eyes burning, Ryder blows out a breath. Crying will get her nothing and no one right now. She opens her eyes, allowing the sting of the light to force a few tears free. Release the pressure. She takes a tentative glance at the woman whose world Ryder just insulted.

Nire still gazes up at the ceiling. "I understand your frustration. All too well. And I should be able to bring you comfort. I'm sorry." She sounds like she means it. Like it pains her not to be able to magic up Ryder's friends and family. "We have both had things stolen from us. I am the Crown of Zentai. By all rights, powerful. I should have armies at my behest. I should have my people placing their faith in my words and actions. I was birthed for one purpose: to rule Zentai. And yet, here I lie. A prisoner in my own dwelling. My faults? Firstly, to be of an age where people await your mistakes with eagerness. And secondly, to have never supposed that those who served me would betray me. I thought the Reigner intended as I, to protect Zentai and all who dwell within the borders." She sits bolt upright, crossing her legs. "But you give me reason to change my low mood, Ryder. You and Aresh both. She has always been kind and just. Guided me when I've lost my way. I will heed her summons. And we will travel to Megnastin as soon as preparations are complete. We will free the Laudine from whatever prison contains her. Our enemies have sought to suppress us both, but together we will shift the flow of this conflict." She pats her hands together, holding them close to her chest like she's praying to whatever gods they have here for help. "I have fought for such a moment as this. When I finally have something the Reigner does not."

This part is said quietly. As though the words should have remained inside.

Ryder floats there, barely aware of the material against her back. Drifting down into the exhaustion which coats her eyelids like lead. All at once, Nire leans over her. Far too close for comfort.

"Show me, Ryder. What power you have. I must see it for myself."

Her enthusiasm bubbles out of her, eyes flashing. But it's more annoying than threatening. A kid on Christmas morning.

"Huh?" Ryder struggles to sit up. Fuzzy headed. "What do you —"

Nire rocks back on her bare heels. "The Commandant told me what you did, back in the cluster. Destroying those Bexsron." She scratches at the top of her hair, bunching the untidy mess into greater tangles. "Did you truly do that? Show me. Show me. Give me some proof that you do not speak lies to my face," she shouts.

"I will not be lied to anymore, do you understand!" She slaps her hands over her mouth. Eyes fluttering closed.

Ryder stares at her. "Are you okay?"

The answer is fairly obvious. The Crown's just had a mini-meltdown. And Ryder gets it. In fact, Nire's shout-fest probably should bother her, but really it's like looking in the mirror. At a person who has just about reached her limits.

"Forgive me," Nire speaks into her hands, eyes still closed.

"We're good," Ryder hesitates, then touches her hand to the Crown's wrist. "I think we both need some serious nap time."

Nire's hands come away from her mouth, teeth bared with a wide smile. "You are certainly not mistaken."

Ryder grins, and stifles a yawn. Meltdowns are kind of exhausting. Even if she wanted to, Ryder's not sure she'd have the energy to put on a Beckoning display for Nire right now. She wasn't joking about needing nap time.

"Oh my god." Ryder holds rock still. "I could find him." Louder, shifting onto her knees to face Nire, she continues. "I could find Lucas for you. There's this thing..." She struggles to recall if the Zentai share the ability to move into the Rising. "It's called Shifting."

The childlike enthusiasm returns. Nire's face brightening. "You can enter the Rising? I thought that was an ability shared only by the Presiderline."

Ryder shrugs. "Yeah, I'm pretty sure that's what Aresh thought too. Help me. Lucas needs—"

Nire nods profusely. "Yes, yes, of course. Find his location, and at least we have somewhere to begin with his rescue."

Ryder drags herself towards the centre of the couch. Laying down. "Okay. Now I think it looks pretty bad when I do this. Like, I'm kind of dead..." Her heart is racing, her throat dryer than that desert they crash landed into.

"Well, we have Bane—"

"Blane."

The queen of Zentai rolls her eyes. "Blane, why must he have such a difficult name? No harm shall come to you, Ryder. You have the Crown of Zentai's word. Besides, this is not the first time

I've been present during a Shift. I was at Aresh's side on more than one occasion." The Crown tugs at her tunic, ballooning the material. "And I have talents of my own. The Zentai have mastered the far-reach, which means I have become most adept at bringing on a restful state."

Nire touches her fingers to Ryder's arm. Ryder's eyelids slide down, lead curtains she can't keep up. A jaw-stretching yawn engulfs her.

"Oh, my apologies." Nire inclines her head. "We don't want you unconscious."

"Not yet, anyway," Ryder mumbles, groggy.

Maybe she should tell Blane what she's doing first. But as she stares up at Nire's face, and the line of freckles that dot her solid jawline, Ryder's concerns fade. Aresh trusts her. Lucas kind of looks like her. And the young woman's quirky habits remind Ryder a lot of Sophie. The two of them would get on like the proverbial house on fire.

"Is that better?"

"Uh-huh." Ryder's chest rises and falls in an even tempo. Her heart isn't trying to tunnel its way out of her chest. She's the most relaxed she's been in… well, in her whole life.

Her eyes flutter closed, bringing Lucas's face to mind. Even through the restfulness, a pang presses at the back of her eyes. And other images force their way in. An image of her dad. He might not have been in Tasmania when all hell broke loose, but he will have heard about it. He will be trying to reach her. Desperate to find her. Ryder rolls her head side to side, the thoughts picking away at her sense of calm. Has Jack told him what he saw? Ryder being dragged aboard an alien ship?

Ryder gasps, her thoughts steaming out of her control. That is what must have happened to her mother, too. Dragged aboard a craft that took her away from everyone and everything she'd ever known. Was she as frightened as Ryder?

Ryder's eyes fly open.

"Ryder?" Nire says. "What is wrong?"

Clearing her throat, Ryder settles back against the mattress. "Nothing." No time to think about that right now. Focus on Lucas.

"Nothing. I'm sorry. I'll try again."

"Very well. I am here. I am not leaving your side." She touches her fingers to Ryder's forehead. The tips are like miniature ice cubes against Ryder's skin. Until now, she didn't realise quite how warm she was. "Ready?"

This time Ryder *is* ready. "I'm ready."

Nire's sedative touch is fast acting. Once again Ryder drifts into a relaxed state.

She forces all other thoughts aside. There is only one face filling her mind's eye. Lucas. Dancing green eyes, smirking smile, the dimples that appear when he laughs. She takes a deep breath and holds it. And when her body ignites, she doesn't fear it.

The heat lifts her eidolon from her body, and she doesn't fight it.

Maybe it's something to do with the Crown's touch, the half-asleep world Ryder rests in, but the Shift is rapid. Ryder catapults into the shadowy interior of the ghost world that lies beyond the dirt and rock and sky of her own world.

Lucas.

Lucas.

Lucas.

Forget everything but him.

Focus.

Ryder moves through the Rising with all the ease of a mist across a moor. A mist that gathers speed. Rushing her forward. Lucas. The pull is undeniable. And with just the thought of moving faster, it happens. Ryder's pace quickens. Moving her through the shadowy world, her flickering watercolour image elongating with the pace. No fear. Just urgency. A sense of utter freedom she doesn't recognise from last time. There are flickers in the air around her. Keeping their distance. Dim forms that move in and out of sight faster than she can focus on them. Ryder is not alone here. And the thought doesn't scare her. It's a comfort. Whatever moves with her, just out of sight, means no harm. She'd bet her last dollar on it.

Even the abyss doesn't phase her. That black void that pulls at her from the moment she enters the Rising. The one that Padellah warned her about. Stay away.

The shadowy images gain greater focus. Not figures now, but higher, broader. No evident shape, or human or otherwise.

Oh no.

Too late Ryder realises what she's seeing. The physical world. Her destination approaching. The veil thinning until it is little more than a blur. And she is still catapulting like a bullet from a gun.

Stop. Stop. Stop.

Ryder's cry rings loud and clear in her mind but does not spill into her ethereal world.

Her trajectory stops. With a jolt that would have jarred a real spine. The shudder of the sudden stop ripples through the shadow world like a brick thrown into a shallow pond.

Right in front of her, a shirtless redhead struggles against the guards who attempt to push him to his knees. A sallow-faced man stands in front of them. Impassive, his face a blank canvas.

Lucas. Ryder's buttery arms move through the air in front of him, but he doesn't notice. Lucas's wrists are bound in a panel of metal that looks like a miniaturised guillotine. The silence that greeted Ryder's arrival, peels back. And voices reach her.

"Yes, Exalted," one of the guards says. "As instructed the blades were removed. But we were not well equipped on the—"

"Do I appear to show any concern that the prisoner still bleeds?"

"No." The guard steps back, lowering his head.

The sallow-faced man appears similar in age to Ryder's own father. And where the Crown has eyes of glinting green with highlights of red, this man shares the opposite trait. Pale red eyes — like he has a major cat allergy — with veins of brilliant green. Markings at the outer edges of his eyes curl like warpaint on his olive skin. He regards Lucas with cool detachment.

"So it is true." The blood-eyed man shakes his head, his grey hair is pressed tight against his scalp, with a braided strand hanging in a loop down to his shoulder blades. "If the genetic test were not enough, to lay eyes on you would suffice. You are just like your father." His laugh is coarse, sandpaper across a piece of timber.

Lucas. Ryder's cry cracks and shivers, but he does not lift his head. *Lucas.*

No response. Ryder's buttery hands reach for him. They are almost upon his shoulders before she notices the bloodstain covering most of his back. The shards are gone. And the man was right. The prisoner still bleeds. Crimson rivulets stain Lucas's pale skin. Ryder recoils, the blurriness of the Rising intensifying. She struggles to refocus. Zoning out of the Rising right now is the last thing Lucas needs. Ryder peers at the surroundings. A cube of concrete-like material with no windows, no furniture. Every inch the prison.

"Varnne, wasn't it?" the Reigner says. "The name your Zentai family gave you? Child of great heart. That's what it means. Did you know that? Or has the traitor Aresh filled your mind with other musings. Like how you will both rise up when the time is right, to take the Presidership from Inel, and the Reignership from me. He has told the tale of Aresh's treachery so many times I believe the Presider actually believes it truth now." The Reigner shrugs. Lucas's gaze burns with hatred. "Did you know he wishes you to live? Inel intends to parade you before the Claven, as evidence of Aresh's betrayal. Proof that she sought to install someone sympathetic to her in the Zentai Vex. In readiness for when she usurped him. But Varnne, I'm afraid leaving you alive does not suit me. You should not be alive to begin with. Your whole family were supposed to be lost during the Treaty Signing assassination attempt. As my mother and the Presider intended." He claps his hands together. "So I intend to finalise now, what was begun that day."

Ryder launches herself at the Reigner at the same time Lucas does. And both attacks are utter wastes of energy. Ryder slides straight through the man's form. A shocking current racing through her, her eidolon contracting in on itself.

Lucas fares worse. He doesn't make it all the way to his feet before the guards stab at him with two-pronged devices that cause his body to jerk and twist. A gargled cry flies from him. Eyes rolling back in his head, Lucas collapses.

Chapter 32

Olessia

Olessia listens to the whispers of those around her. The encounter with the Sretlan Armadel has left everyone shaken.

"So, there can be no denying it now." Maher steers the garreson one-handed, the other toying with frayed edging on his coat. "The war has begun."

"The war has begun," Sen-Bay repeats, both hands firmly clenched on his controls. "Though I'm not sure the conflicts of the past have ever ended, so far as the Presider is concerned."

Christian's gaze still lingers on the sky. Empty now, but the rumble of the multitude of engines seems to linger on the air.

Olessia's elthar glows with a muted sapphire. She flies alongside Teler and Evelyn, readying to join Sebastien who once again scouts ahead. "We are running out of time to reach Megnastin, Sentinel. If we do not hurry, it may be too late."

"Olessia, what if we are wrong," Teler says. "What if Aresh is not in Megnastin at all, and this is a further ploy of the Presider's to trap us all?"

"She is there. I know it."

Teler's eyes narrow but he does not question her further, instead pressing his balled fist to his chest in deference.

Olessia moves ahead of the group, weaving through the Kexen, enjoying the momentary freedom that comes with utilising the elthar. Sebastien slows as she approaches.

"Sebastien, I have had word of Aresh." Olessia pauses. She should have relayed this information some time ago.

"Go on."

"I received a mindreach."

His shoulder's tense but remains focused on what lies ahead, and Olessia continues.

"From Sophie."

Sebastien's flightpath dips, and he readjusts quickly, guiding them through a narrow gap between two Kexen. The space is far too small for the following garreson. Olessia glances over her shoulder, watching the group swing wide to negotiate a more suitable path, leaving Sebastien and Olessia alone.

"Sophie died," Sebastien says. "I witnessed it myself." Cold and flat.

"I don't understand it entirely. The mindreach felt like no other I had received." Olessia falters over another piece of information she has not had time to give. "Well, that is not entirely true. I received communication from the Cyne. Back on Earth. They enabled me to reach Christian—"

"The Cyne? Spoke to you directly?" Sebastien's scowl leaves his eyes in deep shadow.

"Far more than that. One of them pulled me from Aresh's control in a slipstream and guided me to Christian. They said he was our weakness, Ryder and I, and that he had to be protected if Ryder were to be kept safe."

"They endangered you to keep her safe?" Sebastien stops his forward momentum, righting himself to hover upright. "I don't understand this. The Cyne have barely shown themselves in generations, now they interfere with the Laudess of Bax Un Tey? This makes no sense."

"I believe they have shown themselves, only not to us. To Aresh." Humidity dampens Olessia's clothing, and it clings in uncomfortable closeness to her skin. The Kexen whistle around them, though the pitch has deepened, and is thankfully less taxing on the ears. "But listen to me Sebastien. I do not understand Aresh's link with the Cyne, but she has formed a bond with one in particular. It is named Padellah—"

Sebastien turns his head so hard and fast to look at her that Olessia falters.

"Padellah?" he says. "Ryder said that name once. On the Aventar, before she destroyed the Creation in the River—"

Now it is Olessia's turn to scowl at the Guardian. "Ryder? What Creation?"

"The River was being held open artificially, by means I did not fully understand. A device that anchored itself in two Realms. Iondar and the Rising. I myself could not see the Creation, but Ryder could. So could this Padellah, the Cyne, and together they destroyed it. She survived the River, Olessia. We were forced to evacuate the Aventar, and Ryder survived without protection in the River. I barely did so, and would not have, if she and the Celtren had not removed me from it."

"The Celtren?" Olessia holds up her hand, halting her own question. "Never mind. I can barely comprehend everything as it is. Do not complicate it with amiable Arlion creatures coming to your rescue."

Olessia's thoughts swim. Though she stares at a jutting point of a Kexen she does not truly see it. Ryder should not have been able to withstand the River, not without some source of protection. "Sebastien, Maher believes that Ryder may have been responsible for the destruction of the Bexsron in the cluster. Do you believe that is possible?"

Sebastien runs his hands through his hair, rubbing at the back of his skull. "I believe we have no idea how strong she might have become. Olessia… do you sense her? She was so convinced you were still alive… I wonder if perhaps, you feel as great a certainty?"

There is a quiet desperation behind his words, and Olessia regrets not telling him immediately of what Sophie's information.

"I not only feel it, I know it," Olessia says. "Ryder is with J'salax. The Crown's self-same is taking her, along with the Commandant, to the Crown."

"What?" Sebastien spits.

"Sophie said it is what Aresh wanted. They do not intend Ryder harm. Sophie believed Aresh thought the Crown an ally. You and I both know that if Sophie were concerned, it would be obvious. I could learn no more before my connection with her was lost."

Sebastien wrenches his hands from his hair, growling at the nearest Kexen. All at once his chin jerks up. "That is not the only connection that has been lost. Do you sense the others?"

Olessia spins around. She frowns. She had thought herself certain of the direction they'd come, until she peered back that way. A huddle of Kexen stand in the path, far too thick to have simply flown through. The only visible gap is far off to the left. And she does not recall so drastic a directional change.

"No. I do not sense them," she says. "The tone of the Kexen changed before, I noted it but thought nothing of it."

As though the strange plantforms hear her words, the whistling sound alters yet again. It deadens altogether off to the right but pitches high up ahead. Unease grips her. Olessia braces for the familiar curl of the Beckoning, one that comes with a shift in her mood. But there is nothing. She runs her hand across her stomach.

"Sebastien, did we not travel from that direction?" She points at the impassable clump of Kexen.

He scrutinises the plantforms. "That is what I believed." He rotates in mid-air, and gestures in the opposite direction. "Up until a moment ago, an opening was evident there. One I intended to pass through."

The Kexen-heavy way ahead could not be traversed by a shotner, let alone a bi-ped creature.

"Perhaps we have reached the limits of the Dessner Coniva," Olessia says.

Sebastien nods. "And approach the true Arlion Xhentex."

The Kexen fall silent. The only evidence they had made a noise at all is the faint echo of their pitch still ringing in Olessia's ears.

"Sebastien?"

He places a finger against his mouth. Silencing her as he studies their surrounds. A brush of air toys with the lengths of Sebastien's hair. Warm against Olessia's skin. Teler's words return to her: No wind ever touches this area.

The weight of the breeze increases, buffeting the Kexen around them.

"Move, Olessia," Sebastien hisses.

"To where?" Olessia spreads her arm.

"This way. Go." Sebastien urges her forward. Pushing her in the same direction the wind travels. A sensible decision, to move with the flow of rushing air rather than fight their way towards whatever might have stirred it. "Try to rise above the Kexen, we need to make sense of our location."

His loosened hair covers his face as he tries to turn to speak to her.

Olessia does as instructed, her elthar brightening to boost her. Sebastien falls into place behind her. She rises. And rises. Straining towards the darkness of the sky. But just when it seems that she will reach the topmost tip of the Kexen, she blinks and another branch stretches into the blackness.

"There is no end to this," she cries, and the Beckoning emerges. Sniffing at her fear. Twisting and turning within her, as though the Beast too is unsure of direction.

"Keep going," Sebastien says.

Olessia stretches her hands ahead of her, long lengths of elthar whipping from her fingertips. She guides them towards the pointed Kexen branch that arrows upwards. Ever upwards. Seeming to grow before their eyes and strain to touch the sky. She doesn't dare blink, eyes fixed hard on her intended target. The elthar coils around the white tip, minute barbs finding purchase in the smooth surface. Olessia hauls back on the elthar rope, keeping it taunt. Allowing her gaze to shift for the smallest of seconds from her target.

The elthar slackens and she tumbles. Down, down. Ever downward. There is a wild moment when the world seems to flip, and when it reassembles it does so in the wrong way. The blackness of the dayfall sky rests beneath her, but the jagged tips of several Kexen spears towards her at a horizontal angle. Olessia sweeps her hand, and the elthar shatters the Kexen structure, spraying white shards into the air. An air that whips into a frenzy, throwing the pieces in a multitude of directions; left and right, up and down. Some held in position, spinning on their axis. Olessia shields her face with her hands. The shards making contact, setting off sparks from the elthar.

Something slams against Olessia's back.

Panting hard, Olessia stares up at the sky. Back in its rightful place. She has fallen. And now rests on her back alongside the shattered Kexen. Olessia rolls onto her side, crouching on all fours like a vinner readying to strike, Olessia surveys her surrounds. The hem of her tunic flaps madly against the strength of the wind. The clumping of Kexen around her has deepened, a mass of white walling her in.

"Sebastien, where are you?" she whispers.

An answer comes almost immediately. Sebastien's hurtling figure appears out of nowhere in front of her. Olessia utters a brief cry, throwing herself clear of the guardian projectile. His body slams into Kexen wall that has appeared. And his cry speaks of painful contact. Sebastien scrambles to his feet, clutching at his midriff.

"There is a—"

His explanation is cut short by the sweep overhead of an enormous beast. A hantegran. Wings spread. A creature normally sought by the Claven Higher for the fine silky material of its nests. But this hantegran is unlike any Olessia has seen. The creatures would normally grow no larger than one of the black cockatoos that frequented the area around Christian's family cottage. But this specimen is bigger than a fully grown Celtren. The usual downy wings, with feathers soft enough to use upon the facial skin, have been replaced with giant, blade like expanses that make an odd crackling sound as the creature shifts. There is no doubt where the sudden strength in the wind came from. Each down-thrust leaves her struggling to stay on her feet. Olessia morphs her elthar into gauntlets covering her entire arms. Curved blades extend from stubs of metal in her palms. Sebastien's signature blades gleam across his knuckles.

The hantegran are docile. Timid in most cases. Building their nests in hard to reach places is their singular line of defence. They do not attack. A fact to which this bloated version of that creature appears oblivious.

"To your right, Olessia."

She raises her arm in time to meet a forceful downswing of wing. A brilliant explosion of sparks spray from the elthar, an unusual mix of colours. Olessia allows the momentum to push her out of reach, throwing herself to the ground and rolling away. At least, as far as the the Kexen will allow. The space where she and Sebastien stand is not stable. Even now, as she stares, one section of the Kexen pushes in towards them, as though the environment itself is a pliable substance being toyed with by unseen hands. Olessia pushes to her feet, bracing as the land dips beneath her. Once a flat surface, now she and Sebastien fight as though standing upon the slope of a hill.

"We need to leave this place." Olessia grips hold of a length of a Kexen, only to find the piece vanish from her hands a moment later.

"Obviously. Would you care to show me the exit?"

Sebastien slashes at the long slender neck of the hantegran. His blades meet scaled flesh, and the tear of metal against it is horrendous. Distorted and horrendous. The tone echoing around them, as though the Kexen alters it, and then returns it to them.

Again, the elthar releases a spray of brightly coloured sparks. All one colour this time. An emerald green. The world spins. The black of the sky and the stark white of the Kexen forest blur into a contrasting streak. Olessia reaches for a handhold, anything to steady herself, and her hands sweep through empty air. But the upheaval ends, and the world is steady again.

"What is happening?" Olessia says.

Sebastien strikes. The creature does not even flinch from the blow, but the impact pushes Sebastien to one knee. His grim expression seethes with anger, and his eyes churn, the grey so drained of colour to be almost white.

"We are making no impact," he says.

It is impossible but true. Though they have levelled blows at the creature that would have felled a far more powerful being, the hantegran continues its attack. No sign of their blades upon its body. The creature does not utter a sound as it bares down on them. Sweeping wings destroy the Kexen, only for the plantforms to regenerate as the hantegren readies another attack. Olessia swings her arm again, the blaze of elthar casting upon the creature above her, highlighting black eyes as large as her own head, and a beak as sharp as the blades she wields. The clang of both her and Sebastien's metal against the attacking hentegren becomes almost hypnotic. Until the lull is broken by a deafening roar that sets Olessia's teeth on edge.

The ground tilts again, so hard she fears it may flip entirely as it did earlier. She stumbles, landing hard against a branch, a blow that would have winded her were it not for the elthar that now coats her entire torso. The ground tilts at a greater angle, and Sebastien lets out an angry stream of half-coherent words as he is knocked off his feet, sliding fast along the altered ground. His trajectory stops abruptly as the hantegran grips his body in a set of claws larger than the guardian himself. Pressing Sebastien beneath its great weight. The guardian screams.

"Sebastien!"

The roar shakes the air yet again. A sound that could tear the world apart through its volume.

Olessia reaches down into the depths and hauls the Beckoning from where it lies still and unaffected by the circumstances. Her own panic and fear has not roused the beast, and the entity seems surprised by her summons. It struggles against her. Furious, Olessia balls her fists. *Rise.* Her command flows through her, undeniable. Unmissable. The Beckoning relents and claws its way out of the depths. Sending sharp radiating flickers through her senses. Finding every nerve ending and filling them. Olessia lifts her arms. Expecting to see an immediate flare of auras; from Sebastien's under-duress body and the creature who is destroying him.

But only elthar sheds any light. The steady glow of Sebastien's metal, and her own. Olessia takes a deep breath and draws deeper. She grunts, leaning into the touch of the Beckoning against her nerves. The Beast yields to her, her blood heating as though it may boil. Her arms trembling as she raises them.

Finally, the first sign of an aura appears. Olessia's eyes widen. The hantegran life energy is bold and luminous. But Sebastien's seeps from him, rivulets that wind away from his body.

"No," she hisses.

The Beckoning remains in her grasp. Under her control. It is not Olessia who pulls Sebastien's life from him.

It is death. True death.

The tremendous, ear-shattering roar comes again. But Olessia pays it little heed. She runs at the creature. Blade-encased arms raised overhead, a battle cry loosening from her. The slope of the unsettled earth tilts downward, enabling her to gather speed.

Olessia is close enough to swing when the shadow descends. Sweeping down over her. With her arms raised the glow of her elthar casts up against the underside of the four-legged creature, soaring on wide extended wings whose tips shred through the tops of the Kexen.

A Celtren. The largest Olessia has laid eyes upon.

She throws herself to her knees, readying her blades for a new target. But the creature shows no interest in her. Whipping past.

And slamming headlong into the hantegren. The Celtren is only slightly larger than the other, but it is enough. And the hantegran's grip on Sebastien is torn free. The pair of enormous beings intertwine, hard feather and sinewy, bony wings lashing out at one another. Tumbling them further down the unnatural slope of the land.

Olessia races to Sebastien, who sits up, coughing. Clutching at his chest. Bloodstains streaking his cheeks.

"Sebastien. Are you all right?" The Beckoning flows with her concern, a subtle force within her.

"Elthar… protected me." He coughs into his hand. A hand that comes away flecked with dark spots. Sebastien wipes them away against his leg, leaning into her as she assists him to his feet.

"Perhaps the elthar was not protection enough."

The Celtren roars. The sound from earlier. Though now it threatens to flatten them with its ferocity. A great mass hits the ground in front of them, flattening the Kexen that had managed to avoid destruction till now.

"Go, Olessia," Sebastien grunts, struggling to pull his arm from around her shoulder.

She curses at him, jerking his arm back into place. They both know that she will not leave him. Olessia braces. The Celtren heaves a great sigh, showering Olessia and Sebastien in a viscous layer of bodily fluid.

Olessia gasps, blinking through the dripping strands coating her face. The Celtren settles down onto its haunches. The great head is not turned their way. It stares to its left, chin tilted as though something touches at the space beneath its jaw.

Olessia blinks rapidly. Peering at the air beside the creature. A flutter of particles so minute they may be a figment of her imagination. And she is imaging a figure hunched there. Crouched as though they rest their hands against their knees. They shift, a movement of their head that appears as a smear of colour in the air.

"I see you," Olessia breathes.

The shimmering blur jerks, the particles scattering, a dust cloud on the air.

Let him take you. A whisper so desperately fragile, Olessia doesn't dare breathe in case it vanishes altogether. *Get on...*

"On that?" Olessia's surprise overtakes her caution.

Yes. The reply is an exhale.

The particles disassociate, and the figure they had moulded into life vanishes back into the nothingness it came from.

The Celtren swivels his wide head and fixes smouldering firestone eyes on her, releasing another dewy sigh, spittle escaping from its flared nostrils.

"Olessia?" Sebastien shifts his weight, grimacing with the movement.

"I saw her this time. Not just a mindreach."

"Who?"

"Sophie."

Sebastien grunts. "Do not trust your senses, this place is unsettled. Illusion and reality collide here—"

"Sebastien, she wants us to get on this Celtren."

"What?" Sebastien says. "Olessia, we cannot follow a delusion."

"Did I imagine this Celtren saving you from the hentegren? Have you ever seen such a thing?"

The Celtren rests its membranous wings on the ground. A snorted breath stirs shards of a broken Kexen lying before it.

"I have," Sebastien says quietly. His eyes, returned to a deeper grey, rest on the Celtren.

"She was here." Olessia shakes her head at her own words. "I think she brought this creature to us. I believe it was her. I *know* it was Sophie."

A lop-sided smile raises his lip, but Sebastien's eyes hold a tinge of sadness. "Then we had best do as our friend wishes."

Chapter 33

Ryder

Ryder hovers alongside Lucas. He groans, his right arm still jerking with spasms. Whatever device the guards just used on him, it's still having an effect. She tries to touch him, comfort him, tell him everything is going to be okay, but her hands drift through his body. Ryder's a ghost here. The Reigner has just told Lucas he wants him dead, and Ryder is a useless whisper of vapour.

The guards drag Lucas onto his knees. He swears, letting out an impressive stream of curses. Music to Ryder's ears. He's still fighting. The Reigner folds his arms, peering down his sharp nose at Lucas.

Lucas, I'm here. Lucas. There is the barest shift of his shoulders that might be an acknowledgement that he hears her. Ryder's watercolour body shivers with her excitement. But that excitement is forgotten a moment later when a third guard enters the cell.

"Reigner Zetem." The new arrival hesitates, obviously waiting on a sign from their leader to continue.

The Reigner seems lost in thought, still staring down at his bleeding, shaken captive. Lucas raises his chin to meet the Zentai leader's gaze, clear-eyed.

"Don't let me interrupt your war plans, Zetem," Lucas says.

The Reigner's blow is whiplash fast. Lucas is on his back again before Ryder can utter an ethereal cry. The Reigner places his booted foot over Lucas's bound hands. Lucas's lips are tight. His cheeks red.

Ryder's butterflies aren't quite so pronounced here, a very distant flutter at her core, and it is just sheer anger that spreads through her shadow-self, tinting her world with streaks of dark grey. She's not going to watch them hurt him. This cannot be the pool house all over again.

"Reigner, I beg forgiveness for this interruption." The guard ventures a tentative step forward, halting the moment the Reigner's eyes rest on him. "The Presider's Sretlan Armadel approaches. Approximately forty tar from the Xelnor Sector. The attack has commenced as planned."

The Reigner considers the messenger. "The Presider is nothing if not punctual. Have we secured Icewynn?"

"We have dispatched a quadrant to contain Nire. The Crown will be held according to your instruction." The guard gives him a curt nod. "And there will be a full search conducted for the Commandant. Footage retained from the downed Caleax confirms that J'salax retrieved the Commandant from the crash site."

The Reigner releases a sharp exhale. "See that it is done properly this time. I should have rid myself of that cursed soldier long before now. What of those that were monitored with her? Have we identified them?"

Ryder edges back from the Reigner, as though he might suddenly sense her existence.

"No, Exalted. The footage retrieved was... grossly compromised. The interference makes determinations near impossible." The guard pauses, casting a thoughtful frown at the ground. "We believe it was the Commandant purely through a similarity in height and body structure, and the piloting style bore her signature. We can only assume the Commandant was in the company of surviving members of her crew."

The Reigner lifts his boot from Lucas's restraints. "Deal with him, then join the evacuation of Huler-bae. This prisoner, as with all the others, does not survive. Varnne, and all those who did not see fit to follow the Zentai law will be unfortunate casualties of war. I'm sure the Presider will understand."

The two guards either side of Lucas lower their heads. "Yes, Exalted."

Ryder's shadow loses all hint of a humanoid form. Losing herself. Seeping into the Rising. The Reigner's words breaking her apart. They are going to kill Lucas. And Nire, J'salax and the Commandant are to be held prisoner. Ryder needs to warn them. If she goes now there might be time for them all to get out of Icewynn. Including her. Ryder is just as vulnerable. But no one's as vulnerable as Lucas.

Ryder's ink blot edges drift out into the Rising. The abyss tugs at her panic, toys with it. Pulling on a thread of her shadow-self, trying to unravel it altogether. She should go back to Nire. Warn her. Get everyone out of Icewynn. Nire can't help Lucas if she herself is a prisoner. But what information does Ryder have for her? Where is Lucas exactly? Huler-bae. Is that this place? And is it a true name, or a code the Reigner is using?

Lucas glares up at the Reigner. A thin line of blood runs from his top lip. "Good luck with your little war, mate. You're going to need it."

The Reigner produces a sickly, vapid smile. "Your father used to display a similarly misplaced bravado. Astonishing, how you could grow up having never met him, and yet be so irritatingly like him." He turns away. "Was it worth it? Surrendering yourself to us, Varnne. Were the humans worth it?"

Surrender? Lucas, why would you do that?

She's shouting the thoughts, they dart around her, echoing off one another. And of course there is no answer.

"Oh, they're worth it," Lucas replies.

I'm right here, Lucas. Please, tell me you can hear me. Ryder drifts between the Reigner and Lucas, needing to put some kind of barrier there. Even if it is invisible to them both. Lucas is desperately pale, more of a ghost than she is.

"Goodbye, Varnne."

"My name is Lucas."

"It hardly matters."

"It will."

The Reigner snickers, and he turns without another word. Leaving the cell. The third guard rushes after him. Ryder's blurry form refuses to come under any sort of control. She's a maelstrom of soft light. In the shadows around her, others sway and weave, like seaweed in a gentle current.

Help me. Ryder pleads.

But there is nothing. No whispers, no motion that might be an entity moving closer to come to her aid. In the cell, a new movement absorbs all of Ryder's attention. One of the guards settles himself behind Lucas. A splayed device, like half a CD, gripped in his hand. Aimed at the back of Lucas's neck. The cry launches up from the very core of Ryder's messed up eidolon.

No!

Her scream churns at the Rising, whipping up translucent waves that radiate out into the cell. Crashing down on the device in the guard's hand. Wrenching it from his grip. Shattering it against the wall.

A wry grin brightens Lucas's face. *Nice one, Ry.*

Lucas? You could hear me all this time?

Depends how long you've been there. Something is interfering with the mindreach. You're super faint. Must be some kind of shielding in this place. Thought I was just tripping out from blood loss to be honest.

He staggers to his feet.

"Stay down," the second guard bellows, lifting a clenched hand. She clutches another of the semi-circular devices; thin as a knife blade, its prismatic surface alive with colour. Raising her arm, she moves to strike.

Ryder throws herself in between them. Padellah once told her all she had to do was will what she wanted into existence. Well, Ryder wants this guard to stop attacking her friend. She focuses in on the guard's swinging arm. Picturing that fist punching its owner right in the nose.

And the reality plays out before her.

The shocked cry that leaves the Zentai as he punches himself is mildly amusing. Lucas staggers to his feet and swings his bound hands like he's an Olympic weight toss champ. The guard drops to the ground, unconscious. But the momentum throws Lucas forward, his tied hands unbalancing him. Ryder sweeps in front of him. *Stand up. Stand up.*

Like a puppet on tightening strings, Lucas jerks upright. Settling back on his feet.

"Thanks, Ry. You're getting pretty good at this stuff." He crouches by the male guard's side. "Always wanted to see if this would actually work."

What?

He begins unhooking the network of clasps that hold the guard's armour against his body. No easy task when your wrists are bound, Lucas's fingers working like a tiny octopus to try and negotiate the clasps.

Wait, let me help with that. Lift your hands.

Lucas looks around the room, frowning. "Ry? Can you do something about these?"

He hasn't heard her. The interference he spoke about, plaguing them again.

Ryder doesn't bother with a reply, concentrating instead on the bindings at his wrists. Focusing, on what she wants. Release. The binding snaps, falling free of Lucas's hands. Ryder's shadow hums, her edges no longer frayed. It's getting easier, more instinctive to manipulate the strange energy.

Lucas hurries to pull on the guard's clothes. Every move causing him to wince, or grunt.

"No peeking, Ry."

Ryder would have rolled real eyes. But she turns away, gazing deep into the shadows of the Rising, giving him some privacy. Her fellow shadow beings still sway close by. Watchful. Their presence oddly comforting.

Come on, Lucas. Come on.

Finally done, Lucas drags the senseless guard closer to the door.

What are you doing?

"Getting out of here." He plants the guard's palm against a panel to the right of the door. And he is free.

Ryder's delight dances through her shadow-self in tiny pulses of rich orange. But the dance comes to a quick end. An uncomfortable rippling moves through her. And the tug of the abyss deepens.

Lucas. I feel weird.

But Lucas scans the corridor, oblivious. Ryder shirks her shadowy shoulders, trying to dislodge the uncomfortable sensation. Catching sight of her shadow buddies. Their forms are way more discernible now. Slender-man, skinny shapes, gathered off to her right. Like a crowd gawking at a show. The odd rippling intensifies. And the abyss creeps its edges towards her. An enormous tub of tar in the distance. Ryder aches, a feeling as deep as the nothingness calling to her.

All she has to do is let go. Just stop fighting. Drift down.

Don't you dare.

The voices — that slightly off-beat whisper Padellah uses — snap at her, and Ryder jerks, half expecting to find the Cyne right at her watercolour elbow. But there is no one there. Not in the Rising anyway. In reality, Lucas strides past her. Clad in the uniform of the unconscious guard who now wears Lucas's tattered shirt, and jeans. Ryder gathers herself. Scanning the shadows. Her audience has settled back, and the abyss is nowhere to be seen.

"Ryder, I really hope you're still with me, cause I'm going to need you." He glances each way down the corridor. "I have no idea which way to go."

Overhead lights dim. And the floor of the corridor itself brightens with aquamarine light. At the centre, a narrow line of pure white streaks away, headed down the passageway to the right.

A calm, feminine voice fills the corridor. "Attention, Attention. Huler-Bae has been compromised. Fallyn borders have been breached. Emergency procedures should now be activated. Follow directional pulses to reach safety."

The white streak in the centre of the walkway appears again. Over and over, running away to the right.

This way. When Lucas doesn't react, Ryder presses her watery hands to his shoulders. Giving them a gentle nudge. He starts with surprise, but his face smooths quickly. "All right, got it, Ry. Left it is."

Ignoring the ripple that plays at her chest, Ryder moves ahead of him, readying for any obstacle that might make the mistake of getting in their way. But there is no one in sight. Not in the corridors anyway. Several of the cells are occupied. Their hidden occupants calling out at the sound of Lucas's footfall, their voices muffled behind the doors.

Ryder's hands flutter to her chest. She doesn't breathe in the Rising, doesn't need to, there is no rise and fall of her chest, but that area of her body feels tight and restricted. Like she really should take a deep breath. The emergency announcement repeats, over and over. Another left turn, a right, a quick check to make sure Lucas is still close, and Ryder reaches two imposing, solid doors. Ryder moves straight through them, though it takes more effort than she expects. Like she's in a wind tunnel, with the speed of the fan slowly being raised. Forcing more and more pressure against her.

The doors are incredibly thick, at least a metre in width. A bank vault to end all bank vaults. Beyond the doors the light is blindingly bright. Two midday suns sit high in the sky, blazing down on an open area, covered in chunks of jagged stone. Several vehicles, all with caterpillar tracks, perfect for the rough terrain, sit abandoned in a group about fifty metres out.

Lucas's prison is built into a towering lime-green cliff, one whose top is lost in a swathe of bruised cloud. The massive rounded doorway is constructed from a material that matches the green of the cliff so well, a quick glance might conceal the entrance altogether. The evacuation message is instructing empty air. There is no sign of any movement out on the rock field that reaches as far as the eye can see, no hint of aircraft above the giant cliff that dominates the landscape. A perfect natural vantage point to watch for anyone desperate enough to try and flee into the sparse terrain.

Like Lucas. But no one is watching now. Huler-bae is playing a part in a charade. The Reigner has known for a long time what was going to happen here. The Presider is going to land his first blow, and in the process, wipe out the Zentai criminal problem.

Ryder races back through the massive doors. Lucas waits for her there, his back to the solid door, eyes on the corridor behind. "Ry?"

But she doesn't bother trying to speak to him. No time for that. Ryder focuses on the doors.

Open. Open. Open.

There is a mechanical groan, coming from the outer edges of the door, but they themselves don't budge.

The rippling spreads through her shadow, edging out into her extremities. Ryder shakes it off, centres herself. And tries again.

Her buttermilk fingers elongate, spreading like ten snakes. Finding the door. Covering its surface. The hiss of the locking mechanism rises. The rattle of metal under duress presses the air. Ryder's vision blurs, like a cloud has passed between her and the door she focuses on. Lucas is talking to her, but she can't make out his words.

They don't matter anyway. She just has to give him a way out of here. The tightness that has settled over her, spreads. Her shadow is made of lead. Still the door holds. But the scent of burning hits the air. A long, high screech filters through to her muted world.

The panels of the door grind open. Pushing back into the recesses, fighting the mechanics that work against it. Inch by frustratingly slow inch.

In her peripheral vision, Ryder notes the inky blackness. Closer now. Lapping like an incoming tide.

She grits her ghostly teeth, or at least imagines herself doing so. And throws all her energy into one last desperate attempt. The sense of being surrounded grips her. The shadows dance in close, forming a wall between her and the creeping darkness. Whispers fill the air. Voice upon voice. And though most of it makes no sense, she thinks she hears her name called.

The rippling takes hold of her. Shaking every inch of her shadow-self.

And the doors whip open. Sparks fly, the air is heavy with an unpleasant acrid smell. An alarm blares.

Ryder shifts to face Lucas. She can barely make him out in the sneaking gloom. Behind him, more shadows. But these are flesh and blood. Panicked, desperate flesh and blood.

All the cells have opened. Relief crashes into her. Ryder is translucent jelly. Shaking so hard she's about to lose all substance.

Her grip on the Rising is slipping.

And the abyss is moving in.

Go. Lucas, Go.

This time there is no mistaking her name in the cries around her. But all the fight is gone.

And when the abyss draws her in, Ryder melts down into its depths.

Chapter 34

Olessia

Riding astride a Celtren is easily among the most uncomfortable experiences Olessia can recall. Her inner thighs scream with discomfort, her spine assaulted by the wild tilt of the creature's body as it weaves through the seemingly endless expanse of Kexen. At times, the Celtren's movement involves full body rolls. Olessia has survived only with the assistance of elthar, pressing her in place against the creature's back. Sebastien has done the same, seated just in front of her. Their heads have clashed on more than one painful occasion as the creature's unpredictable movement throws them about.

A sudden jerk right causes an uncomfortable crack of joints in Olessia's neck but, at last, the creature is descending. Below, the sharp lines, and jagged points of the Kexan have finally disappeared. But their replacement is hardly reassuring. A white vapour covers everything. Thick enough that Olessia cannot make out anything beyond the tip of the Celtren's wings.

This does not seem to bother the creature though. The descent is taken at a stomach-dropping pace. Sebastien hunches forward, leaning low against the Celtren's back. They burst through the vapour, and the strangeness of this place continues. The Celtren alights upon a long white stretch of beach.

A beach. Sand white as snow. Hugging the edge of an onyx-coloured ocean that stretches out into a murky distance. The far reaches are consumed by the same white vapour.

"This is impossible," Sebastien whispers.

Olessia slides from the Celtren's back, feet sinking into sand. Her knees threaten to buckle and she holds onto the beast's coarse hair until she is steady. The creature swivels its head to watch her, sides heaving. Thanks are in order, but Olessia's disbelief at the surroundings has rendered her mute. She touches the rough fur in an absent-minded pat.

The scenery that lies before them is indeed impossible. There are no such locations on Siros. Nor, so far as she knows, on Zentai. But this landscape is not entirely foreign.

"How can this be?" Olessia stoops to grasp a handful of sand. The tiny alabaster beads are warm against her skin, though there is neither twin confels nor a sun in the sky. Olessia is uncertain of what section of this strange place could be classified as sky. The white vapour trims the edges of this place, as though they hang in a bubble.

"Have we… are we…" Sebastien can't seem to bring himself to say it. "Have we returned to Earth?" He stands at the water's edge. The fluid creeps towards his boots. Moving in a fashion that is reminiscent of Earth's oceans, but with one distinct difference. The inward creep of liquid is slow, while the retreat is spectacularly rapid.

"No. This is not Earth." Though it is similar enough to cause a knot in Olessia's chest; a pang of longing for her time there. "This must be the Arlion Xhentex."

"Clever girl." The voice comes from some distance, and a giggle follows.

Sebastien turns, elthar blades forming. The usual sapphire glow now an intense aquamarine. Olessia's own elthar shines with an equally brilliant shade of ice-blue. As though the very colour spectrum is altered by the Xhentex.

A figure strides down the beach towards them; solid, tangible. All features clear. The shock of red hair is more orange than Olessia remembers but the smile is just the same.

"Sophie!" Olessia says.

Sebastien lowers his arms. "She lives."

Olessia runs, the sand slippery beneath her feet. Sophie's laughter echoes across the distance. Her face bright with delight, floral skirt flowing out behind her. Olessia's arms are raised, readying herself to grasp Sophie in her arms. But she sees too late, that is not to be.

"Oh, Sophie." Olessia stops and lowers her arms.

The beach that stretches far beyond Sophie is faintly visible through the brightness of her clothing. But Sophie's smile remains locked in place. She raises her hands and presses them to Olessia's shoulders.

Olessia sucks in her breath. A subtle tremor runs through her. She can *feel* Sophie's hands upon her. And smell the scent of her perfume. But when Olessia lifts her hand to touch Sophie's she finds her fingers upon her own shoulder. Olessia digs her fingernails into the rough fabric of the certifier garment.

"Sophie… I am so sorry." Sorry for ever coming into her life. For taking that life away.

"Olessia, I'm just so glad you're okay. That you both are." The sense of being touched, fades. Sophie drifts back, and her gaze moves to Sebastien. He stands with lips parted, the sadness returned to haunt his expression.

"Sophie," he says. "Though I wish it were in different circumstances, I am happy to see you."

"Oh, come here, you big softy." Sophie shifts from Olessia to Sebastien's side, in a fraction of a moment. Her hands settle on his shoulders.

Sebastien's posture stiffens, before his shoulders relax. He lowers his head, and the two of them stand in quiet company.

"She's going to be okay, you know." Sophie's voice echoes against itself. "And you and I both know she didn't want to leave you back there. But Ryder had no choice."

Sebastien says nothing, his head hung so his hair shields his expression.

"She's so strong now, Sebastien," Sophie continues. "You should see her, like a supernova."

The inward push of the water makes a sound like heavy rain while the outward drift is more like wind through a forest. Both sounds remind Olessia of her time in Christian's family cottage, and her thoughts settle uneasily on where he is now. Where all the others may be. Her consolation is that they were together. Able to protect one another. But have any of them ever experienced such a place as this?

"And you, Sophie." Sebastien speaks at last. "How are you faring? This must be confusing for you."

Her image flutters, like a shadow passing over the sun. "I'm doing okay. I mean, don't get me wrong, I'm trying not to think too hard about it all right now. Which is surprisingly easy, considering how insane things are right now. I mean, Padellah has got me working like I'm on a million dollar salary, right? And I'm doing what I can, for her, for you guys. For Ryder. I just hope it's enough."

"Sophie," Olessia says. "There is so much I don't understand. How are you here?" She hesitates. "Wherever here is."

Sophie drifts away from Sebastien. Though she takes steps no sign of her passing appears in the sand beneath her. "Well, you're in the Arlion Xhentex, by far the most confusing, minefield of a place I've ever been. But you probably gathered that already. As for what it is exactly, I'm trying to work out myself. It's kind of everywhere and nowhere all at once." Her head bobs. "Actually, that's a darn good way of putting it, if I do say so myself. Like a tar pit where tiny fractures of all the universes are kind of stuck. Or fractions of our memories, maybe? I'm not sure. But I keep seeing stuff that's really familiar. I mean, check out this beach. This is some version of Wineglass Bay. I've been there tonnes of times."

Olessia rubs at tight muscles in her neck. Wineglass Bay. She recalls it all too well, though she could not name the place. This is the beach where she and Christian fled Earth. And where the human woman Petra fell. Sophie continues, not noticing Olessia's unease.

"Anyway, some parts of the pit don't seem to hold anything at all, and they are crazy deep. Infinite, Padellah says. And that is an infinity and beyond you definitely do not want to go to." She seems to be amused by her own comment and looks to them for a reaction that does not come. "Next time you go to Earth, you have to watch Toy Story, promise me."

"Sophie." Olessia is as gentle as her impatience will allow. "Do you know where Aresh is?"

"Right on the edge of one of the infinite bits," Sophie says. "The Presider, her brother, put her there. Seriously, that guy is on track for worst sibling of all time." Her exuberance drains away. "I used to tell Kye how terrible he was at being a big brother but…"

"Sophie?" Olessia says.

Sebastien stays her with a subtle wave of his hand. "I am certain your brother fares well, Sophie. I left him far beyond the reach of those flood waters, and a safe distance from the Paldrian River."

Sophie gives him a grateful smile. "I'm sure you did. I just… I'm just wondering if I'm ever going to see him again."

Olessia senses the pain in her voice but she has no answer for Sophie and does not desire to give false hope. She clears her throat."We must focus on what is happening here—"

"You're absolutely right." Sophie brushes at her chest, as though wiping away the melancholy. "And what is happening here, what is *going* to happen here will be amazing." Sophie's smile is dazzling. Actually dazzling, a light spearing from the edges of her mouth. But just as quickly the light is extinguished. Sophie shudders, hugging herself, as though taken by a severe chill.

"What's wrong?" Sebastien asks.

Sophie tugs at her yellow collar, dragging the material clear of her neck. "Something's wrong. I can't feel her anymore. We've been linked up like she's a cell tower and I'm the phone, but she's gone. Guys, I'm sorry. I have to go. I've lost Ryder."

Chapter 35

Christian

C hristian clutches at his arm. Blood streams fresh and bright from a shallow cut near his elbow. Turns out the weird skeleton trees in this place — the Kexen according to Teler — look like they are made from porcelain but their pointed tips cut like paper against skin.

"Chris-tan, are you—"

Christian waves off Sen-Bay's concern. "All good. Keep going or we will get left behind."

Teler weaves his garreson deftly through the increasingly thick terrain, setting a cracking pace with Evelyn as his pillion passenger. Maher follows next, his passenger seat empty now that Olessia has joined Sebastien to scout ahead. Probably a good thing judging by the way he throws the machine left and right, leaning at wild angles. Sen-Bay grunts and mutters beneath his breath as he follows along. It's not exactly a smooth ride, and the jerky turns are starting to make Christian's stomach churn.

"This place seems intent on ensuring we are left behind, no matter what course I set," Sen-Bay growls.

They gain some ground on Maher, just a few metres separate them now. The humming coming from the trees seems to grow louder, deeper, as they race along.

"Keep down," Sen-Bay shouts, leaning them hard right. Christian tightens his grip, leaning with the Yentern and barely avoiding a low jutting branch. It scrapes at the top of his head, probably taking a few hairs with it, but Christian's not about to let go.

"That branch, it wasn't there a moment ago was it?" Christian frowns.

The pathway was clear, he watched Maher dash down the narrow space just a second ago.

"I am glad you see it too, Chris-Tan," Sen-Bay says. "I was beginning to believe the procedure we endured in the Collective had begun to erode my sane mind."

They heave right, their clear path suddenly blocked by a thick limb with a spear-like tip. There's no wind here, not a breath. No breeze tousles their hair, despite the speed they are travelling. Like they are moving through a vacuum.

"Do you get the feeling this place doesn't want us here?" Christian says. A crazy thought maybe, but the vibe here makes his skin crawl.

Sen-Bay nods fervently, sending dreadlocks jumping. "I share your feelings. But Teler warned us that oddities would arise as we move closer to the Arlion Xhentex. These lifeforms increase their intent to halt us, I fear."

"The trees are trying to stop us?"

"That is my belief."

As if to prove his point, a bulky white limb suddenly blocks their path. Sen-Bay throws them into a sideways slide.

"Lift your leg," he shouts.

Christian's already there, knee raised almost to his cheek. The machine slams against the Kexen. Spiderweb cracks appear at the impact point, racing out along the length of the limb, widening as they stretch back to the trunk, as though the tree is made of the very ceramic it resembles.

Sen-Bay places his hand over Christian's at his belly. "You did well to hold on."

"You did well to avoid a head-on collision."

His hands rise and fall with Sen-Bay's soft laughter.

Maher has managed to turn back despite the narrowness of their pathways. "You two all right?"

"For now, yes," Sen-Bay says. "But this pace is unwise in this terrain."

Maher nods, touching at a tear in his pant leg. "I will not argue with you on that point." He swivels around. "Teler, we need to rethink this pace."

Teler has stopped further ahead, but the section he's reached is far too narrow to turn his machine around. Evelyn, with her veil in place, is almost invisible against his back. Like a secondary cloak.

"We have greater concerns," he shouts across the distance. "The Laudess and the guardian should have checked in by now."

Christian glances around. All that is visible is uneven row after uneven row of the skeletal trees. Even above, they curve over the riders in a canopy of stark white limbs.

"Olessia!" Sen-Bay bellows.

"Quiet! You foolish boy." Teler throws his garreson into reverse, backing towards them as quickly as he'd driven forward for the past half hour. But his trip is cut short. A Kexen appears in his path. Branches fanning out across a passageway that was clear just a few seconds ago.

"Okay. This is officially getting creepy." Christian shuffles in his seat, adjusting his hold on Sen-Bay's waist. Half expecting one of the branches to jut out and smack him off the back of the air-bike.

A crackling begins in the distance, back in the direction they have just come. Christian twists in his seat. The noise shifts. Now it comes in from their right-hand side.

"Teler, any idea what we are hearing?" Maher says. "Or what we should do about it?"

Teler's reply is to pull a device from beneath his cloak and point it towards the Kexen blocking his way. He fires. The blast hits the white branches and the noise is deafening; a giant dropping every pot in his kitchen. Christian crushes his right ear against Sen-Bay's back, covering his left. Chunks of white, like huge jagged pieces of hail, pepper the ground.

Someone is yelling but it takes a few seconds for the blast echo to fade. The cracking sound replaces the gun blast. Louder than before. And coming from all directions.

"What is that?" Evelyn says.

"The Xhentex is deconstructing," comes Teler's terse reply. "Everyone follow me, we must leave. Right now. Move!"

"Deconstructing? That sounds bad. That's bad, right?" Christian says.

It sounds terrible. Like a hundred icebergs splitting around them.

Sen-Bay's stomach tightens beneath his hands, and the Yentern utters a flurry of angry words.

"Hold on, Chris-Tan."

Around them, the Kexen start to fall. Collapsing against one another, setting off a skeletal domino effect. Heavy thuds thunder towards them, plumes of white rising as the fragile trees shatter.

"Faster," Christian yells.

Sen-Bay is already pushing the accelerator, wherever that might be on this floating motorcycle thing.

Up ahead, Teler fires rounds into the sea of white ahead. The Kexen there rise like ghosts to block their way, but behind it's a different story. Christian peers over his shoulder, eyes wide with horror.

"We need to go much faster."

The Kexen dominos sweep in a thunderous wall of white behind them. Pushing a wave of broken limbs towards the fleeing party.

Sen-bay grunts, throwing them wide to avoid the sudden appearance of a trio of narrow kexen. "Any faster and we will be thrown from the garreson. Bletchen bres, where are the weapons on this vehicle?"

He frees a hand from the controls to swipe at the various switches resting between the handles. A touch of his fingers to a pulsing figure eight sets off a spray of darting light from the front of the air-bike. Only just missing Maher who has swung right to navigate a rising trunk of a limbless Kexen.

"Killing me will not enable you to escape this place any faster," Maher shouts.

A high-pitched scream manages to find its way over the chaos. Evelyn has slipped, one leg dangling beneath the garreson, the other hooked over the seat as though she's a rider who only managed to half-mount her horse. Teler grips her, shouting at her to hold on. Like she would do anything else. Maher attempts to dart in closer, presumably to try and help, but the Kexen aren't about to make life easy for them now. The handle of his garreson clips a double-tipped branch, and he's thrown off course, taking out a sapling in the process. Christian ducks behind Sen-Bay, avoiding the shower of debris that follows. When he looks again, Evelyn has managed to haul herself back into position, clinging to Teler's back.

"This is becoming impossible," Sen-bay says.

The sound behind them is a hundred thunderstorms, with a dozen bulls in china shops thrown in for the mix. And no matter which way he turns, all Christian sees is more of the impenetrable forest of collapsing Kexen.

Until, in the blink of a watering eye, they reach the end of the forest. Shooting across a border that no one saw coming. One moment their world is calamitous with sound and motion, the next they are rushing out into an open, silent space.

And straight into the path of two enormous gunmetal-grey crabs.

At least, they resemble crabs. Christian sucks in his breath. Giant ones, at least two-storeys high. Each with four long metal limbs dotted with cogs and spinning wheels like it's just stepped out of a steampunk exhibit, and cradling an oval cabin. A blue light pulses along the rim of the pod. High above the crabs, an aircraft hovers, shaped like the horns on a bull. Easily the size of a school bus.

Teler, Maher and Sen-Bay hit the brakes in almost perfect unison.

"What is that?" Christian whispers.

"Teler, any ideas?" Maher gives the Sentinel a nervous glance. "Do we fire?"

A hissing static noise comes from one of the hulking metallic monsters. "I would suggest an attack is very unwise."

The voice is male, deep and authoritative. Goosebumps bristle along Christian's arms. He's heard that voice before.

Evelyn lets out a short cry. "No. No. It's him."

Teler's shoulders' slump. "Do not fire, Maher. This fight cannot be won."

"No indeed it cannot." The voice booms down. "Unfortunate you did not recognise that before now, Sentinel. Very unfortunate indeed."

Christian draws a jagged breath. "No, no."

"What?" Sen-bay hisses. "Who is it?"

"The last person I wanted to see again." Christian's eyes burn, tears pushing their way clear. "That's the Presider's voice. I'm never going to forget it."

Sen-Bay mutters under his breath, low and venomous.

From the belly of one of the 'crabs' a panel slides open. Armed soldiers float the distance between machine and ground. Their uniforms are like something a medieval knight would wear, smooth gleaming silver covering their upper bodies with sharp points off their shoulders and elbows, and around their wrists. Their faces are covered by a slim piece of metal that stretches from temple to temple, with tear-drop-shaped black lenses over each eye, giving them a kind of bug-eyed look.

They march towards the group, a hook-shaped device in hand, kind of like fancy walking canes, but Christian's guessing they're way more deadly than anything his grandad ever used. Even so, when the guard order them off the garreson, Christian baulks. The thought of seeing that guy, the Presider, with his raging eyes and terrifying presence, is making it hard to stop from shaking. He and Sen-Bay are the last to dismount.

Evelyn extends her hand to Christian. "Come on. We're going to be okay."

Why do people keep saying that? Christian grits his teeth, fighting to keep his expression clear. They are not going to be okay. Not if the guy with fire-eyes is around. Sen-Bay helps him off the air-bike, and Christian takes Evelyn's hand. She must be able to feel him shaking but says nothing.

They are herded beneath the crab. Fear is turning his bones to mush, and he's leaning way too hard against Evelyn's slight frame but she doesn't seem to mind, and wraps an arm tightly around him. The guards surround them, a dull light surrounds them, and the entire group lifts into the air. Pulled up into the belly of the vehicle by a tractor beam. An actual tractor beam, something straight out of *Star Trek*. And Christian's too terrified to care. The network of cogs and wheels along the massive legs spin with a low hum, and the sound hammers at Christian's skull.

"Hold on, Christian. Don't forget to breathe," Evelyn whispers from behind her veil.

The ride is short, and they are sucked into the interior in a matter of seconds. Christian squeezes his eyes shut as they arrive. His insides are hollow, his blood running cold. On the brink of a panic attack. Does he get panic attacks? Christian presses his fingers to his temple, eyes still closed. The black hole in his memories is pulling at him, and it has sharp claws.

"Open your eyes, boy."

A new voice. Not the Presider, but one that Christian recognises equally well. His knees buckle, and Evelyn gasps as she tries to keep him on his feet. Teler steps in, the big man easily taking Christian's weight.

"Easy now," he whispers.

Christian reluctantly opens his eyes. They are standing in a domed room, a confined space just big enough to accommodate them all. Teler and Christian, the tallest of the bunch, could touch the roof easily if they raised their hands.

The figure standing before them draws into focus. Christian whimpers. Teler's grip is all that keeps him from ending up a trembling mess on the floor as he stares at the man who tried to crack open his skull. Made his nose bleed, and his eyes ache like they were about to. The violet-eyed girl had screamed his name. Begged him to stop hurting Christian. Dashel.

Olessia isn't here to protect him now. Christian's breath comes in short, sharp gulps. "No, no." He tries to move, to put more distance between him and the bald-headed man glaring down at him, a vicious smirk on his face.

"Well, we meet again." Dashel's needling gaze moves to Sen-Bay. "You really should choose your company more wisely, Yentern."

Sen-Bay rushes forward but gets no more than a full stride before a guard jabs him with the hook weapon. Sen-Bay screeches as he collapses.

"No!" Christian strains to break free of Teler's grasp. "What did you do? You killed him!"

Dashel sniffs. "Not yet. Not till we see what lies in that rather unfortunate head of his. The same for all of you. This is truly the most impressive collection the Presider has amassed to date. The Sentinel, the would-be Guardian, a couple of humans, and a Yentern. A band of traitors working for a traitor. Fascinating, really. I'm rather looking forward to tearing down Aresh and Olessia's Blackwalls and seeing what this is all about. Truly, it will be most satisfying." He gestures to the guards and they begin to herd Christian and the others across the cabin, towards a section in the wall that shimmers and then disappears altogether, revealing a much larger chamber behind.

"While the Presider deals with the Laudess, we shall spend our time unveiling all the secrets she and the traitor Laudine have tried so hard to conceal."

"The greatest of all the traitors stands before me, Dashel," Teler growls. "You have betrayed your people, and are destroying lives in Siros and Zentai."

Dashel laughs. A gruff, dismissive sound. "The Presider and I have never done anything less than what is best for Siros in this chaotic time." He jerks his chin towards one of the guards. "Remove them. All except the human boy. Leave him with me."

Christian clings to Teler's arm, kicking out at the guard that steps forward. "No, don't touch me."

"Leave him alone," Evelyn launches herself at the guard. But one of the other soldiers thrusts his weapon towards her, and Evelyn screams. She drops to the floor, right alongside Sen-Bay, her body jerking with tiny spasms, her eyes rolled back in her head. Teler roars, releasing Christian and raising balled fists. Ready for a fight. But Christian weaves in front of him.

"Stop! Stop," he pleads, voice lowering. "Don't give them an excuse to hurt you. We need you. Olessia needs you."

He may not understand everything that is going on, but Christian is certain of that much.

Muscles in Teler's throat work as he swallows hard. He nods, cupping a wide palm to Christian's cheek. "And Olessia needs you.

Stay strong. I will take care of your Sen-Bay."

The sob almost escapes Christian, but he bites it back, and steps aside. His heart beats so fast he can't catch his breath. The Sentinel doesn't protest as the guards push him from the room. They gather up Sen-Bay and Evelyn, dragging them out of the chamber. Christian watches until the panel is completely closed. Taking a moment to gather himself before turning to face Dashel.

Chapter 36

Ryder

R yder wakes to the air being forced from her lungs. Blane leans over her, eyes closed. Counting out each compression he pounds down on her chest. Ryder opens her mouth, tries to form a single word. Stop. But it comes out as weird gasp. He's lowering his face to give her CPR before his eyes open.

"Ryder? Oh thank god." He sits back on his heels.

Her joints ache, and she's sweating badly. The tang of sweat fills her nostrils. Ryder moves to sit up, but Blane stops her.

"No. Don't you dare."

The same determined voice she heard in the Rising. Blane's voice filtering into the ethereal world as he tried to bring her around. Shouting at her not to actually die.

He's not shouting now. The guy looks wiped. "I know you told Nire this would happen, but this is way too much. You've been flatlining for fifteen minutes, Ryder."

He's as sweat drenched as she, his fringe plastered to his forehead, a bead running down the side of his face. Ryder presses her hands to her chest, winces. Fifteen minutes of heart compressions is going to make for some serious bruising.

"We have to…" Ryder breaks into a fit of coughing.

"Take it easy," Blane scowls.

But Ryder can't take it easy, she has too much to say. She tries to swat his hands away, but her body is like a balloon filled with sand.

"Where… Nire…" she rasps.

"Here, Ryder. I am right here." The Crown of Zentai is seated at the end of the bed. They are in a different room, much smaller. But the bedding is just as comfortable as the couch. "Please, don't strain yourself."

"Huler-bae," the word bursts from her, rough and dry. "Huler-bae. That's where Lucas is."

Nire clutches Ryder's hands, giving them a gentle squeeze. "I know. You spoke during the Shift. It was the only thing you said. Over and over. I took it to be of importance. And it made sense. Huler-bae is Fallwyn's highest security containment facility. I relayed the information—"

Ryder coughs and its agony for her bruised ribs. "Need to leave here."

Nire's face elongates, then squishes back on itself. Ryder blinks. Her heavy body is light as air now.

"Ryder, lie down," Blane says.

Not until Nire understands. Ryder shakes her head. A bad idea. Pieces of the room tilt at odd angles. She slumps onto her back.

"Leave." In her head the word is clear, but on her tongue it's a squeaky cry.

"How long was she unresponsive?" Blane demands. "When you called me in, you said she had only just stopped breathing."

"She was in no danger, good doctor," Nire replies.

"She was dead," Blane cries.

"Not truly."

"Well, excuse me your highness but not having a pulse classifies as dead in the human world."

"Mr Blane." Nire's voice booms, and Blane jumps. Ryder would probably have done the same if it wasn't exhausting just to blink. "You have taken great care of her, but Ryder has something to say. Allow her to say it."

The Crown of Zentai moves her face closer, strands of her messy hair tickling Ryder's forehead. Taking shallow breaths, Ryder squeezes her eyes shut, concentrating on getting something coherent past her lips. "They are coming… for you… need… to… leave. Now."

She opens her eyes. Nire is inches away, a blurry mass above her. "Coming here? To Icewynn?"

"Yes."

"Who?"

"The Reigner."

Ryder dives into another coughing fit. And each wracking bark brings spots to her vision. She's only passed out once in her life. After giving blood for the first and last time. It felt kind of like this. Something cool presses to her forehead.

"Rest. You've done well," Nire whispers. And the blob that is the queen of Zentai grows smaller. "Mr Blane, all my resources are at your disposal to ensure Ryder's comfort."

Nire's voice comes from a distance. Then sinks into a murmur. Joined by a new voice, deeper. It is not Blane's. Ryder's fairly certain he's the new blur leaning over her. The faint tang of his aftershave, which does not quite cover the scent of sweat, drifts up her nostrils.

"Hang in there, Ryder. Your blood pressure is low." Definitely Blane. "But nothing we can't deal with."

Ryder heaves the dead weight that her skull has become, turning so she gazes towards the cluster of silhouettes over the other side of the room. Nire is given away by her birds-nest hairdo, and Ryder's fairly confident that J'salax is one of the other figures.

Get out of here. They all have to get out of here. But Ryder's tongue isn't playing fair anymore. Her attempt to speak results in a weak moan. Did Nire not believe her? Did the words actually leave Ryder's mouth? Or, is she hallucinating after too long in the Rising?

The answer comes swiftly.

"Mr Blane," Nire's voice fills the chamber yet again. "I am initiating emergency evacuation procedures for Icewynn. I will send an escort for you and Ryder. You are to follow their instructions with no protest."

Ryder's lead-weight body relaxes, and the tension drains from her. Taking the room with it. With a sigh, she slips into unconsciousness.

When she comes to, Ryder is sitting propped up in a circular bed, covered in a blanket of what seem to be feathers – speckled, and so light she can barely feel the fabric against her body. The room has shrunk yet again, and this one has no windows. A low drone hugs the air, and the subtle sway of the room is either her dizziness getting the better of her, or she is no longer on solid ground. Ryder runs her tongue over lips that are even dryer than her throat. On the plus side, the cut doesn't sting quite so much, and no spots clog her vision. The weighty sensation has left her body.

"Welcome back, you timed that very well." J'salax lounges in a chair that looks a lot like an inflatable sun lounge; the base pristine white and the rest the same opalescent shade as the floor in the main chamber in Icewynn.

Ryder tugs the feather blanket up over her chest, even though she's still fully clothed. She wriggles her toes. Mostly fully clothed. Someone has taken off her shoes. She wipes at the corners of her mouth, checking there's no dribble.

"How long have you been there?" Ryder says.

"Not long," he arches his back, arms lifted overhead, stretching. "Nire has been with you since we evacuated Icewynn. She'll allow only myself or the Commandant to sit with you. But my dear self-same is having some issue with convincing the Kali that travelling to Megnastin is a suitable plan of action."

"The who?" Ryder frowns.

J'Salax scratches at the skin beneath his chin. "The Kali are Nire's personal soldiers, tasked with protecting her alone. And they are very unhappy with Nire's decision to split the Kali squadrons, so she might use the majority of their Criterion fleet as decoys. And it is not just the airborne vessels that she has sacrificed. She has sent out all the remaining Taer-lon, in all manner of directions beneath the ground. Hoping the Reigner will be too occupied with the mass movement to notice our little squadron of just two Criterion making its way to Megnastin. Nire and the Commandant are in talks at the moment, and I have to say, I'm quite disappointed I'm not there to witness the shouting."

Ryder swallows, her sore throat niggling. She's guessing the Kali are the exo-skeleton-covered soldiers, the ones who wanted to take Ryder out when the elthar got out of her control. "But we're still traveling there, right? To Megnastin?"

J'salax settles back against the lounge, crossing his arms behind his head. "We are. Nire is determined. But as to what we do once we arrive, I've yet to get a straight answer from my self-same. Would you care to fill me in?"

Ryder hugs her arms around her belly. The growls coming from her empty stomach would be embarrassing in any other circumstance, but J'salax's words plague her, because Ryder doesn't have an answer for him. Or for Nire.

The Crown is playing her part. They are headed to Megnastin. Just as Aresh wanted. But that's the only thing Ryder knew about what the Laudine wanted. Ryder shoves the impossibly soft blanket away and swings her legs over the edge of the bed. She's steady. No headspins. But anxiety knots her stomach.

"I wish I could tell you. But I don't know. I'm not sure what we're supposed to do when we get there." The admission comes easily, and the knot lessens with the release the words bring. Talking to J'salax is surprisingly easy. "I just have to get there. Aresh needs me there."

"Ryder the human, you are most intriguing. You can Shift, you can wield elthar with the prowess of the Claven, and the Laudine of Bax Un Tey is relying on you to rescue her. This is quite the spectacle. And has alleviated the sheer boredom of daily life as the Crown's self-same. So for that, I thank you most humbly."

J'salax's tilted smile makes his eyes sparkle. That, combined with the dusty auburn of his hair, send her thoughts straight to Lucas.

"Did you find him?" Ryder touches her toes to the reflective glass floor. Her skin tingles with the contact. "Lucas, I mean?"

J'salax's smile fades. "No. Not so far as I am aware. You must understand that resources are limited. We have done what we can, but it may not be enough."

Ryder stands, staring down at the floor, her own face reflected up at her. Dark rings lie beneath haunted eyes. No wonder J'salax spoke so gently, Ryder looks like she's about to start bawling.

A section of the wall peels back, and Blane walks in, a tray floats in the air before him, a deep frown marking his face.

"I have no idea what this food is, but it doesn't smell like it's going to kill you, so I guess—" He stops talking, taking in the scene. "Ryder, sit down. For crying out loud, you just came back from the dead. Where do you think you are going?"

"I was just-"

"Sit down," he cries.

Ryder plonks back onto the bedding, bouncing there as it recoils with the sudden weight. Blane is not alone. Nire follows him into the room – a room not designed to hold quite so many people comfortably. J'salax slides off his sun lounge, clapping his hands together.

"Finally, I am relieved of this task."

Nire steps in his way as he tries to leave. "Self-same, one moment."

Blane directs the tray with its steaming bowl in front of Ryder, but she's focused on Nire. The young woman's face bares the same haunted look of Ryder's near-to-tears reflection.

J'salax heaves an exaggerated sigh. "You can have just one moment. I am famished after the boredom. A cup of treyor beckons me."

The Crown cups her hand to her brother's face. "We have received word that Icewynn is destroyed. There is nothing left of our home."

From where she sits, Ryder has a clear view of both their faces. J'salax's reaction is fleeting. A shadow of horror that is quickly swamped by a careless purse of his lips. "You know I never cared much for that place."

He leans forward, pressing his forehead against Nire's. Soft spoken words pass between them, ones that don't reach Ryder despite the compact size of the room. Nire's eyes close, and she nods. J'salax releases her, and strides through the entranceway, leaving them with a carefree wave.

"You are beloved by the people, Nire," he declares. "Icewynn, too, was beloved. The Reigner has overstepped, and this is the beginning of his downfall."

The entrance slides closed. Nire stands, staring at the panel, her face smoothed of expression.

Ryder ignores Blane's fussing and moves to her side. Taking her hand. "We will stop him," she says. Her throat still rasps but there is no waver in her voice. Each word crystal clear. "Both of them, the Presider and the Reigner."

Ryder's not sure she's ever been so determined about anything in her life.

Nire's smile is heavy with sadness, but she doesn't pull away. "It was beautiful, don't you think?"

"Yeah," Ryder whispers. "You had a beautiful home."

And this Reigner guy just took it away. To get what he wants. Just like the Presider took Olessia. And Aresh. And Ryder's mother, just because he could. Ryder stares at the elthar bands around her wrists. The metal is dull and quiet. Who do these guys think they are? The butterflies emerge, rising up and over Ryder's hunger, edging their way up beneath her skin. Like her own private army settling into place. Waiting on the next command.

"Ryder?" Nire says softly.

Ryder's head jerks up. The Crown's smile is odd, her nose puckered like she's just sucked a lemon.

You're about to break a bone in her hand, Ry. Let go.

"Oh god, Sophie." Ryder lets go of Nire's hands, and whirls to try and find her friend. Her hands flutter to her neck, in the vain hope the anvel goggles are still there. She touches the frayed collar of her shirt. Ryder freezes. The goggles aren't necessary. Sophie is right in front of her. Way fainter than with the anvel but still there. Drifting just above the floor of the cabin, her feet much blurier than the rest of her.

You scared me. I felt you slip away. Ryder, what did you do?

Ryder hesitates. *I went into the Rising. I was trying to help Lucas. He's here, Soph. In Zentai. I found him, they had him at this place called Huler-bae. I think I got him out of there, but I don't know for certain.*

Shock fills Sophie's translucent face. *Lucas is here? How is that* — She lifts a hand, shaking her head at her own question. *Ry, I hate to say this. But you can't focus on that right now. Olessia needs you.*

"Ryder? Is everything all right?" Nire says.

"You need to eat something, Ryder," Blane offers up the bowl. The liquid inside is an uninviting shade of green.

Ryder shakes her head. "Just give me a second." She turns back to Sophie. There is a flickering at her friend's core, like when a moth gets inside a lampshade.

Ryder, Olessia is almost at Megnastin. You are close. But they cannot take you all the way. Not in this. I've got alternative transport for you.

What exactly does that mean?

Blane steps between Ryder and Sophie. "Let me check your pulse, Ryder."

She scowls, pushing him out of the way. "I said give me a second. I'm fine."

Blane and Nire exchange a glance but neither of them interrupt.

Sophie?

Padellah has sent her. Her name is Winnie. You need to make sure your friends don't try to shoot her out of the sky.

"Who is Winnie?" Ryder says aloud.

She is a Celtren that Padellah commands. Like Beadsley. And just like that poor guy, she didn't have a name. Sophie's image blurs, then readjusts. *Why do these poor Celtren not have names?* She shrugs at her own question. *Winnie has just taken Olessia and Sebastien into the heart of the Arlion Xhentex, she'll guide you there too.*

"Sebastien?" A prickling runs up Ryder's arms. "He's okay?"

Blane edges in closer, eyes narrowed. Staring at her as though she has gone utterly mad.

He said some nice stuff to me, so he's not okay. Sophie smiles. A shock of light spills from her lips. Ryder flinches, shading her eyes.

"Sophie, is everything okay?"

Oh sorry. She covers her mouth and the sun extinguishes. *Did I beam again? Things are getting weird since I went into the Xhentex. It's a strange place, Ry. But on the plus side, it's like a can of Red Bull for ghosts apparently. I feel like I could light up a city.*

"Be careful, Sophie."

She wiggles her head from side to side. *Not really sure how to do that in here. Still working things out.* She suddenly jerks, and looks off to the right, as though a sound there has caught her attention. The room itself is dead silent, save for the tapping of Nire's foot against the smooth floor.

Ry, things are getting kind of hazy. Don't freak out if I disappear.

The door slides back, and the Commandant and J'salax stride in. He holds a v-shaped glass in his hand, sipping at its contents. The Commandant directs a nod towards Ryder, and then addresses Nire, fist pressed to her chest.

"We're approaching the outer known perimeters of the Xhentex, Lady," the Commandant says. "But we are far too close to the Siros border. There is a significant enemy presence in this area. A squadron of Bexsron patrols in the celestra quadrant, and substantial numbers of sretlan have been detected in the bient quadrant. If we continue on this course, we will find ourselves caught between them. What are your directions?"

Nire turns to Ryder.

"Ryder, we need to take evasive action. Do you have something to tell us?"

Sophie? Ryder punches the side of her leg. Sophie's sudden disappearing acts are getting frustrating. Not to mention frightening. What if she doesn't reappear? Ryder shakes her shoulders, throwing off the unsettling thoughts.

"Did you see any Celtren?" Ryder asks J'salax.

He screws up his face. "Oddly, yes. There was a single creature sighted. But it is over where the sretlan armadel patrols. It would be madness to head towards—"

"It… she is coming for us. For me," Ryder says. "I have to get to her. Winnie is going to take me to Olessia. She's in the Xhentex."

The Commandant's face crumples with a frown. "Who sends the Celtren? Those beasts know no master naturally. Has the Laudine found a way to command them?"

"Not exactly," Ryder says. "Have you heard of the Cyne?"

Any other time, it would be hilarious. The way Nire, J'salax and the Commandant all jerk, looking to one another.

The Crown's bird-like intensity returns. "Of course. But there has been no evidence of their continued existence for so long, we thought them extinct."

Ryder shakes her head. "Well, they are definitely not extinct."

"You've seen them?" J'salax says, his disbelief clear.

"Yes."

J'salax throws his arms in the air. "Now, truly, I do not recognise the world I live in any longer."

But Nire seems far more delighted with the news. A vibrancy lighting her. "And they assist the Laudine?"

"Yeah. Looks like it."

The Crown clasps her hands together. "This is wonderous. The battle is far from lost. We must play our part." She paces, moving past Blane who sits with the steaming bowl in his lap, his face a mask of confusion. "If that celtren is to find its way, we need to move the sretlan armadel."

"And how would one do such a thing, self-same?" J'salax says, slowly.

"By providing them with a target to follow," the Commandant answers, a thoughtful expression on her face.

The Crown nods. "We must draw them away," Nire says. "Allow Ryder time to reach the Celtren. J'salax, you will take a paxen, and transport Ryder. You are by far the most able of the pilots that remain."

"You cannot risk yourself in such a way," J'salax says, his eyes bright with anger. "You are the Crown—"

"And the Crown is born to serve her people. To protect them," Nire draws herself up, dominating the room despite the fact she is the shortest among them. "I have nothing left to protect them with besides this. Aresh can defeat the Presider, her strength rivals his. Threatens his. It is why he imprisons her now. We have an ancient race fighting for her survival, we must aid them in any way we can. And without the Presider the Reigner will fall. This is how we protect our people."

Listening to Nire, to the absolute certainty in her voice, shivers trace across Ryder's skin.

J'salax swallows hard, his throat muscles shifting. Seeming ready to protest, but he bows his head. "As you wish, my Crown."

Nire moves close to him, lifting her hand. He places his palm against hers and something unspoken passes between them. They lower their hands at the same time, breaking contact.

"I'll prepare the paxen," J'salax says. "Ryder, you should follow."

He leaves the room without a backward glance. Ryder stares at the open doorway. Her feet won't follow her brain's order to move. She glances at Blane.

"I don't do goodbyes, if that's what you're about to do," he says, folding his arms

Ryder laughs; a short, sharp sound. "See you when I get back then?"

He twitches his shoulders. It could be a yes, or a whatever, Ryder has no clue. The guy wasn't kidding about not doing goodbyes.

"See you when you get back," Nire says softly.

The Commandant gestures towards the door. "Ryder, allow me to escort you."

Ryder hesitates. One last glance, searching for a red-haired ghost. Only Blane and Nire stare back at her. Forced smiles upon their faces.

She turns to leave.

"Oh wait, Ryder." Blane rushes towards her, holding out Ryder's dirty pair of trainers. He passes them over, and whispers. "See you when you get back."

Chapter 37

Ryder

Ryder grips the edge of her seat in the compact aircraft. A Fegren, J'salax told her. Like she should know the name of the craft she'll be jumping out of. The twin suns she saw hanging over Lucas's prison aren't visible here. This landscape is draped in the darkness of a moonless night.

"Don't lose her," Ryder says. A stupid thing to say, J'salax is every bit the great pilot Nire told them he was and this ship probably has more technology than three NASAs combined, but Ryder has to say something to stop herself from falling apart. Sophie has disappeared again. No matter how much shouting Ryder has done in a mindreach, there's been no reply. *'Don't freak out if I disappear'*, that's what Sophie said. Well, Ryder's not doing so well at following orders.

"We will not lose the Celtren, Ryder," J'salax says, calm to the point of sounding bored.

She's grateful not to hear any irritation in his reply. Ryder's certain the incessant tapping of her feet against the smooth floor is probably driving him mad. The celtren — Winnie — found them first. Five minutes after they jettisoned from the main aircraft, leaving Nire and Blane behind. The Celtren slid towards them, out of the darkness, a deeper shadow against the jet-black sky. It drew in close enough that Ryder can make out her rich brown coat, streaked with bright splashes of pink. The creature's wing tip almost scrapes the side of the Fegren, and she has fixed a wide crimson eye on Ryder since the moment she settled into place.

Winnie is a petite creature by Celtren standards, easily two thirds the size of Beadsley. Ryder presses her lips together. The last time she saw Beadsley was not a good day.

"It is time, Ryder." J'salax's voice makes her jump. "Are you ready?"

"Yeah." Ryder shifts in her seat. "I think so."

Fegren seats are like sitting on marble. The Commandant piloted the same type of craft when she and Blane rescued Ryder from the cluster, and it was just as uncomfortable but had more space than this one. Here, there is barely room for Ryder and J'salax. His arm brushes hers as he shifts the controls, more of those dinner plate things like Sebastien used in the Baershard.

Ryder's fingers tighten on the unyielding metal. She breathes in deep through her nostrils, and exhales through her mouth. As uncomfortable as it may be, Ryder baulks at the thought of leaving the Fegren.

"You need to ignite your elthar," J'salax says, with a gentle undercurrent that tells her he's well aware she already knows that.

In the silence that falls between them, broad daylight marches in. One minute it's dark as pitch outside, the next Ryder's blinking against the brightness. The twin suns she saw over Lucas's prison have appeared in the sky. Not suns, Ryder sees now, but more like comets. Riding so low in the sky it's possible to make out the lick of flames flowing from their tip and stretching back into long sweeping tails. Their light pours down on The Dovers, and the coral pink of the mountain range is an intense glow at the right of the Fegren.

"Dayfall," J'salax says, teeth clenched on the word. "We must hurry."

Ryder flutters her eyelids. A haze grips the landscape up ahead.

"Do you see that?" she says.

Maybe her eyes are still adjusting to the sudden daylight. J'salax nods.

"I do. We are approaching the limits of the Dovers, beyond that, the Arlion Xhentex's influence begins."

"What is the Arlion Xhentex's influence, exactly?"

"It is where reality begins to lose its… well, its reality." J'salax shrugs. "But in truth, there is little concrete known about the region because few of those who enter, ever return. And if they do, their faculties are often profoundly impaired."

"Sounds like a great place," Ryder mutters.

The haze thickens, more of a fog now. Swirling and curling around the ship.

"It is not a place most would choose to venture into, that is for certain," J'salax says. "I cannot travel much further with the Fegren, the craft is under substantial duress already."

"Whoa, wait." Ryder shifts forward but the harness digs in. "She's stopped. Winnie has stopped."

J'salax brings them to an immediate halt. The smoothness of it is impressive, considering how quickly he has to hit the brakes.

The Celtren raises up on her hindquarters, wide wings batting at the air in great engulfing sweeps. The gust she creates, pushes back the snowy haze that is growing thicker with every moment. Winnie bellows, her fire-eyes seem to glow against the backdrop of white. And they do not leave Ryder's face as the Celtren bellows again; like a lion and elephant mixed together.

Ryder swallows. "This is it. I need to go." The elthar glows with dull emerald light but remains as it is. Two slim bracelets. Ryder will need more than that to pull her out of the Fegren.

The sensor panel throws up a series of leaf-shaped icons, and an alarm emits a soft repetitive shrill.

"What's happening?" Her tongue clings to the roof of her mouth.

"You must do so quickly, Ryder," J'salax says. "A section of the Presider's armadel have not followed Nire as planned. They are doubling back towards our location."

The roof of the capsule slides open and the blast of hot air sets Ryder's eyes streaming. It's like gliding through an enormous sauna. Her harness releases. She is free. There is nothing stopping her from lifting up and out of the craft. Though the craft resembles a helicopter, there are no blades overhead. She just needs to ignite the elthar and she is out of here. The coast is definitely clear.

"What are you waiting for?" J'salax snaps. "You need to go, now. Move!"

He's no Sebastien, but J'salax's commanding tone does the trick. Ryder tucks her feet up beneath her, crouching on her seat.

"I'm going." She sucks in a breath and pushes to her feet. The elthar flares, brilliant emerald light bathing her sweaty face. Another heart beat and she's in the air. Her feet are barely clear before the roof of the capsule begins to slide closed. J'salax gives her a grim nod. Then he's whipping the compact craft around in a tight circle and accelerating away.

Ryder's alone.

Well, not so alone. Winnie bays, a long, strained sound that makes Ryder's hair stand on end. "Lead the way."

They jettison into the thick haze. A world of spotless white. The heat here isn't as intense, but it's far from pleasant. Ryder has the sense of being suffocated by cotton wool. Her elthar's light ripples against the starkness, seeping into it, making Ryder's world Kermit green. She keeps her eyes on the Celtren up ahead, but there is something disconcerting about the surrounding nothingness. Anything could be lurking in the depths.

Waiting.

Watching.

Ready to pounce.

The heated air makes her skin tingle, like it holds the hint of an electric current. Ryder suddenly hurtles to the right, her body turning in a full rotation. She cries out, trying to grab hold of thin air. Heart pounding, Ryder shifts herself back into an upright position. At least, that's what she thought she had done. Her hair says differently. The long, tangled strands hang away from her scalp.

"What the hell?" Ryder grunts, trying to shift herself upright. She leans hard to the left, hoping it might start a barrel roll. The idea works. Too well. The roll begins and won't stop. Ryder turns, once, twice, three times.

"Ah, Winnie. Help."

The Celtren bays, but the sound is muffled and distant. And Ryder has no clue from which direction it's actually coming.

"I'm going to be sick." She jerks herself forward, attempting to break the momentum of her spinout. It doesn't work. Now she's doing a head-over-heels forward roll. Her hair slaps at her face, like it's being blown by fans from every angle. The bay of the Celtren rushes in at her, the sound growing louder. Winnie's ember eyes flash into view. Her broad head swings at Ryder. Hitting her square in the shoulder. Throwing her out of the insane rotations.

Now, she's just falling.

And she is definitely going down. Dropping like a stone out of the white sky.

Ryder screams, arms flailing in front of her. Everything is white. And green. The elthar is glowing supernova style but it's just two narrow cuffs around her wrists. Hardly enough to stop a freefall.

The haze sweeps open like giant chiffon curtains parting and a landscape speeds towards her. A beach. Sand as white as the haze; a crescent curve that stretches as far as Ryder has time to see.

"Oh no," Ryder cries. The ground rushes up at a frightening speed. She shakes her hands, trying to get the elthar to do more than look like glamorous jewellery.

"Ryder, stay calm. Don't fight it." The voice calling to her is faint but instantly recognisable.

There, just a few metres away, Sebastien moves at a desperate run across the sand.

"Sebastien, help me!"

"You're not falling. The elthar guides you."

Not falling? Is he blind? Ryder releases a long, high scream. She closes her eyes, arms crossed in front of her face.

And waits.

And waits.

The wind drops. Her hair falls against the sides of her face. And there is pressure against her knees. Gentle pressure. Not the slam of the ground against her kneecaps. Ryder blinks. She is kneeling on the sand.

"Ryder, are you all right?" Sebastien throws himself onto his knees, one arm reaching around her shoulders. She slumps into him. Their heads so close it's hard to focus.

"Yeah." Sand clings to her lips, some of it between her teeth. Ryder screws up her face and Sebastien pulls back.

"Are you going to be ill?" he says, but he doesn't let her go.

Ryder shakes her head. "Just sand—"

His thumb traces down her cheek, brushing away the sand clinging there. Reaching the edge of her lip. Ryder's head is still spinning, her guts still trying to work out which way is up. And now, with Sebastien's finger tracing her lips, she's struggling to remember how to breathe at all.

"I have worried about you." His grey eyes are still, and she can see her reflection in them.

"You too." If one of her new superpowers was the ability to freeze time, Ryder would do it right now. Here in this moment.

"Ryder! Ryder!" Olessia flings herself at them, skidding across the sand on her knees. Sending up a flurry of the delicate grains. But Ryder can't stifle her grin. Olessia throws herself at Ryder with so much force it sends Sebastien toppling, Ryder still locked in his arms. All three of them collapse onto their sides on the sand.

"Did you miss me?" Ryder laughs.

At some point she'll demand to know who dressed Olessia in the crazy folds of material that swamp her. The ruffles at her neck and wrists reminding Ryder of an elegant clown.

"I do not think I can express adequately how much that is so," Olessia mumbles into Ryder's hair. "I was so frightened that harm would come to you."

"Well, I'm guessing there is still time for that." Ryder's laughter dances with nerves.

Sebastien, scowling, releases his hold on Ryder and shifts back. Wiping hard at the smudges of white that cling to his pants. "We have no time for this exaggerated display. There are many who count on us to adhere to the task at hand."

Olessia releases the bear hug grip she has on Ryder and sits up, settling back onto her heels.

"Of course."

The water laps gently at the shore a few metres down from where they sit. A deceptively relaxing sound.

"Olessia, what about Christian?" Ryder says. "He was with you, wasn't he?"

Goosebumps form lines up Ryder's arms. It's cool here, almost chilly.

"He's—" Sebastien begins.

"He's fine. Yes, yes." Olessia nods vigorously. "He is being protected. Ryder, I promise you that. And so is your—"

"Now is not the time, Olessia." Sebastien rises to his feet, dusting off the covering of white that clings to his body. He moves easily, no sign of his old injuries. Aside from the concern that is making all kinds of lines on his face, he seems healed.

"But she should—"

"Focus on the task at hand." Sebastien glares down at Olessia who regards him with slowly-churning eyes of violet.

"What?" Ryder's goosebumps double. "What are you guys talking about?"

"Nothing of import." Sebastien's frown of concern is replaced by a scowl of impatience.

"Are you serious?" Ryder says. "You can't say something like that and expect me to just shrug it off."

"I can, and I do," Sebastien declares. "Tell us of the situation beyond the Xhentex. You were brought here by the Crown of Zentai, was there any resistance encountered?"

Cheeks hot, Ryder holds his intense gaze. "I'm not saying anything until you tell me what you two were just talking about."

"Ryder, I'm sorry but we must—"

"You must tell me who you were talking about." Her heartbeat is shallow and rapid, and the odd flutter in her gut returns. Ryder clenches her hands, certain she knows the answer to her own question but equally sure that won't let this go until she hears Olessia or Sebastien say it out loud.

Olessia's expression grows pained, and for once the Laudess of Bax Un Tey has nothing to say.

"They are talking about your mother, Ryder."

Sophie stands at the water's edge. Though Ryder doesn't have the anvel goggles on, her friend appears as clearly as if she did. In fact, more so. If not for the faint hint of movement of the waves visible through Sophie's torso, Ryder might mistake this apparition for the real thing.

"What did you just say?" Ryder whispers.

"She's alive, Ryder." Sophie replies gently. "I've seen her. And it's incredible how much you look like her. It's breathtaking."

Breathtaking? Looking like your mother isn't breathtaking. Finding out she's alive and well on an alien planet, just as you are about to enter some kind of galactic labyrinth to try and rescue an extra-terrestrial princess is breathtaking.

Ryder touches her fingertips to the sand to steady herself.

"Say something, Ryder," Sophie coaxes. "You're kind of freaking me out."

But Ryder can barely swallow let alone say anything. Her mum is alive. And her best friend is a ghost. Ryder's desperately hungry. Mind-numbingly frightened. And if Olessia and Sophie don't stop looking at her like they think she's about to run away screaming, Ryder will do exactly that.

"You should not have done that, Sophie. Now is not the time." Sebastien's cold hard tone lands on Ryder's pity party. Smashing it into a million pieces. "Ryder, pull yourself together. Your family issues will have to wait until Aresh is safe."

He plants himself right between Ryder and the others. Blocking them from her sight. Ryder's indignation rises.

"My family issues?" She glares up at Sebastien.

"That's what I said," Sebastien says. "Ryder, you need to—"

"You are such a jerk."

"I'm realistic. There is no time for—"

"Well I'm making time." Anger boils beneath Ryder's skin. Her skin is alight with the touch of it. The fluttering beneath her ribcage more violent than before. "You're talking about my mother. Someone that was taken from me."

"Ryder." It's Olessia's voice, coming from some distance away, but Ryder ignores her.

Ignores Sophie too, who is trying to defuse the situation. "Let's all just take a breath."

Ryder hears only Sebastien's smooth words, and they infuriate her even more. "You need to calm down, Ryder."

"Oh really? Well, sorry buddy. I don't want to."

Sebastien eye's narrow. Fixing on something over her shoulder. "I suggest you find a desire to do so. And I suggest that you—"

"Stop suggesting," Ryder cries. "And look at me when I'm yelling at you."

"Ryder, please." Definitely Olessia, and her tone is strained. "Take control of your emotions."

"No, I won't!" The anger is a cauldron inside her, bubbling out of her control.

Sebastien lunges at her, planting his hands against her cheeks, and pressing his lips to hers. The shock arrows through Ryder. Anger gives way to surprise. She is wide-eyed as their lips press. Catching sight of an enormous wall of water over Sebastien's shoulder. Less than a dozen metres away. Ryder gasps, pulling out of Sebastien's embrace.

The fluid arches up from the sand in a curling wave over Olessia. A wave that hovers there, as though held in place by invisible restraints. Droplets rain down on Olessia, dampening her hair. She thrusts her hands at the wave. Shallow dents appear in the wall of liquid, and the entire body of water shudders. The curl of the wave reverses, folding back over itself, crashing down onto the ocean that lies behind it. Sea spray hits Ryder's face. It is icy cold against her skin, still heated from the kiss.

"What just happened?" Ryder says.

"You did," Olessia wipes at her face. "You must be careful with your emotions and your strength in here, Ryder."

"I made that wave?"

Sophie doesn't quite hide her smile before she speaks. "Impressive, I have to say. But probably best we keep things as calm as possible while we're in here."

Ryder stares at the ocean, now almost perfectly flat. The barest hump of a wave teasing at the shore. "I don't understand. I thought it was metal, that I could... like... manipulate or something... but water?"

Sebastien ruffles his fingers through his hair. Droplets spray and catch the light. Ryder forces herself to look away, her skin warming again.

"The normal rules do not apply in a place such as this," Olessia says. "We must be cautious. You and I especially. We must keep control."

Of the Beckoning? Ryder is desperate to ask but Sophie steals the opportunity, waving her hands.

"Um, guys?" she says. "We've got company. And they are kind of in a hurry."

Sophie's company is five glowing figures. Assembled around her in a half-circle. The darting particles of light, vaguely humanoid, that so often made up Padellah's form.

Sebastien edges in front of Ryder, calling on Olessia to step back. But she stares, open mouthed at the strange assembly of figures huddled around Sophie.

"What is this?" Olessia breathes.

"The Cyne," Ryder replies, leaning around Sebastien. "I've seen them before. There's one called—"

"Padellah," Olessia says. "Yes. I know. She has appeared to me as well. Enabled me to save Christian."

Ryder stares at her, opening her mouth to let fly with a dozen questions, just as one of the beings drifts in closer to Olessia, and lifts a glowing, watery hand. Sebastien steps forward, elthar brightening, but Ryder presses him back.

"It's okay," she and Sophie speak in perfect unison.

Sebastien doesn't move back, but neither does he try to get any closer. Muscles work in his lower jaw, his uncertainty lining his face. The entity lowers their 'hand' to the crown of Olessia's head. She sucks in her breath, but holds still, a frown marring her forehead. Her eyes drift closed. The fluttering in Ryder's belly returns. Slinking up through her ribs, spanning out through her collarbone.

Olessia's eyes reopen.

"I understand," she whispers. Whatever it is that she understands seems to pain her. Ryder's never seen Olessia shed a tear but in that moment, it would be no surprise at all to see them fall. "I'm so sorry. Forgive us."

Sebastien ignores Ryder's pleas to stay still. "What is it, Olessia?"

Never has she looked so childlike, pale and small. She lifts sad eyes to find her Guardian. "Something was stolen from them, a long time ago. By those who began the Presiderline. Those whose blood I carry." Her pained eyes find Ryder. "The Beckoning is… was… Cyne,once. But the Claven sought the power of that race, and they experimented then as my father does to this day. The genetic merging of Cyne and Sirosian created the Beckoning. Created the Presiderline."

"Like some kind of chimera," Ryder whispers.

"A what?" Sebastien scowls.

Ryder replies, still at a whisper. "A mythological creature, pretty gross really. A hybrid made from different animals. A lion's head, a goat's body and a serpent's tail." The stories always made her shudder. But now her stomach heaves.

The Presider and the Claven are not the only ones who have experimented. Aresh did too. Creating a child of three worlds.

Ryder is as much a chimera as Olessia.

She curls her hands into fists, nails digging into soft skin.

Even if Ryder does find her mother, who would want a freak daughter?

"Olessia, we need to go." Ryder speaks with a ferocity that surprises even her. "Right now. We find Aresh. We find the Presider. And we end this."

Make sure he pays for all the damage that's been done. To Ryder. To Olessia. To all those beings, scattered across universes, that have been used by the Claven and the Presider.

Olessia tilts her chin. The violet in her irises swirls like mini-tornados. "We end this."

"Ladies, allow us to escort you," Sophie declares, with an overly dramatic flourish of her hands. "Aresh and Padellah have been waiting a long time for you both."

Sebastien's elthar ignites, casting blue light against the grim set of his jaw, and the fierce glare in his eyes. Olessia follows his lead, letting the metal coat every finger, racing up her wrists and disappearing in beneath the puff of material that covers her upper arms.

The Cyne drift closer, forming a full circle around Ryder, Olessia and Sebastien. Close enough for Ryder to make out features within the bubbling light. A face stares back at her, like a sketch on an illuminated page. Wide eyes, a stubby nose, a tangle of hair that hangs around square set shoulders.

It is her own face gazing back at her. Ryder holds her breath. She lifts her hand, and the Cyne copies the movement, a limb forming out of the central mass. A hand appears, fingers splayed just as Ryder's are. She inches her hand in toward the entity, and it does the same. Energy and flesh meet. A tingle runs down Ryder's arm. Soft and gentle, kind of ticklish.

Ryder Carlsson. A cluster of voices all whisper her name. *The child of three worlds, here at the place of all worlds. Let us guide you.*

Her elthar's glow lifts, and the light splinters into tiny fragments, moving around her like snowflakes caught on a breeze.

"Guys?"

"Hang on, Ry." Sophie's voice resembles Padellah's, a jumble of voices talking over the top of one another. "This will be quite the ride."

The Cyne moves closer, so close Ryder feels as though she is standing right in the middle of the entity itself. Her skin is hypersensitive, the slightest movement sending prickly chills across her body. And right at her core something flickers, a brush of butterfly wings against her insides. The sand vanishes from beneath her feet, and the golden glow of the Cyne increases until she can no longer make out the sapphire light from Sebastien and Olessia's elthar.

The brightness is unbearable, and Ryder closes her eyes.

The quickening at her core spreads. Finding her chest, spreading into her arms, reaching into her skull.

And once again, she is falling. Faster than before. Without a lick of breeze in her hair. Just the sensation of moving down. *Soaring down.* The flickering at her core grows stronger. Building. Until it bursts through her pores. Flames the same golden light as the Cyne. Engulfing her. The Beckoning guides her through the strangeness of the Arlion Xhentex. Relishing the new-found freedom.

Ryder throws back her head, spreads her arms.

Here at the meeting place of all worlds, she's never felt more at home.

Chapter 38

Olessia

O lessia's journey through the Arlion Xhentex, encased in the preternatural energy of the Cyne, is spent with the expectation she may be discarded at any moment. Thrown into an oubliette within the infinite folds of the Xhentex and abandoned. After learning the Beckoning was once a part of this mysterious race until it was imprisoned and manipulated by her ancestors, such a fate would not surprise her.

How the Cyne must despise the Presiderline.

And she lays no blame with them for that. She despises herself. So pre-occupied with running from her own fate, she was blind to the burdens of so many others.

Her own people. The captives in the Collective. Ryder. The Cyne. Aresh.

As the Cyne arrow her through the Xhentex, Olessia places her elthar-coated hands to her stomach. The Beckoning lies comfortably within her. No sharpness to its presence now. The energy's heat a pleasant sensation moving through her veins. Olessia does not fight it, and the Beckoning does not fight her. At peace. A strange union taking shape.

Olessia can observe no sign of Ryder or Sebastien but for the first time, in a great deal of time, she is not concerned. Here, for now, she is certain she is not surrounded by enemies. The Cyne protect them, protect them all. And it is more than she deserves.

Olessia. Creation of Inel. You had no part in what has passed. But you will change what is to come. You, and the Laudine. Take your place. Lead them all from the darkness of what has been, and find a new way.

The voices dart at her. A subtle echo upon each word. Gentle against her ears. And there is a notable excitement behind the words. An eagerness.

Her smooth downward path alters, and a jerky, unpleasant shift upwards takes its place. Olessia braces, arms held in front of her. Readying herself for a world that turns on her, turning her upside down and inside out.

We approach.

There is barely a pulse beat between the declaration and the arrival. Olessia's trajectory simply halts. The embrace of the Cyne is removed, the entity forming once again into the vaguely humanoid silhouette at Olessia's side. And there, right before her, in all the glorious shades and angles she recalls, stands Clarendon House. The scent of the human world hangs on the air, the tang of unfamiliar plant life and heavily oxygenated air. A breeze shifts the trees that hug the boundaries of the house.

"Oh my god. Clarendon." Ryder stumbles forward as she, too, is released from the Cynes' hold.

"Are you all right, Ryder?"

She nods, mouth agape. Staring at the wide stairway that leads up to the mansion's imposing main doors, with its subtle lemon-yellow walls and wide rectangular windows. Shadows sit against the house in an odd way, no visible sign of what is casting the light exists. Certainly no Earth moon in the sky. In fact, there is no discernible sky at all. Olessia narrows her eyes. Every direction she looks, the mansion fills the space. As Olessia's gaze traces higher, so too does the mansion. Elongating. The pillars that stand either side of the entrance reach far above her, the sides of the building stretching wide in each direction.

"You recognise this place?" Sebastien is the final arrival, stepping from the Cyne's golden shroud and hurrying to Olessia's side.

"Yes. This is where it all began," Olessia says. "For me, at least. This place contains the slipstream I used to enter the Iondar Realm."

"And Aresh is being held here?"

Before Olessia can answer, Sophie rushes through them, her image sending the barest shiver through Olessia.

"You're kidding me? Clarendon is Megnastin?" Sophie exclaims at a level far louder than is perhaps wise.

"I thought you knew where Aresh was?" Ryder says.

"The general area, yeah. But Padellah wouldn't let me get close." Sophie's eyes are fixed on the mansion. "Said it was too dangerous for… well for someone like me—"

"Then why are you here now?" Ryder glares at her.

"Because you are, Ry," Sophie says. "We've got some kind of bungee string connection going on, I keep rebounding to you wherever I try to go, but let's face it, there's no way I was going to let you come and do this without me anyway." She shrugs. "Padellah just kind of gave up trying to convince me otherwise, she said as long as I don't go inside, I should be okay."

The scowl on Ryder's face could rival one of Sebastien's.

"So, my father's cruelty extends even here," Olessia says.

A metallic clang reaches them, a distant clatter of metal coming from the upper reaches of the mansion's roof.

"Putting Aresh in Clarendon House?" Ryder says, still glowering. "I was just thinking the same thing. You said Aresh used to use the slipstream in Clarendon all the time, to get to Earth. He's done this on purpose. Putting her here. Making her prison the one place that used to be her way to escape from him."

"But is this really Clarendon House?" Sophie's image floats to Ryder's side. The other Cyne keep their distance. "Could we just… I mean… you, Ryder, just walk into a room like Olessia did? Could you go home?"

Olessia notes the tension gripping Ryder. The pained expression that shadows her features. Brought on by homesickness perhaps, but more likely from the way Sophie excluded herself from possibly returning home that way.

"Clarendon House is not Megnastin, it is simply a fragment within Megnastin," Sebastien says. "Any location, in any realm, that contains a river or slipstream is somehow reflected in this place. Teler tried to explain some of the mechanics to me, he said that Meganastin is unstable in the extreme, constantly changing and evolving. No one aspect of this area is static. It would unwise to attempt to return home via this portal."

"But if it is not static, then how has the Presider held Aresh here all this time?" Olessia frowns.

Creation. One of the Cyne, a silhouette that resembles a slowly rotating storm cloud, has edged in closer to them. *Creation. Breaking down. Padellah* holds. Holds fast.

The actual words that reach Olessia in the mindreach are few, but a greater understanding flows with them, as though the entity has imbued her with the knowledge. The Presider has constructed a device that can counter the instability of Meganastin. At least temporarily. But it is failing. This is why Padellah has not shown herself again. The Cyne is all that keeps Aresh from disappearing into the void of the Arlion Zhentex.

The Beckoning shifts within Olessia, emitting its low heat at her centre.

"He has anchored Clarendon here," Olessia utters the words with surprise. And some awe. "How is that possible?"

"This is like in Hobart, right?" Ryder paces up to the Cyne. "That creation we destroyed, the one keeping the River open, the Presider did that too?"

"What was—"

Olessia's question is halted by a crack that rents the silent air. A long, narrow split appears in the far left wall of the mansion, trailing from the roof to the ground where the garden bed bulges. The shutters on the upper windows swing open then slam shut with a clatter of mismatched bangs. There is no breeze. No tangible source of energy that should move the window coverings in such a way.

Ryder turns on her heels and races towards the stairway.

"Ryder, what are you doing?" Sebastien runs after her. Neither of them have ignited their elthar.

"What we are supposed to do," she shouts over her shoulder. "Get Aresh out of there. Didn't you just get that mindreach? That creation is failing, would have failed way before now if Padellah wasn't doing whatever she's doing. Let's go."

Olessia hurries after them, learning quickly why the others had not instigated their elthar. The metal is unresponsive, not heeding her summons to ignite. Sophie appears at her side. The rest of the Cyne remain a few paces back, a glowing escort of gold.

"Sophie, no. You can't—"

"I know, I know. I'm just going as far as I can with you."

They hit the bottom step and Sophie and the Cyne recoil as though they have been struck. Sophie releases an anguished cry.

"Are you all right?" Olessia says.

The others have reached the top of the staircase and she loses sight of them as they race across the verandah towards the entranceway.

"Fine, fine. I just wanted to go further. I think this is where we leave it up to you guys. Go, Olessia," Sophie sobs. "Come back to me, all of you. Promise me. You have to come back. Ryder… has to get through this."

Her anguish erodes her words, causing her image to grow faint. Olessia shakes her head; such a promise is impossible. But she utters a far more human, far more illogical reply.

"I will bring her back to you, Sophie. I promise."

Whimsical, emotional. Olessia flinches at her words, barely able to believe her self-delusion. But the reward comes a second later. Fear evaporates from Sophie's face, replaced with a small, tight smile.

"Thank you," Sophie says.

Not for the false promise, Olessia understands. But for the lie. Olessia returns her smile.

Glass shatters behind her, tinkling as it rains down on the concrete. Olessia's smile vanishes, and races to the top of the stairs. Another great crack has appeared in the wall of the mansion, this one traveling down to meet one of the windows, shattering the panes there. Sheets of material billow from within the house, lapping at the air, lifted by a wind that still does not reach Olessia.

The entranceway to the mansion is open, the double doors wide. She runs through them.

"Ryder? Sebastien?"

The moment her feet hit the interior tiles the doors slam shut behind her. Olessia halts in the hallway, trying once more to ignite the elthar. The metal is unresponsive. Little more than decoration upon her arm. But the Beckoning sends slow licks of heat moving through her, as though to assure her she is not alone. The black and white tiles on the floor, the narrow table beneath the elaborate mirror, all stir memories. She was here for such a short amount of time, but the place is etched in her mind. Even the scent is familiar, the tang of the eucalypt trees that surround the mansion on Earth, clings to the hallway, though it had been oddly absent outside.

"Olessia, upstairs."

Ryder's voice. Clear as though she stood beside Olessia.

"Ryder?" Olessia's own voice is flat, no echo. In the true entranceway of Clarendon House it would have reverberated off the mass of tiles and bare walls.

Vibrations move through the floor beneath her, enough to rattle the gilded mirror and hallway table.

"Olessia, where are you?"

Sebastien's voice this time, sharp with his usual impatience but dulled also, as though he speaks through a heavy barrier. If she is not mistaken the sound comes from a room to her left. Olessia takes a step to follow and a web of fine cracks appear in the tiles beneath her foot. Another step, another set of cracks. Clarendon House is breaking down, just as the Cyne told her. Whatever the Presider has done to keep this place stationery in Megnastin, it is failing now.

"Sebastien, wait for me. Where are you?"

Keeping her eyes off the floor, Olessia rushes into the room. Recalling this place too. Long couches made from the hide of animals, with elaborately embroidered rugs upon the floor. A set of weapons, long swords, displayed on the wall. This is the room where Christian, Sophie and Ryder set up the equipment they believed would enable them to hunt what they referred to as ghosts.

Olessia tenses at the thought of Christian. Countering her unease with the knowledge he is with Maher and Teler; both innately capable of protecting him.

Her present surroundings are of greater immediate concern. She finds herself in the room where the window shattered earlier. Empty, no sign of Sebastien. But most concerning, is what lies beyond the window. No hint of the front of the mansion where Sophie and the Cyne wait. There is, quite simply, nothing. Blackness.

"What is happening?" Her own voice issues forth with the same dullness of Sebastien and Ryder.

Another shudder runs through the foundations. The swords fall from the wall, clattering onto the brickwork laid at the front of a wide fireplace.

"Olessia."

"Olessia."

"Olessia."

Three voices utter her name in perfect unison, but all are distinctly notable.

Ryder, Sebastien, and Aresh.

Aresh is still here. Alive.

"I'm coming!"

Though she says it with conviction, in truth Olessia cannot distinguish from which direction the voices come. She falters, eyes darting between the two options; returning to the foyer and moving upstairs, or continuing through the downstairs area. A pitched sound, a groan of something heavy and under duress, rumbles through the doorway that would lead her to other sections of the ground floor. Dust rains down from the hallway ceiling. The tremor intensifies. Olessia clutches at the couch, her fingers sinking into the animal hide. Her eyes lock on the corridor that seems to be the epicentre of the unrest. Beneath her ribs, the Beckoning stirs. But Olessia holds it in careful check: *stay on high alert, exhibit extreme caution.*

The ceiling in the corridor caves in. Debris floods the passageway, pieces of plaster, timber and whatever else the humans use to build their structures. Through the cloud of dust,

Olessia believes she sees movement. She tilts her head, taking a step closer, hand still braced against the couch. As the cascade settles, a figure is visible further down the passageway. One that stops suddenly. And turns. White hair atop broad shoulders. The silhouette stirs further memories. The wide girth, the slight lilt in the gait. She has seen this very same figure walk along the Clarendon House corridors once before.

"Jack." Olessia intends to yell his name, but it leaves her as a whisper. A heaviness in the air weighing it down.

Olessia takes another step closer. The corridor is empty but for a haze of dust in the air. She sighs, and shakes her head. Ryder's grandfather is not here. He *cannot* be here. She is allowing the Megnastin to distract her. This place is trying to make her exactly as it is. Unstable. Without true focus.

"Find the others." Her instruction to herself rings clear, though still dulled. Olessia swings around, intending to head back out into the foyer. She cries out, stumbling away from the man who stands there. The Presider fixes eyes of fire upon her.

"I must thank you, Olessia. I had deliberated with allowing you to survive. You have shown me how unwise that would be."

Olessia draws herself up. Her father is only a fraction taller than she is, yet he manages to appear as a giant. "I am your heir, your daughter. You would dispose of me, as you seek to do with Aresh?"

She is expecting his answer. If he said anything else, she would know it a lie. Still, the punch of his words renders her breathless.

"Yes. There is no other course open to me, not now. An unfortunate truth, but there it is. A waste of a truly astonishing power, perhaps. And I am entirely to blame. A fool to view you only as my greatest achievement. Ready to overlook what is quite clear now. You are a great threat, an unmanageable risk that must be mitigated."

The words leave her before Olessia can consider their wisdom. "I am not one of your creations." A sharp pain crosses her lower torso. The Beckoning returned to the beast she has fought to control her entire life; unruly, raging, eager to inflict pain.

"Oh, but you are, Olessia." The Presider's eyes have not left her, and their flames scorch her. "Perhaps not mine, entirely, this is true. We are all – you, Aresh and myself – products of generations of the development of the Presiderline. And that bloodline shall continue and improve. Certainly, it will lament the loss of you and of the Laudine. Your contributions would have made Bax Un Tey an immensely powerful force in a far shorter time. A shame you both could not understand what I sought to do here."

Olessia's laughter is brittle. "I understand perfectly well. You are a tyrant, and care nothing for those beneath you, above you."

He purses his lips, and steel enters his posture.

"Above me?" he scoffs. "If you speak of Aresh then you are as deluded as the Laudine has ever been. Do you not see what I've achieved here? I control the Megnastin, the heart of the Arlion Xhentex is manipulated by my technology. No one is above me. Certainly not you, Olessia."

The plasterwork above them tears open, a fist-wide crack tracing from one side of the room to the other. The materials give way with ghastly tearing sounds, screams almost. Through the crevice in the ceiling Olessia can see only darkness. More of that which lies beyond the shattered window. The Presider tilts his head, a smile snaking across his lips.

"You cannot even create a Blackwall strong enough to keep Dashel out." His smile grows larger, more venomous. "How your little human boy screams, Olessia. Shall I allow you access to the mindreach Dashel has sent me?"

Olessia's body is awash with pain, the flicker of each nerve bringing anguish. Her refusal sticks to a mouth run dry with fear and she does not utter a word before Christian's screams fill her mind. Olessia's own cry joins the sound and she sinks to her knees. But within her the Beckoning does not cower. It roars through her senses and she is lifted once again to her feet. Lifted off them. Her elthar is unresponsive, it is the force of the Beckoning alone that raises her. And fuels her.

Skin aflame, Olessia rushes at her father. A throaty cry leaving her.

Heat fills her but does not consume her. The beast does not panic her as it has most of her life. The Beckoning seeks a partnership, not a battle against its host. Olessia thrusts her hands forward. And is rewarded with the sight of the Presider's uncertainty. A lift of his brow, a raise of his hands to ward off what she might direct his way. Energy streams from Olessia's fingertips. Pouring from her skin in a relentless torrent. The source of the power baffles her, there are no visible life auras here, save for that of the Presider. And there is small chance she has tapped into his lifesource.

He summons his own Beckoning, his arms lost beneath a fantastical explosion of light.

The two streams of energy roar towards one another. Impact deadens the world around Olessia, as though it traps them all in a vacuum, sucking the sound from the space. The force of the blow slams her across the room, where she lands dangerously close to the gaping black hole that was the window. Olessia scrambles to regain her footing. A certainty grips her; move too close to that blackness and it will bring about her demise. The Presider takes aim, firing upon her again, the blast no less diminished. Angled so as to force her back towards the glassless pane.

The blow glances against her right shoulder. The scrape of it against her body is excruciating. Olessia grinds her teeth, her expression not altering, but inwardly a panic begins to grow. Her own Beckoning's strength may be magnified in here but so is the Presider's. The ferocity of his blows greater than anything she has witnessed before.

"Cease this futile fight, Olessia. I have them all. Each of those purile beings you are so obsessed with." The Presider's hands brighten once more. "Did you learn nothing from me? Such connections only weaken you. And the bonds you have formed are truly pathetic. Two humans, two traitors, and a low born Zentai?" He swings his head in a slow side to side, the Beckoning's glow upon his features. A madness touching the fire in his eyes. "That is what the Laudess of Bax Un Tey fights for? You are not worthy of the role you were born to. You are no heir, no daughter of mine."

Chapter 39

Ryder

R yder plants one hand against the wall. Sebastien so close his chest brushes her shoulder blades. The entire house shudders around them, its foundations rocked by continuous tremors, rattling loose the thick-framed paintings that cover much of the wall space in Clarendon House. The well-dressed ladies and gents crash to the wooden floors. Glass littering the hallway. But Ryder presses on. Taking step after cautious step.

Ryder. Use haste.

From the moment they stepped across the threshold Ryder heard it.

Padellah's whispery voice. So faint and fragile it's almost lost beneath the groaning, traumatised house. Ryder searches for sign of the entity herself but so far, nothing. For now, she follows the voice alone.

"Ryder, are you certain it is the Cyne guiding you?" Sebastien says. "And not some manifestation the Presider has conjured to keep us from Olessia?"

He can't seem to hear Padellah, even though Ryder's certain the voice is not just inside her own head.

"It's not the Presider. I know it's Padellah." Ryder's never been more certain of anything. Not since all this insanity began. And the butterflies that have made a home in her belly agree. Since arriving here their presence is heavier, like each is carrying a stone. When

Ryder hesitates, unsure which direction Padellah's voice is coming from, the shift in her stomach sways her a certain way. "I know it's her. We need to keep going. Olessia will find us."

They can't stop. Another certainty. Ryder has to keep moving.

A small chandelier swings on its fixture above them. The elaborate cuts of crystal smashing against one another. The chandelier rocks back and forth with far more momentum than even the tremors could produce. The light breaks free from its base, and barrels down towards them.

"Move." Sebastien pulls her back, an arm raised to ward off the incoming projectile. Their elthar has gone dead in here, not even a spark coming off the metal, so it is Sebastien's arm that takes the full force of the blow. He grunts, stumbling back. The chandelier clatters to the ground. Dissolves. The shattered pieces of crystal shrink to the size of rice grains on the hallway carpet.

"You okay?" Ryder says, her gaze shifting between Sebastien and the obliterated chandelier. "How did... did you melt it?"

"No. The Megnastin taunts us with illusions. This is not your true Earth, Ryder, no matter how much it may resemble it."

Ryder decides against asking if what happened to the chandelier could happen to them. Both of them just melt away.

"We have to keep going," she says. "We're so close, Sebastien. Aresh is here."

It's more than a gut feeling, although that's exactly where Ryder feels it. With each step the weight in her gut deadens. Sebastien leads them on. They've gone a few metres when Padellah speaks up again.

Ryder. You draw near. Use caution.

"Yeah," Ryder mutters. "Because I was planning on dancing down the hallway doing cartwheels."

Sebastien glances over his shoulder. "What did you say?"

"Just keep going. We're almost there."

Ryder nudges aside a fallen painting, a bunch of guys riding horses; the men dressed in stiff high collars, wearing tight white pants, ready to a hunt. They stare up at her, their eyes never leaving her. Ryder could swear one of them blinked. Nothing about this place is normal. Her initial excitement about being back in

Clarendon House has crumbled into as many pieces as the chandelier. Whatever this is, it's not home.

Ryder glances back down the hallway. A pang of guilt plagues her. What if Olessia is lost in here? If the instinct to keep going wasn't so strong, Ryder would do just what Sebastien wanted. Find her. But Ryder's feet are moving of their own accord. Like she's on some crazy treadmill. One that's picking up speed. If she stops, she'll go flying off the edge.

Ryder.

A spark of light, no more than the flare of a match being struck, appears over a doorway up ahead. Extinguished a fraction of a second later.

"There!" Ryder rushes past Sebastien, her treadmill in overdrive. "Aresh is in there."

"Ryder, wait. Let me go first." Sebastien pounds after her.

She is turning to tell him there's no chance of that, when the hallway suddenly tilts. Lilting to one side, as though they are on a stricken cruise ship. Ryder stifles her cry, clutching at the wall, legs bent to keep her footing against the slant. Sebastien isn't as lucky. Crashing onto his side, shouting a bunch of definitely curse words as he slams against the opposite wall.

"You all right?" Ryder says.

In answer, he grabs hold of an ornate vase that has come to rest against his head, throwing it down the hall. The vase explodes, shattering into tiny fragments, just as the chandelier did. The weighty fluttering in her stomach makes her cringe. She presses an absent-minded hand to her belly. Her focus on other, more frightening things happening down the corridor. Where the end of the hall had been visible a second ago, an etched rectangular mirror hanging against floral wallpaper, now there is only darkness. A solid curtain that blocks all the light. And black that has swallowed the very corridor itself.

"Sebastien, look." Ryder shifts, trying to stop herself from sliding on the uneven floor. "What's happening?"

He grunts, clawing at the wall to get to his feet. "We are running out of time."

Ryder. The Megnastin overcomes us. You must hurry.

Planting both hands against the wall, Ryder edges sideways down the hallway. It's a slower way of moving, but the slant of the corridor is too great to try and just run for it. She'd spend more time on her knees than upright. As it is, her sneakers struggle to find a grip on the smooth wood, and the trip to the doorway where the light appeared is agonisingly slow.

The room is three doors down. A dozen steps at most. And each of them seem to take an eternity. The doorway is on the high side of the tilt. Of course. Like Megnastin is going out of its way to make things difficult for them.

"Come on, come on," Ryder hisses.

Finally, she reaches for the doorframe, fingers curling around the thick wood. It's unnaturally warm against her fingertips. Ryder grits her teeth, readying for the effort it will take to walk what is essentially uphill. She strains, throwing herself forward. And finds herself pitching headlong into the room.

A room where the floor is once again level.

"Oh!" She cries, her toes clipping the rug that covers most of the floor. Ryder falls to her knees, and her breath escapes in a gasp. "Padellah?"

She scans the room, taking only a second to realise where she is. It's the room where Ryder had her first of many weird experiences in Clarendon House. She stood here clinging to the brass bed frame, so dizzy she nearly passed out. Heavy shadow seemed to suck at the light, and Christian had called to her, over and over apparently, but not a single sound reached Ryder.

Everything is as she remembers: the bed with the burgundy quilt beneath its plastic covering; the creepy porcelain-faced doll sitting against a nest of snow white pillows; the red wood dresser, and the oval mirror on the wall.

The only item Ryder doesn't recognise is an ornate clock on the bedside table. A golden timepiece, all the cogs and wheels on display, rests under a dome of glass. A tiny ceramic fairy wren nods its head in time with the passing of the seconds.

"Ryder."

The voice startles her. A figure rushes into the room. Sebastien barely stops in time to avoid crashing into her.

"Is this it?"

"I don't know."

He scans the room. "Where is Aresh?"

"I don't know!"

She is here.

A shudder runs through the room. The red-wood dresser topples forward, dissolving into tiny particles before it hits the floor. The space where it had been standing is as black as the end of the corridor outside.

"Padellah, where is she? I can't see her." Ryder clutches at Sebastien's arm, readying for another sudden shift in the floor. The door swings on its hinges, slamming closed. "Padellah! What do I do?"

In the centre of the room, shimmering specks of light gather together. Dancing particles that morph themselves into a familiar silhouette.

"Padellah, are you okay?" Ryder's voice cracks beneath the wave of relief.

"Drained. We cannot stabilise this area any longer." Padellah's multi-voiced whisper surrounds them. "The creation must be destroyed to free the Laudine. Where is Olessia? You were to come together."

"They were separated, by this place," Sebastien says.

Ryder glances at him. "You can see her?"

His face tells her the answer before his words do. Grey eyes wide and fixed on where Padellah floats before them.

"I see her. And I hear her." He gives Padellah a low bow. "What must we do to save the Laudine?"

"Ryder must free her. She has the strength. But she will do it alone. If we release our hold, the creation will sink into the sub-levels of this realm, and the Laudine will be lost."

"Alone?" Ryder says. A flutter of panic joins the stone-laden butterflies. "I can't do this by myself."

You are capable.

A terrible groan is followed by the sound of splintering wood. Coming from somewhere beyond the closed door. Pipes bang and hiss beneath the floorboards, steam rising between some of the joins.

Now. Use your will. Bring the creation to you. It is no different to before. Your strength is great here, you must not fear it.

"But I can't even see it." Ryder's panicked gaze shifts around the room. In the Paldrian River, she'd been able to see the creation clearly. But here there is nothing except old furniture. Sweat dampens her armpits, her heart is thumping a mad beat.

Look past what you see. Truly look. And you will find what you seek.

"I don't… I don't see anything…" Her voice pitches. Why can't she see anything? In the Paldrian River the creation shone like a miniature sun. But here, there's nothing. She's failing everyone. Right when it matters most. Messing it up. Like she did with Sophie. Doubt is a tidal wave that threatens to completely swamp her. Ryder hunches her shoulders. Dizzy again. Like the last time she was here. So dizzy she can't think straight.

Sebastien takes her hand, holding tight when Ryder tries to snatch it away.

"Sebastien, what are you doing?"

"Ryder, look at me." He grasps her other hand, placing them both on his chest.

The world is actually falling apart around them, and he wants her to stop and look at him? Ryder shakes her head, ready to tell him what she thinks of his plan.

"Listen to me," he says, his voice soft, his grip gentle. "You do see, Ryder. You always have. That's why you were here to begin with, in this house. Because of the things you saw. I do not doubt that you were afraid then, as now. But you are as strong and brave as any in the Presiderline. Stronger. Because you did not run away."

Ryder stares up at him. Sebastien means well, but he's wrong.

"I should have run," she whispers.

If Ryder *had* run, if she *hadn't* tried to so hard to be strong and brave, then Sophie would still be alive. Sebastien keeps talking but his voice bubbles like they are underwater, the words drowned. An image of Sophie flickers into Ryder's mind. The memory of her friend cradled in her arms. Growing still. Pale. Sophie's eyes lifting to find her.

"You did this," she says.

The words spear into Ryder, blades that cut deep. She pulls free of Sebastien's grasp. Is that what Sophie said? *You did this.* Ryder shakes her head, almost topples over. Sebastien is there to steady her. She cries out and shoves him away.

Sebastien is here. What if she does to him what she did to Sophie?

You did this. But the words don't sit well, the butterflies knock against the inside of her ribs.

"I don't want to hurt you." Ryder waves Sebastien back when he tries to reach for her. "I can't do this."

Is she even still on her feet? Her body shakes, the ground shakes, the very air is unsteady.

"You will do what you must, Ryder. As will I," Sebastien says, the air bubbling his words again.

The Megnastin inflates your terrors. But know this. You did not take Sophie's life, Ryder. She gave it to you.

Ryder's world seems to stop on its axis. *What do you mean?*

The Beckoning inside you is powerful. Like nothing we have seen in our own kind, or in the Presiderline. But it is also newborn. And was weakened after you destroyed the creation in the Paldrian River. When you tried to save those humans, you did not have the reserves required to do as you wished. Sophie offered those reserves, willingly.

I don't understand. Though Ryder is beginning too, and the truth is sucking the heat from her body.

The Beckoning was too weak to take from Sophie by force. Your friend could have easily resisted. But she understood. And so she gave. The humans were saved.

Ryder brought down the helicopter. Jack and Daenara safe and sound on the ground. *We did it.* Those were Sophie's words.

Sophie sacrificed herself to save them? Ryder's eyes burn. The butterflies have all fallen deathly still.

She did.

"Ryder, do you hear me?" Sebastien says. "Take what you need from me. Do what you must. I will remain by your side. Protect you, as you will protect us. I will not leave you, whatever you must do." He grasps her face in his hands, forcing her gaze to meet his. "Do not allow this place to toy with you. It undermines us in every way. Feeds upon our doubts, our fears. Hold your strength."

The world is still crumbling, the room still being picked apart atom by atom, but Ryder breathes with the movement in Sebastien's eyes, slow and sure.

Sophie gave up everything to help Ryder. And as the world implodes around them, Sebastien is offering to do the same. She can't run from this.

He is right, Ryder. The Megnastin distorts our view. I cannot show you where the creation lies. You must see it for yourself.

Ryder wraps her hands around Sebastien's wrists, and gently pulls away. "Let's get Aresh out of here."

Chapter 40

Christian

Christian slumps forward, blood tracing a warm line from his nose to his lip. The salty tang of it makes his stomach roil, but he can't wipe it away. Christian sits on an uncomfortable stool in the centre of an unfurnished room. Pinned to the spot. His hands hang at his sides, wrists encircled by narrow bands. Though he is not visibly chained to anything, it is impossible to raise his arms. His feet, too, are bound by the unimpressive rings of metal. He can barely wiggle his toes, let alone lift a foot.

Aside from a slight shake of his head, he can do little else. And he's tried to do something, anything except scream, as Dashel works to smash the Blackwall Olessia formed in Christian's mind. The only thing Christian knows for certain about a Blackwall, is that it's not indestructible. With Dashel's touch, Christian feels the barrier cracking. A burning ember pushing deeper and deeper into his brain. A girl's face flashes against the back of his eyelids. Memories pushing up like needles through skin. Dashel shifts his fingertips, settling them further back on Christian's skull. The pressure behind his eyeballs intensifies. A fresh scream rips from Christian.

For a moment he thinks Dashel has taken pity on him, because the man releases his grip, and steps back. Blinking through tears, Christian sees pity has nothing to do with it. Kileen has joined them. The guy with eyes like the inside of a cave.

"It has begun," he says, not glancing at Christian. "The armadel has crossed the border. Icewynn has fallen. The Crown has fled, but her freedom will be short-lived."

"Very well," Dashel stretches his arms like a weightlifter readying themselves. "I will be done here momentarily."

He stands behind Christian this time. A drop of blood falls from Christian's lip, staining his white shirt. The first real stain on the material which has managed to stay incredibly clean despite everything. He stares down at the crimson splotch. Dashel's fingertips find he back of his head, right at the end of his spinal cord.

And the torment begins again. Breath-stealing. Pain so intense Christian's scream is locked in his throat. The pressure behind his eyes seems set to push his eyeballs free. Christian squeezes his eyes shut.

And the memories thunder in.

Ryder.

Christian and Ryder in an old house. Filled with antique furniture, and heavy-framed paintings of people in ballgowns and stiff-collared suits. A red-haired girl. She smiles as they huddle over a computer screen that has some infra-red footage on it. Sophie. That's her name. Sophie. And he misses her. Misses her so much his chest aches. For a moment the pain drifts, easing back to allow him to think straight. Friends. Ryder and Sophie are his friends. He loves them. The ache widens, grabbing a hold of every rib. Another image fills his mind. A new face. One he's only seen a glimpse of in the past, before the agony of doing so almost knocked him out.

Evelyn.

An older version of Ryder. Their likeness startling. Unmistakable. And frightening. Another person to add to the list of people he cares about who are in danger.

"My friends," Christian groans. "My friends."

Dashel presses harder, and the pain sweeps in again. Sophie's grinning face shatters, and she disappears.

Christian retches, bile burning up his throat. Dashel takes a hurried step back. He growls, muttering under his breath.

"Who is she? This Ryder," he demands. "Why does the Laudess go to such lengths so conceal her?"

"I thought you believed Olessia's skills in Blackwall lacking, Dashel." Kileen frowns as he peers down at Christian like he's staring at a dog turd. "It would appear she has outwitted you yet again."

The look Dashel sends Kileen's way could melt stone, but the younger man doesn't flinch. This seems to enrage Dashel even more, but he doesn't take it out on Kileen. He turns on Christian, and slaps his face so hard, joints in Christian's neck pop.

"Who is she," Dashel bellows.

Cheeks burning, Christian clenches his jaw. The tiniest of smiles reaches his lips. Dashel isn't getting what he wants. A soothing thought that eases the sting of the slap. And the ache in his skull.

Who is Ryder? She's a friend. Definitely. Christian doesn't need to see it in the memories to know it is truth. The connection is palpable when her face comes to mind. That buzz that comes with catching sight of someone you care about. Someone you love.

Ryder and Sophie are his friends. And friends don't abandon you. They'll search for him. Ryder will hunt for him. And that's bad. Really bad. Because these vicious, crazy guys are hunting for her.

Kileen steps forward. Leaning in close enough that Christian catches a whiff of body odour, and he wrinkles his nose. A bad idea. His entire face aches.

"Did I see you smile, little boy?" Kileen's breath is hot against Christian's inflamed cheek. "The Laudess may believe she is strong enough to defy her father but she is greatly mistaken. When she falls, so too will her Blackwall. All her secrets will be free, and we will have no further use of you."

Christian clears his parched throat. "Good luck with that."

A sneer lifts Kileen's lips. "You would do well to shut your mouth, human."

But Christian's adrenaline is pumping, and opening his mouth is about all he can do. "I'm just saying, a whole bunch of people managed to escape your super-max prison… what does that say about—"

Kileen's fingers find Christian's neck.

"Enough." Dashel appears alongside Kileen. "Return him to holding. Bring the human woman."

Surprise brushes Kileen's face but he's quick to regain his composure. "Evelyn? But Aresh installed the Blackwall in her mind, did she not? Your strength is admirable, Dashel, but why consume your energy with a task set to fail. The Presider will deal with—"

"Are you questioning my ability again, Kileen?" Dashel shouts.

"That's exactly what he's doing," Christian mutters, grateful when no one pays him any attention.

"Bring the woman," Dashel continues. "You have not seen what I have in the boy's memories. There is a striking similarity between this Ryder and the woman sitting in our holding cell. And if the Laudine and Laudess have both seen fit to initiate Blackwalls on these humans, then you can be assured they are both of great importance. Until we learn of the definitive demise of both Aresh and Olessia, we must strive to hold the fullest advantage. This boy and that woman are our security until we learn that no one survives who could threaten the Presider's position as ruler of all of Bax Un Tey."

Christian runs his tongue over cracked dry lips, the coppery tang of blood mingling. A wave of anger washes over him. He should have been stronger, found a way to fight against Dashel. Now Ryder and Evelyn are both vulnerable. And he's let Olessia down. The violet-eyed girl who protected him and made the pain go away when it grew unbearable. The violet-eyed girl whose presence made him oddly calm when his whole world turned inside out.

This guy wants to wipe her out of existence. Christian strains at the bindings around his wrists. He winces, shoulder muscles burning. Kileen calls in a couple of guards. They are in the room before the order is finished. Lifting Christian from the stool, dragging him towards the door. Kileen doesn't step aside as they approach, and they are forced to manoeuvre around him. Christian presses his lips tight, even as the jerky move threatens to dislocate his shoulder.

Kileen and Dashel are watching him. Piercing the space between them. But Christian's not going to give them any more than he already has. Not one single word. Or memory. Or scream.

If Dashel is right, then it's not just Ryder who will come looking for him. It's not just Ryder who is Christian's friend. Olessia and Aresh are too.

The very two people who seem to scare the hell out of Dashel.

Chapter 41

Ryder

Ryder reins in her thoughts. Focuses on the only thing that matters. Finding the creation. Sebastien stands close, but she clears her thoughts of him, of her friends, of all the madness around her. The butterflies are quick to react. Fluttering up out of the shadows within her where they had retreated to while she freaked out. No freaking now.

The energy rises, jumping into Ryder's bloodstream, speeding around her body. Sinking into muscle and deep into bone. No pain, just a touch bordering on ticklish. Laughter catches at the back of her throat. Crazy, maybe. But damn it feels good. To not be afraid. Ryder tilts her head back. And the Beckoning fires up every nerve.

The Beckoning.

She allows the thought in. Acknowledges it. Doesn't, for once, crush it down deeper than the butterflies. There is something within her. A power no other human was born with. And Ryder intends to use it.

Her gaze moves slowly around the room. The Beckoning grants her access to an astonishing visual spectrum. One she's not sure she'll ever get used to. The very energy of life itself. In this room, the furniture is dull and blurred, nothing brightens the dead wood and artificial fabric. There is no miniature sun leading her straight to the creation, either. The brightest thing about the room is

Sebastien's aura; a vibrant blue hugs the silhouette of his body. He watches her, unwavering and unafraid.

Ryder's gaze moves. Searching for an anomaly. Something that doesn't fit. A tiny flicker, a shadow that shouldn't be cast. Anything. She peers at the clock. The butterflies sweep through her, like a flock of birds changing course in unison. Ryder narrows her eyes. *Look past what you see.* Padellah's words. Ryder allows her gaze to soften, her vision to blur. Looking past the spinning cogs, past the white clock face with its black Roman numerals. A pinprick of light appears. The Beckoning whirls like a sandstorm through her body. The pinprick becomes larger. Spreading wider. The illusion shudders, the sides of the clock falling away like petals falling from a dying flower. Resting at the heart of that flower is a very familiar birdcage of light.

Within the cage at least a dozen pin points of light dance around one another; all the colours of the rainbow flickering. Reminding her of a star in the clear night sky back home.

"There," Ryder says, a searing heat stirring beneath her skin. "I've found it."

Padellah appears at her side. Her form noticeably duller than when she first appeared.

As it had to be. I could not lead you to it. Now, use your will. Destroy it, Ryder.

Veins on fire, Ryder steps towards the creation. The windows either side of the bed explode, glass shards rain down on her. A slice against her cheek draws blood, she feels the liquid move down her skin, but Ryder's eyes don't lift from the creation. Her fingertips are flaming, hot enough to melt bone if these were true flames. But this inferno is under her control.

Ryder places her hands either side of the creation: the Presider's prison for his own sister. The creation sends a sharp dart of energy into her body, a protective measure perhaps, and it whips the Beckoning into a firestorm. One that is about to slip from her control. The air pressure in the room drops. Ryder's ears popping with the change. She fights the maelstrom within her. Lose control of the Beckoning, and she loses everything. Beneath her feet, the floorboards groan. Sebastien's aura weaves in tiny tendrils away from his body, reaching for Ryder.

"Take what you need, Ryder." Sebastien moves closer.

"Get back," Ryder shouts. "Get away from me."

The Beckoning is a panicked horse, mindless with confusion and fear, fighting her, struggling to free itself of her hold. But she fights it right back. This is not the weakened energy Sophie gave herself to. Sebastien could not fight this onslaught. Ryder breathes in until her lungs are ready to burst. Grasping at the manic butterflies, gathering them to her. Their senseless whirling begins to slow. Her skin feels fit to burst with the build of energy but Ryder brings the Beckoning to heel. Settling the chaos. Focusing. And the energy that is a part of her, that is her, bends to her will.

Destroy it. The single thought occupies her entire mind, her entire being. *Destroy it.* That is what she wills.

Ryder releases the Beckoning, and this time the firestorm is carefully controlled. The energy tears through her, hot as lava. Pouring from her in a torrent that sends the points of light within the creation into a frenzy. Bright as a supernova.

She's doing it. This is actually going to work.

All at once, the room tilts violently, and Ryder feels her grip on the creation slipping.

"No!" Ryder screams.

Her rage lifts her. And fuels the Beckoning. The energy consumes her, melting her into the firestorm. Someone screams, and the air explodes. A massive blast that sends her flying through impossibly bright light.

Her journey ends when she slams against a solid surface, and a short fall before her backside hits the ground.

Ryder groans. Blinking to try and make out something in the glare.

"Ryder, can you hear me?" Sebastien. Nearby. "Ryder, say something."

"Something."

He laughs. An unsteady and short-lived sound, but definitely laughter.

Spots dance in her vision, but the room begins to take shape again. Ryder has landed against the wall by the mirror. She pushes herself onto her knees. The room has returned to level. Sebastien kneels a short distance away, crouched over a someone. A woman with long lengths of silvery hair.

"Aresh. Oh my god, is she alive?" Ryder crawls to the Laudine's side. Aresh's scar is so much more pronounced, her face gaunt. Her once snow-white hair is tinged silver. It cascades over Sebastien's arm as he cradles her. Aresh's eyes are closed but there is noticeable movement beneath the lids.

She lives.

Ryder's head jerks. Padellah watches from the other side of the room. But Ryder has to squint to make out the entity, she is so faded. Her silhouette is edged with tendrils of light that escape the entity like steam.

"What about you?' Ryder cries. "Are you going to be okay?"

The floorboards release a terrible screech, the timber splintering, swallowing any reply Padellah might have given. A metre-wide crack reaches from one side of the room to the other, a sudden abyss that cuts off their access to the doorway. On the walls, the wallpaper is eroding, sprinkling onto the floor in handfuls of rice-grain fragments. Where it had once covered a solid brick wall, now there are patches of utter blackness. With a slow, agonised movement, the room begins to tilt in a new direction.

"Hold on!" Ryder reaches for the leg of the bed, grasping hold.

"No, Ryder. Let go," Sebastien shouts.

It takes her a second too long to work out why. And in that second, the bed zips towards the fissure. Dragging her with it. She lets go, but the momentum tumbles Ryder into the darkness. The bed vanishing ahead of her in the inky blackness.

Silent, inky blackness. The blaze of light in the room doesn't touch this space. She is utterly blind. But Ryder's barely drawn another breath before she is shooting back out into the light. Crash landing onto a thick embroidered rug, rolling several times before the base of a leather couch stops her trajectory. Her face is pressed up against a material that smells strongly of peanut butter. She wrinkles her nose, sitting up, pressing her hand to her right shoulder. Her body is awash with the heat of the Beckoning, but it doesn't stop the aches and pains.

"Ryder!"

Ryder sits bolt upright. "Olessia, Olessia we found her…" Her words fade as she takes in the view. Olessia is pressed up against the wall, her feet off the floor, her head just shy of hitting the ceiling. A dark fluid runs from a corner of her mouth. A man stands in front of her. He glares down at Ryder. His eyes are two pools of fire.

The Beckoning stirs. The butterflies scattering, diving down into the abyss at her core. Ryder shrinks back, as unsettled by the Beckoning's retreat as she is by the man's frightening gaze.

"You should not have done that." The man's stare pierces her. She's sweating like crazy, her body still warm after the mega-blast from the Beckoning, but a shiver runs through her.

He's not particularly imposing in stature, shorter than Ryder actually, but there is something about this guy that sucks the air out of the place. She swallows hard, not certain she won't throw up. Ryder's got a pretty good idea of who he is. And the Presider is every bit as terrifying as she imagined. He frowns, either oblivious to, or unphased by the sounds around them. The screech of wood under immense pressure. Glass shattering. Heavy thuds that pound at the walls.

"Don't touch her." Olessia struggles against her invisible restraints. "Leave her alone. Ryder run, get out of here."

"There is nowhere she could run that I could not find her." He nods, as though Ryder has spoken. She couldn't if she wanted to, her tongue is stuck to the roof of her mouth. Kneeling before him on legs that have turned to liquid. "You are not leaving this place."

The ceiling tears open, sending a deluge of plaster down on them. Sebastien falls through the opening. He clutches Aresh in his arms, throwing himself onto his back moments before he slams onto the dark wooded dining table. The table shatters. Sebastien lies motionless, but Aresh stirs, easing herself off him. Clutching at her head.

The Presider regards her with eyes that show no white. Only sunburnt flame that moves in fast moving rotations. "None of you shall leave this place."

Chapter 42

Christian

One of the guards kneels beside Christian and presses a square device against the bindings on his ankles. The weight that had locked his feet to the floor vanishes. For a second, Christian considers kicking out at the guard. 9oiSure, it would be satisfying, but would achieve little more than a beating in return. Or worse.

He keeps his feet to himself, and his mouth closed.

"Get up. Move." The guard is short, only to Christian's chest, but he manhandles Christian like a pro-wrestler. Kileen leads the way down a short corridor. His head lowered, fingers drumming against his thighs as he walks.

"You are counting a lot of chickens, you know," Christian says. He's not entirely sure where his newfound bravado is coming from. Maybe he *is* losing his mind after having that guy dig around in it for so long.

Kileen casts a daggered look over his shoulder. "Quiet. I don't wish to hear—"

"Oh sorry, translation issue probably. You guys have chickens? No? Yes?" Christian shrugs. This is insane, purposely trying to irritate an alien but it's all Christian's got. His superpower is being annoying. Like a fly bugging a wolf. "Anyway, there is a saying, about counting your chickens before they're hatched. Which basically means you shouldn't assume stuff. Like assuming you can just get rid of people who are more powerful than you."

He hasn't seen much of what Olessia can do, but he has seen the way people act around her. Kind of wary, and kind of awed. He saw it in the face of that big guy, the Sentinel. And Sen-Bay. Christian's breath catches at the thought. The last time he saw Sen-Bay the Yentern was unconscious. But alive. Then, at least.

Kileen pauses, moves in close. He gives Christian an unkind smile. "The Laudine and Laudess may indeed hold greater power than the Presider, but they are weakened by burdens. Ones such as you, and the others interred here. Olessia did not learn the lesson the Presider sought to teach. She cannot be all powerful if she aligns herself with others. And you will all pay for her mistake."

Christian holds the man's gaze. Jet-black centres in orbs of snow white. A darkness that moves, rotating like black holes. "You need a mint," Christian says. His stomach does a flip at his brashness. This is crazy. The wolf is going to swat him into nothingness. And this little fly can't even raise an arm.

Kileen's sneer returns, and he swings a fist. A thunderous bang against the hull of the ship sends vibrations through the passageway. Vibrations strong enough to throw Kileen off target, swinging wide, almost connecting with one of the guards. Everyone is thrown sideways. Christian bounces off the wall, managing to keep his footing despite the lack of control of his arms. But the pro-wrestler guard and Kileen aren't so agile. Landing in an angry, cursing heap on the ground. Christian bolts. Not so easy when your arms are pinned to your sides. Forced into a ridiculous penguin-like waddle, he races as hard as his until-now exhausted legs will take him. The motion seems agonisingly slow to get going. Like he's dragging himself through syrup. He reaches a curve in the passageway and comes face to face with Evelyn. Without her veil. She does resemble Ryder. But she's not familiar. Not the way Ryder was in his memories; like he knew every skin blemish, every angle of her face. A shiver of something sharp scrapes at Christian's skull. But he doesn't look away. And the pain doesn't build. Evelyn is being held by a single masked guard. Her arms flush to her sides, the metal restraints visible around her wrists.

"Halt!" The guard raises his weapon — another of the walking cane-shaped devices. But the move comes in perfect unison with another heavy blow against the craft. All three of them stumble. Both Evelyn and Christian manage to stay on their feet. The guard leans against the wall, his weapon still pointed at Christian. He shouts into a device at his shoulder, and even though the guard's words aren't clear, his panic is. Either the crab is malfunctioning, or it is being attacked.

Another impact, this one jerking them to the right before the craft realigns. Evelyn does what Christian did a moment before, and takes advantage of the confusion. Only, she doesn't run. She attacks. Somehow, she has freed herself from the restraints. In an impressive manoeuvre she lands a high kick right against the guard's armoured breastplate. The impact sends him toppling onto his back, loosing his grip on the cane in the process. Evelyn darts in, snatching it up, levelling it at the guard's chest. Christian grits his teeth, not sure if he should look way. Evelyn switches her grip on the weapon, and uses it like a baseball bat. Landing a heavy blow against the guard's head. Knocking him out clean.

Evelyn rushes up to Christian.

"Here." She brandishes the square device, a fancy coaster, that the guard used to release Christian's ankle restraints. Evelyn presses it against his wrists and the pressure weighing down his arms vanishes.

"Thanks." Christian rubs at his aching shoulders.

"Let's go." Evelyn grabs his hand. "We've got to get the others out."

The blast wipes them off their feet. Christian's head and shoulder slam against the wall.

"Hold onto something, we're going down," Evelyn shouts.

The craft careens right, keeps tilting. Gathering momentum. But there is nothing to hold onto. It's a narrow, empty corridor. The only saving grace is just how narrow it is. Christian leans against one wall and braces his legs against the opposite. Evelyn tries to follow his lead but she's too short, and her legs don't quite reach. Christian presses his arm across her chest. Like he has a hope of keeping her pinned then when the crash.

"Oh man, this is going to hurt," Christian moans.

The crab-like ships stood a good couple of storeys high. It's a long way to fall. He closes his eyes tight.

I've got you.

The voice is clear and gentle, coming from somewhere at the back of his head. Christian's eyes fly open, narrowing just as quickly against the dazzle of light. He and Evelyn are cocooned in an illuminated sphere, yellow as gold. And in the shimmering air he catches a glimpse of a familiar face. A dizziness sweeps over him.

"I know you." He cries and laughs at the same time, his voice cracking. A strange pressure behind his eyes. "Sophie." She is right by his side. Sophie reaches to touch his hand and her fingers pass straight through his. The pressure behind Christian's eyes gives way, and a flood of memories rush in. "Sophie. I remember. I remember."

Remembers everything; the ghost-hunting, the weekend at Jack's place, the moment they met Olessia. He remembers the time he spent with her, chatting about everything and nothing. The time she helped them all fly. Olessia using a strange metal to lift them all into the sky. Elthar, she called it. And how surprised she was at how quickly Ryder learned to use it. He remembers. Ryder was a natural.

It's almost too much. The downpour of his life. The portions flooding back in, filling the gaps. He sobs, releasing his grip on Evelyn to clutch at his head. Recalling the beach where Olessia and Petra fought to keep him safe.

"Oh no," he groans. "Petra."

Another name resurfaces. Lucas. Petra's son. Does he know? Christian digs his fingers into his scalp. And is Lucas safe?

Chris, you have to get up. Get out of here. It takes a moment to register that they've stopped falling. But he didn't feel a thing. No thud as the crab hit the ground. He can't take his eyes off his friend. And not just because it's been so long since he's seen her.

"What happened?" he whispers. "Is this… a hologram or something?" Sophie is here, but not here. Translucent enough that he can make out Evelyn right behind her.

Not exactly. It's a long story that will have to wait, I'm afraid. Come on, get up. Right now.

Sophie is using her no-nonsense voice. He remembers clear as day now. Ryder hated it, said it made Sophie sound like she was a hundred-year-old school principal. A distant thud sounds, and a faint shudder runs through the metal at his back. Emergency lighting kicks in, a dull glow that emanates off the surrounding walls. With the craft on its side, one of those walls is now the floor. The low bellow of emergency alarms ring in the distance.

"Where is Ryder?" Christian struggles under the weight of his returning memories.

In the Arlion Xhentex. She and Olessia both are. Doing what they have to do right now. And so am I. Keeping the people they love safe. Ryder's not losing anyone else, I won't let it happen. Christian, Evelyn is Ryder's mother. She can't lose her again. She can't lose you either. You have to get out of here.

"Christian?" Evelyn touches his arm. "Are you all right?"

Christian blinks through tears he didn't realise he'd shed. Wide brown eyes fix on him. Features so familiar the tears start to fall again. It's really true. Ryder's mum is alive. Here. Impossible, and wonderful. Christian gave up asking Ryder about her a long time ago. She would refuse to answer, and the questions seemed to cause too much pain. Some part of him had just assumed Ryder's mother had died a long time ago.

"Yeah. Yeah. I'm good," he says. "Did someone attack the ship?"

Evelyn helps him to his feet. "Seems like it. But we shouldn't hang around to find out who. There is so much deception going on, we can't assume whoever attacked the ship is a potential friend. We need to get the others and get out of here."

Christian nods. Searching. Both Sophie and the orb of light are gone. Empty corridors stretch in both directions. Well, almost empty. Kileen lies a few metres to the right, one of his legs twisted at an angle that makes Christian gag. He turns away, catching sight of the guard that Evelyn knocked out. Way down the corridor now.

"Sophie saved us. Did you see her?"

"Who? Who saved us? Christian, are you sure you didn't hit your head?" Evelyn tries to shift his hair off his face, but Christian waves her back.

"Sophie. My friend. She was—

Still is right here. Just struggling with the visibility thing.

He jumps, searching for sign of her.

"Christian?" Evelyn's brow is furrowed.

Get moving, Chris. Sophie trembles into view. Her bright red hair is different though. Less defined. Like someone's done a couple of paintbrush strokes to create it. *We can't do this all on our own, you have to move. Come this way.*

"We?"

Just move Christian! Follow me.

Chris takes Evelyn's hand. "Trust me on this one."

He leads her down the corridor, jumping over the guard without looking down. Too afraid of what he might see. As Christian follows Sophie, something she said earlier keeps playing over in his head. *Ryder's not losing anyone else, I won't let it happen.*

He assumed she was talking about Petra, that somehow Sophie knows what happened on the beach. Christian swallows, his throat tight. Now, he's not so sure. What if Sophie is talking about herself?

A blast blows open a hole in the in the floor behind him. Barely a pace back from where he stands. The blast throws both he and Evelyn forward with so much force they end up on their bellies.

Get up, Chris. Move. Sophie moves in front of him. Get to the others, we will do what I can.

"You keep saying we. I don't see—"

A blast hits the right-hand wall, what used to be the ceiling before the craft crashed. Sophie jumps in with her shielding thing. Surrounding him with golden light. Portions of the shattered wall bounce harmlessly off the barrier. Christian scrambles to his feet, helping Evelyn to hers.

You need to run, Chris.

Sophie shifts and he catches sight of someone racing down the corridor towards them. Bald-head glinting beneath the touch of the barrier.

"Dashel," Christian gasps. Fear takes a hold of his legs, coating them in concrete.

Dashel has both arms raised, fists balled, covered in the blue glow of elthar. "If you run, I can assure you, you will die."

Christian, what are you doing? Run!

Sophie's cry blasts his thoughts, jerking him into action. Christian turns on his heels. Sen-Bay and Maher are coming from the opposite direction. Racing towards him. Sen-Bay's mouth is open, shouting something, but all Christian hears is Dashel's manic cry, high with rage.

"The human chooses to die."

He did no such thing, you jerk.

Three pillars of light stand across the width of the corridor. The central pillar is Sophie. Her superhero red hair the only thing that marks her out from the others. She raises her arms, twin lengths of flickering gold. The moment her fingers meet the other two pillars a huge blast rocks the corridor. Evelyn screams. She and Christian are lifted off their feet and hurtle down the corridor in a soft cloud of gold. Sen-Bay races towards them, shielding his face. Christian hits the ground, the impact slamming his chin against the hard metal. Debris rains down, bouncing off the shield around Christian and Evelyn, but peppering Sen-Bay who drops to hands and knees. Still pushing forward.

"Chris-tan, Chris-tan. Speak, are you harmed?"

Christian lifts a hand, wincing at the spasm of pain at his shoulder joint. "I'm okay. Evelyn?"

She nods. "Shocked but fine."

Christian rolls onto his side, peering back down the corridor. To the place where Dashel had been a moment before. He's not there now. Nothing is. There is a massive hole where a corridor used to be. The dark, outside world replacing it. Sophie stands just above the pebbled ground, her red hair floating in serpentine tendrils around her face. Haloed by the golden light that just protected Christian and Evelyn from the blast. Either side of her, clouds of fireflies brighten the dark night.

"Sophie, did you do that?" Christian reaches for the wall, but Sen-Bay is there already grasping his arm and gently helping him rise. Christian hisses against the stabs of pain that come but he'll worry about injuries later.

"Who are you speaking…" Sen-Bay falls silent, mouth agape.

"Now I see her. I see them all," Evelyn says gently.

The Cyne are kind of shy, but I figured everyone should see who their friends are.

Sen-Bay releases the tight hold he has on Christian's hand.

"Sophie, thank you." Christian stumbles towards her. "You saved us."

She waves off his thanks, all her moves a fraction slower than they should be. Like the gravity is heavier wherever she is. She smiles. The sunshine that envelops her pours from her. Leaking from the edges of her mouth, making her eyes glow like a cat's at night. *I didn't kick all this butt on my own. It was a joint effort. Me and my mini Cyne army.* She gestures towards the clouds of sparkling light either side of her. *Beautiful, huh?*

A lump fills Christian's throat and all he can do is nod.

"Evelyn, get back!"

Startled, Christian whirls around. Sentinel Teler runs down the corridor, one of the walking cane weapons raised and aimed. Maher is right behind him, brandishing what looks like a giant super-soaker, but is bound to do far more damage.

"No, no!" Christian throws himself in front of Sophie, and to his surprise, Sen-Bay and Evelyn do the same.

"Wait, Teler, no," Evelyn cries. "They are not the enemy."

The two men falter, but their weapons remain raised.

"This is not possible," Teler shakes his head. "The Cyne—"

"Are right in front of us," Maher finishes for him. "Very little about all of this is possible, and yet it has come to pass." Maher lowers his weapon. "I thank you." He bows his head. "For what you have done here."

So much more polite than Sebastien. Sophie's giggle dances inside Christian's head. *But you need to tell them your ride is here, Chris. Tell them not to be afraid.* Sophie points to something beyond the jagged opening in the hull. *Come with me.*

"Guys, we need to go." Christian doesn't wait to make sure they've heard him, and follows after Sophie. She and her shining escort float through the shattered hull. Christian ignores Teler's booming voice, shouting at him to stop. Sen-Bay doesn't try to stop him, just follows right behind. They clamber over a warped section of the craft's exterior wall and drop the short distance to the ground. Feet sinking into the pebbled surface.

"Sophie, are you sure about this?" Christian says.

A triangular aircraft hovers just above the ground a few metres away. Jet-black, an onyx so deep it's like looking at a black hole. The sleek design reminds him of the B-2 bomber back on Earth, though this aircraft is definitely larger.

Oh I'm sure. Now we just need to get Ryder back safely, and the whole gang is back together.

"What do you mean?" Christian stares at the craft.

"Chris-Tan, are we safe?" Sen-Bay stands at his side.

"We're safe." Christian has no clue who or what sits behind the deeply tinted cockpit, but he trusts Sophie. Whoever or whatever she has become.

"Get back, you foolish boy," Teler barks, still inside the ruined craft. Evelyn at his side.

"Wait, wait." Maher clambers over the top of a curled lip of metal and drops to the ground alongside Christian. "I recognise that vessel. That's a Zilner. They belong to the Crown of Zentai…"

Christian can't tell if Maher thinks that's a good or bad thing.

"It's okay. Don't be afraid," Christian says.

A section on the underbelly opens, utterly silent. A helmeted figure drifts down to the ground. The headpiece fits as snugly as a balaclava though gleams like it's made of metal. The figure reaches up, and touches at their chin. The helmet folds back on itself, like origami in reverse. Revealing the wearer beneath.

A sob escapes Christian.

"That's Lucas." He races out across the space dividing them. "Lucas!"

His feet slip on the pebbles, their depth more than he bargained for. Stumbling like a drunk man towards his friend.

"Christian," Lucas cries, waving both arms.

By the time they reach one another, Lucas is a just an auburn-haired blur. Christian's tears making it impossible to see straight.

He grasps his friend and they cling to each other.

"You're okay, buddy," Lucas says. "You're okay. Man, your mum she is going to lose it when she sees the state of your clothes."

Christian laughs, a watery, snotty sound. He clasps Lucas tighter, unsure whether to say anything about Petra. Does Lucas even know?

"What are you doing here?" Christian pulls away, wiping at his nose with the edge of his shirt. "This is all so crazy... Ryder is in there, man. In that... place... and Sophie is... Sophie's..."

Lucas plants his hands to Christian's cheeks. "I know, buddy. There are a lot of big things to deal with. But you have to trust Ryder with this one, she got me out of a really bad bind. She's one hell of a bad ass right now. She's going to get through this." His gaze shifts to Sophie who's sunshine-smile is wide. He's thoughtful as he regards her. "Sophie... I'm so sorry..."

Me too, Lucas. About a lot of things. But especially about Petra. It's terrible.

Sophie's voice is clear in Christian's head. It must be in Lucas's too because he nods, muscles in his neck tightening. "A lot about this is terrible. But at least Dashel has paid his price." He jerks his chin towards the wreckage.

"I'm sorry too, Lucas," Christian says. "About Petra. I wasn't sure if you knew and I... I didn't know what to say."

"Cooper told me." Lucas's gaze is stone cold, and the hardness in his tone is one that Christian doesn't recognise. Deep and dangerous. "It's what made up my mind about surrendering to the Zentai. I wanted to get to him. I guess this will have to be close enough." He shrugs, and his dark mood seems to slip away. "Now come on. You all need to get on board. The Presider's troops are occupied at the moment but J'salax can't keep them that way forever."

"Who is—"

"Chris, not the time. Tell your friends it's safe to come over."

There's an underlying forcefulness that Christian doesn't recognise in his friend. In fact it's more than just the voice. Lucas holds himself rigid, as though braced to face whatever comes his way head on. This isn't the guy Christian practised basketball with every day after school, who challenged him to pizza eating contests designed to make both of them want to hurl. In the days since Christian last saw him, Lucas has turned into a soldier.

The crunch of footsteps on the pebbles draws Christian's attention. Teler and Evelyn have joined Maher on the ground. They are all framed by the gaping hole in the metalwork.

"You are Lucas?" Maher keeps it casual, the remark almost flippant. But his arms are folded, and Teler is right at his back, hand tight around the weapon.

"Yes."

"The son of Reigner Bladen."

Lucas's eyes narrow. "The very one. How did you know?"

Christian doesn't love the glare that Lucas is directing Maher's way. "Olessia told them."

Lucas's gaze darts to him. "Why would she do that?"

Christian blushes. "It was to do with me. Dashel was trying to get information about Ryder out of me… and I was a mess. I didn't know what I was saying. Olessia had to give the Presider something."

The tension in Lucas's face eases, and he nods. He turns back to Maher. "I know about you too, Maher. What you did for Aresh. Protecting those from the Collective." His gaze moves to Evelyn. "We all understand what the Presider is willing to do to rule these realms." Amber eyes come to rest on Sophie. "And we understand the sacrifices that have already been made to fight him. We need to be ready and waiting for when Ryder and Olessia return with Aresh. Between us we hold all the truths behind this war. We know all the Presider's secrets. We know all of his lies. Aresh is no traitor, we all know that. Now we need to be ready to do whatever it takes to convince Bax Un Tey of that." He points up to the ship, a hulking body of smooth black that makes no sound as it hovers above the ground. "That's a Crown vessel, I'm sure you know that. I've got it because the Crown of Zentai trusts me. She is with me. With us. Whichever way this day goes, nothing will remain as it was. If we unite, the Presider will fall, today or the next. But he *will* fall."

Despite the dank heat, goosebumps notch along Christian's arms. Lucas appears a foot taller than before, lifted by his own speech.

Sen-Bay whistles. "Show me the way to the armoury."

Maher laughs, clapping the Yentern on the back. "My thoughts exactly."

They gather as a group beneath the craft. Everyone except Lucas and Christian who wait beside Sophie. The Cyne who had joined her have faded away, and she is alone.

"I promised Jack I'd find her," Lucas says quietly. "I told him she was going to be okay. That you'd all be okay. But I'm too late for you Sophie… and Ryder's out there on her own. I'm failing."

Okay, stop that pity party before it's begun. Ryder is not on her own, and she made her own choices. Just like I did, Lucas. I'm not scared. Neither is Ry. Well, that's a lie. We are both terrified, but that's the definition of brave, right? Freaking out and doing it anyway? Jack will see her again before you know it. And he'll know that she's okay. More than okay. Sophie's image flickers, the particles that make up her apparition are more pronounced than before. Pixelated like bad TV reception. But she is smiling, beaming her sunray smile. *Now we wait for Ryder and Olessia to be awesome. And when it's done, Padellah and I will get them the hell out of there.*

Christian's head jerks up. "Wait, what are you talking about Sophie? I thought you couldn't go into the Xhentex."

Can, and I will. Truth be told, I'm not sure I have a choice. There's a connection I can't fight, even if I really wanted to. When I get too far from Ryder, something pulls me back. And right now, it's making it hard keep it together out here. I have to go, Chris.

"Sophie, please. Don't."

Don't leave me. The words burn the tip of his tongue, but even in barely visible form he recognises the set of Sophie's mouth, the thinning of her lips that comes when she's readying for a fight.

Lucas wraps an arm around Christian's shoulders. "Come on. Since when have you ever won an argument with Soph when she's got her mind set on something?" He chuckles, though there's little humour in the sound.

Christian bites down on his lip, and for what feels like the millionth time today he just wants to bawl. While everyone else has some kind of superpower he just has this. Tears. Christian is terrified too. That just when he's got all his memories back, he's about to lose the most important people in them.

Far in the distance a deep, rumbling disturbs the heavy silence. To the west the landscape is swallowed by a dense fog. A thick swirling whiteness that pulses with sudden, violent streaks of lightning. Christian watches it, shuddering. It must be the Arlion Xhentex, but he's too afraid to ask the question. And learn for sure that's where Ryder and Olessia are.

Lucas wraps his arm around him. "Hey, how about you come onboard and I'll introduce you to a Queen and a Crown Prince?"

Christian shrugs. "Sophie? You coming?"

Her smile almost slips entirely, but she grabs hold of it at the last moment. *I'm not one for royalty really. You go.*

She raises her hands, and Christian does the same. They stand there, ethereal palms pressed to flesh and blood. Christian's throat is too dry to utter a word.

When you get home, keep Kye out of trouble, okay? Her smile doesn't dazzle with quite the same intensity. Christian swallows down on the lump in his throat.

"You can tell him yourself."

Sophie doesn't reply. She just stares at him, like she's trying to memorise every line on his face.

Lucas gently pulls him towards the ship. Christian walks with him but keeps his eyes fixed on Sophie, even as he rises up into the air and an alien world spreads out before him. The rumbling sound from earlier is much louder now. Joined by the crack of lightning that seems to energise the air. Prickling all the tiny hairs covering his skin.

Christian ignores it all. Eyes on Sophie, even as the underbelly of a spaceship opens above him and the ruler of a world he never knew existed, waits to greet him.

He watches his friend until the last trace of her sunbeam smile is gone.

Chapter 43

Olessia

O lessia fights against the paralysing grip the Presider places upon her. Pinning her against a wall that threatens to collapse at any moment, her legs dangling above a floor that groans and bends as though an enormous weight presses upon it. Glass shatters, vases and mirrors exploding into razor sharp shards. Heavy thuds flow in from the exterior of the house. This is not truly Clarendon House but it is breaking apart as though it were. Megnastin is shaking itself to pieces. But if the Presider is concerned, none of it shows. There is hunger in his gaze as he stares down at Ryder.

"Don't touch her." Olessia struggles against her invisible restraints. "Leave her alone. Ryder run, get out of here."

"There is nowhere she can run that I could not find her." The Presider raises a hand towards Ryder. She rises into the air, kicking and shouting with all the fervour Olessia directed at him earlier. Olessia's inner voice roars, demanding the Beckoning rise. Show itself. The beast shrinks from her, shifting deeper.

Plaster rains down, and a great rent traces through the ornate ceiling rose, slicing free the heavy ironwork chandelier that hung at its centre. Sebastien tumbles through the opening, clutching a body with flowing white hair in his arms. He throws himself onto his back moments before he slams into the dark wooded dining table. The weight of his arrival shatters the table. Olessia clenches her eyes shut, opens them again. Aresh lies with him, motionless within the jagged nest. A double-banded senlier rests against the Laudine's hair, whose stark white has been dulled to silver. Strands cover her face but Olessia notes the rise and fall of her chest.

"She is free." Olessia's pulses riot. The beast shifts within her.

Ryder has truly done it. Aresh is free.

The Presider's hands curl into fists. There is no white in his eyes now. He regards Aresh with eyes that burn with the intensity of the twin confels. "None of you shall leave this place."

But Olessia takes note of the tightness in his voice, the subtle twitch at the corner of his mouth. Those long hours spent in his over-bearing company as he drove Olessia to utilise the Beckoning are now more than worth the anguish. Inel has been caught off-guard.

He is not fearful, not yet. But the Presider's arrogance has landed him in a position in which he is uncertain of the outcome.

A rare occurrence indeed.

Olessia's body floods with euphoria. Her pulses steady now, but still rapid, and the smile that threatens is almost impossible to restrain.

Ryder is shouting obscenities. Flinging choice human words intended to insult. She is astoundingly confrontational considering the environment and the company she finds herself in. Olessia allows herself a moment to admire the bravery of the human girl. Letting it buoy her further. Her core hums with an energy not born from the Beckoning. A vibrancy she has experienced only once before.

The moment Olessia stepped into the shadowed room at the true Clarendon House. Free. Unrestrained in any way. For the first time in her life.

The Presider jerks his hand. Ryder is lifted from the ground and flung across the room. Slammed up against one of the last panels of plasterwork unaffected by the erosion of the place. She lets out a pained cry, her head rocking. Immobilised just as Olessia is. Living sculptures in the Presider's dissolving gallery. The press of Ryder's body weight against the wall sends hairline fractures fanning out around her, and the blackness fills the narrow lines. There are no elegant gardens surrounding this Clarendon House. Something far more nefarious wraps tighter and tighter around their rapidly-deconstructing surroundings. Clarendon is sinking into the Arlion Xhentex.

"Ryder, stay strong," Olessia calls. "You must fight him."

Instructions that once would have seemed ludicrous. A human girl fighting the Presider of Bax Un Tey? But Ryder was never what she seemed.

She groans, her eyes closed.

The Presider moves no closer but he studies Ryder. His face is no longer expressionless, there is an animation there that was lacking before. A chink in his armour.

"Who works through you," the Presider demands. "How does a human exist in Megnastin at all?"

His voice rises with each word. His fury darkening his face. The floorboards beneath his feet crumble away, but he doesn't even glance down. Simply rises above the pit of black.

"You will learn nothing from us." Olessia's words are strained, her effort to free herself making it difficult to speak at all. "But I have learned everything from you. You are all I desire not to be. Siros deserves better than this. They deserve far better than *you*."

Inel drifts towards Ryder. "Someone like you perhaps, Olessia? A child who abandons Bax Un Tey on a whim, and who would sacrifice herself for the sake of those far beneath her? You disappoint me. You have always done so. I should have replaced you long before now."

He releases the Beckoning. Ryder's eyes fly open. Her mouth stretches wide with an agonised cry.

"No!" Olessia cries.

Ryder's aura tears from her body, streaming away in narrow, faint ribbons of altering shades: the pale green of a forest, the soft blue of a sky, and the burn of an Earthen sun. Her back arches, her mouth wide but not a sound leaving her. The Presider's beast is like no other. A formidable force he wields with mastery. Olessia's own power shudders within her, sensing the massive release of energy.

"Inel, stop," Olessia cries, struggling against her confines. "Stop."

That the Presider can restrain both her and Ryder while controlling the Beckoning is testament to his strength. A strength Olessia has never been able to counter.

"Aresh, helps us!" Olessia screams for the Laudine. Aresh, who fought so hard to protect Ryder, lies helpless in the very same room where Ryder is being destroyed. Aresh and Sebastien remain exactly where they fell. At the heart of the room, where reality still lingers intact. For now.

"Olessia, help me," Ryder cries, her voice choked, as though the Presider's hands are upon her throat. Her aura flares, the colours brightening, the narrow ribbons widening.

"This aura… she is not completely human." The Presider's disdain gives way to open confusion. As rare as his uncertainty. His gaze shifts to Aresh. "You protested the Collective so vehemently. And yet behind my back, it seems you were interfering in other worlds as enthusiastically as I." He shakes his head, and what might pass for a smile touches his thin lips. "For all your desire to be unlike me Aresh, I find that we are one and the same. The lengths we will go to bring about our goals."

Ryder lifts away from the wall, drifting towards the Presider. Her aura fans out from her body, an elaborate cape that flows with her as she moves. She hangs limp, eyes fluttering.

"Come," the Presider says. "You will return with me to Bax Un Tey and I will learn just what you are."

Olessia seethes with anger and horror. He cannot leave here with Ryder.

He cannot leave here.

She calls to the Beckoning, the coward at her core. Her summons is harsh, but the Beckoning answers by burying deeper. Olessia slumps against the wall, desperation pressing upon her. Her capacity to breathe all but extinguished.

Breathe.

Focus.

Her gaze rests on Sebastien's still form.

She fights too hard. Too violently, against the wrong enemy. Olessia is not alone. She never has been. Olessia allows her body to grow limp. Ceasing her battle against the Presider's restraint. And once more, she reaches out to the beast. Coaxing, not coercing.

We are not replaceable.

The flicker is minuscule. Olessia doesn't dare move in case she has misjudged its existence at all.

We are bound, that cannot be changed, and for that I am sorry. For both of us. But let this union transform from what it has been in the past. Let us create a partnership. A new unity between the Presiderline and the Beckoning that will protect not enslave. I ask you to rise with me. An ember flares to life within her, a speck in the darkness. *He cannot be allowed to take Ryder. Too many worlds will be threatened. Including one that was once your own. The Cyne and the humans will suffer, unless we stop him. Unite with me.*

The flames ignite, heat coarses strong and fast through her, through the organs and structures that make her whole. The Beckoning rises, pulling everything together. Merging every cell that defines her. A roar fills her throat, and Olessia throws herself forward. The snap of the Presider's control is audible. The reverberation shatters the wall she was bound to. Leaving nothing but darkness behind. A darkness that flows out over the remaining walls. Eating at them.

"Let. Her. Go."

Olessia launches herself towards the Presider, and with fingers splayed wide, she releases the Beckoning. The energy tears through her, a monstrous wave that does not seek to leave her control. It takes her with it.

The wave strikes the Presider. Inel staggers. Whipping round to face her, naked fury distorting his face into a grotesque mask. He launches a counter-attack. The speed is breathtaking. Olessia has no time to shield herself. The energy sears through her, meeting her own with a bone-jarring shockwave. She spins, head over heels, back towards the gaping black space left by the shattered wall.

"No," she hisses, scrambling to get a grip on the Beckoning.

But it does not race from her as she expects. The Beckoning settles back into her hold, like a weapon returning to the hand.

"You've got this, Olessia," Ryder cries.

She is on the floor, on hands and knees, but there is no anguish paling Ryder's face now. She is bright with the glow of her own life-energy. Her multi-coloured aura cloaking her like a shield, hugging her silhouette. No sign of the siphoning ribbons of earlier.

Olessia's hands tingle with the touch of the Beckoning. The beast senses what she does. The Presider needs all his strength to counter her attack, he cannot contain Ryder as well.

Olessia centres herself and calls upon the Beckoning again. It awaits right at the surface. Eager to move at her summons. Olessia releases. The Beckoning pours from her with a violence that consumes everything in its path. Ripping open what remains of the floor, tracing a line straight to where the Presider stands, arms raised. Readying his return attack.

On any other day Olessia might have feared it. But not today. Today, she is not the one grown rigid with fear. The Presider hurls a calamitous wave of energy towards her.

But the beast already works to protect her, moving without a summons, racing to form a barrier before her. It sets the air shimmering as it creates a wall. Barely has it formed when the Presider's energy hits.

"Ah!" Olessia leans forward, arms held horizontal in front of her, as though she truly does clutch a shield. Her body shakes, her head desiring to snap back with a force that could well break her neck. But Olessia and the Beckoning stand fast before the onslaught. Weathering the tirade. Gathering themselves before the reverberations of the impact have fully ceased. Liquid dampens her face. It may be her own blood that coats her, but there is no time to concern herself with such things.

Olessia seeks the beast and finds it awaiting her summons. Again and again, Olessia and the Presider exchange blows. And each time the Beckoning jumps at her command, works with her to barrage their enemy. But with each blow the intensity fades. The beast is tiring. Olessia's body is soaked with perspiration, a pain grips the back of her head. But the Presider suffers too. The heave of his chest mimics her own. The drop of his shoulders — far broader than hers — is equally pronounced.

"You show great improvement, Olessia," the Presider shouts. "But you delay the inevitable. You cannot sustain this."

Olessia's head lifts. A vitalising thought coming to her. The Presider is tiring, and he has three life-sources in this space; Ryder, Sebastien and Aresh. Two are unconscious, and yet he makes no attempt to take fuel from them. Olessia is too formidable an opponent to take the risk.

The Presider fears her.

The Beckoning rebuilds, bubbling at her centre, feeding with renewed vigour into her veins. Melding both body and beast together. United. She sinks beneath the heat, submerging into a place that may consume her entirely. Olessia looks to Ryder and finds the girl with a smile upon her face.

"It's okay," Ryder says. "Do it."

Olessia nods.

The Beckoning tears through her, taking everything she can offer with it. Hollowing Olessia until she is a mere husk. It pours from her fingertips. Rushing at the barrier offered up by the Presider.

Piercing a hole right through it.

"No!" His cry is rich with desperation.

The Presider slips back. The onslaught overwhelming him. Inching him towards the great and looming blackness that has consumed one half of the room. Onyx depths from which there can be no return. Olessia's vision grows hazy, and the Beckoning digs deeper.

She does not fight it. Olessia is sheer flame and fire as the beast drives the Presider towards the nothingness.

Inel abandons his attempts to use the Beckoning as a weapon. He forms his energy into great blazing hooks, digging them deep into what remains of the room. But still the beast pushes him. The Presider throws panicked glances over his shoulder. He is desperately close to the gaping hole.

"Olessia," he cries, the strain of holding fast to this plane evident in the rise of veins in his neck. His legs lift, sucked back into the vortex. "Please do not do this. I beg you, my daughter!"

The words finds their way through the roar of blood in her ears. Olessia falters. So too does the beast. Her newfound ally's confusion rippling through her.

The Presider seizes on her hesitation. He releases one of the failing energy tethers, and whips it towards her. Snapping it around her waist.

Before Olessia can regather the beast, he is dragging her into the blackness.

Chapter 44

Ryder

Ryder struggles to catch her breath, finally released from the Presider's death grip. Her aura clings to her skin, an impressive rainbow of colours. Pressing close against her now, not drifting away.

The fight between Olessia and the Presider is tearing the place apart. Only two walls still stand, inky black in their place. The darkness creeps in. Like huge lines of ants marching through shattered window frames and up through the cracks in the walls. Ryder pushes to her feet, clinging to the back of the couch. She is shaking so hard it's difficult to stand. Sweat floods off her, her body a sauna. The Beckoning lit her up like the sun when she destroyed both the creations, but here, as Olessia stands like a raging god in front of her father, throwing everything she's got at him, the intensity is far, far worse. Ryder's skin is trying to peel itself off her body. Her heart wants out, punching at the base of her throat like a tiny boxer. And her fingertips are sparking. They are actually sparking.

She flutters her fingers, sending white spray into the air. So what does she do with the power? Ryder watches the exchange between father and daughter; the tsunamis of energy being thrown across the room. If she rushes in, will she hinder, or help? Olessia is handling things, like the queen she's going to be one day. Ryder doesn't want to be the reason she falters.

Twisted with indecision, Ryder looks to Aresh. She is sitting up, staring right at Ryder.

"Oh my god." Ryder vaults over the leather couch, the only piece of furniture in the room still intact. "Aresh, are you okay?"

Stupid question. Aresh is a shadow of her former self. A double-ringed senlier encircles her head, and there is dried blood at her temples where it has dug too deep. Her scarred face is gaunt, her long hair lank about her cheeks. The dirt-brown dress she wears, a formless shift clearly a few sizes too big, swamps her. The only vibrant thing about her is her eyes. And they are churning violet tornadoes. Sebastien is still unconscious, on his back beside her.

"Can I get this off you?" Ryder's hands flutter towards the senlier, unsure if touching it will just make things worse. The Beckoning flutters in imitation of her hands, as though urging her to try. But Aresh pulls away.

"Padellah tried but failed. It is like no senlier I've known. Inel is as intelligent as he is tyrannical." Aresh places her hand on Ryder's. Her skin as cold as if it were actually carved from ice.

"Yeah, well he needs to work on his creations." Ryder offers her a wry smile.

A huge crash shakes the room so hard Ryder braces against what remains of the floorboards. There is an hourglass shape of wood remaining, with Ryder, Aresh and Sebastien at one end, and Olessia and the Presider at the other. Clarendon House is sinking into an abyss, and it is taking them all with it.

"What do I do, Aresh?" Ryder peeks over the back of the couch.

"Let her fight. And ready yourself to do the same."

Olessia seems to have gained an advantage. She's pushed the Presider back towards the black hole where one of the walls used to be. She stands with her shoulders pulled back, chin lifted. The lower part of her face is covered with blood but her expression is fierce. Ryder's skin tingles, and she fights the ludicrous urge to scream like a mad football fan. Urging her on.

The crackle of the Beckoning on the air is unmistakable. Prickling the fine hairs on Ryder's body, and lifting the heavier strands on her hair. Aresh too. Making her look like a silver-haired Medusa.

Olessia speaks to the Presider, her face an angry mask. The words don't reach Ryder but she's guessing they are not words the Presider wants to hear. His sneer bares all his teeth, his expression turns him into less of a man, more of a raging animal. Olessia thrusts her arms forward. Releasing a torrent of energy. The backdraft sucks at everything in the room.

Ryder is jolted forward, the solid arm of the couch catching her diaphram, winding her. Aresh cries out, finding a handhold on the softer seat cushions, grabbing Sebastien's arm with her free hand. Ryder stares in horror. Fine whisps radiate from both their bodies: soft whisps of blue from Sebastien, the white of snow rising from Aresh. Ryder's own multi-coloured aura is untouched, still hugging the curves of her body.

"Aresh—"

"We will give her what she needs. It is all we can offer."

Ryder shuffles on hands and knees to Sebastien's side. The flow of his aura is definitely slower than Aresh, but how much can he handle?

The flutter of butterflies in Ryder's belly is manic. Hurtling against her sides, slamming up against her ribs. Wanting to be a part of this fight.

Olessia thrusts her arms forward, yet again. Another punishing wave is released. The Presider's face is almost comical as his feet slide across the floorboards, his heels carving a path through the wood. He releases two torrents of white-hot energy, three-pronged hooks forming at their ends. He drives them into the floor, attempting to anchor himself in what remains of the floorboards.

"She's winning." Ryder clutches at Aresh's arm.

The Presider releases a rage fuelled bellow. His legs whip from beneath him, flying out into the darkness. The gleaming energy-hooks are all that bind him to Clarendon House.

"Just a little more," Ryder whispers beneath her breath.

Olessia takes a step towards the Presider. He pulls back one arm, and one of his anchors disappears. Replaced with a long shimmering coil.

"Olessia, no!" Aresh's cry comes too late.

The energy whips towards Olessia who is too close now to avoid it. It wraps around her waist. Pulling her towards the abyss.

"Olessia, hold on." Ryder is on her feet, racing towards them. The thud at her core picks up the tempo, like drums on a battlefield. Her fingers burn, her skin smoulders. The Beckoning is all in. Ryder lifts her hands to eye level, fingers splayed. The fireball races up from her core, and spreads through every bone, every vein.

Ryder takes aim at the Presider, holding the Beckoning in check until the very last moment.

Release.

The energy tears from her fingertips. White hot and agonising. But right on target. The energy races towards the Presider, splitting the air. His attention had been wholly on Olessia. Until now.

Now he sees Ryder. Sees what is coming for him.

He fixes on her. And the fire in his eyes extinguishes. Dulling to a washed out yellow. Wide with shock.

And, if Ryder's not mistaken, just a touch of fear.

The Beckoning lands the strike, like a meteor hitting the earth. The Presider's fragile hold is shattered. His sullen yellow eyes do not leave Ryder. In utter silence, Olessia's father drifts into the darkness.

The man who took Sophie. And Petra. And Ryder's mother, vanishes from all the worlds.

But Ryder's made a mistake. A terrible mistake. Her blast didn't destroy the coil holding Olessia. The energy grips her, dragging Olessia towards the abyss. She fights but it's clear she has little left in the tank.

"Olessia, hang on." Ryder lunges for her. Managing to grab hold of her wrist.

"Let go, Ryder." Olessia tries to shake her off but it's like a toddler trying to get free of its parent. "Get out of here, get Aresh out of here."

"You're kidding me, right? Fight it, Olessia."

"I'm trying."

She is, and it's working. Ryder braces, knees bent like she's holding onto the world's largest kite, but her slide towards the blackness reduces to a snail's pace. The Beckoning is just a flicker, a handful of butterflies instead of the usual army, but it's there at least.

The Presider's binding stretches thin behind Olessia. There is no sign of the ruler. The icy touch of the nothingness crawls over Ryder's skin. In agonising slow motion, Olessia and Ryder edge closer towards it.

"Enough, let me go, Ryder," Olessia says. "You can't hold us both."

"I'm not letting you go," Ryder shouts at her. She squeezes her eyes shut. "Time, just need a little time to recharge."

Olessia struggles against her. "Don't be ridiculous. You need to get out of here."

"Absolutely right, Olessia. And you are going with her."

Ryder opens her eyes and chokes back a sob. Sophie stands at the centre of a halo of sparkling golden light. Solid. Real.

"It's time you both left this place," Sophie says. "Clarendon House really isn't what it used to be."

Olessia's grip around Ryder's wrist tightens. "Sophie, you cannot be here."

"That's what Padellah said. But she doesn't have two besties about to be sucked into a vortex, so I decided I wasn't going to listen."

The halo billows out, enveloping Ryder and Olessia, and the relentless pull of the darkness weakens. Sophie smiles and Ryder blinks. It's like Sophie swallowed the sun. She is radiant, a brilliance that swamps the dark. Olessia jettisons out of the emptiness and comes crashing down on Ryder. They lie there clinging to one another. Shattered. Breathless.

A deep rumbling fills the space. Like the distant approach of a storm.

"Thank you, Sophie." Aresh stands beside the couch, swaying like she's just come off an amusement park ride. "But you should not—"

"I should, and I did." Sophie moves to Aresh in the blink of an eye. She brushes her hand against Aresh's cheek, and the movement leaves a trail of white light. "Take care of them. They are going to need you."

She touches her fingertips to the senlier and the metal crumbles away as surely as the rest of the room has.

Sophie's brilliant grin is still firmly in place. Her hair is a mini-halo of superhero red. She drifts back to Ryder's side. "Time to go, Ry. They need you out there."

Ryder tries to touch her, but despite how real Sophie may appear, Ryder's hand sweeps through her. "You're coming with us, right?"

"No." The smile fades. "I can't, Ry. But you are going to do just fine without me. We each have our stories, and this is mine. I get to say how it ends. Tell Padellah I'm sorry. She's not to blame. Tell the people who need to know that I love them. The Cyne are waiting for you. Now go, be awesome, Ryder Carlsson." There is the barest tremor in her voice, but her smile returns. "And don't you dare forget me."

Sophie rises above them, a luminous star against the emptiness beyond her. Her halo casts wide over the wreckage of the room. Aresh moves to Sebastien's side, cradling the guardian's head in her lap.

"Come closer, Olessia, Ryder," Aresh says.

Sophie's light glows brighter and brighter. Olessia pulls Ryder to her feet.

"Come on. We need to stay together."

Ryder nods absently, barely noticing her feet on the floor. She refuses to look away from Sophie. Her eyes water, sending false tears down her cheeks. The real thing can come later. They crouch on the rug beside Aresh and Sebastien, and Ryder takes his hand between hers.

"Stay close," Aresh says. "It will aid Sophie greatly."

"To do what?" Ryder's tongue sticks to the roof of her mouth; she's gripping Sebastien far too hard.

Aresh lays a hand on Ryder's knee. "To gather enough momentum to expel us from Megnastin."

"Can't we do that ourselves?" Ryder asks her second dumb question. She is wiped. Exhausted to the very core. A core that holds a Beckoning equally as drained. She only needs to look at Olessia and Aresh to know how they feel. All the fight is gone.

Beyond the barrier of Sophie's halo, Clarendon House succumbs to the darkness. Snaking lines of tar-black wind their way around the perimeter of the golden shield. And what is left of the room — a portion of the ceiling, the marble fireplace, a lank potted palm that has somehow managed to remain in the last corner of the room — fractures beneath its touch.

Sophie's star rises higher. Higher. Ryder strains to keep eye contact. Her neck cranes, her eyes flood with sharp tears.

"Ready, brace," Aresh says.

The beautiful star goes supernova. Exploding in a blast that hits them with the force of a dozen tidal waves.

Washing them all away.

Jettisoning them out of the mangled chaos of the Megnastin. Ryder moves with unnatural speed through the emptiness. The others are somewhere in the starlight. Ryder is alone. Sophie's star fades, dimming with every moment Ryder rushes away. Until it doesn't exist at all.

Now the tears come. And they keep on falling. As Ryder does. A downward spiral that seems to go on forever. Ending with a rush of whispers, a movement in the darkness. Shadows moving in towards her.

The Cyne.

Waiting just as Sophie had promised.

Guiding them through the Arlion Xhentex. Ryder sees it all through a blur of tears. Unable to makes sense of the shapes around her. All except one. Padellah places herself at Ryder's side. A blur she could never mistake. The shadow that has been with her almost all her life.

The shadow that *gave* her life.

Sophie was determined it should be her who came to your aid. The silhouette shudders. *We were too weakened by holding the Laudine to stop her. And her mind could not be changed.*

"Not once she sets it," Ryder sniffs. "It's not your fault."

Nor yours, Ryder. You have both done a wondrous thing. A new legacy begins in Bax Un Tey.

The hollow at her centre comes from more than an exhausted Beckoning. It's a hole as bleak and empty as anything in the Megnastin. Another great piece of Ryder is missing. And will never return.

"It doesn't feel so wondrous." It hurts more than anything she's endured so far. Ten times more. "And I don't care about new legacies. I don't care about anything."

We do not believe Sophie would approve of your negativity, young lady.

Sobs and laughter mingle together, choking Ryder. The Cyne has just tried to mimic Sophie. It's as beautiful as it is heart-breaking.

"No. She probably wouldn't."

They burst from the shadows and move once again into the heavy white mist. A Celtren waits for them, beating wide dark wings through the swirling air. Padellah guides her onto it. Ryder clings to the muscular back, fingers sinking into the orange-streaked black fur. Finally something that isn't about to crumble away. Numbness digs into Ryder. She lays her cheek against the Celtren's shoulder. Listening to the subtle rush of air that comes with each beat of its wings.

"Let's just keep going," she mumbles into the rough fur.

As far as it's possible to go. And then some. Away from the hurt.

The mist is thinning. Ryder tilts her head. There are hints of land way down below. Another Celtren joins them, Olessia astride. The beasts bay at one another, and the sound reverberates through the creature's body.

They fly on in silence, the image of Sophie, drifting away, leaving her, playing over and over. All at once, Ryder remembers whose hand she grasped as she watched. The fingers that curled over hers. Holding fast. Ryder sits up.

"Sebastien... is he—"

His eyes had remained closed but he'd responded to her touch. Holding her as her world tore apart.

"He has regained some consciousness, though he will need time to fully recover. As we all will. Padellah flies with him." Olessia gestures over her shoulder, indicating somewhere in the depths of the mist. "First words he uttered were to ask where you were. And now you have done the same thing." She pauses, stroking the Celtren's coat. "I have seen how you look at one another, Ryder. He brings you great happiness. I'm grateful there is one aspect of our meeting that brings you some joy. I cannot tell you how much I regret the pain that meeting has also brought." She lifts anguished eyes.

Ryder watches her. "What happened to Sophie was not your fault, Olessia. Don't ever think that. I don't, I want you to know that." Ryder tugs at her shirt, still sweat-soaked and clinging. "That was rough back there, I mean, he was your dad, despite everything. How are you doing?"

Olessia tilts her head back, eyes drifting shut. "I suspect I am the same as you. Not very well." Violet eyes fix on Ryder. "But that will change. We will endure."

"Do you think so?"

"I know so. We have no choice. It is what Sophie would expect from us."

The Celtren drift in closer to one another.

"Yeah," Ryder says quietly. "She would."

"Thank you, Ryder. For all that you have done."

"We made a pretty good team." She tries a smile, but it slips away.

Olessia stares ahead. "We do indeed. There is great change coming for Bax Un Tey. And I would very much like you by my side. Know that there is a place for you at Kinna Bray, when you are ready."

Ryder touches her hand to her stomach. The Beckoning murmurs, deep and soothing. Earth isn't home anymore. Not now. And definitely not without Sophie. But she can't abandon it just yet.

"I need to see my dad, and Jack—"

"Of course, of course," Olessia says, nodding down at her hands, frowning. "I understand that you will want to leave." A pained look brushes her features.

"You didn't let me finish." Ryder rubs at her aching shoulders.

"Oh, my apologies."

"Would I get my own room?"

Olessia's face brightens. "Several. As many as you wish." She grins, settling herself more comfortably on the Celtren.

White mist gives way to the brightness of day. Hovering in the sky up ahead, right in their flight path, sits a ship.

"Oh god." Ryder leans back, trying to find the brakes.

"It's all right. They are not the enemy," Olessia says. "Look closer. Then you'll know for sure."

But already Ryder sees that. This is Nire's ship. The one Ryder and J'salax left the safety of to do exactly what Ryder's doing now. Ride upon a Celtren. The enormity of what has happened in between those two moments makes her entire body ache.

The two Celtren split off in different directions. Ryder's mount sweeps to the left. Soaring in close to the layered metal ship. Passing right by a long, wide window. There are several people standing behind the glass. Two of them wave madly, jumping up and down.

"No way."

Lucas and Christian dance like lunatics, alternating between manic waving and bear hugs. Ryder can't decide whether to laugh or cry, so she does both. Waving back like a girl possessed. Blane is there too, and gives her a short wave but seems more concerned with trying to get Christian to sit down. The doctor's orders fall on deaf ears, both Lucas and Christian run the length of the room to keep pace with Ryder's Celtren. The creature angles in so close to the ship Ryder could touch the glass if she wanted. Instead, she grasps handfuls of fur, trying to keep her seat.

Lucas and Christian stop in front of someone, but Ryder can't make out who it is before the Celtren turns and glides away from the vessel. Sweeping around in a wide circle. Bringing her face to face with Aresh who sits astride a Celtren black as the Megnastin. A smaller creature than Ryder's own. The pair settle in alongside one another.

"Ryder," Aresh says. "I wish I could remove your pain and return Sophie to you. But that is beyond anyone's power. And for that I am deeply sorry." Some of the colour has returned to Aresh's face. Her long silver hair streams out behind her. "What is in my power though, is to return someone else to you. Someone who has been kept from you for far too long. I hope one day, you might forgive me for what I did to protect you."

Ryder frowns. "What are you—"

But Aresh guides her Celtren away, disappearing around the tail end of the craft. Ryder's creature turns in the opposite direction. Doubling back to sweep in, once again, alongside the long glass window.

Lucas, Christian and Blane are gone. A single figure remains. A woman.

She steps up to the glass. And places both hands against it. A woman with a warm smile, and wide brown eyes. Black curls framing a face Ryder recognises all too well.

A woman who has, until now, only existed in old photographs.

Ryder leans from the Celtren, a choking sob escaping her. Sophie is gone, but the other great piece of Ryder, one that's always been missing, has returned.

She touches her hand to the glass.

"Mum."

Also By D K Girl

The Metal Angels Serial **(Science Fantasy)**

Metal Angels - Part One

Metal Angels - Part Two

Metal Angels - Part Three

Metal Angels - Part Four

Short Read **(Dystopian MM)**

Ending Altered

The Diabolus Chronicles **(MM Gaslamp Fantasy)**

The Bandalore

The Verderer

The Skriker

The Greensward

The Dullahan

Dear Reader,

I hope you enjoyed the EXTRA trilogy.

I'd love to know what you thought of Ryder and the gang.

REVIEWS ARE AWESOME!

And really important for authors. It's the best way to spread the word about my stories.

If you have a moment, please leave a review :)

About the Author

Danielle K Girl is an Aussie who lives in stunning Tasmania with her three furkids, cats Luffy, Sweetie (@sweetiebyname) and Ren. Her idea of heaven is a farm full of rescue animals, with a grove of trees that produces peanut M&M's and chocolate wheaten biscuits.

When she's not keyboard-deep in mysterious worlds, she is binge watching K-Dramas, listening to K-Pop or hiking through the beautiful Tassie wilderness.

If you'd like to receive DK's monthly newsletter, and be first to know when a new book is ready, then you are in the right place.

Sign up and receive a **FREE** Dystopian Novella - Ending Altered.

https://daniellekgirl.com/subscribe/

Find D K Girl online:

https://daniellekgirl.com/

https://www.instagram.com/daniellekgirl/

Mikie,
So here we are. At the end of things.
I'm hoping that somehow, impossibly, illogically,
you know that I made it this far.
And that it has only just begun.